The Widow Maker
A Maritime Tale of Lake Ontario

Susan Peterson Gateley

Prologue

The Widow Maker, a Maritime Tale of Lake Ontario

"Ontario" is said to mean Beautiful Lake in the language of the people who lived here before European settlement. On a sunlit summer day its cerulean expanse appears limitless. Though it is the smallest of the five Great Lakes it is a tideless inland sea. There are stories of 19th century British sailors, newly arrived to the military post in Kingston, Canada, who refused to drink the water beside the captain's gig on a hot summer day as they rowed. They believed it to be salty.

Lake Ontario is the last least lowest Great Lake, yet it's nearly two hundred miles in length and big enough to generate twenty foot waves. Watch it on a stormy day while standing safely ashore as white crested seas approach, curling, breaking, then crashing against the stone beach. The wind roars through nearby trees as the surf's thunder drowns out all other sounds. During the age of sail, wooden ships driven ashore on such a day were pounded to pieces in a few hours.

For over 200 years men and women sailed these waters carrying cargoes between the U. S. and Canada. The first shipwreck on the Great Lakes occurred in January of 1679, when a small French vessel carrying a cargo of corn, obtained from the Senecas, went ashore near the Devil's Nose 60 miles east of the Niagara River. In the years to follow, hundreds more sailing ships were overcome by storms. Many wrecks lie intact and almost perfectly preserved on the lake's bottom. As sure as the old salt sea, Ontario, like her four sister lakes, was a widow maker. Yet still the ships sailed. Sometimes they sailed late into November. There was commerce to carry and money to be made.

Our story begins in 1880 during the second Age of Industrialization. It is a time of vast and rapid social and technological change as movements for labor rights and women's suffrage gather momentum. Commercial sail is giving way to steam power on the lake, and railroads have encircled its waters with steel. But family operated schooners still carry grain, coal, stone and lumber between New York and Canada.

Mollie McIntyre, recently married to Will of the small Canadian lake port Eel Bay, is now cook aboard the two masted schooner *Gazelle* purchased by her husband a few months before this tale begins. The vessel is a typical small carrier of her day being 90 feet on deck and 130 foot sparred length. She can carry about three hundred tons of grain or coal. Two McIntyre cousins, Tommy and Nate, along with a neighboring farm lad, Zeb, are crew, while Will's younger brother Ben is aboard as mate. On an April day, the good ship *Gazelle* is about to begin her fourth and last voyage with Captain Will.

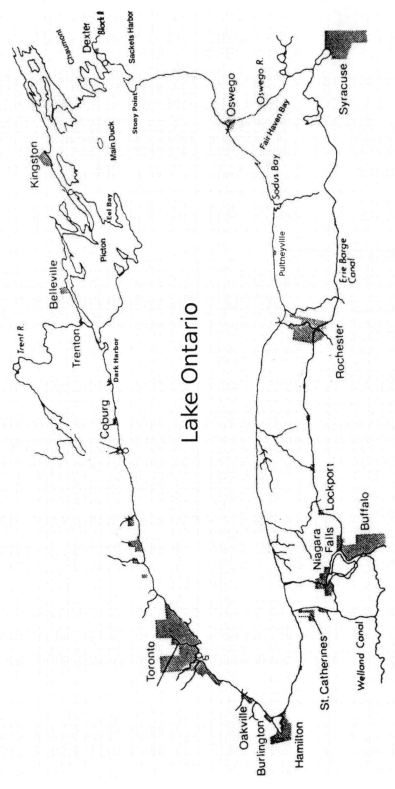

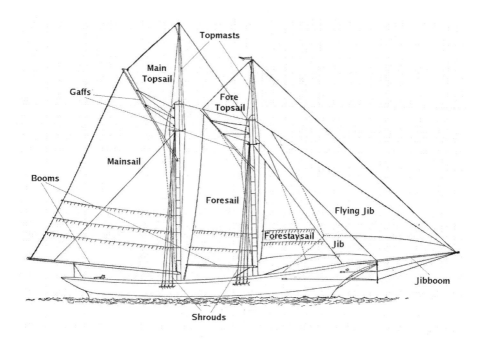

Topmasts

Main Topsail

Gaffs

Fore Topsail

Mainsail

Booms

Foresail

Flying Jib

Forestaysail

Jib

Jibboom

Shrouds

Schooner rig

Chapter One

"Independence is happiness" Susan B. Anthony

On a fine spring morning, a schooner, deep laden with grain and under full sail, ambled over the sun silvered waters of Lake Ontario. Ahead on the horizon the church steeples, city hall dome, grain elevator towers and warehouses of Kingston's harbor were gaining definition. Will McIntyre, a broad shouldered slender man stood at the wheel, his wife, tall dark haired Mollie, beside him.

"So what's our next cargo going to be?" she asked.

"I was thinking about trying for another load of wheat."

"You want to wait around for a new rail shipment of wheat? That could be a week or more. If somebody else doesn't get it first. We can get a load of box boards right away in Port Hope."

Will frowned at her for a moment and then shifted his eyes aloft to the luff of his schooner's mainsail. "We made a good profit on that last run. Besides, I hate box boards."

Mollie scowled as she patted one hand against her thigh. Kingston's elevators could fill the hold with wheat in a few hours, while box boards were slow and devilish to load. They didn't stow closely in the hold and were awkward to stack on deck. The crew had to work them in and out of the ship one plank at a time, one man to a plank. She knew what rough cut two inch thick pine boards did to a man's hands after loading a cargo of them. And the planks piled on deck were an infernal nuisance while working the ship. But the box shop in Oswego paid well, and they could sail to Port Hope for a load in a day.

"You don't even know if we can get another load of wheat."

"Well, maybe we should try."

Mollie's frown intensified as she crossed her arms across her chest. "We can't make any money sitting at anchor in Kingston Harbor. And our first payment on the note is due next month."

Will's hand on the king spoke's wooden grip tightened. Still staring ahead he said, "All right then. Lord save me from a pushy woman! We'll pick up a load of bloody box boards."

Three days later, Mollie wished with all her heart and soul that they had waited for wheat.

Mollie McIntyre had been Will's wife for two years, but she had been a sailor upon the Great Lake for twenty years before marrying. As a child, she had gotten afloat at every opportunity. With no mother and a father often away with his two master, Mollie had split her time between tagging after her Aunt Anna and her Uncle Jack. While other little girls worked on their needlework samplers, Mollie learned to knit a fish net and rig the sails of her uncle's skiff. She'd been rocked to sleep aboard the skiff on Sodus Bay while helping her uncle, and when she grew older, spent many a summer afternoon under sail aboard her father's schooner. As the old *Sheldrake* rose and dipped, she imagined the schooner was singing of travel on wide waters. She had thought of the faithful old vessel as a living thing, like Traveler, her uncle's horse. Even now she sometimes spoke to the *Gazelle* as if the schooner were sentient.

When she left girlhood to put up her hair and don long skirts and petticoats to assume proper womanly behavior, time afloat became even more precious. She didn't worry about being lady-like out on the lake. On the lake, the wind blew free, and the water seemed to go on forever. But ashore was another story. On land, one's proper place was the kitchen or maybe the laundry room on Wednesdays, and there was nothing more important than finding a respectable man to marry and tend to. At least that's what everyone told her. So she had done just that. Now she stood beside the perfect husband this morning. Will was master of his own schooner and an honorable, respectful and loyal man, most of the time, anyway.

On this cool bright April day at the start of the shipping season, it was good to be alive and free out upon the big lake. She decided to let the spat pass and offered, "Well, the freights are up this year anyway. And if we can't get wheat or box boards, we can pick up another load of coal."

Somewhat mollified, Will agreed, "Yes, everyone needs coal."

Mollie looked forward at fast approaching Kingston harbor that the *Gazelle's* bowsprit and jib boom were pointing out with a certain imperative. She could see the windows in the big gray stone hotel on shore and the clock face in City Hall's green copper dome. She could also see the harbor traffic of launches, sailing skiffs and watermen under oars bustling about, as an outbound tug with a big three masted schooner in tow approached.

"Are we getting a tug?" she asked.

"We'll sail in if there's room. Here, take the helm and keep her as she goes."

Mollie stepped up to steer, while Will strode forward and lifted himself a couple steps up the ratlines of the main mast shrouds to survey the harbor. "There's a fine big space at the end, forward of that three master. We'll go for that," he called back to her.

The space didn't look overly large to Mollie, but she decided one argument for the morning was enough. Will rarely turned down a challenge to his ship handling, especially if it would save the ten dollar tow fee. She hoped he wasn't pushing his young crew a little too hard on their second trip of the year. She watched him walk forward to confer with the boys, moving with the lithe easy grace of his that she loved to watch. As he stood next to Ben, his younger brother the mate, she marveled at how different Ben was from her husband. Ben took after Uncle John, with his sandy hair and sturdy build. Like his Uncle, he was quiet spoken and loved to work with his hands. He was not at all like Will whose quick temper and glib tongue sometimes ruffled the feathers of his co workers.

"We'll swing up into the wind, drop sail, then fall off again and coast into the dock," Will told the crew. While he and Ben made sure the boys knew what to do and when to do it, Mollie looked aloft assessing the sail trim. A morning wind was coming up with the sun, getting stronger by the moment, and she exulted as the *Gazelle* slipped along. Look at her go, she thought as she braced herself against the pull of the wheel. We must be doing eight knots deep loaded.

The harbor opened before them, its smooth water glittering in the early sun. The hoot of a train pulling into the Kingston station and the rhythmic slam-hiss of a pile driver at work sounded as they neared shore. Already she missed the freedom and the quiet of the open lake, and a pang of regret struck as she contemplated the end of the voyage. I wish we could keep on going, just slack sheets, put the helm up, and run right on down the river a thousand miles to tidewater and the sea.

Mollie sighed. She'd never see the ocean. Best think about getting into the dock right here and now. She scanned the wharfs and warehouses, aimed for a gap between two fishing boats crossing her bow, and scanned the thicket of spars and masts ahead. Among them she saw a familiar white hull.

With a surge of delight that extinguished any lingering regrets, she called out, "Father's there with the *Anowa*."

"Well, let's make this landing a good one then," called back Will. "I'm not going to disappoint Captain Tom."

Will rounded the *Gazelle* up sharply in the harbor to take the main and foresail off. He signaled Mollie at the wheel as they drew abreast of the wharf, commanding, "Helm down! Smartly now!"

Mollie rolled the wheel over hard and fast. *Gazelle* answered her helm, swinging up into the wind with a loud slatting clattering and flogging of canvas. Nate and Zeb slipped the main halyards on the pin rail as soon as they saw Ben and Tommy taking the foresail down. Mollie worried, had they overshot? The ship forged ahead toward the elevator where there was just enough room to squeeze in. The wharf seemed to be approaching with far too much speed, and the space in front of the three master looked barely big enough for Uncle Jack's fish boat. They were still coasting with their canvas shaking and racketing as the boys heaved hard on the down hauls pulling the headsails down as fast as possible. Will then signaled with his hand-helm up. Mollie spun the wheel again certain they were going to hit the wharf and maybe take out the three master's jib boom and perhaps her head gear, too, on the way in. But the ship responded immediately. Ben moved quickly to the rail ready with the spring line.

Mollie steered close in to the stone pier missing the end of the three master's jib boom by a whisker. She waited for Ben to fling the light heaving line ashore to send the dock line over with. However, he simply leaned out, reached over, and dropped the heavy dock line's loop over the bitts on the dock, and even as it checked the last bit of momentum, Tommy scrambled over the rail and ashore pulling the stern line along after him. He made it fast and then, with a victory whoop, jumped up onto the bollard.

"Nicely done," said a quiet voice nearby, and Mollie turned to see a slender gray haired man standing on the dock a few yards away.

"Father!" she exclaimed.

The moment the boarding plank was down, Mollie hastened down it and rushed to embrace Captain Tom.

"Oh, it's grand to see you again, Father."

"When I saw you coming in, I thought I'd be walk over to ask how the new ship was coming along. But after that entrance I think I know the answer already."

"Oh, she's a peach, and the crew is doing well, too. Will's cousins are shaking down as deckhands. Tommy is strong as a bull already even if he is only sixteen. Cousin Nate is very sharp at steering and sail trim. And Ben is as steady as they come. It's hard to believe it's only been two months since we got the boat. You'll come for noon day dinner won't you Father? We'll be at the elevator unloading, so we'll have time for a proper meal."

"I'll be there. I wouldn't miss a chance at your cooking for a cargo of coal."

Mollie gave her father another quick hug. Then she turned away, "I'd better get busy in the galley then. See you at noon."

She watched Captain Tom walk away with that odd lurching stride of his. Years ago, her father had smashed his knee against the ship's bulwark after being flung across the deck during a bad blow on Lake Michigan. She felt a pang of sadness. Captain Tom had never remarried after Mollie's mother died in childbirth. He loved (and seriously coddled) his only child, but sometimes Mollie wondered if he should have remarried. Now and then she caught him looking at nothing, his eyes empty, still missing his Catherine, for twenty two years now. Her own life would surely have been different had she grown up under a mother's watchful eye ashore.

The next day, the *Gazelle* set sail for Port Hope. No boat ever made money sitting at the dock. Best to load the next available cargo before someone else did. The crew sailed through the night and hove to off Port Hope's entrance at dawn in a brisk southwest wind to wait for the tug. Port Hope's channel was far too narrow for even a bold sailor like Will to chance under sail on a lee shore. The dock lines had scarcely been secured to the quay before the boys had the hatch covers off and crew and skipper alike were loading a consignment of rough cut boards for Oswego's Standard Oil Box Shop.

It was grueling work, lifting, moving and stacking thousands of heavy splintery ten foot planks. Each board had to be taken from a stevedore, carried across the deck and handed down to the stackers in the dimly lit hold. When Tommy and Will had crammed the space below decks full, the boys stacked more planks on deck to nearly the height of the booms. It took them all day to load with time out for a hasty noon meal. Ben drove the last spike in to help hold the top layers of the deck cargo together late that afternoon, and *Gazelle* cast off immediately for Oswego.

After the supper dishes were cleared away and the galley cleaned and secured for the night, Mollie went on deck. Will headed straight for his bunk after supper. Zeb was forward as lookout, while Nate and Tommy were also below for a few hour's sleep before their watch. Mollie made out Ben's square shoulders and sturdy form at the wheel. She thought as she approached, that if Will were a horse he might have been a high stepping hackney, while his younger brother was more of a reliable robust Morgan. Ben was a quiet man, unlike his brother. She thought of him as a follower rather than a leader, reticent, and possibly a little shy. As she approached the helm she realized she really knew very little about him.

The light wind that shaped *Gazelle's* canvas into curves overhead carried a touch of winter's chill that still lingered in the lake's icy depths. Slate colored low clouds cloaked the evening sky leaving a narrow crack of pale yellow light along the western horizon.

Ben looked to starboard at the sun's sallow disk just touching the dark gray water's edge. "I think it's going to work around into the north. The glass is dropping, and it may get dirty."

Mollie drew her wool cloak tighter against the gathering night. "Would you like me to spell you for an hour or two before dark?"

His quick smile was like a sudden beam of light in a shadowed room. Ben left the wheel and walked over to the rail to stretch and groan. He rubbed his back saying, "Those box boards take some pushing."

Mollie now on the helm, surveyed the stack of lumber filling the deck before her. "I guess you pushed a few thousand of them today."

Ben sighed and slumped down on the deck and leaned against the bulwark. He was too tired to answer. Silence prevailed disturbed only by the quiet murmur of water under *Gazelle's* stern and the occasional clunk of a block or creak of rigging overhead as Mollie steered with the practiced ease of long experience. She thought of the dinner yesterday with Captain Tom and his talk of more steamers and lower cargo rates on the lakes. He had spoken of a big new steamer made of steel that could load a thousand tons of coal in just a few hours. She wondered how they would manage with their own small mortgaged vessel this season. I must ask Will when the next payment is due on the note, she thought.

Mollie steered a steady course as she brooded about her exchange with him a few moments ago. While cleaning up, she had found the bill of lading for their cargo underfoot on the cabin sole. It had been stuffed among a bundle of papers that Will had crammed into a satchel and tossed into the spare bunk. The satchel had popped open, and when Ben went through the cabin and opened the cabin door to go on deck for his watch, its contents took flight in the draft.

Will had been sitting already half asleep at the table, and after stepping on the business document and picking it up, she said, "Will, you can't just throw these important papers in with everything else. There's a file for ship's business!"

Will roused with a start. He sat up and scowled at her. "Stop nagging. I run the ship. You run the galley. I'll deal with paperwork as I see fit."

"You may be captain, but you're also the owner, so you have to take care of the ship's business, too."

Will stood up and shoved his chair back sharply. He slammed his open hand down on the table. "Can't you be still? I knew where that paper was!"

"Yes, right here on the floor, and now it has a boot mark on it. How will that look when you take it into the Box Shop office?"

"I don't give a damn what it looks like. I'm sick of you telling me how to do everything. Just get out of here and let me get some sleep."

Now, in the gathering dusk, Mollie glanced down at the illuminated compass watching her heading for Oswego as she said, "I wish I was more help on board."

Ben looked over. "What do you mean? You cook. You clean. You work on deck. You're a first class lake sailor."

Mollie, still looking at the compass card, answered, "Will thinks I'm too bossy. Maybe I shouldn't even be here."

Ben suspected that Captain Will had told Mollie to shorten sail. It had been easy enough to hear angry voices in the main cabin as he stood steering a few feet away on a quiet night.

"Nonsense. No one wants you to stop helping work the ship. We need you. You're as good on deck as an extra hand."

Mollie felt her eyes sting as she shook her head. "They say it's not lady-like to haul on a halyard or steer. A lot of people think female cooks aboard ship are a bad thing."

"Most people squawking about female cooks are the wives of mates and captains who can't keep their hands to themselves. Will's proud of you. He says you're the best helmsman aboard excepting Nate." Ben sighed and added, "My brother does have a temper though. Sometimes he acts before he thinks. His back was probably bothering him. He twisted it trying to keep up with Tommy. He couldn't do it either all cramped up below in the hold so that probably made him mad."

Then Ben chuckled. "Did anyone ever tell you how Reuben's great grandmother came to us?"

Mollie looked over. "Reuben the cat?"

Ben nodded still smiling as he stretched out in a comfortable slouch against the bulwark. "I was eight so Will was twelve. We were walking home from the store when we heard a racket and saw Artie Boggs and Sammy Wilson and two other boys teasing Mrs. Pearson's terrier in her yard front of her house. 'There's trouble' said Will. Artie was the town bully. He had a little gray kitten. He'd hold it up and dangle it over the dog, and when dog jumped for it, he'd yank the kitten away. We went over to the picket fence. 'Stop it. Leave it alone,' said Will.

"Artie just laughed at him. 'You want to stop me?' And he gave the kitten a good squeeze so it let out a yowl.

"Will jumped the fence as quick as could be and punched Artie hard right in the face. Will was skinny, but he'd worked all summer on the Holmes's schooner scow, and he was hard as wire. Artie was a lot bigger, he was a good fourteen years old, but he was soft and used to bluffing and bossing little nippers. He went right down on the ground and dropped the kitten. I crawled through the fence took a handful of dirt and threw it in Sammy's face and grabbed the kitten and ran. Sam and Artie went after Will.

"I ran down the street hooting and hollering, and a couple of men came running. As soon as they saw Artie and Sammy, they figured somebody was getting a licking. Mrs. Pearson's dog was yapping and jumping around, and when the men pulled Artie off Will, she came out into her yard. The gang ran off. Will was a sight, his nose was bleeding all over his shirt, but he grinned and said, 'I knocked one of Artie's teeth out!' Mrs. Pearson took us in to her kitchen and washed Will's face and gave us some lemonade. I asked if she wanted her kitten. 'Oh it's a stray,' she said. 'The mother had them under the porch and I couldn't catch any of them to drown.' So we took it home.

"That was Reuben's great grandmother. She had seven toes on both front feet just like Reuben. She was a brown tiger tabby, and she was the best ratter we ever had. I saw her take a rat half as big as she was once.

She followed me and Will around like a dog. Uncle Rob and I even took her out on the fish boat." Ben paused and studied the tips of his shoes and then looking up at Mollie said, "My brother doesn't like to see anyone pushed around and not get a fair chance. That goes for women as well as cats. He might say something sharp when he's mad, but he wouldn't want you to go ashore. Except for pure strength, a women can do 'bout anything a man can. You belong on this boat."

"Thanks. I don't ever want to give up sailing on the lake. I love it out here with the sky and..."

She sneaked a quick look at Ben. He seemed to be nodding in agreement. Then his head fell forward onto his chest. He's as tired as Will, Mollie thought. She stood on tip toe trying to see forward over the deck load. I hope Zeb's awake up there. Then she looked over at Ben again, fast asleep right on the deck. Steady Ben. He never complains. I wish I could be more like that. I need to learn to curb my tongue.

Mollie scanned the empty horizon. The wind had picked up, and she now had to brace against the pull of the wheel. She thought of the day just two months before when Will had led her down to the quiet icebound harbor to show her the new ship. He had been so proud and puffed up that day- a lot like Uncle Jack's tom turkey courting the hens. Will had boasted of *Gazelle's* rugged hull and spent a good hour taking her around to examine every detail of deck and hold. Mollie's gaze shifted to the sturdy oak timbers and the oversized freeing ports of the bulwark beside her.

Will had told her the *Gazelle* had been built by Jamie McPherson of the little bay port of Cat Hollow. Jamie was one of the best shipwrights on the lake. She's built to last, he'd told her. Our grandchildren will be sailing this schooner in 1930, he had laughed. *Gazelle* was nearly twenty years old, but the oak frames and planking of her green painted hull remained stout and strong. Back then, they had used well seasoned timber, and she had been salted by her builder to prevent rot. She still rated A-2, good enough for grain. She even retained a bit of fancy work with trail boards on her bows and a carving on her transom of a leaping antelope, reminders of a time before railroads when ship owners could afford a bit of embellishment.

She sighed and thought, I didn't know Will's back was bothering him. I could have gotten some liniment out for it.

Two hours later, Will Tommy and Nate came on deck for their watch. Mollie Ben and Zeb headed below glad to go to their warm bunks. The raw lake wind lanced deeply through the men's wool shirts and Mollie's cape, and her legs were stiff as she walked through the darkness to the companionway.

Ben paused to speak briefly with Will. "Wind's going into the north. She'll build more."

Will nodded, "We'll take in the topsails, now."

As Mollie settled under the covers, she heard Will's muffled commands and the rattle clunk and thud of gear as the crew moved about. She hoped it wouldn't blow too hard as she dozed off. The night wind was already plenty cold up there, and the boys were still pretty green at handling sail in the dark. They had only set and struck topsails a couple times and that only during daylight. She was glad she didn't have to go aloft to furl and lash the canvas on a black overcast night.

Chapter Two

"We shall someday be heeded" Susan B. Anthony

Near midnight, the wind veered more into the north. Will ordered Nate on the wheel to fall off one point. Then he went forward to help the inexperienced crew jibe the foresail to run wing and wing. After the foresail boom was secured, he and Tommy climbed up on the deck load to put the preventer tackle on the main. Though the rough cut boards were close stacked, the surface of the load was somewhat uneven. Tommy caught the edge of one plank with his foot as he made his way toward the boom and nearly fell.

"Cmon, Tom hop to!" snapped Will who was already at the boom leaning hard against it to hold it out against the wind.

Tommy scrambled across the load and added his weight and considerable muscle to the boom. Both men pushed and shoved on the spar to force it out to where Ben waited holding the heavy preventer tackle block. When secured and tightened, this would keep the boom from making accidental jibe as the ship ran downwind. It was a routine maneuver, even in darkness, one that Will had done a dozen times as a mate on other larger schooners. The *Gazelle* took a bigger wave on her quarter and lurched underfoot, and Tommy grunted and staggered as he strained against the boom.

But the wind got around behind the sail. Just as Ben was reaching up to hook on the boom tackle, the *Gazelle* yawed slightly. The boom end lifted. Then in the blink of an eye, it whipped back across the deck in a flying jibe. Tommy saw the massive spar coming and dropped to the deck load flattening himself against it. But the boom struck Will squarely and knocked him overboard.

Mollie awoke to the ship's sudden lurch and a loud crash followed by shouts, banging rattling sheets and blocks, and flogging thundering canvas. Then she heard a cry that shot a flood of cold terror through her.

"Man over board! On deck everyone- man over board!"

Mollie grabbed her cape and sprang up the three steps of the companionway. The ship had rounded on to a reach. Her noisy sails luffing in the darkness overhead, shook the rig and hull. Mollie saw Nate's

16

pale face in the binnacle's dim light as he stood frozen at the wheel. Ben came running aft followed by Tommy.

Ben pushed roughly past her as he headed for the small yawl boat that hung aft in davits, hooked to a tackle at its bow and stern. Tommy leaped to the starboard davit and uncleated the line that lowered the boat. It had been a week since the yawl boat had been used, and the swollen wet manila wouldn't run through the blocks on Ben's davit. Tommy had already started to lower his end of the yawl boat.

"Wait, Tommy," called Ben. "We've got to get the way off the schooner."

The *Gazelle* was still moving ahead under luffing sails and clattering banging sheets and blocks. If the yawl were lowered now it would capsize and swamp before the tackles could be unhooked. Mollie hurried over to Nate. "Go help Zeb get the jibs down."

Nate gave Mollie the wheel and ran forward. As she spun the wheel down hard to turn the schooner into the wind, she heard the davit blocks squeal behind her as the yawl boat finally began to descend.

Ben had the yawl ready, but now he shouted, "The oars-Tommy, where are the oars?"

Tommy sprinted forward to where the boat's oars had been stowed on deck after being painted the day before. He came pounding aft gasping and half sobbing and dropped them into the boat. Then abruptly Ben was over the rail, into the yawl and gone into the night.

Mollie called out, "Tommy, we need to get both jibs and the foresail down. We've got to heave to and jog. I'll keep her head to. Set up the weather staysail sheet hard after you get the jibs down."

The blustery wind had rolled up a choppy five foot sea. Ben would have a rough time out there alone in the little yawl boat. In the intense darkness of an overcast night twenty miles offshore, Mollie saw only the occasional dim flashes of wave crests breaking near the ship. Her stomach knotted with fear. What if both Ben and Will vanished. What will we do then? The flogging canvas and clashing iron hardware of the jib sheets quieted. The boys had the foresail most of the way down. Mollie let go of the wheel and turned to haul in on the heavy mainsheet, trying to pull it in tight. Tommy came hurrying aft to give her a hand.

"Is the staysail backed?" she asked,

"Yes'm. Any sign of him?"

"Nothing."

Hove to, the ship was much quieter. Mollie slipped a lash on the wheel and went to the leeward main shrouds. The crew stood rigid as they listened taut with fear and hardly daring to breathe while the *Gazelle* slowly drifted. Now and then a small creak or groan from the ship sounded almost like a distant cry for help. Once Mollie started upon hearing a high thin call. Her skin crawled. It was merely a gull startled from its sleep by their ship. Or was it? Only the slosh and thud of water against the hull answered. Only the swish and snarl of a nearby breaking wave came to her ears. The implacable void of darkness around them revealed nothing.

Mollie's hands grew numb from gripping the shroud. She no longer felt the burn of her bare feet on the deck. She began to shiver from cold and dread. Where was Ben? Had the yawl boat been swamped? Only the sound of wind and water came to their ears as the crew stood by. Soon Mollie's whole body was shaking with the raw wind plucking at her thin night clothes.

After what seemed like hours, they heard Ben's hail. Then abruptly the yawl was alongside. He tossed the bow line up and quickly followed it, timing his exit from the yawl carefully as the small boat leaped up and down beside the rolling schooner. Ben was soaked. As the wind struck him, he shivered. Without a word he turned away to stare into the night. Then looking at the spot on deck where Will had gone over the side, he said, "We'll jog 'til morning. Then we'll search again."

Time crawled as *Gazelle* lurched and rolled heavily in the waves while drifting slowly downwind. For hours her crew watched and waited, each standing tense and vigilant peering into the unrelenting darkness, listening for any sound and searching for any hint of Will. A few hours before dawn the wind freshened and began moaning through the rigging, and the night grew colder. Occasional rain from several sharp passing squalls pelted against their wet clothes. Will's loss and the increasing cold soaked into their bones, yet no one left their station or went below even just to fetch their oil skins.

No one spoke. Nate, Zeb, and Tommy stood forward by the windlass scanning the night, while Mollie and Ben were aft, one to each side of the ship. Mollie clung to the weather shroud cable gripping it with unfeeling hands. She stared into the blackness straining for sight or sound.

In the night's wee hours, as the initial shock wore off, she gave in to grief. Waves of despair and anguish swamped her. She leaned against the aft main mast shrouds. The deep bass notes of wind in the rigging groaning overhead sounded a dirge. She clutched the heavy steel cable with both hands and pressed her forehead against it. The words 'he's dead, he's dead' pounded repeatedly through her mind. Her eyes filled, and she began to weep. Soon she gave in utterly, abandoning the vigil. She heard nothing of wind and waves. The enormity of Will's loss roared in her head. *It's no use. We aren't going to hear anything. He's gone.* She sobbed in great racking shudders of grief that she tried to muffle lest Ben hear her over the moaning wind.

Why? Why was he gone? Why had she insisted on box boards? Oh Will, I'm sorry. If I had only listened to you. Oh dear God in Heaven, why did you take him? Why didn't I leave it alone? I made him go to Port Hope. If only we had waited in Kingston. It's all my fault. I could have stopped it.

She pictured Will struggling in the lake, gasping as icy water washed over his face. She imagined him thrashing, choking, his arms flailing. She saw him disappear as his heavy gear and boots pulled him down. That thin wail in the night sounded in memory again. Had it been a gull? Could they have found him if she had called out to Ben in the yawl? She imagined Will's lifeless body sinking slowly drawn down into the black depths of the lake. Mollie had never seen a dead sailor washed ashore. But she had heard of pallid corpses found on the strand. Would Will come ashore on some lonely wave washed beach, cast up like a bit of debris for the gulls to pick at?

Another spasm of grief wracked her as she gripped the heavy shroud cable. She told herself, "Hang on. Hold on. You must keep watch". But she couldn't stop the pain. It poured out again in noisy sobs. She gulped, drew a deep breath, and told herself, hold and belay, right now. You've got to stop.

Could he possibly be alive? The violent slam of the main boom that had awakened her, the heavy shock of the spar as it fetched up to leeward- she had felt the whole ship tremble with its force. No, he's not out there. Not in that cold water. But still they stayed hove to. Drifting. No one suggested they get underway. No one left the deck. They stood trembling in the bone chilling rain, muscles cramping with the cold, hands numbed, staring and listening to the sighs and moans of the wind passing through the ship's rigging.

Gradually the blackness paled to show the lake around them. The rain ceased. In the east a crack of dim sallow sky showed between the clouds and the dark horizon. The wind freshened more as night gave grudgingly away to a gray dawn. Around them the crew saw an iron colored lake liberally splashed with the dirty white crests of eight foot rollers streaked with foam. Not even a gull appeared overhead that bleak morning. Caught between the low cloud and the dark water, *Gazelle* drifted hove to, completely alone on a lifeless lake.

There was no more reason to wait. Zeb and Tommy stumbled forward to let the windward jib sheet go, while Mollie stiff and aching shuffled to the wheel to head the ship up into the wind. With the boys on the peak halyard and Ben and Nate on the throat halyard, they raised the reefed foresail and trimmed the jibs. Mollie then put the helm up to bear off on a broad reach.

The schooner felt heavy and dispirited beneath their feet as she rolled and pitched. The bitter wind raised its voice to an occasional wail in her stays, while some bit of loose rigging kept up a constant whimpering noise. At times, the wash of water under her counter flowing past her rudder gurgled and sobbed.

After changing into dry clothing, the crew gathered aft near the wheel to take comfort in each other's presence. No one wanted breakfast, but Mollie brewed strong bitter black coffee. All hands took a mug together with Nate once again steering. He had scarcely spoken since they had hove to. His cheeks were wet, though no spray had come aboard.

As he scanned the waters ahead, he spoke, "I thought I heard him say 'Fall off' but he must have been telling me 'Steer small.'"

"No," said Ben. "It happened before you did anything. I saw it. It wasn't your fault."

Nate made no reply as salt water silently ran down his face.

Mollie stared at the deck load of lumber and thought how Will hated box boards. He hurt himself trying to get the entire load on in a day. Oh, dear God, why didn't we stay in Kingston and wait for wheat?

Ben finished up his mug with a long draw and handed it to Mollie to take below. "We did what we could. We must bear up and go on to Oswego."

A week later in Eel Bay, redwing black birds shouted from the fringe of cattails at the head of the harbor while the silvery trill of ardent toads singing of spring love sounded under a strong May sun. A breath of wind from the south shifted the white curtains at the open kitchen window of the McIntyre home bringing the fragrance of early blooming lilacs into the room. Five people sat at breakfast. There was little talk among them of yesterday's funeral.

A strange funeral, with no procession to the grave yard with its black limbed locust trees still bare of leaves, and no body to lay beside the other McIntyres and close the grave over. They had only the service inside the small white wooden church and the clang of its bell sounding a solemn toll afterwards, announcing the passing of yet another mariner from the little bay port.

Would the family someday put a stone up, a cenotaph with "lost upon the lake" on it at the cemetery beside the church? Mollie looked down at her breakfast eggs. Some of the words of the minister echoing in the sanctuary stillness of the little church the day before came back to her.

"We are all preparing to cast off. One and another and another, we all must depart to that unknown coast. But there shall be no night there. Do not grieve, for we sail into the morning light and to a finer safer harbor above. God forbid that we should ever bury our love. The jewel that was Will lies not here. We bury merely the husk when we bury the dead. Will McIntyre's spirit is is now one with the wind. He has reached that further shore and resides now in a better world. He lives on in our hearts, and someday we will all join him."

Mollie looked away from her plate at the window. She listened to a robin's loud warbling nearby. She felt strangely detached as if she were viewing the room before her through the wrong end of Will's spyglass. The contrast between a cold and gray April night on the lake and this green sunlit early May morning added to the sense that Will had died a very long time ago.

She heard Ben saying to Uncle John, "If I had only gotten the preventer on a few seconds earlier, I never heard a thing after he went. I rowed around for maybe an hour- nothing. I think the boom hit him so hard that it knocked him out. Will was a good swimmer- we would have heard him yell. He could have stayed up a few minutes even in that cold water, and we did get the boat stopped pretty fast. That's why I think he was hurt when he went in, and he went right under. I don't think he felt a thing after the boom hit him."

21

"It's hard on the ones left behind, but it was a mercy for Will, if it was his time for the Lord to take him," sighed Aunt Sara.

Mollie felt a surge of resentment and anger. She knew Aunt Sara was right. Dying slowly, freezing in icy water alone surrounded by darkness would not be her preferred method of departure from this world. Better to be slammed on the head. But she wanted to shout- He was only twenty five years old! It never should have happened! She pushed her rage back into a dark place of the mind, clenched her hands in her lap, and remained silent. A knock sounded sharply on the front door, and Aunt Sara went to answer it.

On the step stood a short stout man wearing a well tailored dark gray frock coat. He was leaning upon a silver headed cane as he tapped the ground lightly with one foot. Behind him a sharp rig with a gleaming bay gelding in harness stood at the roadside. Without removing his black coachman's hat, the man spoke.

"Ned Sloan. I'm looking for the widow Mollie McIntyre."

Seeing the group at the table within, he limped past Aunt Sara, entered the kitchen and fixed his gaze upon Mollie.

"I'm here to foreclose on the note." Seeing the looks of confusion turned toward him he added impatiently, "The terms are quite clear if you had troubled to read them. Payment within ten days or foreclosure in the event of a sale or change of ownership of the vessel."

Mollie's father was the first to gather his wits about him. "Ah, won't you sit down and have coffee with us Mr. Sloan?"

"No, I will not. I've come to serve notice of foreclosure or collect the money." He drew out a document from his coat pocket and tossed it on the table.

Mollie dropped her fork with a clatter and sat back as if repelled by the man standing before them. "How much?" she asked.

Her father drew the paper across the table, unfolded it and scanned it. Then he looked up with eyebrows raised. "Twelve thousand dollars? Isn't that quite a sum for a wee little two sticker nearly twenty years old?"

Sloan's frosty gaze took in the table as he replied coldly, "I wouldn't know. All I know is that the stated value of the vessel as collateral is as herein, and that's the balance due."

Ben spoke, "But what if we don't have it?"

"Then I shall auction her off for what I can get."

Mollie's father said in his best dealing with a difficult port official voice, "Now Mr. Sloan, do please sit for a moment. Perhaps we can work something out."

Sloan leaned a bit more heavily on his cane and with his other hand gestured impatiently towards the paper as he ignored the Captain.

"I am a busy man, Mrs. McIntyre. Do you intend to pay off the note within ten days?"

She looked back feeling the room closing around her, the walls pressing in, squeezing the breath from her lungs. She felt trapped, like a bird inside the house beating its wings against a window. Helplessly, she dropped her gaze down at the table, though not before everyone saw her eyes shining with unshed tears.

"No," she said in an almost inaudible voice.

Ben got up suddenly. He put a hand on Mollie's bent shoulders.

"Come, Mollie, let's get some air."

Silently she rose and followed him out the door into the sunlight. Once outside she began to weep. Ben took her in his arms and held her gently as one would comfort a small child.

"I know," he said. "Let's go down to the harbor. We should check on the boat. No one has tried the pump for over a week."

Mollie dragged along behind Ben down the path to the little harbor. She didn't see the old gnarled willows at the head of the harbor glowing green- gold with their lace work of tiny new leaves. She didn't hear the cheerful twitter of the barn swallows swooping overhead gathering midges for their clamoring youngsters in the nests under the boat shop eaves. Nor did she notice her favorite flowers in the dooryard, the cheery yellow daffodils now fully open and welcoming the morning sun. She knew she could go back home to live with Aunt Anna and Uncle Frank on their farm beside Sodus Bay. But the thought of giving up Will's vessel and leaving the family and village that she now loved like her own, twisted a knife blade of grief deep into her heart.

And what would she do back in Sodus Point? She couldn't just live off her aunt and uncle. They had a hard enough time supporting themselves on their little patch of land. There were the hotels and taverns. Perhaps she could find work in one of the hotels as a scullion or cook. The thought of being shut away from the open lake and never again feeling a deck alive underfoot, the brave schooner leaning to the wind, rising, then plunging to shoulder aside the seas, engulfed her in a new wave of grief.

Tears again flooded her eyes and blurred her vision as she plodded down the path.

Aboard the now familiar ship, she shuffled after Ben as he went forward to check the pump. For two months they had worked hard and long, but they had worked together. Now, she thought, she would never sail aboard the *Gazelle* again. Perhaps she would spend the rest of her days inside a dark smoky tavern scrubbing floors or scouring pots, fetching and carrying and serving drunken and dissolute patrons. How long could she endure their demands and their unwelcome unwholesome attentions? Like a hatchling turtle ashore surrounded by greedy gulls, a young widow in a tavern would be easy pickings. She remembered her neighbor's daughter who had worked at Harris's Hotel and come home with bruises on her face and her dress torn. Deliberately she steered her thoughts onto another tack.

What will become of the *Gazelle*, she thought as she watched Ben try the pump handle. The *Gazelle* had lost her captain. Who would guide her course now? We're both adrift it seems.

"Not a bit of water," he said. Then he sat down on the anchor windlass and stared at the deck.

"What will the boys do?" asked Mollie. "What will you do without the ship?"

"I don't know about the boys," answered Ben. "Perhaps I'll go work with Uncle John in the boat yard." He sighed deeply, and his shoulders slumped. He seems lost without Will, Mollie thought. Well, she felt lost, too. Adrift and awash, foundering in a dark sea.

"Twelve thousand dollars," said Mollie. "How could Will have possibly borrowed so much?"

Ben shook his head. "She won't bring that at auction. Not this season anyway. We'd be lucky to get half that for her with things so slow."

"So what about the rest of the note?" asked Mollie.

Ben shrugged. After a moment he said, "I guess it's in your name, now, and you don't have any money, so the bank has to write it off as a bad debt."

Mollie walked to the rail and looked down at the water beside the ship. In the clear shallows a school of minnows turned and swirled the silver of their sides flashing and flickering in the water alongside.

"So everybody loses."

Ben nodded silently staring down at the deck as he scuffed his foot along one of the plank seams.

Back in the kitchen Ned Sloan glared at the door after it closed behind Mollie and Ben and then turned back to address Captain Tom and Uncle John. "Well then, I must be going. The sheriff will be down to post bond on the ship shortly. And don't get any ideas about moving her anywhere."

Sloan limped down the steps and out to his waiting carriage, thinking of the rest of his day's tasks, especially the meeting with the bank's board of directors that afternoon. They would be wanting to know what he proposed to do about the McKenzie Starch Factory loan that had gone sour. He cursed his gouty foot. He wished he could go home. He badly needed some cash liquidity right now. He cursed McKenzie's investment in unsound railroad bonds. Any fool would have known that an interest rate of 18% was a rank gamble. Why had he listened to his son- in- law Jared Kraut who had urged the board to back McKenzie. Jared is bright and ambitious, but he's also impulsive and greedy, and now I must clean up that mess. He cursed the sharp pain again as he lifted himself into the carriage and reached into his pocket for the flat sided small bottle. He took a healthy swallow before starting the horse. As he did so, he briefly recalled the young widow, her face pale against her gleaming dark hair. He remembered her gray eyes filled with pain. Well, yes, he thought. It is a rotten world. But life goes on and debts must be paid. He started the horse with a sharp slap of the reins.

Captain Tom, who had walked to the door with Sloan to open it for him, returned to the table. He looked down at Uncle John who was still seated and now contemplating a large blue- bottle fly washing its face while it sat on the rim of his coffee cup. "How could we hang onto the boat?" the captain wondered. He pictured the schooner as she sailed into Kingston last week, tall sparred and still holding her springy sheer line even after twenty years of cargo carrying. The vessel was solid and sound and had looked so grand, especially with Mollie at the wheel. In his mind's eye he saw the *Gazelle* running into the harbor, broad off the wind, the sun glinting on the wake aft and a tall strong woman at her helm. He had been so proud of his daughter that day. His pride had risen right up and near choked him so that he had turned to Mr. Jenks, his mate, and said with studied nonchalance "That's my girl there on the wheel."

Captain Tom was thinking hard as he sat down. "How much money have you got John? I've an idea."

Chapter Three

"If a woman is proved competent for duty, and anxious to perform it, why restrain her?" nineteenth century newspaper op ed

It was a simple idea. As Captain Tom explained while standing upon the *Gazelle's* after deck two days later, "A bird in hand is worth two in the bush to any banker."

He and John McIntyre had hatched a plan of action that morning in the kitchen. They would go to Picton and offer Ned Sloan three thousand dollars, the combined sum of all their savings, for the first payment on the *Gazelle's* note.

Captain Tom told Mollie and Ben, "He's no fool. He knows he won't get his twelve thousand dollars from an auction sale. He'd be lucky to get half that. This way he has a quarter of the money right now, and he can still sell the ship later. He probably figures he'll get at least one more payment out of us before then."

The meeting with Sloan had been unexpectedly cordial. "He said he was in a tight spot for cash. The big bugs on Wall Street down in New York City were battling each other again. Their manipulation and foolery disrupted the market, and with bonds being called in to cover positions, everyone needed to raise cash. Then, he said, one of his biggest loans went bad because of a railroad bankruptcy. So he took our money and said we had until the end of September to make the next payment."

"How much will that be?" asked Mollie.

"Another three thousand with the balance by the end of the year."

Ben and Mollie exchanged anxious looks as Captain Tom continued, "Well, it gives us a few months. We'll raise the rest of it somehow. We shall proceed one day at a time."

Mollie asked, "You didn't put up your share of the *Anowa* did you Father?"

Captain Tom looked off across the water for a moment before answering, "Not all of it anyway."

When Ben looked hard at his uncle, John said quickly, "Nope. No debt for us. Strictly cash. There's nothing in the shipyard to mortgage anyway."

Mollie felt a cold pool of dread settle in her midsection at the thought of Father putting up his share of the *Anowa* to keep the *Gazelle* going.

Seeing the look on her face, Captain Tom said, "We're not whipped yet. The lumber wholesaler -Isiah Fitzhugh- that we're meeting with, he's from Oswego, and he's a good man. I've dealt with him for years. He's honest and fair, and he's in Deseronto right now. I telegraphed him while we were still in Picton and asked if he'd meet with us. He answered 'yes' right away so I think he'll help us out."

The quickest way to get to Deseronto at the north end of the Bay of Quinte's Long Reach was by boat, so Captain Tom had rounded up Tommy, Nate and Zeb with a hasty explanation of the plan, and they, along with Ben and Mollie, set sail with *Gazelle* right after breakfast. He put the boys to work, swabbing and cleaning once they got under way.

"I want that deck clean enough to eat off of. I know Fitzhugh, and if he has any use for a little two-master he'll help us out. But he's got standards, and we'd better measure up."

No one grumbled. In fact it felt good to turn to and spruce up the ship. Tommy even ventured a few verses of The Sailor's Alphabet as he scrubbed the deck. Mollie followed suit below, sweeping, mopping and stowing in the galley and main cabin. She even got the stove blacking out and applied a coat of it to her little range and polished the nickel plating of the oven door. As she worked, she was amazed at the industry the ship's spiders had displayed below decks during the brief layup after Will's funeral.

The wind came up with the sun, and before long they made the turn at Indian Point and began sailing upwind on the protected waters of the eastern reach. It was tack and tack about, and it kept everyone busy, too busy to think much. All morning, they worked up the reach under a blue spring sky as the land off to port grew higher and more rugged. By noon, they had passed the gray stone buildings of the Glenora Mills and the Little Giant Water Wheel Works tucked away under Lake of the Mountain's steep slope. By then, the schooner was heeling to a brisk westerly funneled by the lofty steep sided limestone escarpments that flanked both sides of Picton Bay.

Once around the corner, they started their sheets. *Gazelle* sprang forward like her namesake and foamed along, light and flying at twelve knots, the water hissing along her lee side as she tore open the green waters of the bay. It was the grandest sailing of the year, as they romped up the narrow waters of Long Reach, and Mollie's spirits rose with the fresh breeze. Now at leisure, she went forward and settled against the pawl post to listen to the rumble of the water surging under the bow. As she watched the patchwork of verdant pastures and farm fields, split rail fence lines, and the barns and houses on the low lying mainland to starboard slip past, she pondered future possibilities.

Bright green fields of newly sprouted barley and wheat promised harvests and cargoes to come, contrasting with darker green pastures and the hay meadows rippling in the wind. Occasionally the fragrance of cedar came to them from the tree clad highlands of stony Prince Edward County to windward. The sun warmed deck under her and steady rush of the water nearby gradually pulled her out of the deep well of grief, and she indulged herself in a few glimmers of hopefulness.

It was good to be under sail again. She had missed being afloat. The liquid croon of the water moving past the ship's side and the gentle motion over the calm bay waters made her feel like a babe gently rocked in Mother's arms. Could they possibly keep the ship? Ben had gotten his ticket last year, he could be captain. Ships *Gazelle's* size didn't need a mate with papers. She could help out, and Nate could be the mate. Mollie tried to count up how many trips carrying lumber they would need to make over the next five months to pay Sloan. Assuming current freight rates held, after wages, port fees, duties and other expenses they might be able to clear just enough to meet the September payment.

"But," she said out loud to the *Gazelle*, "you'll have to step lively. No time for delays or break downs."

"What's that?" a voice asked. "What did you say?" She turned to see Ben leaning against the hatch companionway behind her.

"Oh, I was just trying to figure out how many trips we'd have to make between now and September to make the next payment."

"How many would it take?"

"I'd guess maybe twenty."

Ben shook his head. Mollie could see grief etched deeply on his face as he said,

"That's a pretty fast turn around." After a lengthy pause spent watching the shore go by, he continued, "Look, Mollie, maybe if everything went exactly right, the winds were perfect and every cargo was unloaded with no delay, no waiting for a berth and nothing to hold us up, we might be able to make the note payment. But it won't be easy. That waterfront is rough over there. Those dock workers and stevedores..." Ben grimaced in recall. "There were all sorts of labor troubles over there two years ago and there's plenty of bad feelings still."

Ben had been in Oswego as a deckhand then with Jack Parson on the old *Red Rover* during a wildcat strike by the stevedores. The walkout had been in sympathy with a series of violent railroad strikes in Pennsylvania coal country. It had been sudden and vicious, touched off by the beating of a stevedore by two policemen and fueled by whiskey and starvation wages. Rough tattered men had converged on the lumber docks like angry hornets swarming around a kicked nest.

Suddenly a mob was cursing, scuffling, and then brawling with the out numbered constables. A huge bear of a man picked up a broken spar from the wharf and ran with it at the warehouse door. He slammed the door twice before it fell open. More men drawn into the fray, immediately began looting. They had acted like a pack of starving dogs, snarling and shoving their way into the warehouse to grab anything they could lay their hands on. Those of the mob unable to reach the warehouse began seizing planks from the lumber stacks to sell or take home to burn for heat. When a couple of men tried to board the *Red Rover,* the fight quickly spread to her decks.

A hulking dockworker, with fists hard as horses hooves, reached the head of the gangplank. He slammed the mate square in the gut and then kicked him in the knee. The winded man dropped to the deck. Ben had jumped into the fray then. He went for the giant with a hard punch to the face. Bright blood gushed from a broken nose as the man staggered back. From the corner of his eye Ben saw the glint of a knife blade as another stevedore lunged at him. Ben got an arm up, then abruptly his attacker staggered aside and fell. In the nick of time, old Jack had laid the man out with a belaying pin grabbed from the pin rail.

"I darn near got killed there. And another thing, even if this Mr. Fitzhugh does give us a charter, when I was mate Will did all the paperwork in port. I've never done any of the accounts or the customs reports."

"Maybe I can help with that," said Mollie.

Ben brightened a little. Then he frowned again. "I can just picture how those dock lumpers and coal shovers will take to being bossed by Mate Mollie over there. They won't like it at all. You'll have to lay low when we were in port. And Will had a run in with one of the customs men on our last trip, so we're already on his bad side."

30

Mollie's face was beginning to assume that set look that Ben by now had come to recognize very well. "I can be pretty persuasive if I have to be. Maybe I can use some womanly wiles on the customs man."

Ben shook his head. Womanly wiles just didn't seem to be part of Mollie's suit of sails as far as he could see. He walked over to the forward shrouds and stepped up onto the rail. While holding the shrouds he leaned out to take in the view fore and aft. He was silent for a spell before remarking, "She sure is going along." He remained standing on the rail for a minute or more, watching the *Gazelle* moving through the water and remembering when he had first seen the boat.

Jamie McPherson had built her. Old Jamie had launched a half dozen schooners out of his South Bay shipyard. His last two, the *Gazelle* and another similar sized boat, the *Antelope,* had been built for his two sons. The *Antelope* had been cut down by a steamer up on Lake Erie fifteen years ago and went down with all hands. Tim, his other son, had lost *Gazelle* to the bank. Arthur Stevens bought her at auction. He kept her busy and profitable, too, until he died. She was a good carrier and fast for her size.

But times were changing. Steam was taking more and more of the trade once handled by schooners. Ben remembered an exchange a few days ago in *Gazelle's* cabin between Will and Mollie. They had been arguing about plans and prospects for the season. Will was ready to go out and buy another boat though he'd hardly gotten *Gazelle* shaken down. But Mollie had argued for caution saying that the steamers were getting bigger so coal was cheaper for them to carry, and cheaper for the steamers to burn, too.

Mollie had said Captain Tom told her of a propeller called the *Ketcham* up on the upper lake that had all her gear and machinery aft. Her whole deck opened up to load and unload through five hatches far faster than a schooner could.

Will, the ambitious dreamer, had objected, "But it takes twenty men to run her. We can sail with five and the wind costs nothing."

Mollie had argued back, "When they start building iron lake steamers here, you watch out. They'll take our timber, grain, and our coal trade, too. The steamer makes three trips to our two and carries five times as much as we do. And her insurance rates are lower in the fall."

"No filthy smoking steamer manned by lubbers and landsmen will ever out sail my ship!" Will had argued back.

Ben stepped down onto the deck again. His eyes lingered over the vessel, and he noticed again the quality of the detailing and the good finish that the boat still had. There were the small things, too, like the way the belay post for the foresheet was set to take the line's lead easily, and the tight fitted scarfs in the bulwark cap rail by which he now stood. She's well made, he thought. If any schooners could still make a living on the lake, this one would.

Mollie broke into his reverie. "Ben, we can do it. I know you can handle the boat. You're as good a sailor as Will was. And I can do the port business. Please let's just try it until September and see where we are. If we have to hire a captain we can't possibly make it pay."

They both looked aft to where Tommy was at the helm listening to one of Captain Tom's endless supply of lake tales, standing much like Will had in that place just two weeks before. Ben thought of Uncle John's offer to work with him in the yard a few days ago. He ran one hand over the bulwark rail cap. He thought of the yawl boat he had built last winter, now hanging at *Gazelle's* stern, and the satisfaction he had felt when she had been launched. She had floated pretty as a swan on the bay then. He propped his elbows on the rail, leaned out and studied the curl of white water coming off the *Gazelle's* bows, wondering for the fiftieth time, how her builder had shaped that entry to make her cut so cleanly through the water. He deliberated over his choices as he stared down at the foam alongside.

He loved building. Shaping and fitting wood to see a boat take form from a collection of oak and cedar lumber was the best thing he had ever done. But then he remembered the day two months ago, when Will had come into the boat shop, like a gust of wind, full of energy and noise. He had envied his older brother that day, and his own dreams of doing grand things had stirred as he listened. It had been easy to let Will's enthusiasm carry him along when he'd asked Ben to come as mate. Will's vision had drawn Ben as a candle flame brings in a moth.

"Ben," Will had said that day, "I've done it. I've bought a ship."

Ben had been working down an oar blade. He put his plane down deliberately, careful as always not to rest it on the iron. Without speaking, he looked at Will who stood before him fairly vibrating with excitement. He had a feeling that his brother had plans for him. He wondered how he was going to like those plans.

"It's the *Gazelle*. You know the boat. I can get the cousins for crew and Mollie will go as cook, but I need a mate. You'll come won't you, Ben?"

Ben picked at a curl of shaving stuck to his wool shirt. Then he looked across the shop at the nearly complete yawl boat he had built to his own design. He remembered other adventures that Will had talked him into. Like that time when they were kids, and they had set sail for the Duck Islands, a ten mile sail to the east. He'd nearly drowned that day.

Will had found an old beat up fish boat on the beach and purchased it for two dollars. He poured some pitch in her gaping seams, nailed a couple of tin patches over the worst splits in her planking, and after soaking the boat up for a couple of days in the bottom of the harbor, the boys bailed her out and set sail.

About five miles out, the wind picked up sharp from the southwest. The lake soon kicked up a nasty steep chop. Before long the little skiff was laboring hard. Ten year old Ben was too, bailing for his life trying to keep up with the skiff's leaks. It was time to turn back. The water rose over the floorboards despite Ben's efforts. Will put the helm up and headed for home, cussing the rotten old boat and bad luck. But while he bailed, Ben felt the boat's quick rise as she sped along lifting to the four foot waves chasing them. He scooped up the bilge water and tossed it over the side, silently urging her on. It felt like the skiff wanted to live, too, that day. She was doing her best for them. Ben scooped and dumped until his arms ached as the boat surfed down the waves and the distant line of dark trees on the horizon ahead drew slowly closer.

At last, they reached the stone ledges offshore in the lee of Long Point and got around the corner and into the shelter of Eel Bay. Soaked chilled and wobbly with fatigue, Ben clambered out and helped Will drag the skiff up out of the water at the shipyard. Will left it without a backward look. But Ben lingered. He unstepped the mast, furled the sail, and carefully bailed the boat dry. He tied the painter to a log on shore and only then did he follow Will home.

Later, Uncle John asked Will what he planned to do with the boat.

"Burn it!"

"Why not give it to Ben? He could fix it up," suggested Uncle John.

So Will did. That winter with help from his uncle, Ben brought the little fish boat back to life, making her strong and young again with new steam bent oak ribs, gunwales, stem, and several new cedar planks. He had relished the process of restoration, and when he was done, he knew he wanted to build boats more than he wanted to sail them.

So two months ago on that March morning in the shop, Ben had looked at his older brother and opened his mouth to say, "I want to stay here with Uncle John in the yard." But somehow out had come, "I guess I could give it a try."

Ben's face twisted in a wry smile as he looked at Will's widow. He felt some of the same feelings now that he'd had toward the hard pressed gallant little skiff more than a decade ago as he looked at Mollie standing there, her chin up and her eyes bright as she met his gaze squarely. He remembered Will's jubilation back in March after he had been pestered into going as mate. The schooner had been Will's dream. Ben returned Mollie's direct look.

"All right, I'll give it a go for one season."

Mollie impulsively reached out and put her hand on his arm. "Thanks, Ben. We'll pay that note off. With a ship and crew this good we'll make money hand over fist. You'll see, Captain Ben."

They reached Deseronto as the sun was flooding the western sky with orange and gold, anchored, and then lined the vessel into a dock to await their meeting the next morning with Fitzhugh. There was little talk as they ate supper together. Each wondered about the man who could determine their future with a piece of paper and the stroke of a pen tomorrow.

Chapter Four

"I would have girls regard themselves not as adjectives but as nouns" E.C.
Stanton

Fitzhugh arrived at precisely 9 am as his agent had said he would.
Mollie expected that a wealthy lumber baron would look a lot like Ned
Sloan, the banker. She expected to see an old man with a gut like a shad
and a face like a Yorkshire boar pig. Her father had told them that
Fitzhugh owned tens of thousands of acres of forested land in Michigan,
Minnesota and in Ontario. So Mollie was surprised to see a slender man,
who stepped lightly down from his carriage and came aboard, moving
with easy grace and a quick smile to meet Captain's Tom's handshake.

"It's good to see you again Captain Tom, good indeed."

Then he turned to look upon the ship's company. The boys under his
scrutiny shuffled and shifted a bit, doing their best to hide behind Uncle
John, Ben and Mollie. Though Fitzhugh's hair and neatly trimmed
mustache were well silvered, his face was unlined, and his pale blue eyes
were keen. Mollie got the distinct feeling that he wasn't missing much as
he sized the young crew up.

Captain Thomas introduced Ben and Mollie explaining, "This is the
new owner I wrote you of. She's hoping for a cargo."

Fitzhugh shook hands around, and took his silk top hat off to Mollie.
As he straightened up from his courtly little bow, Mollie saw an odd look
flit across his face. Then he stepped back and scanned the decks as he
said, "*Gazelle*. There was a ship who lost her captain just two weeks ago.
Wasn't her name..." Then realizing why the *Gazelle* was here to see him,
Fitzhugh said to Mollie's father, "I'm so sorry Captain Thomas. I didn't
realize..."

Mollie's father said quickly, "Well, let's take a look around the deck
shall we? She's a fine ship, and her crew is one of the best on the lakes.
Come, I'll show you the hold if you like."

He started off to lead the way forward towards the now open main
hatch. But Fitzhugh lingered, his eyes falling upon Reuban who was
perched upon the deck house watching the proceedings. That stupid cat,
thought Mollie. I should have shut him below.

"Now who is this noble fellow?" he asked extending a hand towards the cat. Reuban sat up and graciously accepted the gesture. He closed his eyes in bliss as Fitzhugh rubbed his ears with a practiced hand, and a purr began to hum from his chest.

"That's Reuban. He's part of the crew," said Ben.

"Every grain carrier needs a cat. I'll wager this fellow earns his pay," said Fitzhugh as he ran his hand down Reuban's back. Then he turned and followed Mollie's father forward.

"We're cooked," Mollie heard Nate murmur behind her. "He'll never give us a charter with a brand new Captain twenty three years old." But Tommy reached out and punched his cousin Ben lightly on the shoulder, "Sure he will. We got the best wind wagon driver on South Bay here. And besides, he likes cats."

Ben tried to smile. He reached over to pet Reuban and said, "Cross those seven toes for luck, Reuban."

Then they all stiffened as Captain Thomas and the lumberman came aft, Nate looking particularly pained. Fitzhugh addressed Ben, "You have a fine vessel here, sir. She's well made. Those grown knees are absolutely splendid, and that planking-some of those strakes run sixty feet without a knot. How much does she draw loaded?"

Ben said, "With her board up about seven feet sir."

Fitzhugh nodded, "She is exactly what I need. I have a mill on Dark Harbor where the river has silted in the harbor, and the steamers and big schooners can't get in to the wharf anymore. You're little *Gazelle* will be of great help to me." He turned to Captain Thomas. "Shall we have a business meeting in the cabin?"

Mollie moved quickly to open the door. "I'll start the coffee right now."

The business arrangements were simple enough. Fitzhugh would charter the *Gazelle* for three months until the barley harvest came in. Then he would release the ship, so her crew could pursue the higher freights of grain. She would carry high quality graded pine between Dark Harbor and Oswego, though there might be an occasional run to Charlotte.

He gave them a fixed rate of freight for the duration of the charter. Mollie sucked in her breath. Seeing the look on Mollie's face he said firmly, "It's a fair rate, Mrs. McIntyre. I believe reliability is vital to good business. I like long term relationships and workers that I can count on. It's far cheaper and more profitable to me in the long run."

Some of Mollie's excitement must have appeared on her face because Fitzhugh smiled slightly and said, "If this charter works well for us all, there will be others. I can keep your *Gazelle* on the run for as long as you want."

Fitzhugh detailed the arrangements and terms, wrote down the names of his agents in Dark Harbor and Oswego, and assured them that he would at least occasionally see them himself over in Oswego where he made his home. Then they sat down to a mid day dinner followed by coffee and conversation, both favored occupations of Mollie's father whenever he was in port. Before long, they were discussing trees and lumber, topics of keen interest to both men.

Captain Thomas spoke of the great fires that had burned for weeks in the pine forests of the upper midwest, darkening the skies last fall and laying a heavy haze over the lake in Michigan. He told of an accident involving a schooner and a steamer not far from where his own ship had then been. "The smoke was so thick that the two collided. I was about five miles away and it was as being in fog- no more than a few hundred yards visibility. Even when it lifted the sun was pale like the moon at mid day. You could smell it, too, a burned bitter smell."

Isiah looked grim as he spoke of the tens of thousands of acres of desolation left by the fires."The rivers ran with mud. I saw vast rafts of dead fish floating down to Green Bay. They were killed by the mud and silt that choked the rivers after the fires. The very soil burned down to naked rock. Some of the finest pine forests on earth were lost, and with only sand and gravel left behind, they will never recover. I lost a magnificent stand that contained many splendid mast pines- some over 200 feet tall. It's nothing but worthless black charred trunks as far as one could see now."

Mollie's father sighed, "Such is the price of progress, I guess."

Mollie was surprised by the anger in Isiah's reply.

"It is not an inevitable consequence of progress. This ruthless destruction year after year is careless and senseless, but not inevitable. Man is everywhere an agent of disturbance and destruction in nature. But as he advances his civilization and depletes the soils and waters, he sows the seeds of his own doom. However, just as we destroy, we can also rebuild. I have a book you should read, my friend. It's by George Perkins Marsh, and it's called *Man And Nature*. He has described these cycles of destruction and ways in which European forests are being now restored."

At this point Isiah was beginning to lean forward a bit as his voice took on urgency. He declared, "I am adopting these practices, as we log our holdings. We will leave mother trees to re-seed, not the broken twisted rotted trees, but rather, the very finest tallest most vigorous specimens that will produce strong offspring."

Captain Thomas objected, "But those are the most valuable timber trees."

Isiah replied, "Surely. And we won't leave all of them! But we will leave every tenth one, a sort of a tithe for the forest."

He went on to tell of his purchase of vast tracts of cut over land for pennies an acre in both the Midwest and in Ontario and of his plans to experiment with active re-seeding. He described a tree nursery he had seen in Germany and how he had begun to experiment with such seedling cultivation in the midwest. Though there were some who said pine could never grow again where it once stood, Isiah had seen otherwise.

"I have young trees planted five years ago that are now fifteen feet tall. It's true, it costs money, but consider the costs of forest destruction. Think of the great damage done to streams and rivers by these careless practices. Think of the fish killed and the soils lost. Fishermen and those who do business with them, like the boat builders and net makers will not recover those losses for many years. And it will be many more years before the fish runs resume in clear running streams."

This prompted an interjection from Uncle John. "I build fish boats. My father was a fisherman, and my brother is a fisherman now. Fifty years ago there were salmon runs here that packed the rivers solid. You could walk across a stream on them they were that thick. In a single night my father speared enough to fill four barrels. You could reach down and catch a hundred fish with your hands in an hour. And the ciscoes..." He shook his head at the devastation of the lake's silver hordes remembering beach seines that had bulged with tens of thousands of small fish.

"We would bring in fifty barrels in a single haul. Sometimes we couldn't even bring the net up on the beach, it was so heavy with fish. Now it's hard to believe it was ever like that. No one thought we'd ever catch them all. Now they're gone. I remember the spawn drifting on shore three inches deep during the fall runs. We salted down 800 barrels a year in just in Eel Bay. There'd be twenty boats out there during the run. You're lucky to see a small school of 'em out there now in the fall."

Isiah said, "Not all of those losses are the result of deforestation, of course. But they are all part of a pattern of great constancy. As man advances his so-called civilization, he disturbs nature's harmonies in a relentless cycle of thoughtless exploitation and destruction. If we continue, in another generation there will be no more forests and rivers and fisheries to destroy. I, too, recall the salmon runs when I was a boy. The Oswego River had salmon as you describe. Tremendous beautiful silver fish- thirty pounds or more. Once, when they were running near our home, I saw a team of horses fording the river spooked by the fish hitting their hooves." He paused and lifted his empty coffee cup and Mollie refilled it. Then he went on more quietly.

"I have a son, Daniel. You'll meet him in Oswego. He's about your age," he said looking at Ben. "He's a fine lad and a great help to me. I want his son to still be harvesting timber from our lands when he is my age. And I want him to be able to take his boy fly fishing to catch a salmon dinner as I did when I was young. I believe it can be done. We shall show the lumbermen of Michigan and Wisconsin how."

They talked on about fish, forests, lumber, and ships, Isiah obviously enjoying Captain Tom's company until the late sun slanted long shadows across the deck. When Fitzhugh got up to leave he said, "You must come and visit me this winter in Oswego with more of your stories. I ask you every year and you never come. And bring your daughter and Captain Ben, too!"

When he had gone ashore, the ship's company looked at one another in amazement. Then Tommy let out a long loud two fingered whistle, while Zeb did a little victory shuffle. Even Nate was smiling. They agreed to get underway at once for Dark Harbor, about fifty miles up lake, passing by Eel Bay to drop off Uncle John and Mollie's father. Reuban was winding around the crew's feet reminding them it was getting close to supper time.

Ben scooped him up and cuddled him ruffling his fur. "Nice work, Reuban. We should promote you to sales agent- that's chow every day from the table."

By late afternoon the *Gazelle* was romping out of the Bay of Quinte with the wind well aft over her quarter. But ten miles from Eel Bay, the breeze softened and then faded away leaving *Gazelle* becalmed. The ship's company accepted their lot stoically. The wind would return. While they waited, Mollie cooked up a victory supper of ham and navy beans and dried apple pie. Afterwards, the men sat on deck got their pipes out and settled down for a yarn or two as they awaited the wind.

Uncle John was very quiet. Mollie had noticed his sober look and furrowed brow. Now he stirred on the deck box he had staked out for his roost, sighed and reached into his pocket for the comfort of his clay pipe. He held it in his hand and asked Mollie, "Did you ever hear of how Duncan, Will and Ben's Pa, was lost?"

She shook her head.

"Well you shall hear of it now." John packed his pipe and lit it. After a long draw to fire it up properly, he fixed his eyes on Mollie."You should know the story if you plan to sail the lake this fall." He puffed away for a bit leaning back against the aft rail. Then he began his tale.

"It happened on a November night in '75. Twas late in the season. Freights were down, wages and insurance up. It were lean times. Everyone was driving their vessels hard. Freights had been low for years and profits scarce. Boats were sailing short handed and overloaded and corners were cut. Gear that should have been replaced was patched and lashed and cobbled together and many a late season trip that should never have been made was taken.

"Duncan was master and part owner of a canal sized schooner, the *Ellen Murton*. She was laden with wheat from Milwaukee for Oswego. It was her last freight and last chance for a profit, too, that season. She sailed in late November from the Welland Canal and ran the length of the lake in a rising wind. After she passed Charlotte, it chopped around into the north and turned bitter. By nightfall, it was blowing a living gale and spitting sleet, while the decks were icing up. They reefed her with two tucks on fore and main and kept on. With the lights of Oswego ahead and fifteen foot waves behind, Duncan called everyone aft including the cook. That would be Tommy's older sister Annie. He told them the harbor entrance would be bad, and that they would have to wear ship to get in. Between the backwash from the jetties, the river current, and the harbor bar, it was going to be rough. The tug wouldn't be able to get a line on them until they were inside, and if they struck bottom on the bar or broached, Oswego harbor would be their grave just as it's been for a lot of other ships.

"Duncan told Annie to go below and put on a pair of his trousers. He said a soaked wool dress was the last thing she needed if she had to make a jump for the jetty. He had the crew lash a pair of oars and extra bailers in the yawl, and they overhauled the tackles to be sure she'd be quick to lower. When they reached the entrance, they jibed her over and the rotten old foresail split with a bang. They'd patched 'er one too many a time.

"Then a big wave lifted the *Murton* and flung her towards the jetty. Duncan was on the wheel and he managed somehow even without the foresail to keep her from broaching. They almost made it in, but then they dropped into a trough like a hole in the water and the *Murton* hit the bottom. She hit hard and shuddered like a dying thing. Then she started to fill. The next wave lifted her off and threw her against the stone pier.

"Annie said it was all a muddle after that, but she remembered the *Murton* laying over and water over the decks up to the cabin side. They got the yawl launched and the crew all in it but one man and Duncan. Duncan was back by the stern rail, and he saw a wave like a mountain rolling down on them and shouted pull-pull into it! He threw them the painter and jumped for the rigging.

"Rob Mears was the mate and he was at the oars. He got the yawl around facing into it. She climbed up the face of that wave until they thought she'd fall over backwards. The top broke over them and filled half the boat. Annie said the water was up to the thwart. They all bailed while Rob kept her straight somehow and headed into the waves even half swamped. After that, there came a bit of a smooth, and they got turned back around and pulled for the *Murton*. But both men were gone. The ship had been completely swept by that wave.

"They managed to get to the pier. It was all frozen, and Annie said more than once she would never have made it crawling over the rocks solid with ice if she hadn't been wearing Duncan's trousers. The *Murton* pounded to pieces by morning. The harbor backwaters looked like barley soup with all the grain floating around. There wasn't a stick three feet long left of her two days later."

John knocked the ash from his now cold pipe. He shook his head slowly and looked at Mollie seated on the deck leaning against the deck house. "It's a mean lake, and Oswego is the worst harbor on it. The lake has killed a lot of ships and schooner men. It's scarce a month since the *Northman* went down and nothing but her yawl boat and a water cask found. The oars were still lashed to the boat's thwart- so you know she went down fast. Eleven men aboard. He turned to look at his nephew. "You watch yourselves. You watch every day. Don't take nothing for granted out there. The lake don't give second chances."

A breath of air cooled Mollie's face and filled the mainsail over their heads as it rippled the water around them. She needed little reminding of the lake's indifferent cruelty towards the careless, the threadbare, and the inattentive. She loved its wide waters and free winds and its magnificent sky borne cloud shows and sunsets. But always, after a lifetime afloat, she was keenly aware of the lake's relentless demand for respect.

She got up and walked to the rail as Tommy went to the wheel, and the rest of the crew moved off to trim sails. The evening wind still held a hint of winter's chill from the lake's depths, and Mollie, watching the small wake growing astern, shivered with the dampness. Back there astern was Eel Bay, a snug harbor. Ahead in the twilight, lay a vastness of gray water.

Looking upon it, the magnitude of the challenge before her loomed like a breaking rogue wave. For two hundred years ships had sailed and died here. A thousand men had slipped beneath its surface. French, British, Canadian, and American bones lay on the bottom. Other men, like Duncan, had died on the very doorstep of a safe harbor, their schooners smashed against merciless stone.

Mollie felt her sturdy ship's rail under her hands as she closed her eyes and thought of Will. Soon they would set sail again, this time without him. How many more lives would the lake claim in the season to come?

Chapter Five

"We live in deeds not words" Dr. Mary Walker

The *Gazelle* made excellent time with her first delivery for Fitzhugh's docks. With a cargo less weighty than coal and a brisk west wind, the schooner lived up to her name, arriving off Oswego the morning after her departure from Canada. Nate now was watch chief on deck during the day, Ben took the watch after dark, and Mollie filled in at the wheel for two hours after supper to give their new captain a brief break.

But near Oswego shortly after sunrise, the wind faded away leaving them becalmed. After observing that the dead fish littering the lake off the harbor entrance had stayed alongside for over an hour, Ben called out to Tommy to strike the masthead fly for the tug. Soon the little *James Moray* came puffing out leaving a cloud of dark coal smoke hanging over the calm water behind her.

As they towed in, Mollie and Ben watched the rows of close packed brick and stone buildings, the weathered wooden towers of the grain elevators lining the waterfront, the timber trusswork of the coal trestles and the iron bridge over the river grow distinct and detailed. To starboard the inner harbor light tower stood, a lonely sentinel beside the river entrance. To port in Grampus Bay, several schooners lay at anchor tucked under Vinegar Hill, waiting to move into the docks and add their cargoes to the twenty foot stacks of lumber already piled ashore. Over it all, brooded the gray stone casements and buildings of Fort Ontario atop the low bluff east of the harbor. A powerful tug hurried past with a roll of white water under her bows as she headed out to take another vessel in tow, as Mollie watched a waterman rowing his skiff across the harbor with strong sure strokes.

She wished she could turn the clock back to her own care free days of rowing around Sodus Bay on spring mornings like this. A distant bugle sounding morning muster at the fort was all but drowned by shrieks from an excited flock of gulls swirling through the air behind a fisherman's sailing skiff nearby. The smell of the river, foul with city sewage and the starch factory's waste, wafted over the water. Neither spoke of other arrivals here, especially their last. But Mollie remembered.

How could a person so full of life suddenly cease to be? Surely Will was still alive somewhere. He couldn't just not exist any more. Had his vital force truly been no more than a mere candle flame extinguished by a puff of wind? And how would they manage without him?

Ben, standing a few feet away, thought about port officials and businessmen and wished Will was with them. He missed his older brother's brash confidence and quick decisiveness. What would Will do about the return trip? Go empty? Load with coal? What was the best cargo to seek, and where and how would he find it? Ben longed for the peaceful boat shop back in Eel Bay where a man could work at his own pace to create something beautiful and strong. He wished he was there instead of trying to figure out where to load three hundred tons of coal.

By mid morning *Gazelle* were fast at the dock waiting to clear customs. When the officer stepped out of the white building on the end of the pier and started for them, Mollie heard Ben draw a quick breath. She glanced over to see him rubbing his starboard sideburn, his storm signal for approaching heavy weather.

Seeing her raised eyebrows, he said, "That's Ulysses Holmes, the collector that Will ran afoul of on our last trip."

Mollie squared her shoulders and stepped forward to meet Holmes. One small butterfly tumbled around in her stomach as she watched the official waddling down the dock towards them. She didn't like the petulant look on his puffy face. Holmes clumped up the gangplank, shouldered past her, and stopped before Ben holding out one hand. "Ship's papers?" he demanded.

Ben, with what he hoped was a respectful nod, gestured toward Mollie, "Right there sir."

Holmes spun on his heel, and seeing Mollie with the documents, scowled as he looked up at her. "Since when does the cook declare the manifest?"

"Excuse me, sir," said Ben, "she's the owner."

Holmes snapped, "Women cannot own ships. It is neither legal nor natural." He snatched the paperwork from Mollie and scanned it briefly. "Where is William McIntyre? This states he is the owner."

"I'm Mrs. Mollie McIntyre. I'm acting on behalf of his estate, and I will soon be the owner." She held out another document. "Here is the paper that confirms my appointment as executrix of the estate."

Homes lips drew back in a sneer. He glared up at her his eyes narrowed in scorn. "Estate? A woman ship owner? Not possible."

Mollie's grip on the papers tightened. Her face darkened, and as the documents wrinkled, Ben hurriedly stepped forward and nudged her elbow. "Perhaps we should all go below and see if we can sort this out."

Mollie eyes blazed as she met Ben's warning look. She opened her mouth to say something, then abruptly turned on her heel and stomped aft. After some backing and filling, a grumbling Holmes followed her.

Mollie had previously laid out the manifests, their clearances from Canada and other documentation on the table in the main cabin. Holmes settled his ample bulk upon the chair with an audible plump. Clearly still unhappy about dealing with a provisional owner and a female one at that, he flung his hat down on the table. He muttered and fussed as he went through the paperwork often scanning a page three times. Though he found nothing out of order, at one point he threatened to turn the affair over to his superior (who was not on duty until Monday) declaring this was all highly irregular if not outright illegal.

Mollie watched with increasing anger. At the thought of losing a day stuck in port waiting for paperwork because of this horrid little toad, she clenched her teeth. They could ill afford more delay. May was more than half over. After that, only three months remained until the next payment on *Gazelle's* note. Every day counted now. She felt as if Holmes had his grubby hands around her throat squeezing her life out.

"Please Mr. Holmes, you must understand. My husband died just a fortnight ago. All the proper papers have been filed."

Hearing the strain in her voice, Holmes sat back. His eyes narrowed as he studied her. She knew exactly what a mouse under Reuban's steely gaze felt just before the cat pounced.

"Now, I'm a very busy man, but I might be able to take on the extra paperwork associated with the change of ownership for a fee."

Mollie gritted her teeth and focused her eyes on a large grease spot decorating Holmes's shirt front. "How much would that be?"

"Twenty five dollars."

Mollie heard Ben grunt softly behind her. Her anger surged as she raised her eyes to Holmes's triumphant leer. She drew a deep breath longing for a belaying pin in her hand. She imagined smashing the hardwood pin squarely into that smirking face. She clenched her hands into fists at her sides under the table, her whole body taut with rage, as she locked her eyes on Holmes. Then she felt Ben's hand gentle on her shoulder. The touch brought her abruptly to her senses.

She shoved her chair back sharply, got to her feet and choked out, "If you'll wait a moment I'll get the funds."

She took two strides to the corner of the cabin with its small built in desk where the ship's papers and other important items were kept. She opened the lid of the metal strong box she had gotten out earlier, noting with some irritation that her hands were trembling. I will *not* show him how angry I am, she thought, as she extracted the bribe. The money lay heavy in her hand. Abruptly her rage ebbed away, even as the knot in her stomach tightened further. So few coins still lay on the bottom of the box. We won't even make it until the end of the month now.

After wordlessly handing over the silver, she and Ben silently escorted Holmes up the companion way and across the deck to the boarding plank. Here, Holmes stopped and turned to fix his eyes upon her with a look of utter contempt. "A woman has no business owning a ship. Your place is below in the galley not here on deck. Or better yet ashore. No good will come of this unnatural authority you have assumed." He stuffed the money in a pocket, stomped down the boarding plank, and waddled away.

"A fair wind for pirates in Oswego today," said Ben dryly.

Mollie glared after the disappearing official. "What a filthy arrogant beast. He's a leech- a bloated blood sucking leech. We should have waited until Monday for his superior."

"His boss might have asked for fifty dollars," said Ben with a shrug. "Well, we'd better get started unloading."

Mollie nodded and went back below to put the last of their cash and the ship's documents away. She sat down, filed the papers, and noted the fee in her account book. As she did so, the last of her anger ebbed away, replaced by a wave of despair. Her shoulders slumped and she fought back the sting of tears. What would Will have done? This wouldn't have happened if he had been here. He would have stood up to that fat little worm. Holmes wouldn't have pushed Will around. But what could a woman do? It wasn't fair that she should have to deal with this on top of everything else. And now here was twenty five dollars gone-only a few dollars left for to feed the crew, pay the tow bills, and cover all the other costs of ship keeping for the next two weeks. Everyone had worked so hard. The money had vanished in a moment. What was the use? Why even keep trying?

As she sat staring numbly at the bulkhead, Reuban glided silently into the room and jumped up on her lap. She picked him up and clutched him to the her chest. Several tears escaped and rolled down her face to wet his fur.

"I wish Will were here. You miss him too, don't you?"

While the crew were clearing away for discharging cargo, a well dressed man arrived seated alongside a teamster aboard his heavy wagon pulled by two black cart horses. Several scruffy laborers straggled along behind. The young dandy jumped down and Mollie guessed from his fine silk vest and five dollar topper that this was surely Daniel Fitzhugh the lumberman's son. Would he be another Holmes? she wondered as she watched him stride up the gangplank. Mollie felt herself being measured by the young businessman's keen brown eyes as he paused to look over the ship and its owner. It made her uneasy and a little resentful, as if he had caught her not quite fully dressed. She wondered if she saw a hint of mockery in those eyes.

Daniel turned away to confer briefly with the burly teamster who evidently was the work gang boss. Soon the cargo of box boards was passing in a steady flow over the Gazelle's rail. Then Dan crossed to where Mollie stood. He doffed his hat and bobbed his head in a quick blow. "Mrs. McIntyre I have looked forward very much to meeting you." His dark eyes met her gaze, and again Mollie felt uncomfortable under the intensity of his stare.

"Yes. Well, shall we go below and take care of our paperwork?"

A shadow of some emotion passed over Dan's face, and he ran one hand quickly through his curly hair. Was it more disapproval of a woman in charge? To her relief he said no more though she thought she caught a glint of amusement in his eyes. She clamped down hard on the wave of rising anger and quickly turned to lead the way to the cabin.

Here, to her relief, he was brisk, efficient and silent. When they had finished and he got up to take his leave he said, "I looked forward to meeting you after Father telegraphed of your arrival. Perhaps another time we can visit a bit more. I see you have business to attend to now. However, before I go, I must tell you that Father directed me to bring an associate down for introduction. I'd like to do so later this afternoon if it's agreeable. I'll bring your payment then, too."

Mollie wondering what sort of business this associate might be in, nodded her assent as she kept her eyes fixed on the cabin sole. "Why surely Mr. Fitzhugh," she answered, though she couldn't stop herself from fiddling with the end of her braid as she spoke.

A ringing peal of laughter made her look up. "Mr. Fitzhugh is my father. Please! Call me Dan. And perhaps someday you'll permit me address you as Mollie?"

Before she could gather her wits to reply, he went briskly up the companionway steps, turned toward her as he put on his derby with a flourish and said, "Until this afternoon then."

He walked off with a long legged stride dodging piles of timbers, stacks of rough cut lumber, men carrying boards, piles of horse droppings, and the general bustle of the wharf. Mollie watching him go felt that somehow she was missing something here in this encounter, but she wasn't quite sure what it was.

Later, she shared that thought with Ben. "That Dan Fitzhugh, he kept staring at me, like my face was dirty or something."

Ben replied, "Didn't you see him look at that photo of Will you keep on the bulkhead by the desk? I saw him look at that and back at you at least three times. He knows you're a new widow, and he wishes you were available. I think we're going to see more of Dan Fitzhugh aboard this boat."

With the ship's business completed for the moment, Mollie decided to escape the noise and disorder of unloading cargo. She badly needed a change of scene. That fat lump of a collector followed by young Fitzhugh making eyes at her-blast these men. Why couldn't they deal with a single woman? She just wanted to run her business and be treated like every other ship owner-with respect, as Will would have been treated.

With an alarmingly large portion of what was left of the ship's ready cash and her market baskets in hand, she headed ashore for the chandlery a few blocks away, to get provisions. As she walked away, she heard Ben and the boys hard at work transferring the deck load ashore to the longshoremen who were quickly building yet another towering stack of planks on the wharf already jammed with high piles of boards.

At Peter Pearson's chandlery, Mollie was working her way through the turnip bin trying to find a few roots that weren't too shriveled or soft, when the door closed loudly behind another customer, an older sailor that Mollie remembered seeing around the waterfront on previous trips. The man went straight to the counter and said to Peter, "Did you hear what happened this morning down at Rathbun's wharf? Constable Hogan arrested Don Burton of the *Black Oak*. We heard a general ruckus aboard and some shouting and language to shame a stevadore. Then Burton and his cook came tumbling out of the cabin and the lady was a-cussing him somethin' fearful. She had an iron skillet and when he went after her, she let him have it with both barrels and brought him up all standing. She knocked him right down on his beam ends. Then the mate and a sailor from the *Minnie Blakely* jumped aboard and separated them. Burton was spitting nails. Blood was running down his face. He was a sight. But the lady had spunk, I tell you. Constable Hogan took 'em both off."

Pearson, the shopkeeper said, "Don Burton, didn't he get into trouble a couple years ago for assaulting a cook?"

The old sailor nodded. "He got off on that, but they say he had his way with her."

Peter Pearson shook his head. "He's a mean old goat. He shouldn't be allowed to have a female cook aboard. Do you remember that boy who made a pierhead jump here last year? Burton near pounded that poor kid to death. Why, I saw him after he skipped. He had a shiner and a big bruise on his arm. He said he had two cracked ribs from Burton kicking him."

"Yeah, he beat that kid fearful bad," agreed the sailor.

Mollie had drifted over to the counter to listen. She asked, "What does this Burton's ship look like? Where does he sail out of?"

Pearson answered, "The *Black Oak's* a two master, about 150 ton or so. Goble built and he sails out of here. Right now he's carrying box boards and coal. You'll know him if you see him. He's about six foot tall and someone rearranged his nose awhile back. And if I were you, I'd stay out of his way." Glancing at her basket he added, "I'm sorry the stock's so low now. We're betwixt and between, too early for new goods. I've got some of last year's potatoes and yellow turnips over here that aren't too bad yet."

Mollie left the store with a selection of shop worn root vegetables and walked along thinking about Burton and the *Black Oak's* cook. Clearly, as a female ship owner her world would be very different than when Will was alive. She suspected Burton wasn't the only loathsome sewer rat lying in wait in this man's waterfront world. And she wondered how she would cope with the next one she crossed tacks with. That woman cook had courage. I'd shoot the skunk. If I had a gun. Will's pistol is still aboard. I think I'd better get it out and learn to use it.

An unexpected outbreak of shrill cries and heckling from around the corner ahead assaulted her ears. It sounded like a flock of crows mobbing an owl. Curious about the cause, she quickened her step and at the intersection looked down the street towards the disturbance. She saw a small woman wearing an odd looking short dark skirt and leggings besieged by a swarm of tattered canal boat children, all boys. They shouted and jeered; "Is it a man or a woman? "It's a she-male!" "Freak", Freak," "It's witch ugly legs," and a dozen other insults.

Mollie spotted one boy nearby drawing back to throw a rock. She dropped her basket and grabbed him. Her grip strengthened by regular hauling on downhauls and sheets was not gentle, and the startled urchin let out a yelp. The rest of the pack looked towards her, and as her captive squirmed in her hard grip, they took to their heels, scattering like sparrows before a hawk. Mollie released her prey with a none too gentle shove towards the disappearing scamps, and he scurried away and ducked into an alley.

The object of the pack's harassment came over to help pick up the scattered turnips. "Thank you," she said in a surprisingly low strong voice. "I didn't see that rock coming."

Mollie, evaluating the woman's odd dress from the corner of her eye as she collected her wayward vegetables, said, "Why, no thanks are in order. But what is that costume you're wearing?"

"It's something I devised. It's modeled after the reform dress much like the bloomer outfit."

The turnips having been rounded up and restored to Mollie's basket, the woman introduced herself. "I'm Dr. Mary Walker. And you are?"

"Mollie McIntyre, of the schooner *Gazelle*."

Dr. Walker's gray eyes twinkled as she smiled. "A mariner. Well, I can see why you might be interested in the short skirt then. I need not tell you how unhealthy and how unhandy long dresses like the one you're wearing are. You know how it drags filth and disease from the street back aboard your boat and into the kitchen. But what you may not know is that the long skirt and corset are shackles put upon us by men to keep us subservient and weak. Come. Let us walk together."

The two women started down the street heading towards the docks, and Mollie listened with growing interest as Dr. Walker explained how the clothes designed by men for women's use damaged the health and physical well being of the wearers.

"It's all a very deliberate attack on our strength and independence. The corset is nothing more than a coffin contrived of iron bands and whale bone. By constricting the lungs and by restraining movement, such fashionable clothing weakens women. We need physical activity. You can't be strong and active in conventional dress. And that's precisely what men want. They want us dependent, physically confined, and as nearly helpless as possible. Everything that makes women independent of men is condemned by a certain class. The current fashion in dress, moreover, was devised by the prostitutes of Paris and is totally unfit for a proud modest woman to wear."

"But," said Mollie, isn't it un-lady like to exercise or run about? That's what I've been told."

"Hardly. Exercise is essential for your health. Many physicians now agree that physical activity is important in combating female hysteria, depression, and prostration. Fresh air, sunshine, and exercise are the essentials of the Swedish cure and are a great medicine for women. Many ailments result from unhygenic dress that cramps and hampers the body."

As they walked, Mollie learned that Dr. Walker had been a battlefield surgeon in the Civil War. During that service in tent hospitals near the front lines she had worn men's trousers. She crossed enemy lines to render surgical service several times and on one occasion was taken prisoner by the rebels and held for being a spy. "I spent four months in that filthy disease ridden prison at Castle Thunder. The men who tried to impose more lady like dress upon me did not succeed, though they tried to starve me to death!"

Since the war, she had insisted on continuing to wear trousers. Her voice rose a notch as she told Mollie, "These aren't men's clothes they are *my* clothes. Even so, I have been arrested several times for public indecency. I am a woman, surely, but it is my right to dress as I please in a free America on whose tented fields I served four years in the cause of human freedom. God has given to women just as important rights of individuality as He has to men."

At the bridge Dr. Walker stopped, explaining that her way lay across the river. "Thank you again for your assistance. And do consider the advantages of reform dress. I am certain you will not regret it as you move about your vessel. More and more women are adopting the bloomer outfit. Oswego's very own Elizabeth Smith Miller, the daughter of Gerritt Smith who owns five piers in the harbor, is an ardent supporter. She devised an outfit modeled after that worn by the Indian women of the Oneida nation."

Dr. Walker then drew her self up to her full height and declared, "For your own sake and health, make such an outfit. Remember, the Deity has given you a mind to decide for yourself in *all* things. You will not be respected if you don't respect your own individuality."

After the two women separated, Mollie walked along slowly as she considered Dr. Walker's comments. Mollie thought what an odd little woman she was. And she certainly was outspoken. But what she said made sense. She probably had to be outspoken to give men orders during surgery in a battlefield hospital. And she surely had earned the right to wear men's pants after years of military service.

Men were physically stronger than women, yet they tried to make women even weaker than they naturally were. Look how the fine ladies of Oswego had to wear corsets beneath their clothes to train their waists. A woman could scarcely breathe let alone do anything with such a binding on them. What was wrong with a strong independent woman like Dr. Walker? Just because she acted and dressed differently, shouldn't she be allowed control her of own body? Surely this was the most basic of all human rights.

I have been fortunate, Mollie thought, as she walked along. Most women don't have men around like Ben or Father who respect or even encourage a woman's ambition. She glanced at her reflection in a shop window and wondered why men like Burton or that odious little customs agent hated independent women? If you stick your head up, they bite it right off. Long dresses and skirts were an intolerable nuisance. On Lake Michigan there had been a move to prohibit female cooks aboard schooners a few years ago because, it was claimed, when a ship got in trouble, a male cook could turn to and haul and pull while a hysterical female just added to the crew's troubles.

Mollie recalled Uncle John's story of the shipwreck and the trousers that had saved cousin Annie's life. She muttered as she walked along, "I'm going to catch hell for it, but I *will* make one of those outfits. It's time for some changes on this old waterfront."

Mollie's step quickened as she approached the river. She spotted *Gazelle's* masts among those of the half dozen or so other schooners at the timber docks. The sight of her little ship's sheer line and the jaunty angle of her jib boom lifted her spirits. The crew had cleared the deck already, and boards were flying out of the hold. As she neared the wharf, Mollie looked up at the proud tall spars and her mood rose another notch. She had a grand little ship and a good crew, too. She would make several of those bloomer outfits the first chance she had.

Mollie had just lit the kindling in her range to prepare the fire for supper when Daniel Fitzhugh returned bringing a most welcome payment and another man, almost as short as the custom's official and even fatter. They made their way to the after deck where they could stand clear of the unloading activity.

Dan introduced his companion, "This is Sandy Parsons. He's a business associate of many years with us. He brokers cargoes."

Mr. Parsons bowed low removing his hat with a flourish. Sandy he might have once been, but now he was bald as an egg. He beamed up at Mollie. "I so wanted to meet the lady of the lake, Mistress Mollie of the *Gazelle*."

A little wary Mollie answered, "I'm pleased to meet you Mr. Parsons."

But now Parsons replaced his hat and swept his gaze over the ship and became business like. "What's your capacity in coal?"

"She can carry three hundred fifty tons on a ten foot draft," said Mollie.

"Hmm," said Parsons as he continued to study the *Gazelle*. Let's make that three hundred or perhaps a tad less for the fall season." He turned back to Mollie "If you like, I can set you up for the duration of your charter with Isiah with return cargoes of coal. We should be able to route you mostly to Port Hope so you'll be close to Dark Harbor and your lumber."

Mollie said hesitantly, "You'll make all the arrangements?"

"For a fee of course. Ten percent is customary."

Mollie remembered how Will had spent two days tramping around the waterfront trying to get their last cargo of coal for Kingston and how they had been delayed at the loading dock for another half day. She thought to herself that this was an extreme bit of good fortune and a real courtesy on

53

the part of Isiah to put a word in on their behalf with the plump little deal maker who now stood with his shrewd eyes upon her, awaiting her answer.

Mollie said, "We would be very pleased to work with you."

"Well, consider it done. A friend of Isiah's is a friend of mine. You warp on over to the trestle when you have finished here, and you'll take on three hundred tons of coal for Smith's in Port Hope. I believe three hundred tons is quite enough for your little vessel, at least until the summer season."

Mollie nodded, "Yes, Mr. Parsons. We'll do so. We should be finished unloading tomorrow."

"Very well. You'll be dealing with Robert Howard at the Conger Coal company. Just ask for him when you are ready to load."

Chapter Six

"Being persons, then, women are citizens" Susan B. Anthony

After that first round trip, the *Gazelle's* company began to settle into their new routine, carrying lumber between Dark Harbor and Oswego and returning to Canada with coal. Isiah occasionally routed them to Charlotte with lumber, but here, too, Parson's contacts got them prompt return freights. The work brought in a steady flow of money, enough to pay the boys their twelve dollars a month and cover port fees and ship keeping with some left to put away towards the next note payment. But it was hard work. Hard on men, woman, and ship alike.

The runs between ports were short. The hours ashore working cargo and afloat working the ship were long, and the work was heavy. Each fresh sawn spruce or pine board had to be wrestled in and out of the hold by the crew who then passed it up to or took it from the lumber shovers ashore. To carry the largest most profitable load possible, the planks had to be carefully stacked below decks. Handling the thick splintery lumber in the cramped space tried body and soul. Once Tommy jammed a plank into place only to hear Nate bellow "Avast you jackass!" More than one board carried blood stains that day from Nate's mashed fingers.

Once the boards had filled the hold, the crew crammed shorter lengths of plank between the side of the ship and the piles of long lengths to keep them from shifting. Then they stacked more lumber on deck, leaving just enough room to get at the pump, the windlass and the centerboard lifting tackle.

Sometimes the run to Oswego was slow enough to snatch a few hours of sleep. Rarely, they ended up with a night in port where no one had to stand a watch, and all could enjoy the luxury of eight uninterrupted hours in the bunk.

Coal loaded faster than lumber, but when the first tons of coal cascaded down from the trestle pocket and thundered into the hold, Mollie standing aft with Ben watching the chute, winced at the impact. "I hope those old fastenings are still up to this."

Ben watching the dark cloud of gritty dust rising up from the hold replied, "Don't worry. She's Cat Hollow built by Jamie McPherson. Nobody built a better two master than Jamie. She's still stout."

Mollie watched the steady stream of glittering black anthracite chunks flow steadily down the chute. As it filled the hold, she thought of the grave and of burials. Perhaps it was the hint of sulfur smell in the air.

"I don't like coal. There's something about it. Maybe it's the mines it comes from. Did you see that article last week in the *Palladium* about the explosion in Pennsylvania? Five men were killed."

Even as she felt the ship settle under her feet, she thought of men at work deep beneath the hills of eastern Pennsylvania. Entombed in clammy dripping chambers, they swung their picks and sledges. Glistening black caverns echoed to their labor as they burrowed like blind moles following the turning twisting seam. Hard coal. Black diamonds. Mollie despised coal. It was hard on men and ships alike.

"Yes," said Ben. "But it loads fast and it pays the bills. Besides everyone needs coal these days. Where would the railroads and factories be without it? How would Vulcan Iron and Kingsford Starch here in Oswego keep running without coal? There must be a thousand men working in just those two factories."

Mollie shook her head as she looked at the black scum on the water alongside *Gazelle* where the coal dust had settled. "I know we need coal. But every time I see some old cut down hulk towing behind a steamer, I can't help but think coal is killing off the schooners one by one. And it's so dirty. I hate how it gets on the sails. Even Reuban's feet are gray."

Ben sighed and turned to pick up the coal shovels leaning against the deck house. "I guess we'd best get at leveling her off."

He rounded up the crew and passed out the shovels. The boys and Ben toiled below in the hot airless hold for several hours, shoveling tons of coal to trim ship. Each toss of the shovel raised more dust as the crew coughed and panted in the gloom. They came on deck afterwards blacker than Andre the smith except where sweat had made little white trails on their skin. But when Mollie fretted over the beating they were all taking, Ben told her not to worry. Trimming coal, he told her, was a nice change from pushing lumber. And Tommy grinned and flexed his grimy arms showing off his growing muscles.

Mollie had her duties, too. She rose before dawn each morning to prepare breakfast- a schoonerman's breakfast designed to power a body through moving ten tons of coal or fourteen hours of shoving lumber. She served fried ham and potatoes, eggs, with hot biscuits or rolls, or sometimes griddle cakes for a change. Hash was a particular favorite of Ben's. He would pack away a great pile and ask for more.

After breakfast clean up, Mollie found an hour or two to do her marketing, sharpening knives, or mending. There was baking ahead for the main noon day meal, and hard on its heels came supper. Monday was laundry day, and Friday was cleaning day, and every afternoon and evening when underway, Mollie tried to pitch in where she could on deck. She continued to take the wheel for the short "dog watch" after supper. With no mate aboard, Ben had double duty as captain and as a regular watch stander. The surplus cash account built slowly, and the days flew by.

She did find time to tailor herself several bloomer outfits made from suitably dark material for a new widow. She fashioned the loose fitting pants and short skirt of light weight cotton and wore them aboard the boat where they were a great help in getting around as she worked with the rest of the crew. The first time she put one on she hesitated for a few seconds before going on deck. She remembered the canal children jeering at Dr. Walker and the stares from men and women walking by. It was the right thing to do, but she wondered what Ben would think.

Ben was back by the helm and Tommy was near by securing the yawl boat while Nate drove wedges into the hatch cover down on the main deck to batten it down as they towed out. She stepped out on deck with her head high, and braced herself for the crew's reactions. She expected that the conservative country boys of Eel Bay would be free with their opinions.

Tommy's eyes grew wide. He let out a loud whistle, "Look at our cook," he exclaimed. "She's ready to go aloft now."

Zeb sniggered and then quickly ducked behind Tommy.

Nate looked aft, stared at Mollie's cloth covered legs, blushed and quickly looked away. Ben's brow creased as he gazed upon the outfit. Mollie felt a twinge in her stomach as he studied her bloomer.

Then he said, "Well, it's different."

"It's healthier and safer," answered Mollie. "If I'm to do anything aboard this vessel, I can't do it with three yards of cotton wrapped around my legs. I need to be free to move about."

To her relief, she saw Ben nod in agreement. "I guess no one said we had to do things the same as everyone else aboard our schooner. We're in charge here, so we'll do what we think is best for us."

With the longer days of late May, came hot weather. Memorial Day felt more like Independence Day as the peonies ashore quickly dropped their petals and lilac blossoms shriveled. The lake's shallows and beaches were littered with windrows of dead sardine-like shadines, and Oswego harbor's fragrance intensified as its water turned green and slimy. Even offshore on the open lake where winter's chill had lingered well into late May, the crew began stripping down and wrapping wet bandannas around their heads as they worked on deck under the blazing mid day sun.

On land, the unusual early heat frayed tempers in the home and workplace, as it affected animals and humans alike. Cranky babies, irritable fathers, and sleep deprived mothers coped as best they could, while hens stopped laying and cattle lucky enough to have a pond or creek in their pasture spent the most of their day standing in the water.

One sultry afternoon, Mollie was trudging through the thick air along River Street when she saw a hubbub ahead. A horse was down, and the driver, a young man dressed in a fine dandy's outfit, was whipping the animal mercilessly. She caught a glimpse of the man's face twisted in rage as he beat the struggling animal. Mollie turned her head away sickened by the cruelty as she passed. She knew it would be useless to try to interfere, but, as she thought this, a wave of intense frustration and self loathing washed over her. She hated herself for being so timid. As she hurried away from the scene and her own cowardice, she heard shouting and cursing behind her as a male bystander scuffled with the driver to take his whip away.

Unable to contain her distress, she traded looks with another passing pedestrian, a sturdy gray haired woman with market basket in hand and two little ones in tow. The woman shook her head. "That Jared Kraut, he thinks he owns the world, just 'cause his Canadian father in law owns a bank in Picton." Mollie nodded thinking he's another, like Captain Burton of the *Black Oak*. Then she wondered who Kraut's Canadian relative was. She could only think of one bank in Picton, the one that held her mortgage.

On a muggy early June evening in Oswego after loading coal and washing down the decks, Mollie escaped the stuffy galley after supper to sit on deck with Ben and the boys for a rare hour of leisure before she went to bed. Tommy was trying to teach Zeb how to tie a crown knot and making a hopeless snarl of it much to his friend's amusement. Nate had his charcoal and paper out and was sketching a gull sitting on a nearby piling. Ben sat with his back against the cabin's aft side with a book in hand. Mollie, perched on a deck box, looked over and envied his peaceful demeanor. She had again been thinking about the ship's finances. Reuban was the only crew member with enough energy to go ashore that evening. No one else felt like getting up much less taking a hike even as far as the Great Laker Tavern after shifting twenty tons of coal. The cat slipped down the boarding plank and disappeared.

"What are you reading?" Mollie asked.

"It's Will's book, *The Pathfinder Or The Inland Sea*"

"What's it about?"

"It's about a frontier scout called Natty Bumpo during the French wars here on the lake. Oswego was a frontier post then, and it was all wilderness around it-wonderous fine tall trees and no starch factory waste or coal dust in the river then," said Ben with a laugh. "There's a fine sailor lad in the story-Jasper, master of a handy little cutter, the *Scud*." Ben looked down at the page and read, "'She is easy on her rudder but likes looking up at the breeze as well as another' -sounds like the *Gazelle* doesn't it?"

Mollie allowed herself a slight smile at Ben's pride in his command's ability to work up to weather in a wind as she nodded.

Ben continued, "The scout, Natty Bumpo, likes to say we all have our own special gifts and must be true to them. I guess that applies to women as well as men, and schooners."

Mollie, thinking of Dr. Walker's struggle to be accepted as a battlefield surgeon, was about to respond when Nate who had been sketching a trim three master lying unloaded and light across the river with his charcoal and paper, spoke up. "Is that the old *Telegraph* there?"

Ben looked out over the rail at the passing steamer with her consort in tow. "I think it is. Marty Stoud used to have her didn't he?"

Mollie watching the forlorn grimy old hulk following at the end of the hawser recalled the *Telegraph,* once a smart tall sparred Oswego-built two master. Now she was barely recognizeable cut down and converted to a coal hulk

"I don't like that word 'consort' used for a barge. It reminds me of too many women and the situation they're in- captive and powerless."

Ben shrugged, "Hey, she doesn't have to worry about where her next cargo is coming from." He looked over at Nate and added with a wink, "She's being looked after now."

Mollie failed to see Ben's smile as she watched the hulk's slow passage. She had never been tolerant of teasing. "That's no way to live being dragged around by the nose all the time!"

A angry wailing battle cry sounded forth from the gathering evening gloom nearby interrupted whatever witty response Ben might have been preparing.

Reuban had faced off with a big black and white tom who had been skulking around near the ship. Now the two stood toe to toe on the wharf, backs arched, tails bushed like squirrel tails exchanging truly frightful curses and threats. Tommy had just picked up a bit of coal from the scuppers to chuck at the intruder whose threat had escalated to an ear splitting shriek when two stevadores came around a pile of coal. They were evidently homeward bound from a voyage to an uptown alehouse when one of them saw the cats intent on their dual. He veered off course and approached the battlefield quietly. Unseen by the combatants, he stopped few feet away and swung his foot in a mighty kick.

Fortunately for Reuban, the kick was badly aimed and caught him a glancing blow as the two cats broke and ran. But it was enough to send Reuban scrabbling perilously close to the wharf's edge and the dark river below. With a laugh the drunk followed up for another attempt to knock him into the harbor saying, "Go for a swim. That'll cool you off."

At the first assault, Mollie jumped up, bloomers and all, and rushed to the rescue, while Tommy shifted his target and threw the coal at the drunk instead of at the cats.

"Leave our cat alone!" shouted Mollie as she flew down the gang plank.

When the coal hit him on the shoulder, the lout lurched around. Upon seeing Mollie's approach he called gleefully to his comrade "What have we here? Is it a man, a monkey or a female? What happened to your skirt and petticoats Missy?"

His companion, a tattooed giant of a man, sniggered and snatched at Mollie's bloomer skirt saying, "Hey, let's see some more of your legs dolly." Then something went past her in a blur, shoving her aside, as it jumped on the big docker driving him back into the pile of lumber.

The cat kicker lunged forward to his friend's aid. Then Nate and Ben arrived, each grabbing a combatant and pulling them apart. Nate gripped Tommy's shoulders while Ben pushed his man back to separate them. Mollie and Reuban decided a rapid retreat was in order and both made for the *Gazelle* at top speed.

"Leave 'em be Robbie," said the cat kicking stevador. "You don't want that witch. She'll likely cast a spell on you."

Ben released the big man who staggered away a few feet snarling something about sea hags and unnatural females. Still cursing and muttering the two men stumbled away down the dock. Back on deck, Mollie picked up Reuban and carried him aft to the main cabin, telling him, "You'd better stay aboard tonight. I don't think either of us wants to run into those men again this trip. I wish they hadn't seen my bloomers."

Two weeks later, near the end of June as they towed into Dark Harbor, Mollie confided to Ben that though their cash balance was rising slowly, she feared they couldn't make enough trips to meet the September payment. There had been the unexpected increase in the insurance premium and the regrettable loss of their much patched inner jib that had finally split into tatters after Zeb had mistakenly grabbed the wrong line while tacking. "If we could carry five thousand feet more on deck each trip it might be enough to make up the difference," said Mollie.

Ben shook his head "I think we're carrying all the lumber we should. Remember what happened to the *Waubuno*?"

Mollie did. The steamer *Waubuno* had been the talk of the waterfront last fall, mostly because of Mrs. Doud's dream. The Douds had been passengers aboard the vessel, sailing for Parry Sound on Georgian Bay. It was the last trip of the year, as Mollie recalled her father's account of the tragedy. The steamer had been heavily loaded with supplies being hurried north before the freeze up. The cargo included over a ton of whiskey in barrels bound for the lumber camps. The ship's captain had refused to take it, there being no room in the hold. But the whiskey went aboard anyway. It was stored away on the upper deck twenty feet above the water without Captain Burkett's knowledge or consent. The *Waubuno* was a little vessel. With her seven foot hold she was not even able to carry as much as the *Gazelle*. And she was long and narrow so she was a roller even on the best of days.

"I remember they said Mrs. Doud dreamed of a great weight pressing down upon them all. And after they heard about her dream, some of the people got off the boat and took the train," said Mollie.

"And after the *Waubuno* disappeared, they found all the lifeboats and every one of them was empty. No one had time to get off," said Ben. "She rolled right over with that weight on her upper deck. The boat, crew, and all the passengers died because of overloading."

Mollie patted her right hand against her thigh, silently. She pictured the passengers asleep in their cabins, the black gang sweating in the engine room as they fired the boilers below, the captain and mates on deck peering into the November darkness. The wind strengthened, and with it came snow falling hard and thick. The seas rose quickly, and the heavily loaded steamer struggled through the night pitching and rolling. The seas began coming aboard and soon the pumps were running constantly. As the water in the bilges rose, the *Waubuno* battled on. Then came that fatal wave, bigger than all the others. Perhaps it leaped aboard crashing over the rails as the ship rolled. Mollie imagined the decks awash, the weight pressing the vessel down, until the next wave, the last one, followed it. They had died very quickly that night in the bitter black waters of Lake Huron. Not a single survivor remained.

Mollie shook her head and looked Ben in the eye. "That was in November. It's summer now. We won't see those big waves until September. We can carry more lumber at small risk today. If we don't, we are certain to lose the ship to the bank. We can increase the load. Lumber is a light cargo compared to coal."

Ben, still thinking of the *Waubuno,* shook his head. I shouldn't let her talk me into this, he thought. But reluctantly he agreed. She was right about summer weather. Prolonged winds and seas over eight feet were rare on the lake in June and July. But still, there was always the chance of a line squall. As he turned away, he saw Reuban crouched on the cabin top. Reuban looked back and in his intense yellow gaze Ben saw disapproval.

They loaded the next day starting at dawn to fill the hold with pine. Then the boys and Ben reefed the sails, two-blocked the halyards and slacked the downhauls off to raise up the booms and make room. Under a scorching sun, the boys then piled the biggest pile of boards ever upon *Gazelle's* decks. When the decks were filled, they lashed the stack down and cast off. Soaked with sweat and exhausted with heat, the crew got the load underway for Oswego without so much as a break for supper.

The boys and Ben slept on deck. Mollie sweating in her bunk below longed to strip all her clothes off. After midnight the fitful south breeze dropped off completely, and the schooner lay with limp sails and slack sheets upon a motionless lake with nary a whisper of wind. At dawn the sun rose out of the haze to glare at them with an angry red eye. By mid morning the deck was too hot to walk on with bare feet. The pitch in the deck seams softened and grew sticky, and Mollie let the galley fire go out after breakfast. They made their dinner on bread and cheese and a bit of smoked sausage.

After cleaning up, Mollie joined the crew up on deck. "It's like an oven down there even without the stove," she said to Ben. The schooner crept along at a snail's pace over the calm water an almost imperceptible ripple flowing off her bow. It seemed as if she were too hot to move.

"It's a scorcher alright," agreed Ben, sitting on the deck box where the tow hawser was stored. He was whipping the end of a dock line winding the marlin around its end in a continuous comforting routine of binding. Sweat darkened his shirt and he had exchanged his beloved brown cap with a brim for a bandanna to keep the sweat out of his eyes.

The boys were sprawled on top of the deck load in the scant shade of the sails when the sun faded bringing a slight coolness. Nate sat up and looked aloft. Ben squinted at a cloud edge overhead, looked into the haze to the west and said, "There's weather coming."

Then they all heard it, a faint rolling rumble in the distance. Everyone looked off to the west. Tommy nudged Zeb and got to his feet frowning at the horizon. Ben set his rope work aside. Already the gray haze looked distinctly darker. Another louder grumble rolled across the sky, followed by a deep boom. Ben cursed softly, got up, dropped his rope work in the locker and shouted, "Get those topsails in and take the outer jib off her. We'll squat the main and foresail."

The vague darkness to the west intensified quickly. Mollie felt the air pressing down on her. Her palms were slippery with sweat as she gripped the weather rail. The pewter colored water around them lay slick flat and oily. Not long now, she thought. This one's coming on fast. Tension clamped hard upon her and panic flickered for a moment. She forced it down. Already she distinguished the lighter gray leading edge of an approaching roll cloud forming against the darkening slate colored sky. She called to Ben up forward, "It's going to be bad."

Ben shouted, "Help Nate with the main halyards."

Mollie, grateful for the order and action, hurried forward to the pin rail by the mast to help lower the sail. The now clearly visible squall edge advanced with the speed of a fast freight train. Distant flashes of greenish lighting flickered behind the cloak of rain. Rumbles and growls of thunder were now nearly continuous. Glancing to the west as she worked, Mollie saw the fast approaching roll cloud forming a rising broadening arch that spanned much of the western sky. Its pale pus-like gray contrasted against a nearly black backdrop. The air beneath the arch of vapor had taken on an ominous tint the color of corroded copper. The rapid changes in the sky were mesmerizing. Mollie kept glancing at the squall as she slipped the halyard as fast as she dared, while Nate dropped the peak. She thought, *Hurry. Only a minute or two now before it hits. We're going to really catch it this time.*

The squall raced across the water towards them, shreds and tatters of cloud trailing at the bottom of its leading edge. Wind ruffled and darkened the lake surface a mile or so away. Mollie had the halyard slacked off, but would there be time to lash down the loose sail she wondered? The wind darkened water was advancing quickly. Streaks of ripples shot out ahead of the squall reaching towards them. The light south breeze suddenly shifted to the northwest. A cool puff touched Mollie's cheek with the delicacy of a lover's soft kiss.

Seconds after a brilliant flash of lightning and a simultaneous ear splitting bang overhead, the wind slammed into the *Gazelle*. Even with main and foresail squatted down to the second reef, the schooner was knocked down on her beam ends. Mollie, who had gone aft to where Ben was at the wheel, watched unbelieving. First the deck edge, then the top of the nearly waist high bulwark amidships vanished under the water. Mollie no longer heard the wind screaming through the rigging or felt the sting of hard driven rain against her face. She watched with horror as the water rose to cover the entire side deck. All she could think was *We're going over*. Frozen in place, Mollie watched the water creep quickly up the deck house side towards the open ports. The schooner lay at an impossible angle. Minute details burned into Mollie's conscience, the astounding angle of the deck, the main boom end now submerged in the lake, the seething foam along the lee side.

"Hold fast everyone," Ben roared.
The ship was capsizing.

Chapter Seven

"The best protection any woman can have is courage" Elizabeth Cady Stanton

Mollie clung to the wheel housing as her feet went out from under her. Ben left the wheel to crawl forward over the steeply slanting deck to release the foresheet. The main boom was now submerged for over half its length. A water barrel lashed forward of the deck house broke loose. It shot down the steeply angled deck barely missing Tommy in the narrow space between the deck house and the stack of lumber as he scrambled to help Nate who was struggling to cast off the halyards to drop the squatted fore sail. Then, incredibly, the ship went even further over.

Mollie thought *This it it. We're all going to die. It's in God's hands.* With a strange detachment, she watched the water foaming over the deck and climbing the deckhouse side. It reached the open ports and began flooding into the cabin, as the *Gazelle* struggled to right herself. As if in slow motion, she saw the ends of several two inch thick planks on the top of the deck load lift. Then the boards rose and flew off like leaves on the wind. Suddenly the whole deck load began to slide with a low rumble audible even over the scream of the wind.

"Nate, Tommy, Zeb-look out," roared Ben over the shrieking wind.

A sharp crack sounded immediately followed by a brief roar, and then it was over. Within seconds the *Gazelle* had staggered upright and was on her feet again turning up into the wind. Her thundering canvas flogged so violently it seemed the sails would simply shred or the masts would snap off as the whole hull shuddered underfoot. The three boys jumped down from the rigging, wide eyed with amazement. The entire deck load was gone. It had slid over board taking most of the port bulwark with it.

Ben put the wheel hard up, and the *Gazelle* fell off the wind to run down the lake. As the flogging sails filled,` it grew quieter except for the pelting of the wind driven rain and the snarl of the waves alongside. Already some of the bigger seas were slopping aboard as the schooner rolled downwind. Spindrift and streaks of foam covered the lake surface. Mollie, soaked to the skin and still clinging to the rail, stared unbelieving at the empty decks and the gap in the bulwark.

Ben shouted to Nate, "Check the pump!"

Nate hurried forward and worked the handle.

"Nothing! She's bone dry."

Ben turned to Mollie his face streaming with rain,"I don't think we damaged the deck any. As soon as this goes by we better rig a lifeline there."

With the crisis over and *Gazelle* running before the wind under control again, Mollie spoke little as she stood by on deck over the next few hours. But she was very busy with her thoughts. And they were not kind.

She had badly overstepped her authority by persuading Ben to take on the extra load. And she had been wrong. Again. This time no one had died. But the ship had been injured and there was the lost cargo, all 8,000 board feet of it. Perhaps the insurance would pay for it, but it wouldn't be delivered on time. She remembered Isiah Fitzhugh had said reliability was vital for any contractors who would do business with him. Perhaps we'll lose our charter. And now there's time and money lost for repairs. How could I have been so stupid? Several tears seeped out and rolled down her face as she wallowed in self loathing while staring off to leeward into the gray rain. After just two months with barely a good start on the season, this could be the end of it. The lake did not suffer fools, and she knew she had deserved its reprimand.

By the time the ship reached Oswego, the seas had built to eight feet, but the *Gazelle* now under just her foresail and fore staysail, slipped handily over the bar and into the harbor with Nate's steady hand on her helm. This time Oswego's backwash from the breakwaters, the rocks below them on the harbor bar, and the river current spared her. There would be other days of higher seas and stronger winds.

"I'm glad we got in before dark," said Ben as they towed up the river behind the tug.

"I wish we'd never left port this morning," said Mollie.

"Well, it'll work out somehow," said Ben.

For a moment Mollie resented his serene faith in the future. Then she cursed herself for resenting him.

Supper that evening was somber with little conversation among the weary crew. Mollie, her decks awash in self pity, picked at the stew and dumplings she had cooked. She dreaded explaining the deck cargo loss the next day and wondered if it would be her last day of doing business with Fitzhugh and Sons.

Ben seeing her distress, tried to cheer her up. "It could have been a lot worse."

"Yes. Someone else could have died. And it would have been my fault. Again. Just like in April."

She stood abruptly to clean up the galley.

In the small hours of the night, she lay awake thinking of how much worse it almost was. What if Tommy or Ben had gone overboard? Or we had lost the rig? Two summers ago the waterlogged hulk of the two masted *Baltic* had been found on the open lake. She had been knocked down and dismasted by a squall. Her decks had been swept clean, and not a soul was found aboard as she drifted off the False Ducks. She had capsized, drowned her entire crew, and then come back up again to float on the lumber in her hold. That could have been us, thought Mollie.

Or if they had stayed stayed afloat, they might have been blown down into Mexico Bay, the lake's graveyard. Every year at least one schooner hit the beach there, to then be swept, smashed, and broken by the biggest waves on the lake. Only a year ago the schooner *General Andrews* had gone ashore there and been pounded to pieces. Her entire crew had perished including the captain's wife, who was aboard as cook, and their baby, found dead on the beach.

The deadly trap of Mexico Bay at the lake's east end had claimed a dozen ships within Mollie's memory-*Medora, Black Duck, Ariadne* and others. The lake's bottom rose towards the surface at its east end to drag on, slow, steepen, and then trip the waves. After westerly gales drove the seas down the entire 200 mile fetch of the lake, they slammed into the shores of Mexico Bay with savage power. The seas grew higher than a house when they felt bottom here before they were transformed into breakers. No sailing vessel afloat could fight her way out of that bight against such waves, even if she did still have her rig and sails intact. Oswego in a westerly gale was the last chance harbor for a ship running before the wind along the south shore. Pass Oswego, and cold death waited under your lee. Molly finally dropped off to sleep, a sleep troubled by dreams of slanted decks, surging waves, and the roar of flogging canvas tearing itself to shreds .

Dan Fitzhugh arrived the next morning as Mollie was cleaning up after breakfast. Ben called down announcing his presence, and she went up on deck wishing she could stay below and leave the whole affair for her captain to deal with. Dan was surveying the clean washed empty deck and the broken bulwark.

"Ben tells me you have devised a new rapid unloading technique. Now if you can just improve its accuracy so the boards land on the wharf..." His grin faded as he saw Mollie's face.

Without meeting his eyes, Mollie said, "It was my fault. I told Ben to load the extra on."

Dan started to offer another witty remark but seeing Mollie's face, thought better of it. "Well, fortunately no one was hurt. Ben tells me he can easily repair the bulwark. In fact, I think we have on hand some good white oak from Michigan that was due to go to a shipyard on the coast. I'll speak to Father about sparing you a bit of it."

Mollie now finally pulled up enough courage from her depths of despair to look Dan's eyes. He added hastily, "Oh, not as a gift. We'll charge you wholesale price."

Mollie said, "I'm sorry we lost your property. I know your father prizes dependability. It won't happen again."

"I'll tell him what happened. He wanted to stop by to see you anyway. I'll send him right down."

Dan turned away to go ashore. At the head of the gang plank he paused and gave the intact starboard bulwark cap a pat saying, "I'm glad old *Gazelle* brought you home." Then he hastened down the gangway.

Ben told Mollie, "Don't worry. We'll make it up. Uncle John and I can fix that bulwark in a day, and I can do without my pay this month."

Mollie looked at Ben her eyes bright with unshed tears. "Ben, I was so stupid. Look what I've done to the ship and we almost lost Tommy. We could have lost everything." And to her intense chagrin tears began leaking down her face in a shameful display of female hysteria. This made Mollie feel even worse, and the salt water flow promptly increased.

Ben stared down at the deck. Then he reached out and took one of Mollie's hands in both his own and squeezed it gently. "Hey, I've made a mistake or two in my time. If you never make mistakes it means you aren't doing much."

He released her hand and announced, "I'm going to start on the hatches. Will you go get Tommy to give me a hand?"

They were well into discharging the remaining cargo when Isiah and a young woman no one had ever seen before appeared working their way around the stacks of lumber. With an appraising look at the girl's red gold hair green eyes and slim figure, Tommy said, "I didn't know he had a daughter. She's a trim looking packet."

This earned him a poke in the ribs from Nate's elbow. "Come on, let's get back to work. I don't think they need us here."

Ben directed a quick look at Mollie that he hoped conveyed support before following the cousins and Zeb back to the hold. Isiah and his female companion came up the boarding plank and stopped to look at the splintered deck timbers and the large gap in the port side bulwark. Mollie's heart sank when saw Isiah purse his lips and frown before he came briskly up to her.

"You had a time of it I see. The squall hit hard here, too. We lost a fine big oak tree from our yard. It snapped right off. They say it hit seventy knots inside the harbor."

Mollie said, "I'm sorry. It won't happen again. I know what I did was wrong."

"The important thing is that you are here now thanks to your stout little ship. But in the future I would prefer my cargoes to come in late and whole rather than as speedy partial deliveries. You might not be as lucky next time." Isiah paused and studied the shattered bulwark assessing the damage before continuing. "As owner it is your responsibility to look after the safety of your ship and her crew. A ship has only one captain, and it is he who has the last word concerning safety. You must remember that while you have rights and responsibilities, he is the ultimate authority. I know it is difficult, but you must help him as much as you can."

Isiah continued as he still studied the splintered bulwark, "Well, that's enough lecture for now." Isiah turned to the woman beside him "I'd like to introduce Hannah Redfern. Hannah, this is Mrs. Mollie McIntyre, the owner of the *Gazelle*."

Mollie looked down on the petite neatly dressed assistant. She felt ungainly and awkward standing upon her damaged deck in her bloomers. Hannah had her golden red hair up in a bun, and was wearing a dark, simply styled, well cut dress. Mollie was keenly aware of her own wind burned complexion and her now worn bloomers, as she met Hannah's cool measuring green eyes. Isiah's assistant looked like she was all business.

Isiah continued, "Hannah will be in charge of the office for several weeks. I'm sending Dan up to Michigan as I have more need of him these days with our expansion there. Hannah has been with us for two years and is an extremely capable young woman." He added with a slight smile, "You and Hannah also have some common interests, I believe. I shall leave you now in her hands."

As he started ashore he paused and looked back. "Mollie, please do not hesitate to tell Hannah if you have needs. She will see to them. And we have some excellent Michigan white oak on hand here, should you deem it worthy to join to your Canadian timbers." With that, he walked briskly down the boarding plank.

Mollie watched him off, then turned to see a tentative smile on the clerk's face. "Let's go below. I've got everything laid out there," she said shortly.

Hannah nodded and followed her down the companionway. The office assistant proved to be as efficient and knowledgeable as Isiah had promised, as she quickly adjusted the cargo manifest for the lost lumber. Mollie relaxed a bit, watching the quiet competence of the young clerk reconciling her accounts. She wondered what interests she could possibly have in common with this prim and proper girl with her flawless face and gleaming hair. She barely came up to Mollie's shoulder and didn't look a day over sixteen.

When Hannah had finished, Mollie said, "Would you like some tea before you go? There's still hot water from lunch."

Hannah accepted, and Mollie assembled their cups, tea, and some strawberry preserves and fresh bread to go with it.

Hannah remarked, "At least the squall brought cooler air in with it."

Mollie placed the teapot on the table and said, "I wish we had gotten more rain though. It's dry on our side of the lake, and if the heat continues, we'll be losing crops soon. We need a good barley harvest."

Hannah agreed. "It will be the last year for some of our farmers, too, if we don't get more rain." Hannah appeared to be deeply interested in the blue willow pattern on her saucer. Then she looked up and across the cabin at the painting of the *Gazelle* that hung on the bulkhead."It feels good to be afloat again. Sometimes I do miss it."

Mollie's curiosity was aroused. "Have you sailed much?"

"My father and uncle had a two master about the size of your *Gazelle*. I sailed as cook, and my two brothers worked on deck aboard the good ship *Mustang*."

"Where did you sail out of?"

"We sailed out of Little Sodus. We mostly just traded around the lake. Father didn't have a lot of ambition, he really wasn't interested in getting a larger boat and going west. He had the farm, too. I would have liked to get off the lake though, and maybe see Lake Michigan and Chicago or even sail on salt water."

Mollie sighed remembering her own longings. She, too, had dreamed of sailing down the St. Lawrence all the way to tidal water. "How long ago was that? Maybe we saw each other."

"I guess it was five or six years now. Time surely moves along."

"That was before Will and I sailed over here on the *Alma*. We were only together two years."

Silence settled over the cabin as each woman considered her memories. Mollie's thoughts drifted to a long ago trip when she and her father had sailed together alone. She was ten years old then. On a gentle summer day they had traveled from Great Sodus Bay to Charlotte. She had climbed all the way to the main mast spreaders that day to see if she could spy the Queen in faraway Canada. The crew all jumped ship in Charlotte to sign up and collect Civil War bounty. Just the two of them had sailed the vessel back to Sodus Point. She steered while her father trimmed the sails to catch the fitful breeze. For lunch she cooked and proudly served her father a plate stacked with griddle cakes. Captain Tom had pointed out an eagle soaring along the shore, and in the morning, after leaving the Genesee River entrance, they had both seen the great brown sturgeon gliding beneath them in the clear shallow water just east of Irondequoit Bay. That day on the lake with Father and the old *Sheldrake* all to herself remained cherished in memory.

The scrape and bang of boards passed and dropped on the stacks along with the occasional shouts and banter of the men at work nearby filtered in through the open ports. Mollie asked, "Would you like more tea?"

Hannah studying the photograph of Will on the bulkhead in the alcove that passed for a ship's office, looked away and said, "Yes, that would be nice. What happened to your husband if I may be so bold to ask?"

Mollie told her. At first, she was going to deliver the abbreviated two sentence version, but Hannah's quiet interest invited more. Before long, the teapot had been drained, and the whole story had come forth. For the first time since Will's death, Mollie was able to recall and speak about that night in detail to someone. As she told of Will's end, she felt again the raw piercing wind, the pelting rain on her face, and the utter despair of finding him afloat.

"I was so afraid we'd lose Ben, too, when he went after Will. It seems like some awful grotesque dream. Sometimes I can hardly believe even now that Will is gone."

Hannah was a good listener, and Mollie found sitting and talking to another woman was unexpectedly pleasurable. Neither wished to break the visit off. After a companionable silence during which Reuban wound himself around the chair legs, Mollie asked, "Why did you leave your ship? And how did you come to work for Isiah?"

Hannah heaved a deep sigh, and Mollie heard pain in her reply. "It's a rather long story." She paused and sipped her tea. "Fair is fair. I guess it's my turn to stir up old bones."

Chapter Eight

"one code of morals for men another for women" - Elizabeth Cady Stanton

"Four years ago Dad was driving the team. It was late fall, the boat was laid up for the season, and we had gone to the marsh to cut flag for the cooperage in town. They used it to caulk the barrels for the distillery. It was windy, and we were on our way down the hill when a gust knocked a big tree limb down. It spooked the team, and they bolted. One wheel caught in a rut and upset the wagon. Dad got caught under it and broke his neck.

"He sailed the lake for twenty years, made it through the blow of '75 and crossed the Oswego bar in a gale more than once, and he got killed by a bit of a breeze on dry land. He died a half mile from home. My brothers and I, we couldn't keep the farm going without him, so I went to work and sailed as cook. I sailed aboard a couple different boats before I signed up with Burton."

"The captain of the *Black Oak*?"

"That's the man. Or I should say the rat. He offered twenty dollars a month. I should have known there was a reason he paid such a high wage. You know what it was like two years ago. Ships laid up everywhere and scarce a job to be had anywhere. I was happy to get a position. I'd been months looking for something. A lot of people turned me away saying it was wrong for me to take a man's job.

"At first, Burton was gruff and short but he kept his distance. I didn't like the feeling at the dinner table though. No one said anything. Not the captain nor the mate. It was so different from being on the *Mustang* with my three brothers and Dad. No jokes or talk of the next port or what we would do there or where we might go next. It was awful. I had no one to speak with at all. I felt like I was being shunned.

"About a month after I had shipped aboard, I was below scrubbing a pot. We were inbound for Oswego, and I was trying to get things shipshape before we towed in. I felt I was being watched. Then I heard footsteps and smelled him. It was Burton. I knew his pig stink. He was right behind me. I turned to look, and he grabbed my arms with a grip like steel.

"He said, 'I've watched you flirting your tail around- you're a flash packet and I've a cargo for you.'

"Then he shoved me across the cabin and over to the bunk with one arm and started pulling down his suspenders with the other. I tried to scream. Burton pushed me down on the bunk and crammed his hand so hard over my mouth I could hardly breathe. I tried to kick him, but he just slammed me hard against the bunk frame. He ripped my blouse open, stripped my clothes, and forced himself on me. Oh, it hurt. It felt like like he was tearing me open. I tried to scream again, but he jammed his hand over my face so hard- I thought he would kill me. I think I fainted for lack of air-at least I don't remember anything else. When I woke up he was gone."

That night while the schooner was in port, Hannah escaped. The thought of being under Burton's control and being violated again was unbearable. She would die before she let that happen. Hannah waited, lying sleepless and rigid, as the night crawled by. When the solemn tones of the city hall clock tower tolled three times, she slipped out of her bunk. With pain stabbing in her ribs and throbbing deep inside, she crept slowly and soundlessly barefoot with her shoes in hand across the cabin and out on deck. It was a frosty September night, and the chill air cut through the thin shawl she'd hidden in her bunk earlier. There was no moon, only darkness with an immensity of stars, and the luminous milky way overhead to light the decks. After she got off the schooner, Hannah blundered about the wharf in the intense darkness of its shadows for what seemed a nightmare of eternity. Once she knocked over a pile of blocking that fell with a clatter. She froze, her heart thudding against her chest. Had Burton heard it? Behind her, the *Black Oak's* deck house ports remained dark. At last, she worked her way through the piles of lumber and reached the street. She bolted then, running through the empty streets until her lungs burned, and the pain could no longer be endured.

She walked through much of the night up hill and down moving in a maze of the unfamiliar city roadways. Her only thought was to get as far from the waterfront as possible. Now and then, a dog's barking followed her as she hurried along. She came to a church and tried the door. Locked. No sanctuary there. The night's cold air gnawed relentlessly as she pulled her shawl tight around her shoulders. Once she heard voices behind her. Was it Burton? A snatch of bawdy verse from a hoarse tuneless drunkard, a burst of obscenities-two men homebound from a tavern cruise. A wave of terror washed over her. Panicked she ducked into the Stygian space of a narrow alley close at hand. It reeked of garbage and offal, and in the darkness she stepped on something that squirmed underfoot. Startled, she jumped, lost her balance, and fell hard into cold mud. The drunkards were only a few yards away, and she froze into stillness while they passed by the alley.

Finally, near dawn, she stumbled up a flight of stone steps, collapsed and huddled in a doorway. When the sun rose, its light found her, mud spattered and soggy, curled up at the entrance of a large house on the hill just west of the harbor.

"As luck would have it, that house belonged to a man named Edward Pound who was a business associate of Isiah's. Pound didn't know what to do with me, so he introduced me to his 'eccentric friend'. He told me, 'Isiah takes in all kinds of oddities and waifs.'

Hanna smiled, "Pound and Isiah both are fly-fishermen. Pound took me up the street to the front door of a splendid big stone house. When his friend came to the door, he said 'Look at this fine catch that landed on my doorstep!' So Isiah took in another waif.

"Before long, he found out that I wrote a neat hand and asked me to work in the office. I liked figures, so I assisted Isiah's chief clerk to learn the accounts. I hope to soon take over the Oswego office."

Hannah paused for a sip of tea before continuing. "For months I felt shamed by what had happened. But I now know I was not at fault. This man, if you could call such a creature that, and his kind are all around us. But they will not stop me from living *my* life. And I thank the One Above for men like Isiah."

Mollie nodded thinking of Ben and the crew of the *Gazelle* who had stood by her after the squall. We all make mistakes Ben had said. She wouldn't overload her ship again, that was certain. She asked Hannah about their mutual benefactor.

"He's a widower with two sons, Michael up in Michigan and Dan the younger. Some years back he worked with Gerritt Smith on real estate. You know Smith. He's the abolitionist. Isiah's family made a good deal of money from their land holdings when the canal first went in. He used that money wisely in his own ventures. He has many business interests besides lumber wholesaling. I know he has stock in at least one bank, but I don't know much about his other investments. I have heard him speak several times of purchasing a ship. He believes it's unwise to have all the freights under the control of the railroads."

"What of his wife?"

"I'm not sure what happened to her, but I know she was sick for a year or more before she died. It may have been consumption. She's been gone for over ten years now. I know also, that he still misses her a great deal. He called her 'My conscience' and says it was his Alice that opened his eyes to the need for the woman's reform movement. Just recently he spoke of the shabby treatment that Dr. Mary Walker has received from our local justice system. She was arrested again and fined last week for wearing men's trousers, you probably heard."

"I hadn't heard that. I don't see what's wrong with her trousers. She told me that dragging the hem of a long skirt around in the slop of the street brings filth and disease into the house. I decided to make a bloomer dress to wear aboard ship after talking to her."

"Perhaps you should start wearing your bloomer dress ashore," suggested Hannah.

Mollie hesitated, "The stevedores despise it."

"Well, that's their problem not yours. You should be able to wear bloomers or men's trousers, for that matter, if you want," retorted Hannah. "I had decided to make an outfit myself even before I saw yours. Isiah has said it will make my work inventorying lumber in the yard much easier. He says women should be physically strong and active. He has told me more than once to go out and take a brisk walk at the dinner hour. Isiah is well acquainted with Dr. Walker and her views on women's health."

They talked for more than an hour, speaking of schooners and sailing and of good times afloat aboard family ships. After Hannah went ashore, Mollie cleaned and stowed her galley. As she worked, she thought of the girl who had been through her own stormy seas, but was now under full sail again. It seemed that rather than breaking her down, Burton's rape had hardened and tempered her. Hannah was a survivor to be sure. Yet, she had said before she went ashore that she envied Mollie, owner of her own schooner. "Well," said Mollie to Reuban who was sitting nearby, "I don't own all of the *Gazelle* yet. There's still the bank, Father, and Uncle John to pay off."

The next morning, as the last of the lumber was leaving the hold, a large powerfully built man with lank greasy hair down over his collar, an unkept set of black whiskers, and a complexion darkened by coal dust stopped at the gang plank. He scanned the deck with narrowed eyes and then roared, "Where's the captain of this cisco boat?" Ben and Mollie along with the boys, who were all forward shoving plank, paused in their various activities. The men moved over to and gathered by the rail near the gang plank while Mollie stayed aft.

"I am, and who might you be?" replied Ben.

"I'm Captain Burton of the *Black Oak*." Eying the broken bulwark he said, "Is this the ship with the female owner who don't know how to carry a deck load?" When Ben didn't respond immediately, he continued, "I came over to tell you to keep your damn cat off my ship. I hate the stink of cat piss, and if I catch him aboard again, I'll break his neck and throw him overboard."

Mollie back by the ship's wheel felt an immediate and visceral dislike of Burton. She took a couple steps towards the crew grouped by the rail. Ben flashed her a quick warning glance, and she paused.

He turned back to Burton and replied, "Captain, we'll be sure to do that. We're sorry and apologize for his bad behavior."

Burton hawked and spat into the river. He bared a row of crooked yellowed teeth and snarled, "You keep him off my ship or I will. And while you're at it, keep your damn deck cargo aboard, too." He turned away muttering something about lubbers and boy captains strewing good lumber all over the lake creating hazards for other vessels, and strode off.

Mollie went to Ben's side. "So that's Captain Burton. I don't think I'd like meeting up with him in a dark alley."

"We'd better watch Reuban at night and try to keep him aboard," said Ben.

They finished unloading the lumber before supper, and as there was no space at the coal trestle, they stayed at the wharf for the night. With a rare few hours of leisure, the boys decided to go up to the Great Laker Tavern to sample some of the local malt houses' output. Ben went along telling Mollie, "I have to keep the squall wind strength below force twelve and the waves under twenty feet as they tell of our near escape from Davy Jones Locker."

Mollie rounded up Reuban and carried him below. Still tired from the night before, she went to bed shortly after sundown. She was rudely awakened sometime around midnight by Reuban jumping on her bed and landing on her stomach. She was about to toss him off when she heard a small scrape somewhere forward.

That was no rat, she thought. Reuban, still crouched on her chest murmured a faint growl deep in his chest. She lay tense and listening under her covers. Another soft clunk sounded. Someone was aboard the ship. Someone who didn't belong aboard. The boys weren't back yet. She would have heard them come aboard. Mollie gently pushed the cat aside and got out of bed. She crept across the cabin to the companionway steps and slowly placed her feet on each step to avoid a squeak from the tread. When she poked her head out of the companion way, she saw only an empty deck. With a tight knot in her stomach, Mollie padded across the deck and peered around the corner of the cabin.

A waning moon flooded the ship's decks with pale light. Mollie saw a dark figure emerge from the foc'sle. His face was shadowed by the hat he wore. He moved with stealthy short steps. There was something familiar about the man, something odd. Mollie was certain she had seen him before, though where and why she didn't know. It was the way he wore his hat, low and pulled down over his ears. She had seen him recently.

She was alone on the boat. Alone with a thief. While she watched, he slipped silently over the rail and landed lightly on the wharf and disappeared into the shadows of the piled lumber carrying something in one hand. As he moved off, she saw a distinct limp before he blended into the darkness.

When the boys came back an hour or so later, Nate and Tommy found they were both missing money. (Zeb had spent all his). Nate also found a new pair of boots gone. They listened to Mollie's account, and after some choice remarks on the thief's ancestry, intelligence and physical attributes, they turned in. The next day they shifted the ship to an opening on the trestle and that afternoon loaded coal and sailed for Kingston.

After unloading the coal, Ben set a course for Eel Bay a half day's sail distant. As he explained to Mollie, he could repair the bulwark far faster with his full tool kit there with Uncle John's help. Besides, it was high time for a day or two in homeport. Since mid May, the crew had scarcely had a day's rest. For six weeks, seven days a week they had either been loading, sailing, or unloading. They all needed a break.

Chapter Nine

Man himself stands appalled at the results of his own excesses... Elizabeth Cady Stanton

The *Gazelle* sailed into Eel Bay in late afternoon, tacking up the narrowing cove against a brisk hot southwester that brought the dusty smell of land with it. On shore, recently cut hayfields lay sere and brown looking more like late August than June. Surveying the parched fields, Mollie dreaded the possibility of a meager barley harvest. Unless rain came soon, there would be little grain to carry in September and little money to be made carrying it. But the whole crew felt a lift of spirit at the sight of the familiar cluster of houses and buildings by the water as the ship coasted into the inner harbor. *Gazelle* was home again.

Mollie worked ashore helping Aunt Sara make strawberry and raspberry preserves, pickling, weeding, watering, and doing other kitchen and garden chores, while Ben and Uncle John transformed Fitzhugh's lumber into a sturdy new bulwark. Near noon time on their first day home, the two women sat down for a brief break. Aunt Sara fanned herself with a folded up *Picton Gazette*.

"It does get warm in this old hole. I should get the men to move the range out into the summer kitchen while Ben's here." She looked over at Mollie at the sink silently washing up, "How you doing?"

Mollie shook her head and mumbled, "I miss Will."

Aunt Sara sighed. "I know. There's not a day goes by when I don't think of my Duncan drowned in Oswego. Will was a good boy, though he did have a temper. Duncan took him over his knee once when Will was a little tyke. He could be ornery even then. He kicked a hen off her nest after she pecked him when he was collecting eggs."

Mollie leaned her elbows on the dry sink and stared at the kitchen wall. "Maybe we should quit."

"Nonsense. That's the last thing you should do. Ben's good for it. The cousins are game."

"I almost killed us all."

"But you didn't. You all pulled through. Now you need to snap out of that blue slump young lady. Hitch up those bloomers of yours and keep going. Everyone makes a mistake now and then."

Mollie dropped her gaze to the wash water. Outside the window she heard the wailing crescendo of an early cicada heralding high summer's arrival, and the knock of mallets from the shipyard where Ben and Uncle John were at work on the *Gazelle*.

At the end of the second day in the cooling dusk, Ben laid down his plane and surveyed the new rail, still pungent with the smell of freshly worked oak. It felt good to finish a job and see it complete. A little oil and paint and that bulwark would be good as new. Working wood was so different from the day after day relentless grind of being in command with always another task, another port official, another crisis to deal with. Never an end to it. Here, he had something to show for his day of labor.

He sighed and glanced over at Uncle John with a small smile. His Uncle nodded and pronounced the rail first rate. They both sat down upon the deck box in front of the main cabin house to pack their pipes for a smoke. The fierce heat of afternoon had waned with the setting sun, and the heavy fragrance of Aunt Sara's mock orange bushes just up the hill drifted over the harbor.

After lighting up, Uncle John looked over at Ben and said, "It's been good to have you around for a few days. I've missed you in the yard. How is it being Master after God?"

Ben smiled a bit ruefully, "They're both a handful at times- Mollie and the *Gazelle*. But it keeps a man busy."

Uncle John remarked, "Mollie seems pretty quiet these days. Is she still missing Will so?"

"We all do. But she's feeling bad about losing the deck load, too, and the waterfront stiffs and idlers have all made sure she knows that a woman can't possibly manage a vessel as owner."

Ben puffed on his pipe for a few seconds, as the sounds of a summer evening on the harbor surrounded them. The deep roars of a trio of bullfrogs debating ownership of the marsh at the head of the bay, a sharp cry of a lone gull overhead, and the quick chatter of barn swallows swooping low and dipping down to the calm water for a late evening midge emphasized the tranquil calm of the harbor. Ben watched the v shaped wake of a muskrat as the small brown swimmer passed by, its tail sculling it steadily to its burrow. In the distance beyond the field behind the boat shop, a fox cried out her sharp short squall, perhaps calling her pups together for the night.

Ben said, "It sure is peaceful here- the waterfront in Oswego is an ever lasting chore-people there, they act like they run the world. That big deck load –I don't think it was Mollie's fault at all. That wind would have knocked us down anyway. Why, maybe the bigger load helped it all slide off faster. We might have been better off getting shed of it as quick as we did." Ben shrugged. "Anyway, we came through. I don't see why everyone has to keep on croaking about it like we're all as brainless and foolish as spring lambs. Other boats were damaged in that blow. The *Ella Murton* lost part of her deck load, too, but no one in Oswego seemed to notice that."

Uncle John nodded his sympathy. "There will always be those that know what's best for everyone else, nay sayers who will tell you it can't be done or it should have been done this way or that way. You just keep on as you are, and you'll be fine. By the way, how much money have you got set aside for the next payment?"

Ben frowned, "Not enough according to Mollie. Only about 500 dollars so far."

"Well, you've got three more months. And barley and wheat freights will pay good money come fall."

Ben nodded, "I guess that's about our best hope. Honestly, I wouldn't mind being back here in the shop, though."

Daylight had faded, and the mosquitoes were beginning to whine around them. Uncle John stood up with a groan. "Time to get up to the house for dinner."

He and Ben stretched, and the two men pocketed their pipes, gathered up and stowed their tools, and walked ashore. Ben turned to look back briefly at the schooner, her spars and rigging dark against the rose and lavender of the hazy evening sky. He felt a warm contentment at making things right and shipshape with her again. He thought to build a ship like the *Gazelle,* a brand new schooner, would be a fine thing for a man to do. Then he sighed, turned away, and followed his uncle up the hill. It wasn't likely any new schooners would ever again be built at Eel Bay. So he'd better keep this one working.

Five days later, the *Gazelle* was back in Oswego unloading another cargo of lumber. By mid morning the pace had slowed as the sun rose high overhead and the heat built. Mollie, still in her bloomer outfit from the crossing, came on deck for a breath of air. In the oppressive stillness flags hung limp, dogs panted in the shade, and horses and men alike drooped. The river's scummy surface lay glassy alongside as she stood watching the dock workers carry and stack the planks on the wharf. No one was moving very fast. She wiped the sweat from her face as she watched the load going ashore. She noticed one man in particular, a man with a slight limp.

She went down to the main deck and called to Ben in the hold asking him to come on deck for a moment. When he emerged, his shirt dark with sweat and his hair wet on his forehead, Mollie pointed out the stevadore. "That man there, he's the thief."

"Are you sure?" asked Ben.

"He has a limp and he wears his hat pulled down. I'm certain of it."

Tommy Zeb and Nate climbed out of the hold and joined Mollie and Ben at the rail. The break in the flow of boards brought the work boss Andy Doyle over. Doyle was a bull necked man with a thick beard and powerful arms and shoulders developed from years of shoving timber. He did not look happy as he strode down the wharf toward the ship. Mollie saw his face darken further as he took in the idle workers and her bloomer outfit. She stood her ground, thankful to be on the deck of her own ship.

"What's the problem here?" he demanded.

"That man over there, I wish to speak to him," said Mollie.

"Why," growled Doyle.

"Because he's a thief."

"Now look here missy, there ain't no thieves in my gang."

"Then he won't mind telling me where he was two Thursdays ago at midnight."

Then she called loudly jabbing her finger at the accused, "You. Come over here!"

The stevedores had been slowly gathering by the side of the ship, drawn by the work stoppage and exchange between Mollie and Doyle. They were silent but an air of malice hung heavy over the dock. As word passed quietly among them, a low buzz of discontent began to rise. Comments passed back and forth as the volume grew.

"The witch called Abe a thief"

"What does she know"

"She can't even load her ship"

"It's that cisco boat from South Bay again"

"That she thing who dresses like a freak..."

Nate spoke loudly above the growing growl and muttering of menace. "Those are my boots!" as he pointed at the feet of the stocky stevadore, Abe, who had sidled off a little distance from the main group.

The accused spat vigorously and snarled, "You lie. I've had these over a year."

A man near the front of the group suddenly yanked the ties of his heavy protective apron loose and threw it on the ground, "I'm not touching another board until the witch apologizes."

Others followed suit, stripping off their gear and flinging it down as they took up the demand for an apology.

Nate flushed red and shouted over the clamor, "He stole my boots!"

Nate's shout was lost in a general chorus of curses and jeers. Doyle's voice boomed forth, "That's it men. We're done. We're off this job!"

The group dispersed, teamsters going to their wagons, lumber pushers leaving their leathers on the dock where they had fallen and walking away, a few turning back to shout a parting profanity or snarl an insult over their shoulders.

Ben was as angry as Mollie had ever seen him. "What kind of a damfoolishness is this? Where are these jackasses going?"

Nate with uncharacteristic passion and clenched fists said, "Those were my boots! I know they were."

Mollie stared after the disappearing workers. She felt the sweat trickle down her neck as she gritted her teeth in silent fury. Then she whirled around and stomped across the main deck to where a board lay. She bent over, seized one end, and lifting it shouted, "We'll unload and stack it ourselves!"

"Damn right!" shouted Tommy.

He and Zeb leaped ashore to receive the planks and carry them away to the stack as Ben grabbed the other end of the plank Mollie was holding.

Two hours later, Isiah and Doyle, the crew boss, arrived with the stocky stevedore Abe in tow. The *Gazelle's* crew stopped work and gathered on deck. As they stood mopping their faces and relishing the light cool breeze now coming off the lake, Isiah told them, "Mr. Doyle and I have agreed that everyone should knock off until five o'clock. Then the gang will return to unload in the cool evening hours. Now, on what basis do you accuse Mr. Harris of being a thief?"

"He's got my boots on," said Nate.

"Can you prove they are yours?"

Nate looked down at Abe's feet muttered something and shook his head.

"Very well then. Mr. Harris, you are free to go."

Silently *Gazelle's* crew watched him limp away. When he was out of earshot, Isiah said, "I believe you, Nate. And you, too, Mollie. There have been at least three other ships robbed over the last two weeks, but without proof there's little I can do. The dock workers are still touchy after that strike last month out in Buffalo, and this heat isn't helping. I did speak to Constable Mallory, and he says he'll be around the wharf a lot more after dark. For now we had best drop the matter lest there be more trouble."

The rest of the cargo went ashore with no further incident, and the next morning they moved *Gazelle* across the river to the coal trestle. By late afternoon, the cargo had been trimmed, the hatches secured, and the schooner was ready to cast off. But Reuban was nowhere to be found. He didn't like loading coal any more than the rest of the crew, and usually took refuge from the noise and dirt in Mollie's bunk in the main cabin. Mollie searched her quarters thoroughly, opening doors, moving storage chests and boxes, and peering into lockers. No Reuban.

She came on deck and noting the sweet cool west wind that was rippling the harbor waters said in some annoyance, "I've looked everywhere for that foolish cat. He's not in the cabin."

Tommy standing by the main mast pinrail ready for orders to strike the masthead fly for the tug, shrugged. "We searched the foc'sle. He's not there. He must have sneaked ashore."

Mollie said, "If we wait much longer, it'll be too late to get the tug, and we'll have to wait until morning to leave. We can't afford to miss another day."

"We can't leave without Reuban," said Ben firmly.

Mollie set her jaw. "We lost three days last week with repairs and nearly another because of the dock workers-we need to get underway. Now. We can tell Hannah to watch for Reuban."

Ben scowled, "Reuban was Will's cat. He's part of the crew, and we don't sail without him."

Arguing with Ben was like telling a stone wall to get out of the way. He was not going to give in.

Mollie said, "Damn that cat. Doesn't anyone care about keeping this ship?"

She stomped off to the galley and with an angry clatter and banging of pots and pans began preparing supper.

Even after twilight grayed the sky and the night hawks began swooping over the elevators and city streets, their strange sharp cries echoing off the buildings, no Reuban came gliding up the gangplank. Ben worried silently about their wayward crew member, then took the boys and went ashore to search. Mollie sulked for awhile and then, as it grew dark, joined them in walking the docks peering around the stacks of lumber calling out for the lost one. Only after it was too dark to see the bats zig zagging overhead, did they give up and return to the ship.

"I hope he shows up. He's our good luck cat," said Tommy.

Ben looked glum as he replied, "Maybe someone tossed him in the river."

No one said much after that as they turned in.

Mollie lay awake in her bunk. Despite the open ports, the thick night hung heavy in the cabin. Not a breath of air stirred as she turned and twisted and shifted her pillow a dozen times trying to find a little comfort. Finally, she tossed all the covers off and lay on her back sweaty and sleepless. The distant solemn bong of the city hall clock sounded once, twice.

That stupid cat- off hunting for mice or love in the night. She pictured Reuban prowling the wharf the next morning looking in vain for his ship after they had sailed. Perhaps he would run into Burton or a stevedore- a swift kick, a small tawny body arcing through the air landing with a splash, a brief struggle in the filthy brown water. One more corpse floating in the foul river.

What good will it do anyway, to leave in the morning? We'll never make the September payment. In two months we've barely cleared five hundred dollars. At this rate we'll never raise 3000 dollars by September. Why keep working ourselves to death? The lost deck load, the torn jib, the wildcat walkout, the constant taunts and leers, the endless ridicule, and rudeness-if only Will was here. They wouldn't dare insult us if he was Captain. She felt her eyes sting as a bitter wave of loneliness and grief swamped her. What's the use? Will's gone, and the ship would soon be sold.

Before the dark flood of despair could fully engulf her, Mollie swung her legs over the side of her bunk and got up. Moonlight from the ports illuminated the stuffy cabin as she easily found her way through the familiar space to the companionway and went on deck to stand aft near the wheel.

It was better here. No mosquitoes yet. At least it was a little cooler with slight offshore wafting down the river. The sleeping city, the deck washed with soft silver light from the nearly full moon high overhead, and the gleam of moonlight on the calm water soothed her. The smell of long dead fish mixed with sewage and rotting seaweed reminded her that summer was moving on. She leaned upon the stern rail watching the splintered image of the moon dancing on the water and thought about last few weeks.

I've been selfish and stupid. We could have lost the ship in the squall. Now the stevedores won't work with us. I've fouled up everything. I couldn't even keep track of the cat. A sensation of unease moved over her as she stared at the black river. What if Reuban's disappearance really was unlucky? Now Ben was mad at her. The crew is falling apart.

She turned away from the rail and walked across the deck to the wheel where she had lately spent so many hours as assistant helmsman. She grasped the king spoke and gave it a slight pull, comforted by the familiar feel of the grip's polished wood. At least *Gazelle,* now newly repaired, still floated solid and true under her feet.

A memory surfaced from her talk with Hannah last week. Just before parting, she had said something to Mollie like, "You must hold your course. Other women need to see you in control of your life." She also remembered Isiah saying that owners must consider the welfare of their vessel and crew, and that a vessel has one captain. What if they had lost Tommy in that squall? She thought of Aunt Sara who had lost her husband and her oldest son to the lake. The sturdy old woman's words echoed in her mind- you got to keep going.

Her gaze traveled over the familiar deck before her. She took in the newly repaired bulwark and looked up past the tall strong pine spars at the moon floating serenely over the lofty mastheads. Father and Uncle John had staked their life savings on the first payment. They believed in her. As did the boys, and Ben the reluctant captain. We can't quit now. We must continue.

Somewhere in the distance out on the dark lake a loon called, as she turned to go below. Its cry sounded strong and wild and free. The long wail touched something deep in her. The call sounded defiant.

She squared her shoulders and said to the schooner and the sleeping city around her, "I'm not quitting. I'll apologize to Ben in the morning, and we'll search every wharf, warehouse and elevator in Oswego for Reuban. We'll find him if he's there to be found."

Chapter Ten

"women their rights and nothing less..." Susan B. Anthony

While sipping his coffee the next morning Ben said, "Maybe we should ask Hannah to look for Reuban and get underway."

Mollie said, "No. We'll keep looking for him. You were right. We have to stick together, and Reuban is part of the crew. Maybe if we look one more time he'll turn up."

After breakfast, the crew went on deck and began discussing who would search where for the cat. Abruptly, they were silenced by an ear splitting blast that shattered the morning. The echo was still rolling off the elevators, malt houses and warehouses along the waterfront when a confusion of distant shouts broke out. A hundred dogs on shore set up a howl and a baying like hounds from hell.

Tommy exclaimed, "Look! Out there on the river!"

Mollie and Ben hurried to the rail. "Oh dear God," Mollie murmured in horror.

A tug with a schooner alongside lay dead in the water. The ruined tug on the schooner's quarter was quickly settling into the river under a cloud of rising steam dust and smoke. The water had already reached its deck.

"Her boiler blew!" exclaimed Tommy.

Distant figures, partially obscured by the mist and smoke, moved around the schooner's decks. Mollie saw no movement or visible life on the wreckage of the tug. Several dark objects in the water, possibly men's heads, were scattered near it.

Ben snapped, "Get the yawl down. Maybe we can lend a hand."

He and the boys pounded aft to launch the boat.

Moments later Mollie Zeb and Nate stood by the rail watching the yawl race off. They saw several other boats converge upon the wreck their crews rowing frantically. The little tug *James Moray* got underway from her berth and made fast to the schooner to tow her back to port. Rescuers began pulling the victims into their boats. Ben and Tommy disappeared behind the wreck still rowing hard.

After perhaps a half hour, Mollie sighed with relief at the sight of the returning yawl. As it came alongside, Nate caught the line, and Ben looked up and gave Mollie a reassuring we're ok gesture.

After they climbed aboard he said, "It's bad over there. The explosion killed the engineer and a stoker. Another man is missing, and one of the tug deck crew was scalded. He'll die soon." Ben paused and let out a long breath from pursed lips and shook his head slowly.

Tommy said, "The mate of the schooner -a piece of iron hit him in the head. It smashed him right open. We could see blood and brains and-"

Ben cut him off, "There's no sign of the tug captain. Maybe he was blown overboard. It was the first tow of the day, and they were just getting ready to shift from the schooner's quarter to take her in tow, so the schooner's mate was aft next to the tug. I doubt the scalded man will live out the day."

Ben grimaced at what he had seen. "The mate was lucky. He died instantly."

Mollie murmured, "Those poor men." Four people had died in an instant. Another now lay in agony. Though life on the water was uncertain and filled with hazards, seldom did death strike as suddenly as this. And what of their families? Some of the dead surely had been married and probably had small children. Nate's voice broke into her morbid musings.

"Hey, look whose here."

It was Reuban, scampering up the gangplank. He bounded onto the deck and then, tail held high as a flag of truce, trotted over to Ben who picked him up and gave him a gentle squeeze. "Where have you been you deserter? Did that noise scare you out of your lady love's house?"

The crew crowded around to pet the cat and examine him for any damage from his extended shore leave. Ben passed him over to Mollie. Purring loudly, Reuban worked his paws kneading Mollie's arm as she held him close to her breast. Then she looked over at Ben and said quietly.

"You know, if he had come back last night after dinner, we would have been the first ship to tow out."

"And the *Nellis* would have had us alongside when her boiler blew," Ben finished the thought.

Mollie bent down and set Reuban gently on the deck. *And Ben would have been back aft beside the tug to shift the lines.* She stood and looked at each member of the crew as she gathered her thoughts. Her eyes glistened with unshed tears as her first words came with a slight tremor.

"I guess no one knows why things happen as they do." She paused and took a deep breath. "We may not make enough to pay Sloan in September, though we will try. But from now on the ship and crew come first. Cargo comes second. We'll load no more than three hundred tons of coal, and starting in September we'll stop at two hundred fifty. We'll give Sloan all the money we have at the end of the season, and we will have done our best. But nothing is more important than this family."

She looked down. "Yes, you, too, Reuban."

Reuban wove in and out among the crew's legs. After a moment of watching the happy cat, Ben said, "Well, perhaps we should strike the fly for the tug and get this family and our freight underway."

Gazelle cleared the harbor and set sail, shaping a course for Kingston on an easy reach. The strong June sun had heated her decks, and the galley, too, by the time Mollie had cleaned up from the mid day meal. She left the stifling space to go topside and walk forward to sit by the windlass. Here, a cooling breeze deflected downward from the staysail washed over her. Lulled by the gentle motion of the ship nodding along and the steady rumble of the bow wave, she thought of the morning's events.

Steam was a vast power for both good and evil. It drove great ships and locomotives, raised heavy loads of coal and grain, and pumped huge quantities of clean water to the homes of those who lived in cities. Yet, it could also destroy life in an instant. Death, so distant on this gentle summer day on the lake, yet able to strike on a calm morning right in harbor. Without warning, a piece of steel smashes, spattering the life force in an instant. Or in an eye blink a boom sweeps across the deck at night and flicks a man overboard.

What whim had sent Reuban off into the alley ways of Oswego and kept him there when he usually spent the night on her bed? If the *Gazelle* had been towing out, Ben might well be dead now. Could the boiler explosion have been avoided by taking a little extra time during start up? But time is money these days. Or was it simple bad luck that a chance bit of debris had blocked the tug's boiler water supply?

Watching a white winged gull skim off to leeward over the waves, Mollie thought that their lives was little more secure than that of the bird's. There were thousands of iron fastenings holding the *Gazelle* together. If should just one fail with three hundred tons of coal in her hold, she would sink in minutes.

Last November, she remembered, the old canal sized schooner *St. Michael* had cast off with a load of coal for the Welland Canal and Lake Erie beyond trying to get one last trip in before winter. The day had been mild, the wind south and the lake flat. A half hour after the vessel had left, word came by wire from Chicago of a great gale moving east. The *St. Michael* was less than an hour's sail from the entrance of the canal at dusk when the storm struck. Assaulted by heavy snow and bitter winds just five miles from safety, the schooner had to give up and turn to run with the wind back towards Oswego.

In the early night darkness she showed a flare for the tug off Sodus Bay. The tug went out and chased her down the lake. Somewhere near Fair Haven an hour later, the schooner went down. There was just enough light for the tug crew to see her give a lurch and then disappear. There were no survivors.

Had she left Oswego an hour earlier she would have beat the weather and made it to Port Dalhousie. Had she sailed an hour later, word of the storm would have come in time to prevent her departure. That was luck. But her captain had chosen to make one last trip. That was judgement, and the lake rarely forgives bad decisions in November.

Yet to never attempt anything, to stand on shore and look out at the horizon longing for freedom while growing old and useless, what kind of life would that be? Will's time had been brief, yet filled with vitality and ambition. Would you rather be a dour hopeless old widow woman simply existing for thirty years? Maybe you can't determine the ultimate course fate sets for you, but you can at least cast off and adjust your sails to the shifting winds. Fate, luck, and your own choices- it's all a blend.

She sat gazing off at the mesmerizing rise, curve, and collapse of breaking waves all marching in an endless fluid procession down the lake to Mexico Bay. The lake could take life in an instant. But it also gave. Thanks to the lake, she might be able to carry cargo, earn money, and keep the *Gazelle* and her crew at work. The lake might allow her to determine her own course through life as an independent woman.

Reuban strolled up and requested a lap. She took him aboard comforted by his bright little spark of being. Reuban was here. Reuban, Ben, Zeb, Tommy, Nate- the crew's presence surrounded her. Their energy buoyed her spirits and her courage as they went about their routine tasks of steering, trimming sail, standing lookout, or working the pumps. Their combined strength was united by the *Gazelle*. They had worked together to keep her and her cargoes moving along. We're a ship's company, she thought as she cuddled Reuban.

"You're the slayer of rats and guardian of cargo. We all have jobs to do," she said to the cat.

As she smoothed Reuban's fur she thought, Perhaps we'll fail. But we've held this boat together for three months now. Maybe Lady Luck will give us a little slack.

The ship reached Dark Harbor shortly after midnight and hove to until dawn to wait for the tug to come out and tow her into the small harbor. Here Isiah's manager Grant Hurley greeted them with the news of a load for Charlotte this time, explaining that Isiah thought a brief break in the association of the *Gazelle* with Oswego's dock workers might calm troubled waters. Handing Mollie a letter, he added "If you reach Charlotte by the seventh, Isiah wants you to try to attend this lecture."

Later, below decks at her desk Mollie opened the envelope finding within a handbill describing a lecture program, in Rochester, a piece of folded paper, and a neatly penned note that read:

> Dear Mrs. McIntryre,
>
> I believe you will find this program of interest. If you can possibly attend, please use the enclosed small cash advance to hire a rig, the church in Rochester where the lecture takes place being about eight miles from the harbor.
>
> Miss. Anthony is a noble woman of the highest possible character. She has campaigned as an abolitionist and for the temperance cause for many years and has been a stalwart for the cause of suffrage. I have heard her speak and found her logical and persuasive. She is a brave single woman of integrity and courage, not unlike the owner of the *Gazelle*."
>
> Respectfully,
> Isiah Fitzhugh

93

The handbill announced a lecture by the prominent speaker on rights for women, Susan B. Anthony, to be held at 6 pm at the First Presbyterian Church of Rochester on July 7, admission fifty cents.

She sat back and stared at the bulkhead listening to the slosh and gurgle of the water against the hull and feeling the gentle sway and lift of the schooner underway. She recalled her encounter with Dr. Mary Walker a few weeks ago. Dr. Walker had spoken emphatically (and sensibly) on the need of individual physical freedom for women. Anthony was advocating for a more general form of freedom. Maybe it was time for some new ideas about a woman's role in society. And business. A woman's place couldn't be at home with her children if she were single and childless. Women needed more equality in the world of work and less protecting and coddling in their long skirts and petticoats. Women also needed respect. No one should ever have tolerate behavior like that of the *Black Oak's* captain. Yes, Mollie decided, she would attend the lecture if the *Gazelle* got there in time. And she would wear her bloomer outfit.

Chapter Eleven

" This Government ... is an oligarchy of wealth, where the rich govern the poor..." Susan B. Anthony

The passage to Charlotte was uneventful with a hot gusty southwester sending the close hauled schooner over to the south shore at a brisk pace. She made her landfall several miles to the leeward of Rochester, and after slogging upwind along the shore to the mouth of the Genesee River, arrived in late afternoon. Mollie hurried ashore to a livery stable near the harbor and hired a trap to take her downtown. She traveled alone. On a muggy evening after a long day of pushing plank, none of the crew felt a need to learn more of the women's movement. They opted to stay behind for a few hours of leisure at a nearby tavern followed by an early bed.

Mollie located the church easily by the many parked carriages and wagons and by the people arriving on foot. After securing her horse, she joined the throng climbing the steps of the large brick building. Inside the sweltering sanctuary, women of varying ages and fashions of dress, stood or sat, many with fluttering fans. Women were packed in the pews along with a goodly number of men. Most of the seated women were well outfitted with expensive clothing lavishly pleated, embellished with lace and ruffles, and shimmering with color. Many had enhanced their outfits with gold and silver jewelry, and most had stylish hats sitting on their laps. The workers with their worn shirts, patched trousers, and simple dresses stood in the back of the church or along the side aisles. Mollie was one of a handful of women wearing bloomers.

She made her way to a small space near the door where a faint stir of air found its way in to the stifling space. Clearly many leading Rochester citizens were keenly interested in the suffrage movement. Mollie didn't like being packed among them like a plank buried deep in *Gazelle's* hold and was grateful for her marginalized location. She felt sorry for the seated ladies in their layers of fine clothing, pressed together in rows in the stuffy air of the oven-like sanctuary.

From her spot she could see the distant podium beside the pulpit. As she waited, Mollie listened to two men standing in front of her discussing Miss Anthony's exploits. Unlike most of the spectators standing in the back, they carried well tailored dark jackets and wore silk vests and dress shirts. From the way they spoke, she suspected they were lawyers.

The first man was saying, "Do you think she'll be so bold as to speak on the social evil tonight?" when a sudden hush fell over the packed hall as the speaker stepped through a door at the front of the church. Susan B. Anthony was a tall woman. She wore a dark gray dress with a simple white collar. Her costume bespoke her Quaker heritage as she strode straight and proud with head up to the podium. Her graying hair was pulled back into a neat tight bun, and as she turned to face the audience, Mollie saw a strong featured woman of dignified bearing with a serious but not unkind face. She began to speak simply and plainly using no notes. Her clear voice carried easily to the back of the sanctuary where Mollie stood.

She began by explaining that she wanted to share information from the book she was now compiling, *A History of Woman Suffrage*. She said wryly with a small smile, "Although I would prefer to make history than to write it, I felt it essential that we record the facts lest they be forgotten or misinterpreted in the future. So much of history, you see, has been written by men who somehow have managed to overlook the contributions of the other half of humanity."

A ripple of amusement passed through the audience which then became still again as she continued. Only now, she told them, could she undertake the book project, having at last paid off the 10,000 dollar debt incurred by her women's newspaper *The Revolution*.

"When I gave up the paper it was a very deep sorrow- it was like a mother binding out a dear child she could not support. I was advised to declare bankruptcy but would not do so. I traveled over 13,000 miles and spoke 108 times in one year alone. Nearly all those speaking fees I sent to my creditors until at last, after six long years, the bond was paid off."

Mollie clenched her hands at her sides into fists. She thought, If she can do such a thing so shall I. I will pay that note off. Somehow. Her thoughts broke off as an uneasy murmur around her brought her attention back to the speaker. Anthony was now talking about something called social parity.

"Today there are far more women in poverty than there were twenty years ago. Work once done in the home by women is now often performed in factories by women paid a wage inadequate to meet their needs. This poverty and economic dependence of women as well as the passions of men are the true causes of prostitution."

Another louder ripple of sound passed through the crowd at the sound of the ugly forbidden word, and there were a few scattered boos and hisses. Unfazed, Anthony went on. "We must lift the vast army of poverty stricken women who now crowd our cities above the necessity to sell themselves for bread and shelter. Girls, like boys, must be educated to some lucrative employment, and women, like men, must have an equal chance to earn a living. For whoever controls work and wages controls morals."

A heckler standing a few yards from Mollie called out, "No whore will ever take my job!" She turned to see a small wiry weasel faced man standing a few yards away. He made an insulting gesture to the people around him who were hissing and saying; 'shut up', 'pipe down', 'if you don't like it get out'. Mollie feared more hecklers might join him as a brief scuffle broke out around the small man. Then a well groomed dark haired gent with a magnificent mustache pushed past her, grabbed the heckler by the arm, dragged him off, and ejected him out the church door.

Anthony's voice grew more impassioned as she spoke. Sweat gleamed on her brow, but her voice rang like a clear trumpet in the now quiet sanctuary. "Women must be educated out of their unthinking acceptance of financial dependence on men. We must have women employers, superintendents, committees, and legislators. We must have woman preachers, lawyers, and doctors, so that wherever women go to seek counsel be it spiritual, legal, or physical there, too, they will be sure to find the best and noblest of their own sex to minister to them."

"Here, here," said Mollie loudly amid an outbreak of other similar supportive exclamations, hand clapping, and stamping of feet from nearby female listeners. Mollie noticed the two men in front of her were also applauding vigorously. Many people stood to applaud. She listened raptly to the rest of the lecture, as Anthony called for joint ownership rights to earnings and possessions for married woman and said that with the vote, women could help write laws on marriage, divorce, rape, and adultery. Her clear compelling logic held Mollie spell bound. She had never before considered the world of government policy as something that she herself might have the power to change.

Anthony concluded her lecture with quiet passion. "The vote will come to women. Perhaps I shall not see it, but it is inevitable. It will not be wrought by the same disrupting forces that freed the slave but it will come, and I believe within a generation. Failure is impossible."

Mollie joined nearly everyone in the hall in prolonged standing applause for the lone woman on the stage.

As the horse jogged easily through the quiet city streets back to the port of Charlotte in the last of the summer twilight, thoughts swirled like buzzing flies in Mollie's mind. A woman's purpose in life was not simply answering to the needs of a man. You must be more useful and rely upon yourselves, Anthony had said. Yet how could you do so without a job?

Only the right to vote will bring about the change we need the speaker had said. You'll never sing or pray or talk down institutions of evil voted into existence by men. Mollie also recalled Miss Antony's concluding declaration. "It was we the people, not we the white male citizens that had founded this country." Allowing only half the nation to exercise its full power was wasteful and stupid, she thought. Hannah was a perfectly capable clerk and accountant. Yet few men would have hired or trained her. She was lucky to have crossed tacks with Isiah.

Why should women take only jobs chosen for them by men? Far too many, like Burton the *Black Oak's* captain, treated women like dogs, or worse. They view us as mere property. We went to war to liberate the slaves twenty years ago, yet we're still under the yoke. Why should anyone care if I wear bloomers or work the deck on my own ship? Don't I have a right to run my own business? It all comes down to money, and we need the right to make our own.

Darkness had fallen by the time Mollie had returned her rig to the livery and walked the last few blocks to the river. She found all quiet and dark aboard the *Gazelle*. Either the crew was still ashore or more likely, Mollie suspected, in bed after a long day of unloading lumber. As she approached the ship, a soft night wind blew up the river bringing with it the aroma of mud, marsh and city fouled water. She paused for a moment before going aboard. She considered her schooner's well being, making her usual check of the dock lines and her vessel's trim. All was ship shape, thanks to her good crew. The sail covers were on, the decks clear, and the lines and gear neatly secured and stowed.

She thought, too, as she stood by the river, about Anthony's declaration that things were worse now than twenty years ago. Children as well as men and women worked fourteen hour days in factories. Wages and freights alike were lower now than they had been during the war, and everyone was doing more with less. There had been that bloody strike breaking and riot in Pennsylvania's coal fields last winter when several miners had been killed. She wondered would the tug's boiler have exploded if her engineer had been given more time for maintenance? Increasingly fouled rivers flowed into the lake, while the destruction of forests and depletion of the lake's fishes grew ever more relentless and savage.

As Mollie walked up the boarding plank, she recalled Anthony's declaration, "Only the right to the vote will give women the power to re-write the laws of the land." Yes, Mollie thought, and women must also be allowed to run for office. I must talk to Hannah about this.

The *Gazelle's* return cargo of coal from Charlotte took her to the city of Cobourg, a short sail from Dark Harbor and Isiah's wharf where she loaded select graded pine for Oswego. The summer heat intensified, softening the pitch of the deck seams by mid morning and turning the galley's butter supply into a yellow puddle in its dish. The crew held up to the relentless labor of sailing and ship keeping under a burning sun, but it was weary work.

On shore Mollie could see the effects of the heat and the continuing lack of rain. The hot winds that swept the lake and powered *Gazelle* on a fast broad reach back to Canada from Charlotte, had also scorched and shriveled the farmers' fields. In Cobourg Grant Hurley, the agent, told her that if it hadn't been for a light shower last week things would be even worse. "It's been a month since our last good rain. If it stays this hot and dry, there'll be precious little grain to ship out this season."

That evening after supper Mollie joined the crew on deck to escape the stifling cabin warmed by the galley range.

"Not a breath of wind. No point in leaving now," said Ben.

Mollie nodded, "We should get what rest we can though it's so hot down there I won't sleep much."

"I'm bringing my bed up on deck," said Tommy. Zeb and Nate murmured agreement. Tommy went on, "What's gonna happen if it don't rain?"

Mollie, seated on a deck locker, gazed into space as she answered, "We will default on the next payment of *Gazelle's* note. Barley is the only cargo we can get that pays enough to possibly raise the money by the end of September."

After that, the conversation lagged. Then the first hungry mosquitoes arrived, and everyone including Tommy, who changed his mind about sleeping on deck, retreated to their airless bunks below.

Mollie tossed and shifted sleepless for several hours thinking how something always went wrong just when they seemed to be getting a bit ahead. Squalls, breakdowns, wildcat strikes, walk outs, and now this early season drought. Perhaps suffrage could make some things better in the workplace, but it wouldn't help with the weather.

When the schooner had tied up at Isiah's wharf late the next day, Mollie and her crew looked ashore to see an astonishing sight. Hannah was riding at an amazing rate of speed towards them down the wharf astride a two wheeled contraption. Her mechanical steed was painted bright red with yellow pin striping on each of the wheels and moved at railroad speed among the stacks of lumber. She pulled up, dismounted with a flourish and bounced up the gangplank, to greet Mollie with a big grin. She was garbed in a bloomer outfit much like Mollie's, and her faced was flushed with color. The crew stared open mouthed at the device left behind on the quay.

"What in heaven's name is that thing?" asked Mollie

"It's a Velocipede. Isiah had it shipped up from New York City to help me get around the waterfront. It makes my job so much easier. I can go from here back to the main office in minutes aboard my wheel."

The crew had gathered to watch her approach. Now they straggled down the boarding plank taking Hannah with them to examine the machine. They saw that the velocipede consisted of a metal frame connecting two light steel wheels together, the front wheel being slightly larger. Two pedals on the front wheel had allowed Hannah to propel herself down the wharf and along the level regions of the street.

Hannah said, "I kept up with Mr. Fitzgibbon's prize pacer last week. There are claims of men riding a hundred miles in five hours on level ground, though I don't believe it myself."

Ben peered closely at the contraption. "How do you steer this beast? Where's the rudder?"

"This is the helm," said Hanna gripping the horizontal bar attached to the wheel. "It turns the front wheel like a tiller turns a rudder. And this is the brake."

"Why, it must be terribly rough to ride," said Mollie

"It has a padded seat, and see how this thin steel attached to it flexes? It's a spring. It's not that bad-no worse than a carriage, really. You can lift yourself up and sort of stand on the peddles when the road is really bumpy." Hannah demonstrated briefly. She went on, "When women are riding the wheel, our own powers are revealed to us. Our systems are invigorated, the spirit refreshed and the mind swept clear of cobwebs. And what a sensation as you rush down a hill- I feel like a gull sweeping across the water on a gale of wind."

"Isn't it dangerous? What if you fall?" asked Tommy.

Nate shook his head. "It ain't proper."

Hannah responded with some passion, "When a woman wants to try anything new or do something useful like take a watch on deck or if we want to have any fun at all, someone always starts croaking about how it's our duty to stay home and protect our health. Women work in factories fourteen hours a day. They stand behind counters closed up in stores from morning to night, or bend over a sewing machine for five cents an hour and that is perfectly ok for their health. But let us find a way of getting fresh air and exercise and just listen to men howl about how dangerous and unhealthy it is."

Mollie decided it was time to steer onto a new conversational tack. "Speaking of work, have you heard anything about the situation with the stevadores?"

Much to Mollie's relief, Hannah answered, "The dock workers are, if not exactly pleased with a female ship owner, at least willing to handle her cargoes again. Isiah smoothed things over with the work gang on the wharf after he returned from Michigan. He talked to Andy Doyle, the crew boss, and told him that you need to wear your bloomer outfit because as ship owner you must look after your vessel and assist your crew in any way that you can. You must have freedom to move around on deck as well as below, and it's your responsibility and duty to do so. Doyle understands." Hanna paused to laugh. "Besides after the Velocipede he's hardly going to notice you steering the *Gazelle* in your bloomer outfit."

Mollie said, "I surely hope so. He's a mean looking brute."

Hannah answered, "He is rough, but dependable. He's a hard worker, and he respects others who work. He keeps the dock lumpers in line and needs to be pretty tough to do that. "Oh," she added, "they caught Harris robbing another ship, the *Wood Duck*, last week. He's no longer in the gang."

The two women adjourned to the cabin, and after the paperwork was in order, Hannah leaned forward a bit on her chair and said, "Now tell me about the lecture. What did Miss Anthony say?"

Mollie summarized the program telling how the crowd, much of it initially hostile, had warmed, applauding long and loud at the conclusion.

Hannah shook her head in admiration. "She is a tireless worker for our rights. Do you know she said she believed that the wheel will do more to emancipate women than anything else in the world. She wrote 'I stand and rejoice every time I see a woman ride by on a wheel.'"

Mollie nodded. "She spoke forcefully of our need for autonomy and independence. She says women must be free to establish their own identities physically and legally and must have access to the political systems of America through suffrage to do so."

"She's right," said Hannah. "The only way a woman can own a ship or anything else now is by inheriting it. We'll never get anywhere until we can make and keep money on our own to achieve self sovereignty."

"It's more than money," said Mollie. "Men control the newspapers, the courts, and the pulpit as well as the banks and the government. We need our place there, too. As long as they say we're all hysteria and weakness, we're going to be patronized and pushed around. And I'm getting darn tired of it."

As Hannah was about to answer, they both heard a knock on the aft bulkhead by the companionway followed by a hail. Recognizing the voice Hannah called out, "We're here, Mr. Fitzhugh. Come on down," adding to Mollie "He said he might stop in."

Isiah came down the four steps into the cabin, took off his hat and greeted them with a courteous bow and smile. "I thought I should come by to see if you were satisfied with the stevedores."

Mollie said, "Yes, they seem to be back on the job. Thank you for your help. How were your affairs in Michigan?"

"Ah, it's still far too dry out west. There have already been several small fires, as yet none on my lands and none too serious. But we are being very careful and trying to impress upon the crews the need for every precaution. With luck we may escape."

He looked over at Mollie. "I am curious as to your opinion of Miss Anthony."

Mollie and Hanna invited Fitzhugh to sit a moment which he did, and Mollie gave a recap of the lecture. Fitzhugh nodded when she spoke of Anthony's courage in standing alone in her act of defiance at the polls in Canandaigua.

"Yes, that's when I first heard of her. That same year another brave woman also attempted to vote in Michigan."

Hannah asked, "How did you become interested in the cause of suffrage and the rights of women?"

Isiah looked off across the cabin. For a moment he seemed lost in thought.

"It's an interesting story. It has to do with a truly remarkable woman, that woman I just spoke of who tried to vote in Michigan. She was like no other that I have ever known. She changed my life, and I have ever after seen the world differently because of her."

When he fell silent, both Hanna and Mollie demanded,

"Tell us more!"

"Who was she?"

"What did she do?"

Isiah glanced at the ship's clock on the bulkhead. "I really should get back to the office."

Mollie said, 'Why don't you come for a late day supper? And you, too, Hanna. I'm going to the market –it's cool enough to bake today, and it's time I cooked the boys a oven meal. I was going to get a good cut of meat and some cherries for the first fresh fruit pie of the season."

Isiah brightened. "I would like that very much. What time should we return?"

Mollie told them to come back around 7 pm. Isiah promised to bring some Bordeaux. After they left, Mollie wondered how the *Gazelle's* crew, all confirmed ale drinkers, would react to wine with their supper.

Chapter Twelve

"The good old way is a righteous way, I mean to take the kingdom in the good old way." Sojourner Truth

They reacted very well. A pot roast with brown gravy, new potatoes, and fresh peas were disposed of with dispatch, and by the time the cherry pie was served, all the diners were on a first name basis, and everyone had achieved a well stuffed contentment derived from gluttony and modest overindulgence of spirits. A toast to the gods of fortune, the gods of rain, and the gods of wind, had been followed by several more to great women, great men, great schooners, and even to the greatest and luckiest cat on the lake.

As Mollie and Hanna cleared the table, the ship's company and Isiah alike sat back to fire up their pipes or to simply digest and to sip the last of the wine as they praised the meal and the tender crust of Mollie's pies.

Ben asked if Isiah had heard anything more of the *Woodruff,* reported over due.

"That turned out well. She was anchored under Long Point awaiting better weather. But did you hear of the *Ariadne?* In the same squall that knocked you down, she lost 20,000 feet of pine for C.W. Post. So you weren't the only vessel to contribute lumber to Neptune's winter home. Not only that, she also split a jib and her foresail came off the gaff and mast hoops. She was in a state, if I do say, worse than the *Gazelle* because she couldn't sail."

Mollie listening as she collected the plates, considered the squall's unbiased treatment of male and female ship owners alike. Then she decided to change the subject, for she still felt guilty about not listening to Ben.

"Have you heard what the latest predictions for the grain harvest are?" she asked.

"No, only that western wheat shipments are expected to be down in volume here, thanks to the toll reduction on the Erie."

"We need that enlargement of the Welland locks so the ships will come straight through to Oswego instead of transferring to canal boats at Buffalo," said Ben.

Mollie offered "Perhaps barley will hold up. If the freights are as good as last year we should be able to make 200 dollars a trip."

"But we won't be able to make as many trips as we can now if we have to go around to South Bay, Black Creek, Stella, and six other places to load it one two- bushel box at a time," said Ben.

"Let's hope we can load at the elevators in Kingston," said Mollie.

"Well, demand for pine remains strong on the East Coast," said Isiah. "I might be able to raise the freights a bit, if you decide not to load barley this fall."

Tommy said, "We had better load barley. If we keep pushing plank until November my arms will be as big as my legs and I won't have any shirts that fit anymore."

This prompted Nate and Zeb to tease him about needing new shirts to impress the maid in Charlotte he had met last week. As this was going on Isiah sent the last bottle around saying, "It will only turn to vinegar if we don't drink it all."

Hannah spoke up. "I want to change the subject. Please tell us how you became interested in women's rights, Isiah."

Isiah settled back and sipped his wine. "Very well. It came about after I attended a talk years ago while I was in Michigan. It was in 1872 and the speaker was a woman named Sojourner Truth. She was the most powerful speaker I have ever heard. Sojourner Truth is still alive, though she is now, alas, too frail to continue what she calls her testimonies, for she is surely well past her eightieth year. She is a Negro, tall and spare and even in her old age, strong and straight. She has a deep powerful voice like thunder and great stage presence though she can neither read nor write. She also has a sharp and droll wit and a truly remarkable talent for singing.

"She was born a slave named Isabella Baumfree, but took her name Sojourner after she became a wandering preacher. Truth, she said, is the last name of our Lord, and in the custom of blacks in bondage, she took her master's name as hers for, she said, He was her only master.

"She spoke in Michigan after she had attempted to vote and been turned away. She had heard of Susan B. Anthony's action in Canandaigua and wished to act in support, as Anthony had hoped many women across the land would, but few actually did."

Isiah paused and looked around the table. "Perhaps you men from Canada can't appreciate just what an act of courage this truly was. Not only was she a woman alone, she was also a black woman. But such was her power and the respect people held her in, the police made no attempt to jail or quiet her as they did to Anthony. She truly has the heart of a lion. " Isiah paused for a sip of wine and then went on.

"In Michigan where I heard her speak she made such an impression on the stage with her eloquence and strength that she was accused of being a man. She opened her blouse to reveal her breasts! Nearly thirty years ago she attended a meeting in Boston that is still spoken of to this day. A large group of whites and black freemen had gathered on the eve of the Civil War and feelings were strong. John Brown, Frederick Douglass, and others were calling for a slave uprising of revolt and retribution, and the mood of the crowd was dangerous. After hearing Douglas shout for the men to take up arms for it would never be done otherwise, Truth called out from her place in the audience, 'Frederick. Is God dead?' In a flash the mood of the audience shifted, and their blood lust was stilled.

"At least one other time, she single handedly confronted a mob. As I heard the story, it went something like this;"

Some years ago a camp meeting was held just over the state line in western Massachusetts. A party of wild young men had assembled, hooting and yelling, to disrupt the services. Those in charge of the meeting tried to quiet them and then sent for the constables to take the hoodlums under arrest. Things became very tense. A hundred angry young men gathered and threatened to fire the tents. Sojourner, seeing the confusion and fear around her, caught the contagion, and fled to a corner of a tent and hid behind a trunk. She thought, 'I am the only colored person here, and on me, probably, their wicked mischief will fall first, and perhaps fatally.'

But as the riot grew and the very tent began to shake, she thought, "Have I not faith enough to go out and quell that mob, when I know it is written–"One shall chase a thousand, and two shall put ten thousand to flight"? I know there are not a thousand here; and I know I am a servant of the living God. I'll go to the rescue, and the Lord shall go with and protect me." Suddenly then, she said, she felt as if she had *three hearts* and "they were so large, my body could hardly hold them!"

She came forth from her hiding-place, though several others who had hidden with her urged her to stay telling her the mob would surely do her harm. The camp meeting tents had been pitched in an open field. On this night a full moon shone over all. Sojourner left the tent alone, and walked some thirty rods to the top of a small rise. Here, she stood proud and straight in the moonlight, threw back her head and commenced to sing with all the strength of her powerful voice. She sang of the Easter resurrection of Christ.

It was early in the morning, it was early in the morning,
Just at the break of day-
When he rose, when he rose, when he rose,
And went to heaven on a cloud.

They say all who have ever heard her sing this hymn remember it as long as they remember her. The hymn, sung in the open air with the utmost strength of her powerful voice, must have been truly thrilling.

As she commenced, the mob of young men rushed towards her. She was immediately surrounded by a mass of rioters, many armed with sticks or clubs. As the circle narrowed around her, she ceased singing, and after a short pause, she inquired, quietly but firmly, 'Why do you come about me with clubs and sticks? I am not doing harm to anyone.'

'We ain't a going to hurt you, old woman; we came to hear you sing,' cried many voices. 'Sing to us, old woman,' 'Talk to us, old woman,' 'Pray, old woman,' 'Tell us your experience.'

'You stand so near me, I cannot sing or talk,' she answered.

'Stand back,' shouted several voices. The crowd suddenly gave back, the circle became larger as they clamored for singing, talking, or praying. Several men declared on oath, that they would '*knock down*' any person who should offer her the least indignity.

She looked about her, and thought to herself–'Here must be many young men whose hearts are susceptible of good impressions. I will speak to them.'

She did speak; they listened, and then asked her many questions. It seemed to her at the time that somehow she answered with truth and wisdom beyond herself. Her speech was like oil on agitated waters; The crowd fell silent, and only clamored when she ceased to speak or sing.

They assisted her to mount a wagon, from which she spoke and sang about an hour. She told them, 'Well, there are two congregations on this ground. It is written that there shall be a separation, and the sheep shall be separated from the goats. The other preachers have the sheep, *I* have the goats. And I have a few sheep among my goats, but they are *very* ragged.' This produced great laughter.

At length, wearied with talking, she began to cast about for some way to induce the mob to disperse. But when she paused, they clamored for 'more,' 'more,'–'sing,' 'sing more.' She motioned them to be quiet, and said: 'Children, I have talked and sung to you, as you asked me; and now I have a request to make of you; will you grant it?'

'Yes, yes, yes,' resounded from every quarter.

'Well, it is this,' she answered; 'if I will sing one more hymn for you, will you then go away, and leave us this night in peace?' 'Yes, yes,' came faintly from a few.

'I repeat ' says Sojourner, 'and I want an answer from you all. If I will sing to you once more, will you go away, and leave us this night in peace?'

'Yes, yes, yes,' shouted many voices. '

A third time she spoke. "I repeat my request once more,' said she, 'and I want you *all* to answer.'

This time a long loud 'Yes–yes–yes,' came up, as from the entire mob.

'AMEN! It is SEALED,' repeated Sojourner, in the deepest and most solemn tones of her sonorous voice.

Her words ran through the multitude, like an electric shock. Most of her audience considered themselves bound by their promise. Some of them even began to leave. Others said, 'Are we not to have one more hymn?'

'Yes,' she answered, and she commenced to sing:

I bless the Lord I've got my seal today and today-
To slay Goliath in the field today and today-
The good old way is a righteous way,
I mean to take the kingdom in the good old way.

Before she had concluded, the crowd began to turn from her. Then they were running as fast as they could in a solid body. They were like a swarm of bees, so dense was their movement, so straight their course, so hurried their march. As they passed with a rush near the stand of the other preachers, the onlookers were smitten with fear, thinking that the mob was attacking with remorseless fury. But their fears were groundless. Before they could recover from their surprise, every rioter was gone. Not one was left on the grounds or seen there again.

After relating the account, Isiah paused for another sip of wine. Except for the soft creak of a dock line, the cabin was silent. The ship's company sat with their eyes fixed on Isiah.

"Sojourner Truth challenged injustice wherever she saw it, though never by violent means. She believed women were the equal of men and should have their rights. I remember she said that Eve, the first woman God ever made was strong enough to turn the world upside down all alone.

"Some church men have argued that because Christ was male, and because of Eve's sin, men should have dominion over women. But Sojourner Truth said, "Where did your Christ come from- from God and a woman. Man had nothing to do with it!"

"I remember that night in Michigan, when I heard her speak, she told the crowd that was nearly all white and with many unfriendly faces, "We will have our rights-see if we don't. You can't stop us from them. You may hiss as much as you like, but it is coming." As she spoke, you simply had to believe it would be so. It gave me a chill to hear her speak with such assurance and certainty. And, do you know, by the end of her talk the sneers and jeers had turned to respect and even admiration. Nearly every sentence she spoke was followed by applause."

"She never advocated violence or revenge despite her own very hard years in slavery. I remember she said that one should not presume bad intentions of a person, and that one should ascribe the best possible motive for their actions until proven wrong. I have found that advice quite useful in business, though many would say me a fool for following it."

"I have never forgotten her speech that night in Michigan. I have since supported the work of Anthony, Stanton and others with financial donations. Sojourner Truth is a great hearted woman whose wit, strength, courage and self assurance will long be remembered. I do believe her words are a prophecy. Rights for blacks and women will come."

In the quiet that settled over the table, the distant chime of City Hall's clock drifted in through the open ports. Ten times the bell tolled and, as if in response, they heard a stir of wind in the rig overhead and felt the vessel shift against her lines. Isiah extracted his pocket watch and checked it.

"Hannah, we must let these hard working mariners go off to their bunks. They have three hundred tons of coal to load tomorrow."

With pleasantries and promises for another dinner soon, the ship's company bid Hannah and Isiah farewell. Mollie walked her friends to the head of the gang plank. Isiah thanked her for the good food and stimulating conversation. He tipped his hat, bid her good night, and walked off.

Hanna said, "Thank you so much. It was a splendid affair- and so good to talk of strong women."

Mollie put her hand to her chin, hesitating for a moment. Abruptly she asked, "Hannah have you ever thought of running for election to an office?"

An odd look crossed the clerk's face as she looked off across the river. Then she met Mollie's gaze and nodded slowly. "I might consider it."

Chapter Thirteen

"I have plowed and planted and gathered into barns and no man could head me. Aren't I a woman?" Sojourner Truth

With a fresh morning breeze filling in nicely from the west, Captain Don Burton ordered his mate to strike the *Black Oak's* masthead fly for the tug. Up the river at the Fitzhugh wharf, Andy Doyle, the crew boss, had stopped by the office to confer with Hannah on the day's schedule. As they stood on the wharf, they were joined by another stevadore, Red Fields. Hannah noticed the *Black Oak* and the nearby *Gazelle* getting underway. The rest of the group followed her gaze to watch the two schooners preparing to set sail, Mollie standing tall at the wheel aboard *Gazelle* as the boys hoisted and trimmed with swift efficiency.

"Looks like we might have a little race between Burton and the *Gazelle*," said Fields. He gestured toward the *Black Oak* to which the tug was making fast. "I just heard one of the *Gazelle* lads betting Burton a week's pay they'd be in Kingston before him."

Hannah frowned. "Burton should be in jail, not out there on the lake. You know the story about how he ended up with the *Black Oak* and what happened to his partner."

Doyle nodded, "Yep, poor old Marty. He shoulda stayed ashore that day. He was just a mite too old and stiff. When his body came on the beach, he had a big bruise on the side of his head, and his lungs were free of water."

"He never drowned. Burton knocked him overboard. Everyone knows he did."

Doyle sighed, "Burton's old man was a terror. He tried to pull a dirty trick on the gang that was running Buffalo harbor and ended up on the bottom of the canal. Captain Burton was just a brat, then, but he learned fast how to get by on the waterfront. I know he ain't good with women. He was carrying on last night about Miss Mollie at the Laker Inn sayin' how she shouldn't be allowed on the lake after dumping her cargo all over for ships to run afoul of. He said if he ever got a chance, he'd teach her a lesson or two about how a real captain manages a ship and crew."

Down by the trestle as the crew of the *Black Oak* prepared to get underway, Burton shouted over to Nate getting ready to cast off from their spot just astern, "You'll never get that little tub out of the harbor with her at the wheel."

Tommy up by the forward pinrail leaped up onto the bulwark and shouted, "We'll be at the coal dock in Kingston before you're half way across."

"A week's wages says you see my transom before we're out of sight of Oswego," jeered Burton.

"You're on!" roared Ben at the jib halyards. "Come on, Tom, heave away!"

Tommy leaped down onto the deck and ran over to lend a hand. He matched Ben's grip, and the two men pulled together rapidly hoisting sail. Nate then joined Ben at sweating it taut leaving the halyard ends to be coiled up later. As the jibs luffed cracking and snapping in the fresh wind, Nate jumped ashore, cast off the last forward dock line and shouted to Mollie, "We're free forward."

As he did so, Ben and Tommy were hauling both jibs to windward to back them and pull *Gazelle's* bow off the dock. As she pivoted out into the harbor, Nate ran aft and leaped aboard over the widening gap of water. Mollie spun the wheel steering for the harbor entrance, while Nate and Zeb hauled in the heavy dock line trailing in the water. She looked back over her shoulder and smiled. The ship was underway and halfway to the channel under all lowers with scarce a command given, the while the *Black Oak* was still making fast to the tug.

"We'll get the topsails on her as soon as we're clear of the harbor," said Ben.

"The race is on," shouted Tommy as he began coiling down the halyards.

"*Black Oak* slow poke!" shouted Zeb back towards their dock bound rival as he helped stow dock lines.

On the wharf, Hannah watching *Gazelle* get underway said, "That's the best ship and crew in the harbor-Mollie will leave *Black Oak* in her dust."

"Would you put a wager on that?" asked Fields

"I don't believe in gambling, but I would if I did," answered Hannah.

Doyle spoke up, "I'll take your bet, Red. I think Miss Hannah's right about the Canadians."

Red grinned, "You're on, boss."

Before the two ships had cleared the harbor, word of the race had gone around the waterfront faster than a gull with a gale at its tail. Doyle, who wanted to keep his gang busy with Isiah's steady work, backed Mollie, covering a dozen bets. Another of the gang did one better, taking odds of two to one saying, "Burton's a rotten skunk. He killed my brother's dog, shot him in the head with that revolver of his."

Surprisingly, Clancy, the man who had tried to kick Reuban into the river, also put his money on the *Gazelle*. "The witch can handle a boat, and Burton's a rat and a bastard. I saw him grab that last cook, and she was right to take a skillet to his head bone."

Though most of the dockers shared Clancy's views on Burton's ancestry, they still bet enthusiastically that he would show his schooner's transom to a female owned ship especially with the female at the wheel.

Gazelle slipped past the pier head and began to lift to the waves of the open lake. Wave crests flashed white around her against the sapphire blue water and a few wisps of white cloud hurried by overhead bright against the clean washed blue sky.

"I think it's going to freshen," Ben said to Mollie after joining her back by the wheel. "We'll see about the topsails."

Mollie, about to object, remembered who was captain and held her tongue. Ben glanced over, saw the slight tightening of Mollie's grip on the kingspoke and laughed. "All right. Boys- get those gaskets off the topsails!"

Tommy and Zeb both whooped and raced aloft.

Gazelle, with every stitch set, leaned to the wind and tore open the waves. Spray and a bit of solid water boarded the lee decks and ran out the scuppers of the deep loaded ship. The bow wave rumbled under her forefoot and hissed aft as the lance of her long jib boom lifted and plunged stabbing at the horizon out ahead.

"We're getting rid of the coal dust now," exalted Tommy.

"Nothing can touch her on this point of sail," agreed Nate.

Zeb peering aloft said, "Look at those topmasts- they're bending like whips."

Ben looked aloft, too. "She'll stand."

Mollie glancing off to windward saw that the *Black Oak* had dropped her tow after working upwind of them and was now getting underway.

"If this wind we could be in Kingston by 7 o'clock," said Mollie.

"It'll hold. I think it'll pick up some yet," said Ben

Gazelle sailed on a broad reach leaving a boiling wake of green water white foam and breaking waves astern. She flung occasional cascades of sparkling spray aft over her bows as she crashed through the seas. The boys made up and stowed the halyards and dock lines and had the sheets ready to run. With one long tack ahead, only minor sail trimming was likely to be needed for the next forty miles. Mollie braced against a strong pull on the helm as the *Gazelle* sought to pass the *Black Oak*, now only a few hundred yards to windward.

Mollie exalted, "Look at her go. This is some sailing!"

"We're taking him," Ben answered. "If those topmasts hold, we've got him. We're makin' ten with a full load right through his lee!"

An hour later, the *Gazelle* had edged several lengths ahead, and Mollie who was still steering said, "I suppose I should get us some dinner.

Ben looked over with a grin. "Hey. We had a big breakfast. If we're going to beat *Black Oak* we'd better keep the best man on the wheel."

Tommy perched near by on the windward bulwark added, "I've got a week's wages on this. Who needs hot food?"

Already the south shore of the lake lay dim and low astern, the tawny faces of the shoreline bluffs west of Oswego fading into the blue haze. Ben went forward with the two cousins to trim the jibs in hopes of squeezing another tenth of a knot of speed out of the ship. Mollie, as she watched the ease with which the crew worked together anticipating each other's actions, thought that there was no other place on earth she'd rather be right now. If only Will could be here.

She glanced to leeward where the foaming water was rolling off *Gazelle's* lee bow. Farther away, she saw Tug Hill's blue loom rising over the lake's east end as flashing wave crests gleamed against the green-blue swells of water that rose and fell as they drew away to leeward down the length of the lake. For a moment Mollie imagined him standing on the angled deck, his head up, a grin on his face as he watched *Black Oak* fall astern. He had been a bright burning flame, and she felt a brief sharp stab of grief.

Before the stiletto of pain could slip in deeper, she looked forward at the luff of the main and adjusted the wheel slightly. She would not let the tears come. This is not the time. She caught Ben's eye as he looked back from his post by the foresail sheet. He raised one hand in a quick sign of encouragement, and she was struck by how much like Will he looked when he smiled. No, there would be no mourning. There was a race to be won.

An hour later *Gazelle* had gained a more than a mile on *Black Oak*. Mollie turned the wheel over to Ben, saying, "It's high time for a hot meal."

The cousins, now remembering how much coal they had trimmed that morning, were sprawled on top of the deckhouse. Mollie looked aft at the *Black Oak* following them with a white bone of frothing water in her teeth. The schooner shouldered aside a wave, plunged down, and took a dollop of solid green water onboard. Her topsails bulged taut with the wind, visibly bending her topmasts. Mollie knew she was a reflection of their own hard driven vessel- tearing through the water more than a little overpowered by the fresh west wind. She went below to the galley glad to rest her aching muscles after two hours on the wheel.

After dinner, Mollie came on deck and rejoined Ben who was steering. She looked aft at the distant *Black Oak,* now a good half mile behind and to leeward.

"What a grand day," she said.

Ben nodded, "Best sailing of the year."

"Maybe our luck is turning. Things might be looking up. That was a good dinner last night. Isiah and Hannah are fine people. I really like Hannah."

Ben nodded again, "She's sensible and level headed. I can certainly see her staying in business and doing well at it-that is, " he added with a small smile, "if she doesn't get too caught up in the suffrage movement or kill herself with that wheel of hers."

"I never realized so much was happening," said Mollie. "Twenty years ago hardly any women spoke in public. Now Susan B. Anthony travels alone all over the west lecturing. And she's right, too. Women do need the vote to protect themselves. No one else will do it. It's up to us."

Ben replied, "We could all use some protection these days, from the big bugs and wheeler dealers of Wall Street. There's way too much greed running free down there."

After a pause during which Mollie watched the *Black Oak* surging along astern, she said, "Will would have loved this day. I can't believe he's been gone four months. It feels like a lot longer, and yet sometimes it still seems like he should be coming on deck any moment."

Ben sighed, "I know. I still half expect to see him at breakfast with you when I come down into the cabin sometimes. I heard a noise the other day- it sounded almost like his laugh." Ben deliberately turned his gaze upward to study the topsails' trim and then looked away from Mollie gazing forward over the bows.

Mollie said suddenly, "Ben. Do you have any regrets? Leaving the shipyard to stay on as Captain, I mean?"

Ben did not answer immediately. He seemed to be chewing his reply over as he made a slight adjustment to the helm in response to a small wind shift. Finally, he answered while still looking forward, "Like the Good Books says, there's nothing more wonderful than the way of a ship on the sea. What makes her go and how she behaves- sometimes she seems almost alive. How the builder shaped her keel or how she's loaded-there's so much to understand in what makes a vessel sail. It's such an amazing creation. I think a good ship carries a little of her builder's soul. Just using the wind, a breeze that can barely lift a flag sometimes to move 300 tons of cargo- it's sort of astounding." Ben paused and turned to meet Mollie's gaze-"We may never see a new schooner like this launched again. I wish I could have built one."

Mollie saw the almost tender way he handled the helm as he again turned to look forward.

"Well," she said with deliberate lightness. "You never know. Perhaps someday all the coal will be mined out, and we'll only be able to move cargo by wind again. Trees grow back. Coal doesn't. I think there'll still be at least a few schooners sailing the lake a hundred years from now. And maybe one or two shipyards will still be building them and a McIntyre will still be sailing one, too."

"Maybe so. I don't mind being a captain on a day like this. It's about the grandest thing I can think to do. Of course, come November, then I'll wish I was back in Eel Bay in a warm boat shop while someone else drives this old wind wagon through the sleet and ice."

"Oh, yes. November. I guess we'll be dealing with that soon enough," said Mollie soberly.

"Do you think we'll get the note paid off?"

"I don't know. I think there's a fair chance we'll make September's payment, but after that it just depends on the freights and the weather..."

Ben braced against the wheel box at ease as he steered. He thought-whatever happens it will be the most interesting season I've had. It's been good for Tom, too, he's really growing up. He'll be a good schoonerman, just like Nate. We could do all right with this old boat and the boys if we got her paid off. Jamie McPherson would be pretty pleased right now if he could see her out in front of the *Black Oak* like this.

Mollie standing off to the side looking back at the *Black Oak* thought, If we don't make it, I don't know what I'll do. A queasy pang almost like seasickness knotted her stomach as she worried about being beached ashore. I don't want to be alone. I don't want to leave Will's family-my family now. I don't want to crawl back to Sodus Bay on my belly like a kicked dog.

Then someone called out, "Hey there's the Ducks! We're almost across."

Kingston and its harbor rose up over the horizon faster than Mollie had ever seen before. They were a good mile ahead of the *Black Oak* when they entered the St. Lawrence River, and the wind shifted ahead and dropped a bit, forcing the *Gazelle* to tack. Now the *Black Oak* gained quickly as she still had the fresh lake breeze well aft. She came romping up through the upper gap her dark hull looming astern as they dawdled along in the lighter wind.

Though on port tack and being the give away boat *Black Oak* drove straight for the *Gazelle*.

"What's he playing at," shouted Tommy.

"He's not giving away!" Ben spun the wheel hard shouting, "Ease the main, Nate!"

The *Gazelle* obedient as always, swung off the wind and passed *Black Oak's* stern. Burton's jeering comments were lost on the furious crew as they rushed to tack their own ship and follow him into the river.

As they closed with the harbor, the *Black Oak* was only a few hundred yards ahead. Several of her crew shouted taunts across the water "Where's the witch's broom?" "Gotta weed on your rudder?" "Who forgot to pull up the anchor?" The boys remained silent, concentrating on trimming sails to gain another quarter knot of speed. As they neared the entrance, Ben left the wheel telling Mollie, "You take the helm. We'll keep everything up and follow him in." Ben went down on the deck to get the dock lines out.

As the two schooners came booming into the river with every bit of canvas set and top masts bending with the strain, groups of idlers gathered to see who would reach the coal trestle first. The late daylight touched their masts with gold and gleamed off their bow waves as the schooners swept past Garden Island. Onlookers clearly saw the leaping antelope on the trailing two master's transom as the two schooners swept past, and word went around-it's the McIntyres of Eel Bay in a race to the end with Don Burton.

Inside the harbor where the west wind was blocked by buildings and trees, it dropped further and became shifty. The two schooners still slipped along, *Gazelle* steadily gaining on her rival. *Black Oak* now sailed only a few lengths ahead. When Burton rounded her up near the wharf, a dozen onlookers stood ready to take her lines. Mollie saw a crew man heave the light messenger line off from *Black Oak*'s deck. "They're going too fast," she murmured to the *Gazelle*.

The line missed the outstretched hands of the men on the dock and fell with a splash into the water. Burton let out a roar of abuse and a string of curses as the second line also missed. Mollie glimpsed him furiously spinning the wheel as he bore off to go around again. It was her turn now to try for the dock.

"I hope this is right," she breathed, and she turned the wheel down as fast and hard as she could, just as she had three months before when she and Will had made that trip into Kingston a lifetime ago. *Gazelle* swung up into the wind, her sails luffing, blocks banging, jibs flogging and Nate Tommy and Zeb flung their heaving lines ashore with perfect aim. As the ship continued to coast Mollie saw the men on the dock pulling the heavier dock lines in furiously. Then the first, and immediately after, the second line was snubbed and slipping on bollards and bitts as *Gazelle* tried to pull the wharf up the river after her.

"We done it, we got her!" shouted Ben as he went for the halyards. Within a few minutes, the sails were down and the noisy canvas quieted. The dock lines were hauled taut and a score of idlers crowded the wharf exclaiming and laughing over the close finish and the showy ship handling.

Mollie tried to look nonchalant as she watched Burton going around to come in to the wharf under sail behind them, though she could feel the venom in Burton's look as he went by. Tommy Zeb and Nate climbed up on the deckhouse to watch. Tommy yelled, "Nice second place finish!"

Ben made no attempt at modesty. He grinned widely and said, "That was a helluva landing, Miss Mollie."

She smiled back. "Why, thank you Captain Ben. That was sharp line handling, too."

As the crew dispersed to furl and stow canvas and lines, Mollie went below to get her paperwork ready for customs and for the cargo discharge. The Customs officer, Jerry McLeod, now well known to the ship's company, appeared walking briskly down the dock swerving among the dispersing idlers. He stumped aboard with a cheery greeting saying "That was some entrance. Did you race from Oswego?"

"All the way," said Ben. "We led from the start and were well ahead when he got a lucky wind shift near Simcoe Island."

"That was smart ship handling," said Jerry.

"Tell it to the helmsman," answered Ben with a smile-"or I should say the helms- woman."

When Mollie and McLeod emerged from the cabin after clearing customs, Mollie sought out Ben who was at work on the fore hatch saying, "Mr. McLeod says they expect the *Anowa* to arrive within a day. She was reported off Port Hope at 3 pm."

Ben said, "What about a lay day after we unload? We can give the crew shore leave-Tommy's got some extra money to spend-and I can take care of a few jobs that need doing. I want to check a couple things aloft."

"Done," said Mollie.

Burton sent his mate over to pay the wager. After he had counted out the coins and handed it to Tommy he said, "Stay out of Burton's way ashore. He's a sore loser."

The mate turned to go saying to Mollie "And he don't forget neither. He told me next time you won't be winning."

Chapter Fourteen

"as an individual, (a woman) must rely on herself" Elizabeth Cady Stanton

Late the next day, the old white *Anowa* came plodding along from up on Lake Erie with her load of timber for Calvin's Lumber on Garden Island. Mollie stood on the dock to greet her and her captain as they eased alongside. When the ship was secured and cleared, Mollie skipped up the gang plank to the main deck where Captain Thomas stood tall and straight and with his arms out. She embraced him saying against his chest, "Father, it's so good to see you again safe and well."

He held her close, then at arm's length. "And you Mate Mollie- You look fit and strong. I am glad to see you. I spotted your ship out there at anchor. Is all well?"

"We're fine, we decided to take a lay day when we heard you were due in. Ben had some things he wanted to take care of. We haven't had a lay day in ages. Can you come out for dinner tonight?"

"I certainly can. Tell me the time and I'll be there."

Dinner was a festive affair with Captain Thomas's favorite fish chowder, fresh baked rolls and gingerbread for dessert. There was much news to catch up with, too. There was more talk on the upper lakes of a seaman's union with higher wage scales for any work above the deadeyes or forward of the knightheads and on the jib boom. Business at the coal trestles in Fair Haven and Sodus was strong though, and Captain Thomas had managed to get back home briefly several times. Aunt Anna was well, and Petunia the goat had produced a pair of beautiful twin kids. It looked like wheat freights would be about a penny higher than last year. There had been a bad collision on Lake Erie off Cleveland between two steamers in early summer fog. A dozen people were still missing though neither ship had foundered. And yes, they had experienced the same front that had knocked *Gazelle* down. *Anowa* had lost a jib in the squall.

Gazelle's crew all talked about the great race and the decisive humiliation and defeat of *Black Oak*. Then talk shifted to more somber subjects including the boiler explosion and the squall. After awhile Zeb and Tommy started to fidget a bit.

Ben said, "Perhaps you'd like to take the yawl boat and go ashore?"

That was exactly what they would like. Nate considered a bit, then decided he'd go along just to keep an eye on them. After they left, Ben with a quick glance at Mollie and Captain Thomas remarked, "I think I'll turn in. I've still got some catching up to do on my sleep, so I'll leave you two."

After Ben had gone up the steps and forward, Mollie got up to make a fresh pot of coffee. There was more talk yet to be had, for much water had passed under the bows of *Gazelle* and *Anowa* since early May.

Mollie told her father about the Anthony lecture and her encounter with Dr. Walker. She spoke of Walker's ideas about the importance of physical freedom and activity for women and Anthony's call for women's suffrage. She also told of her first encounter with waterfront corruption, the robbery and the stevedores' reaction to reform dress worn by a bossy woman shipowner.

"I'm sick to death of being stared at, called a freak, or a witch, or worse just because I wear my bloomers and try to do things myself. It was grand to whip Burton today, but when we go back to Oswego nothing will have changed. Men everywhere want women to be little white lily maids who simper and beg and hang on to their man's arm. Hannah calls them silly little noodles."

Her father shook his head saying, "Many do believe a woman's only purpose is to be a wife and mother, and that women, like children, should be seen and not heard. Guess they never knew any of the women in my family," he laughed. After a sip of coffee, he changed the subject. "How's the mortgage fund doing? Is your little ship paying her way?"

Mollie frowned, "We might make the September payment. But I don't see how we can possibly have the balance by the close of the season. At least not unless we see some record high freights this fall." She paused, took a deep breath and continued. "I don't want to go back on the beach. If I lose the ship, how can I ever earn enough money to pay you and Uncle John back?"

Mollie and Captain Thomas both studied the table with its freshly washed table cloth, laundered in honor of the dinner with Hannah and Isiah a few nights before. Then Mollie said, "Maybe I should go ashore and look for a rich husband and try to be a silly noodle myself. Dan Fitzhugh has had his eye on me more than once. It really is true- a single woman is a nobody without a man."

"No," said Mollie's father sounding a bit gruff. "I'll hear no talk like that. You must be yourself, before you can be a wife, a daughter, or a mother. You can't do any of those things well unless you believe in yourself. You have to stand on your own two legs in this wicked old world. Tell me, what happens to the 'helpless noodle' if her husband dies or divorces her? What if he's a drunkard and beats her? You're young strong and healthy. You have skills, you're the best cook on the south shore, and you can steer and trim."

"I guess you're right. If I tried to be Dan's good little wife and stay home and have tea with the ladies of Oswego, I'd go crazy."

Captain Thomas reached across the table and patted her hand. "That's my Mollie. It won't be easy, but you'll do it." He sipped his coffee, then putting his cup down said, "I almost forgot. I must tell you about a Canadian woman I encountered in Michigan about two months ago. Her name is Fannie Buell and she's the master of the three master *Maud S.*"

Mollie's eyebrows lifted. "A woman? In command of her own schooner?"

Captain Thomas nodded. "Yes, indeed. We were in Alpena loading lumber and I noticed her on the deck of the vessel ahead of us that was also loading. She was conferring with the mate and I took the liberty of going forward to the bows and hailing her to ask was she indeed the captain? She assured me she had been in command since 1875 and would I like to come aboard? I did so, and talked with her of your own chance acquisition of a two master.

"Captain Buell started sailing as a cook when she was seventeen, and after she married a captain from Kincardine she sailed with him for several years on the *Annie Watt*, a two master. Her husband was lost overboard during a bad blow, and she had two small children to care for, so she had to find work again to support them.

"She told me she left her two boys ashore with her sister and took a job aboard the *Maud S* as cook. The *Maud S* is a timber hauler, a fine vessel built by Shickluna here on Lake Ontario, but she rarely trades on the lower lakes now. She's a canal sized schooner, and sets a raffee and three jibs.

"After several years, she and the *Maud S's* captain and part owner were married and sailed together. He was considerably older than she. He fell ill late in the season one fall, and she took the vessel into port. He never recovered and that winter she took her exam, got her ticket, and continued as captain and half owner after he died."

Mollie listened with intense interest. "How old was she, Father? What happened to her children? What was she like?"

"She's a little slip of a woman, would hardly come up to your shoulder, but she is very well spoken and has great self assurance on deck. She sometimes wears trousers when working on board her vessel, but she said she prefers her skirts ashore. I don't know about her children. Perhaps they're grown by now. I would say she was at least forty five. She also said she could never have kept the *Maud S* without a good crew. The mate and two of the sailors have been with her for five seasons. When I told her of your situation, she said tell your daughter ' It won't be easy but it is possible. She must treat her ship and crew well, and they will take care of her in return.' She also said, 'Don't let anyone tell her it can't be done.'"

Mollie sat her mouth open a bit, her eyes shining. "What a wonderful thing that you met her. I would so like to speak with her myself."

"Well, there you are," said Captain Thomas. You pay attention to what Ben does, learn a bit of piloting, and you could sit for your ticket and take over in a year or two. You'd be the first female master on Lake Ontario."

Mollie said thoughtfully, "I don't know if I really want to be captain of the *Gazelle*. At least as long as Ben is willing to do it, I think I prefer being more of an assistant. That squall was pretty bad."

"You could do it. You just need a little more experience in heavy weather. But as long as Ben is willing, he's a good lad to have on the after deck."

Mollie nodded, "I think we're really a pretty good team right now. He appreciates my work on deck. I take care of the business ashore, and he does the ship keeping that I don't know how to do. It's a good partnership if I can keep him."

"He would rather build than sail wouldn't he?"

"Yes, but no one is building new schooners now. So maybe he'll stay with *Gazelle*. That is, if there's another season for any of us."

Captain Thomas sighed and stretched. "Well, there is going to be another day, and it'll be here soon, so I think we'd both best get to our bunks."

Mollie saw him over the side and in the stillness of the summer night watched him fade into the darkness in his yawl boat. She listened to the quiet dip of the oars for a long time while she held Reuban for comfort.

Then she went below, still carrying the cat, but feeling more hopeful about the future than she had in several weeks. Be true to yourself- Dr. Walker, Susan Anthony, the woman called Sojourner Truth, Captain Buell- and Hannah, too- they were all doing just that. It wasn't easy for them. Yet, they had stood up for their rights and kept doing their work. We had a rough start, she thought. But maybe things are turning around now. If other women can keep going I must do the same. Take care of the ship and she'll take care of you.

The *Gazelle* towed into Oswego a few days later with another load of pine lumber. It had turned sultry again after the welcome cold front that had pushed *Gazelle* to victory over the *Black Oak*. The late afternoon haze dimmed the shoreline into a blur only a mile offshore. The south side of the lake had not received any rain worth mention for well over a month. Here, the garden bean and corn rows drooped and shriveled, and hayfield stubble had burned brown. The Oswego river level had dropped to where its sluggish flow could no longer flush the foul inputs from the city's sewers and factories. The *Gazelle's* company smelled the river before they saw the harbor entrance through the humidity.

The tug picked them up outside the jetties where they waited hove to amidst the white bellies of countless floating dead fish mixed in with thick gray mats of rotting vegetation. As they towed up the river against a light southerly wind that was thick with the smells of decay and filth, she worried about the mood of the stevedores.

"I hope Doyle and his gang aren't too ugly today," she said to Ben.

He rubbed his sideburn and shook his head. "Hotter'n the hinges of hell. Hard to think anyone would be happy shoving a shipload of lumber in this- you could fry an egg on the deck."

After they were cleared by customs and the hatches were off, she watched nervously as a group of a half dozen men approached. She recognized among them Doyle's bulky shoulders and the stevedore Clancy, Reuban's nemesis of a few weeks ago, as well as a strange teamster with a full rigged red beard and a belly to match. What do they want now, she wondered. The whole gang came clumping up the boarding plank and from the irregular path some of the men steered, she suspected a bit of drinking had been going on. This may not be good, she thought.

As the clot of men reached the deck, to her surprise she saw Clancy and the red headed man were wearing wide smiles. Doyle was poker faced as he carried a keg before him. He set the container down on deck, and everyone doffed their hats except for Clancy who had his hands behind his back.

What on earth are they up to, she wondered. Clancy produced a fresh lamb kidney which he announced was for Reuban, and Doyle stepped forth and nudged the keg with his foot."This is for your crew- it's Oswego's best pale ale." Seeing her look of utter bewilderment, he laughed a great booming laugh. "The boys here, Red, Clancy and meself, made over a hundred dollars on the race."

Red, the teamster, added, "Don't' worry Mz McIntyre, the boys we scalped ain't mad at ye-no one likes Burton. He kicked his last cook so hard, she hadta go ashore. He shot Paddy's dog dead – he even 'bused my Prince-threw a firecracker under him while he was in harness two weeks ago and spooked him so bad he almost went down. He coulda broke a leg. They're all glad he lost."

Ben took the keg up and said, "Mr. Doyle, that is right white of you. We thank you."

Doyle turned abruptly away and cupped his hands to his mouth and bellowed to the gathering gang ashore, "All right boys-let's get to work and unload this here packet so she can be on her way back to Canaday"

Despite the cooperative dockers, *Gazelle* was still at the Fitzhugh wharf two days later waiting for a spot open up on the coal trestle so she could move over and load. Hannah had stopped in for lunch and now the two women were on deck visiting. Hannah was about to leave when an elegant phaeton pulled by a sleek long legged dapple gray pulled up nearby. A woman, clad in a dark green lavishly frilled silk carriage dress descended from it. Her white leather boots were spotless, and her outfit was topped by a large hat of the latest style, trimmed with egret and heron plumes. As she picked her way around the horse balls and debris of the wharf with her dress hem held high, Hannah whispered,"That's Abigail Potter, the wife of Isiah's chief rival in lumber forwarding. She's very rich. What on earth can she possibly want?"

Mrs. Potter stopped on the dock a few yards from the *Gazelle* and looked across at them. Hannah went over to the rail. "May we be of assistance?"

"I wanted to see the Canadian ship owner who defeated Captain Burton in the race."

Mollie stepped forward to the rail. "Here I am," she said with her head held high and a trace of defiance in her voice.

"Good gracious. They said you were six feet tall and had the arms of a stevedore. You actually look quite normal." Mrs. Potter craned her head to look up at the spars and looked forward along the jib boom. "Do you really climb up there and go out on that pole thing?"

Mollie remembered Isiah's story about Sojourner's Truth's advice of never assuming evil intent until it was proven. She took a deep breath. Then she said, "I can, but I don't usually. And I certainly wouldn't if I were wearing this skirt!"

Mrs. Potter was not deterred by Mollie's cool tone. "Your ship looks so big. How on earth can you possibly manage?"

Mollie and Hannah exchanged a quick look. Then Hannah said, "It's not difficult, but it takes team work. Mollie, let's show her how two people can run up a staysail."

Mollie nodded, "It's not hard at all at the dock in a quiet harbor." With that, skirts and all, she set about casting the gaskets off the staysail. Then she and Hannah went to the dockside pinrail near where Mrs. Potter stood watching.

Mollie lifted the coil of line off the belaying pin explaining, "This is the halyard to pull the sail up. See, it leads through that block there and then aloft."

She pointed out the blocks and the lines called sheets used to control the sail after it was raised. Then she and Hannah each took a grip on the halyard. Placing their hands alternately and saying "hey yah, pull ya, hey yah" to set a rhythm, the two women pulled together each placing her hand above the other's as they pulled downward to raise sail in a smooth unbroken effort. The sail rose quickly, and when it was two-blocked, Mollie called to Hannah, "'Vast and hold." She belayed the halyard, and in the harbor with no wind to flog the staysail, it hung aloft quietly.

"There, you see how that went?" said Hannah. "Women can do many things if they work together."

Mollie added, "If we had five or six women willing to learn, we could take the *Gazelle* out ourselves. We aren't as strong as men, so many things would take longer to do and would need an extra set of hands, but we'd get it done."

Mrs. Potter was visibly impressed. "And the bloomer outfit you wear when you're on the lake, you could go up the mast with it on?"

Mollie nodded.

Hannah said, "Women can do a lot if they aren't wrapped up in corsets and whalebone and long skirts. Sailing a schooner is a lot like the Swedish cure-fresh air, sunshine, and exercise."

"Except your hands get a lot harder than they would with lawn tennis or a stay at a spa," Mollie said with a smile.

"Living proper and ladylike doesn't mean being lifeless weak and ailing," said Hannah. "Dr. Mary Walker says it's well known that repression and physical inactivity cause mental weakness and prostration. Sunshine, work, and sleep, not coddling indoors are a great medicine for women. Control of your body gives you control over yourself and your soul."

Mollie nodded, "Physical control is the most basic right that many men would deny us."

Hannah, out of long habit, was making up her halyard coiling it to hang on the pin. She paused, fixed Mrs. Potter with a hard look and declared, "All women should be treated as humans. You are as intelligent and worthy as your husband. But until we attain the right of suffrage, you will continue to be a nobody. You're little better than a slave to your husband. If you don't vote you don't count. What if your husband divorced you? What would you do? Where would you go?You have no more status than a dog. And that will not change unless we change in the laws, and we need the vote to do that."

Mollie reached over and cast off the halyard to let the staysail fall. As she did so, she remarked with a wry smile, "We're not saying women are better than men. We haven't wrecked railroads or corrupted legislatures or done other wicked things that men have, but then we've never had the chance."

She gave the sail a hasty furl as the still obviously intrigued Mrs. Potter moved to the very edge of the quay. She wanted to know more. She asked about suffrage and how mere women could operate a schooner and who made bloomer outfits in the latest style. After several more questions, Mollie invited her aboard and walked her around the decks pointing out the heavy gaffs and booms, the big wooden blocks and the various tackles, and the pinrails with their coils of manila line neatly hung from the belaying pins. She pointed out the lines used to raise and control the sails and led Mrs. Potter aft to the wheel and binnacle where she explained the basics of using the compass to keep the vessel on course.

Hannah then offered to supply their visitor with literature from the women's reform effort on setting one's own course through life. Abigail Potter was clearly interested in both the reform movement and sailing a schooner. She stood aft by the wheel looking along the main deck towards the distant jib boom, "Is it difficult, steering a big ship?"

"In a gentle wind, no. But in a storm it can be very difficult," answered Mollie.

Potter took hold of the wheel and gave it a tentative turn. "It must be exciting out there on the lake. I wonder what it would be like to direct the path of a ship like this? And did you say there are other women who sail on schooners?"

The deep tone of the city hall clock tower sounding once for the end of the noon day dinner hour struck their ears. Mollie was surprised by the anxious look that immediately shadowed Abigail Potter's face. With a glance ashore towards the hill where the city's wealthiest families resided, she said, "Oh dear, I must be going. I was supposed to be back home by now." Mollie saw her brow darken as she paused and then continued with a hint of defiance in her voice, "But first, I would know more of these things you speak of regarding women's rights."

Hanna said, "I'll go ashore with you. I need to get back to my own work. I have some literature at the office I can give you on the reform dress, suffrage, and the Seneca Falls Convention last year."

"I'll drive you to your office in my carriage."

Hanna flashed a quick smile back over her shoulder at Mollie as she followed Abigail Potter down the boarding plank. Mollie watched them go. She shook her head as she watched the upper class lady pick her way across the wharf to her carriage. Her longing look over the ship's bows had been clear. She's like a pretty little bird in a cage, with no freedom to ever fly about. Then Mollie smiled and said to the *Gazelle*, "That Hanna. The Swedish cure- next she'll be taking the ladies aboard and making sailors out of them aboard our schooner spa." Still smiling Mollie went below to clean up from lunch. Hannah will be up there on the stage next to Susan B. one of these days she thought.

That evening after supper, the whole crew sat or lounged on deck taking advantage of the scant stirs of an evening land wind moving down the river. "I sure wish it would cool off," said Tommy. Gesturing toward the cat sprawled flat and full length at their feet he added, "Look at Reuban. He must be three feet long."

"If it keeps up much longer it'll burn up the crops," agreed Mollie. "We really need another good rain."

"We'll wish we had some of this heat three months from now when we're watching those snow squalls roll down the lake," said Ben.

"What's it like, being in a snow storm out there?" asked Zeb.

Ben and Mollie both laughed, "You'll find out soon enough," said Ben.

Mollie added, "Will and I were in one on the old *Alma* last year. It snowed so hard it piled up on the sails and came sliding off on us in masses. We all worked with brooms to sweep it off the decks. It's strange out there in a snow storm. It gets real quiet, and you can't see the waves. It's worse than fog because it's so cold. All that white stuff swirling and slanting-it got rough as we ran from Kingston across to Oswego, and when we took a wave aboard, it froze right up solid. We didn't have a salt barrel with us, and in no time the deck was so icy you could hardly walk on it. The halyards on the pinrails froze stiff. We had to beat the ice off before we could lower the sails."

Ben said, "I remember one snow storm when we came in here they had three feet on land. We were darn lucky to find the place. We had a little bit of clearing near shore, or we would never have found the piers. Ships can ice up quick. The weight up high has capsized some steamers."

Seeing Zeb's look, Ben assured him, "We'll have lots more good days before then. Sometimes it doesn't snow at all until late November. And September can be fine out on the lake-real yachting weather."

Mollie said, "Abigail Potter came by-she's a rich lady from up on the hill. She wanted to gawk at the she-freak. That Hannah." Mollie broke off and laughed. "She had Mrs. Potter about talked into going yachting with us on the *Gazelle*. She told Mrs. Potter it would be as good as a visit to the spa, all that exercise, fresh air and sunshine."

Ben chuckled, "You know, Hannah's no fool. She might have something there. Sailing in early September can be pretty nice. Maybe we could take a yachting party out- if they'd pay enough."

Mollie said,"You're not serious are you?"

Ben answered, "Hey, you never know- you cook 'em a good lunch, take Hannah along as mate, let 'em steer a bit, come back in by sunset. It might do wonders for your reputation ashore. What do you suppose we could charge?"

Mollie stopped smiling and looked thoughtful. "Maybe it's not so crazy an idea after all."

"Do any of those old rich ladies have daughters?" asked Tommy.

Expecting an early move to the trestle tomorrow Ben announced he was turning in. The rest of the crew followed his lead. Mollie caught Reuban as he was about to sneak ashore and took him below with her. She lay awake for awhile thinking about Hannahs' remarks and wondering if it would be worth organizing a yachting party. She was thinking about the menu when she drifted off to sleep.

In the stillness of the sultry night a hundred yards or so from the wharf where the *Gazelle* lay, a half smoked cigar smoldered in a bit of hay beside the stevedore's horse barn. City Hall's clock chimed once as uneven limping footsteps faded in the distance. Softly the whisper of night wind passed over the sleeping port. An ash glowed red, then brightened. A flicker of flame awakened, and a grass stem flared abruptly. Tiny flames licked at the weathered boards of the barn wall.

It was very dark when Reuban jumped on the bed and landed on her stomach waking her up with a loud Miaoooww. He clambered all over her still yowling as she asked Reuban, "What's wrong?" Then she smelled smoke. She threw the covers off. Something was amiss.

Then close by a man shouted, "Fire, Fire! Rouse out there aboard the schooner- the warehouse is on fire!"

Chapter Fifteen

Never wound a snake. Kill it. Harriet Tubman

For two months the sun had withered baked and scorched the countryside and Oswego's waterfront with scarce a sprinkle of moisture. Now fire fed greedily upon parched boards, crisp trash, scrap wood, and curled shingles. Whip-like snaps, crackling, hissing, and a deepening roar sounded loudly in the night as greedy flames spread devouring the warehouse. As the fire leaped thirty feet in the air, Mollie saw a fountain of sparks and a few bits of burning wood fly up from the building. Some landed on the roof of a small shed across the road and immediately flickered into life. *The whole west side could go. We could lose half the city,* she thought.

Men and boys dashed through the shadows and flickering orange light as a wind shift sent a dense mass of smoke rolling across the scene. A horse screamed in terror nearby. Mollie coughed and choked turning away from the flames and smoke. A shower of sparks, burning bits of shingles and red hot embers landed on deck near her. She leaped onto them stamping out a half dozen glowing coals smoldering near a coil of dry manila line.

Behind her, Ben shouted at the crew, "Wet the sails!"

The canvas would ignite in a moment. If the blaze then spread into the tarred rigging, the ship would be lost. It would be over in minutes as it spread through the rig. A flicker of orange licked briefly over the furled outer jib's sail cover before Tommy and Zeb clambered out on the bowsprit with their buckets flinging water over the sail to douse it.

Mollie ran to the bilge pump, seized the handle, and began working it up and down to draw up and spill any free bilge water upon the decks to wet them down. There was little they could do for the masts and the bone dry tarred rigging aloft though. Just aft of them, she saw another schooner with a flicker of flame running up one of the foremast shrouds towards her furled topsails. A hot blast of air blew across *Gazelle's* decks, and Mollie fought rising panic as she worked the pump. A huge curtain of orange flame leaned towards the several schooners tied to the wharf. *We should cut the lines and push out into the river before it's too late.*

A sudden brilliance flared nearby throwing her shadow against the deck. It was the schooner behind them. Someone shouted, "Cut 'er loose!" Another voice, a woman's, screamed "Help!" Ben rushed past Mollie, his sheath knife in hand. He joined another man on the quay slashing away at the lines to free the vessel. Several other men leaped aboard and were dousing the flare up that had ignited her furled foresail as she drifted off to safety.

Mollie heaved away at the pump handle her heart pounding. She heard shouts and curses from a gang hauling a hand pumper onto the wharf with Doyle in the lead. A dozen teamsters and dockers that usually worked the lumber wharf were at the handles. She also saw Reuban's one time nemesis, Clancy, running towards her bringing more buckets to help wet down their own sails with river water.

A pile of lumber flared up in a sudden explosion of bright yellow, the blaze leaping high into the night. The pumper began to draw from the river, and a stream of water hit the pile extinguishing it in a cloud of acrid choking smoke. The firemen began wetting down the other stacks of boards nearby. With the schooner's sails and decks now well soaked, Tommy and Zeb pounded down the gang plank buckets in hand and ran off to join a group forming a bucket brigade to save the office building. Across the road, she saw several men passing buckets up a ladder to the roof of a burning barn, while others led a pair of frantic mules and a horse out of the building.

The urgent clamor of a bell heralded the arrival of the Kingsford Starch Company's steam fire engine, drawn by a team of snorting horses. Mollie saw the animals and men silhouetted against the lurid glow of the blazing warehouse as the engine crew raced to get the hoses out and drawing. She heard Doyle shout, "The Northwestern-it's going!"

The two crews turned away from the doomed warehouse to concentrate on saving the large elevator. A scant month from now schooner loads of barley from Canada would be coming into port. Losing the elevator would devastate the barley trade.

Tommy noticed another flare up among Isiah's piles of stacked lumber. He snatched two buckets, shoved one at Zeb, and they sprinted across the dock to put it out. Mollie had joined Ben and Nate in scooping buckets of water from the river to wet decks and sails of another neighboring schooner. She glimpsed the two boys running by the hellish inferno of the warehouse. The docks and lumber piles around them were lit as bright as day by the flames.

Then she heard someone shout, "Watch out!" followed by a shriek of terror and pain. Nate dropped his bucket, bolted down the boarding plank and disappeared into the steam and smoke ashore. Over the crackling and roar of the flames and the shouts of the firemen, he heard Nate crying, "Tommy, look out!"

Horrified, Mollie watched the roof of the warehouse collapse in a great blaze followed by the outwards fall of the timbers of a flaming blackened wall. The still burning timbers descended with horrible deliberation upon the spot she'd last seen Tommy and Zeb.

"Oh dear God," she whispered as she watched, frozen in place. The heavy beams crashed onto the ground in an explosion of sparks and a great leap of brilliant flame.

Then Ben gripped her shoulder, "There they are."

Tommy was hobbling towards them limping heavily while Zeb, doubled up with pain, his shirt stripped off, was following with Nate's help. Ben ran down the boarding plank to the dock to assist as Tommy cried, "Zeb's burned!"

An hour later, the *Gazelle* lay safely in the river. Ben with only one able bodied crew man left, had cast off the dock lines to save his ship, as several other schooner crews had already done. The *Gazelle* drifted off the wharf to the open river where he and Nate could drop anchor. Mollie had dressed and bandaged Zeb's badly blistered arm and several other burns. Tommy's ankle had been assessed as probably sprained but possibly broken. In the darkness, only an occasional bit of flame still flared briefly as the fire brigades patrolled the blackened remains of the warehouse and some of the lumber piles.

The next morning with the push of the *James Moray* on her quarter, the *Gazelle* returned to the wharf. Isiah arranged for Tommy and Zeb to go ashore for further medical care. Now, with the reek of fire's aftermath in the air, Dan, Isiah, Mollie and Ben stood on the dock and surveyed the charred timbers.

Isiah spoke. "We were very fortunate. Thanks to Doyle's volunteers and the Kingsford Pumper, our losses were small. The *Grampus* lost several sails, but on the whole, the waterfront came through very well. Had there been any wind I believe we would have lost the entire row here along the river as happened back in '51 instead of just two buildings."

"I heard there was a rumor about arson," said Mollie.

Dan said, "Doyle thinks Harris might have been involved. Remember him? The thief. It wouldn't have taken much. A careless pipe or an innocent cigar -in this weather nobody would think it was an arsonist's work. At any rate, a couple of our men had a little talk with Harris this morning, and he decided to leave town."

Mollie, looking at the blackened rubble ashore, marveled at the pain and hardship a single vindictive moment could cause. It was a miracle no one had been killed in the blaze.

Ben said, "We're going to have to sign on a couple of hands for a trip or two. I'd guess I'd better get the word out."

Mollie sighed. "We'll miss them. Zeb bless his heart, he plugs along even though I bet he'll head back to the farm after this season. And Tommy is a rock. He's not real ambitious, but he's strong and willing-he'd make a wonderful mate someday for someone."

"And he's loyal," said Ben. "You know, that day you were at the Susan B. lecture in Rochester? He stood up in the tavern and recited the whole Minerva McCrimmon ballad start to finish in honor of his female ship owner. A sailor there bought a round for us he was so impressed."

Mollie smiled. "Tommy really is quite the tavern room baird. He's got an amazing memory. And I don't know anybody better with the mouth organ."

Then she sobered as she thought of the girl who had inspired the ballad. "Minerva did have spine, I will say that." She recalled the incident when the young Canadian had saved her family ship, and the subsequent ballad that had gone around the lake's various waterfronts endlessly last fall after the incident. She struck a pose and recited;

"Through the howling wind and the hail,
"Dad, I see the light of Oswego,
You'd better shorten sail.
Show the torch and blow for the tug,
Dad and I'll head her for the pier,
And have your heaving line handy,
Dad We're getting mighty near."
We blew and blew our lungs out
But no tug would hear.
And the "Dave Andrews" drove like a wild bull

Right straight for them old wooden piers.
With one little girl at her wheel, boys,
A little thing plucky and thin.
With her mother's old grey shawl
Pinned underneath her chin.

We got everything off but the staysail.
The "Dave Andrews" was jumping like mad.
Nerva drove straight through the breakwater gate
And called, "Get your lines out Dad!"
We didn't snub her the first try,
But the next we caught one spile,
Two dockwallopers dragged our spring line out,
Which held us for a while.

I rushed aft with the Old Man
To lift Nerva from the wheel.
Her frozen hands was bleeding.
Her feet she could not feel.
Her hair was iced to her back boys,
And it seemed to me a sin,
For her mother's old grey cradle shawl
Was froze beneath her chin."

Dan applauded, "Bravo!"

Ben grinned, "You're not too bad with a recitation yourself. Well, I'd better go find us a crew so we can get underway."

That afternoon, while Mollie and Nate were cleaning up the ship, a stranger approached. He was tall and powerfully built with a bull neck and broad shoulders. Lank greasy brown hair hung down over his forehead and his collar. He stopped at the boarding plank and called out "Ahoy the *Gazelle*. I hear you're looking for hands."

Mollie and Nate came over to the rail, and Mollie said, "We are. We need an able bodied seaman for a couple of weeks."

The stranger grinned displaying two rows of crooked discolored teeth. "Well, I'm your man. I'm looking for just a trip or two before I head home to Michigan."

At their invitation, he strode up the plank and introduced himself as Joe Blake, explaining he'd been beached for a spell looking after his poor old Dad, but now he was free to head home again. "But I needs a few dollars in my pocket first."

They learned he had sailed aboard big three masted four hundred ton grain and lumber carriers on the upper lakes for several years as an able bodied seaman and that in his opinion their little cisco boat would be a snap to sail.

Though Blake was civil enough, Mollie took an immediate visceral dislike to him. She sensed something intensely disquieting behind his heavy lidded impassive gaze, and as he looked at her she felt a sharp stir of unease. She didn't like him calling the *Gazelle* a little ciscoe boat, either.

"The captain isn't here right now. He'll be back soon, if you care to wait."

Blake said, "Sure, I'll wait." He flopped down in the shade of the deck house to sit and watch, while Nate and Mollie finished up cleaning and stowing gear from the night before.

Ben hired him, telling Mollie later, he's big and strong, and we need some muscle aboard now. Ben had also recruited another sailor, a fourteen year old lad, small but willing. He was the youngest of Clancy's brood. Clancy, the would-be cat kicker had confronted Ben ashore with the youngster in tow saying, "He's a good worker. Take him on and teach him to drive a wind wagon. He thinks he wants to go to sea. I'd rather he went anywhere but to sea!" Clancy had said with a laugh.

So Ben had agreed, for the boy, Patrick, known universally as "Mouse" appeared bright and eager, and he assured Ben he was not afraid to go aloft. Though he was light, he was wiry, and he had an air of determination that Ben liked.

Three days later, they sailed with three hundred tons of coal and two new hands. They set course for Kingston, and even before they cleared the harbor, Mollie knew she was not going to enjoy having Joe Blake aboard. Blake was seldom without a twist of tobacco either on his person or in his mouth. After they struck the fly for the tug and were waiting for its arrival, he directed a load of brown juice at the base of the main mast.

Mollie spoke sharply, "Mr. Blake, kindly direct your emissions over the leeward side. My ship's deck is not a spittoon."

"A little 'baccy juice helps preserve the wood."

"The masts have already been oiled. Now wash that off you please," Mollie pointed at a deck bucket.

"Since when does the cook give orders on deck?"

Mollie folded her arms across her chest. "I am the owner of this ship. And you will wash that deck. Now."

Blake stared back at her with venom in his pale eyes. For a moment, she thought he would defy her, and her heart pounded as she braced herself ready for the worst. But then he dropped his gaze and slouched over to the buckets in their rack, muttering something Mollie couldn't quite catch, and snatched one up. He went to the rail, dipped up a full load of river water and directed it with a careless toss towards the mast. The water splashed and splattered, some of it wetting Mollie's bloomer. Then, with a look of pure malice, he challenged her eye waiting for a comment before turning away to put the bucket back.

Mollie moved aft trying not to hurry. She didn't want Blake to think she was afraid of him, but she wanted to keep her distance from his hostility. This man is trouble, she thought. He's a powder keg. He could blow anytime. Best to limit contact with him as much as possible for this trip.

As they towed out, Mollie relieved Nate at the wheel so he and Ben could get ready to hoist sail. With a light west wind darkening the calm lake with patches of ripples here and there, Ben ordered Blake aloft to cast off the lashings on the topsails.

Blake nodding toward Mouse said, "Send the kid up. I've got a bad knee. I'm supposed to work on deck only-Dr.'s orders."

Mollie saw the look of annoyance on Ben's face. Blake hadn't said anything about any physical issues or limits before being hired. Ben gestured toward the halyards. "Very well, you help Nate raise the main. Mouse, come with me. I'll go up with you. It's a good quiet day to show you around up there." He moved off with the boy to the foremast ratlins.

Once on the open lake, the tug changed course, towing them into the wind. The mainsail then rose slowly, followed by the foresail, jibs, and finally the two topsails. Back on deck, Ben showed Mouse the lines for setting and sheeting the topsails, The boy was as eager as Blake was slothful. While Blake used the minimum amount of energy he could get by with, Mouse turned to with a will, hauling and pulling with all his slight frame's strength, and moving quickly around the deck as directed by Ben.

After the ship was under sail and the tow line had been cast off from the tug and dragged aboard, Nate began coiling the many yards of line left lying about from raising sail. Mouse pitched in, following Nate's example, while Blake sat on the main hatch to take his ease. Ben, also making up lines, said "Lend a hand here, Mr. Blake, and let's get this gear coiled down and stowed."

Blake said, "Hey, the kid there needs to learn the ropes. Let him do it."

Ben replied, "As short handed as we are he'll learn them soon enough. Right now I want these decks cleared and made ship shape. At once." He added as Blake showed no sign of turning to. Blake then heaved himself to his feet with exaggerated weariness and dragged himself over to the rail to begin coiling down, his languor in marked contrast to Mouse's diligence.

Mollie and Ben exchanged quick glances, and Mollie shook her head slightly as she turned away to answer the galley's dinner time duty call. She saw dark clouds on the horizon for the good ship *Gazelle* and her crew.

Chapter Sixteen

"Men make the moral code and they expect women to accept it."
Emmeline Pankhurst

Over the next few days, the pattern set upon their departure continued. Mouse was a quick study, eager to go aloft, or to swab and stow. Ben soon had him trimming sails and working aft at the helm mastering the basics of steering a compass course. He told Mollie the youngster was a pleasure to teach. "I believe he might truly run away to sea. He talks all the while of clippers and brigs and barkentines built of iron. He knows the rigs and most of the courses and headsails by name."

But Blake, the powerfully built experienced sailor from the upper lakes that they had counted on for help with the ship's heavy gear, was lazy slack and sullen. He used Mouse as a personal servant, making him fetch and carry, and did as little as possible. Nate found him asleep once when he was supposed to be on watch. After unloading her coal in Kingston, *Gazelle* sailed for Dark Harbor and enroute Blake's carelessness caused a near disaster.

They were sailing in a brisk northeaster with the wind well aft. Blake had just taken the helm after dinner, and Mollie was below in the galley cleaning up, while Ben sat for a moment of relaxing at the table with his pipe.

"I'm thinking of trying to find another hand at Dark Harbor if I can persuade Blake to go."

"I wish we could get rid of him. Honestly, he scares me," said Mollie. "But he's an American, and he might refuse to go ashore in Canada."

Ben was about to reply when the deck lurched abruptly under their feet, and simultaneously a loud crash sounded overhead. Ben jumped up from the table swearing and bounded up the companionway, while Mollie grabbed for the pot of stew that was headed to the low side of the table.

When she emerged from the deck house a few moments later, she saw Nate on the helm and heard Ben berating Blake furiously. She also saw Mouse standing forward, crouched sightly his eyes wide, as she heard Ben shout, "He nearly went overboard- he could have been killed. You were two points off course for no reason. It's broad daylight, hardly any sea, what's your excuse?"

Blake muttered something about being tired and sleepy, and Ben snapped, "You've done half the work of a fourteen year old kid this trip and slept twice as much. Now get back on that wheel and mind your course!"

Blake moved to obey, but the look of venom that he gave Ben as he did so chilled Mollie to the bone.

Mollie went down onto the main deck and asked Mouse, "What happened?"

"I saw the boom coming and I ducked, but I forgot about this thing," the boy said gesturing toward the heavy iron traveler on which the foresail sheet block was shackled. The big lower block had slammed over to the lee side of the traveler missing him by inches.

An image seared through Mollie's memory like the flash of a lighthouse beacon. A black night in April, another accidental jibe, Will overboard, the sails thundering, the ship rolling and pitching as Ben and Tommy struggled to launch the yawl. Impulsively, she hugged Mouse and then released him quickly. "Thank Heaven you weren't hurt." She looked aft to where Blake and Ben were and shook her head. *Oh please not again, not ever again* she thought.

Mollie was back below finishing up in the galley work when she heard a light knock. She called "come in" and saw Mouse entering hesitantly.

"Mrs. McIntyre, I need to tell you something."

"Sit down. What is it? Are you all right?"

The boy sat stiffly and refused Mollie's offer of a second piece of pie. "It's about Mr. Blake."

Mollie sat down opposite of Mouse and fixed her gaze upon him. "Go ahead. I'm listening."

Mouse hesitated and then said, "Earlier before dinner, I smelled booze on him. I think he's got a flask in his pocket."

Mollie nodded, "That would explain a few things."

"Don't tell him I told you," said Mouse quickly.

"Better to know now before someone does get hurt," said Mollie as she dismissed Mouse who was eager to leave.

Ben confronted Blake after he came off his watch, and after Blake denied the accusation Ben demanded, "Then what's this?" as he held up a flat sided whiskey bottle.

"You've got no business in my things. You can't be going through a man's private possessions."

"You could have killed someone today. You darn near did. Now I'm telling you once and once only. This is a dry ship. And if you have any more of this stashed anywhere, you better leave it all in the bottle until we get to shore."

All night long the *Gazelle* made good time loafing along easily with no cargo and a fair wind. As dawn paled the east showing a clearing sky of broken cloud, the schooner arrived off Dark Harbor where she hove to and jogged drifting slowly offshore nodding to the easy rollers to await a tug. Mollie served the crew breakfast, and then as she and Ben ate alone, they discussed Blake.

"He's a drunk, and I don't want him aboard."

"Well, now that he knows we're believers in temperance under sail he may not stay anyway," replied Ben.

"I hope he doesn't. There's something about him. I'm afraid of him. It's as if there's a rattlesnake inside him coiled to strike."

Ben gulped down the last of his coffee before going on deck. He put down his cup and got up from the table saying, "I know. Sometimes I think he's going to bust loose. Maybe if he stays off the booze we'll be all right. We need his muscle for loading and unloading. But if you want me to beach him, I will."

"No, you're right. We do need him. I'll just stay out of his way. When we get to Oswego, we'll get another hand."

To Ben and Mollie's surprise Blake pitched into the job of loading lumber with far more vigor than he had shown in Oswego, though he was sullen and said little. He pushed and shoved with a will, trying to outpace Ben and Nate by loading his side of the hold first. Mollie hoped that things might work out for a few more days. They didn't quite finish the deck load, however, and Blake headed ashore steering a course for an uptown tavern after dinner. When he came aboard three sheets to the wind in the small hours of the morning, Ben was waiting.

He confronted Blake at the head of the boarding plank while the sailor was still on the narrow board. "If you've got any bottles, hand 'em over now."

"You're not pushing me around again, Cappy Ben."

Ben moved into a fighting stance and raised his fists. "Then get ready to go for a swim."

141

Blake swayed a bit on the plank and glanced down at the water. Then, with a snarl about Ben's ancestry and manhood, he reached into his pocket and drew forth a flat sided whiskey bottle and handed it over. Ben stepped back and let him aboard and then stripped him of two more flasks telling him, "You'll get your truth serum back when we reach Oswego and no sooner."

Blake cursed and blustered, and Ben braced himself again for a fight. Blake dropped his fists and snarled, "Ok, Cappy, have it your way. But payday's comin', Bennie Boy. You'll be wishing otherwise soon enough."

The next morning they finished building the deck load, signaled for the tug, and by 9 am the *Gazelle* was towing out. The day was clear with a light west wind, and once the sails were up and the tow line cast off, Ben and Blake went below. Blake was hung over and in a foul mood, and Mollie had done her best to avoid him at breakfast. Now he was out of the way and with Mouse as lookout and Nate on the helm, Mollie settled on a deck locker just forward of the house to catch up on the mending. As she stitched away, the gentle motion and the quiet sounds of the ship loafing along on a reach with a moderate breeze on a fine late summer day lulled her, and Mollie relaxed even as she thought of Blake's smoldering hostility and the contemptuous looks directed at her during breakfast.

Before Will's death, she hadn't crossed tacks with men like Burton of the *Black Oak* or Blake who despised a female that dared to set her own course. Every man she had ever sailed with had treated women with respect. Her father, Will, and Ben, too, they all had worked with her. The entire crew of the *Gazelle* had backed her quest to be the self supporting owner of a profitable vessel. None had ever questioned the propriety of it. Blake's dark presence had brought constant tension aboard ship. She hadn't seen Reuban for a whole day though he was aboard somewhere. Blake was like a dynamite stick with a short fuse when in his liquor. She would be very glad when he was gone and Tommy and Zeb were back aboard.

A shadow fell over the mending in her lap, and as she looked up, two hard hands seized her. One covered her mouth, the other hand and arm wrapped around her body pinning her arms to her sides. A strong smell of whiskey surrounded her as Blake said in a low voice, "Now we'll see who's boss on this boat."

The deck load of lumber forward and the house aft screened Mollie and Blake from the view of Nate at the wheel and from Mouse on lookout up in the bows. Mollie struggled with all her wiry strength, but Blake pushed her up against the forward wall of the deck house with ease. "You tell anybody what I did to you today, and I'll see that Ben McIntyre goes overboard."

Blake pressed her hard against the deck house. He jammed her head against the wood while keeping one hand over her mouth and started working at her clothing with the other. Mollie, with the strength of desperation, managed to plant a solid kick on his shin. As Blake winced, thrown off balance for a moment, a roll of the ship made him reach to steady himself. Mollie pushed against the deck house and managed to tear loose from his grasp enough to get one brief shriek off before he slammed his fist into her face. She slumped against the deck house stunned.

Nate, a few yards aft heard Mollie's single short panic stricken cry. He left the wheel and rushed forward to see Mollie lying limply on deck with Blake tearing at her clothes. Nate launched himself at Blake grabbing him by the shoulders to pull him away. With the speed of a striking rattler, Blake whirled around and punched Nate in the stomach. Nate doubled over gasping. Blake followed up with a hard two handed blow to his neck. Nate went down out cold.

Eyes blazing, Blake now turned back to Mollie who was beginning to stir feebly at his feet. "Now it's your turn," he snarled. But as he stood gloating for a moment, the laws of physics asserted themselves.

With her helm untended, the *Gazelle* had begun a slow swing into the wind as all properly balanced sailing vessels will. As she headed up, the jibs began to luff. Mouse, on lookout up forward, turned at the sound of the sails and looked aft wondering what was wrong. He saw the wheel untended. He scrambled up on to the deck load and saw Nate lying on deck and Blake bent over Mollie's body ripping her dress open as she batted at his face. Mouse bolted for the nearby hatch to the foc'sle where Ben slept in his bunk below.

Gazelle meanwhile continued to work up into the wind. Blake undid his belt and dropped his pants. As he did so, the foresail sheet slackened when the wind spilled from the sail as it began to luff. Then the boom swept inward. Ben came leaping aft just in time to see the heavy foresail sheet block strike Blake on the side of his head. Blake staggered off balance. Mindful of the man's strength, Ben quickly followed *Gazelle's* first strike with one of his own, lunging forward to knock Blake down with his shoulder. Then, before Blake could get up or go for his knife, Ben had his own blade out.

"Stay right where you are, and you won't get hurt," said Ben.

Blake froze, locked eyes with Ben, and measured the distance between them. Could he lunge far and fast enough to get past the blade? If he could get his hands on Ben's throat, he'd finish this business in a minute. Mollie, meanwhile, staggered to her feet. She stumbled around the deckhouse and took the companionway stairs with a jump. Below she flung open the lid of the small built in desk and grabbed Will's revolver by the handle. She sprinted back on deck with it in hand, praying Blake wouldn't call her bluff on the unloaded gun.

He didn't. When he saw the barrel of the heavy Colt pointing at him, held two handed but steady by Mollie, he slowly drew his knife and tossed it on deck by Ben's boots.

"Now get forward," snapped Ben.

Blake went, followed by Ben who locked him in the forecastle. "I ought to put you in irons, but we don't have any. You get in there, sleep it off, and we'll deal with you in Oswego."

The rest of the day passed quietly. Ben confided his suspicions to Mollie that he had overlooked some of Blake's liquor. He told her he had looked in on the prisoner at the lunch hour and found Blake snoring loudly with the smell of whiskey strong in the forecastle.

Mollie said darkly, "The influence of alcoholic spirits on a man like that-it's no wonder some people would close down the saloons."

Ben merely grunted. He was not a temperance man, but he had seen enough trouble caused by booze aboard ship to believe in keeping his schooner dry.

"It's maddening, not to be able to do anything," continued Mollie.

Ben nodded agreement. "You'd be wasting time to have him arrested. He would say you asked for it, and the judge would agree and let him go. Why give up several days of sailing? We need to make them all count now."

Tight lipped and scowling, Mollie nodded in silent agreement. There was nothing she'd like more than to see Blake cooling his heels in the county jail for a few days. She hated the thought that instead he would walk off free to prey on other women sometime somewhere. But at least he would be out of her life.

As they towed into Oswego, Ben paid Blake off. The moment the ship was secured to the dock and cleared through customs, Blake shouldered his kit and clumped ashore and strode off without a backward glance. Mollie felt a weight like a full load of coal lift from her shoulders as she watched him go. He had scarcely disappeared around the corner of the warehouse when she saw Hannah approaching, her copper colored hair coiled up in a neat braid and her binder of paperwork under one arm as she rode down the dock in her blue and white bloomer, steering her velocipede one handed. The sight of her friend brought a quick lift to her spirits. Hannah had survived far worse than what she had just experienced. Now Hannah was flaunting her bloomers and running the entire Oswego lumber operation for Fitzhugh and Sons.

When Hannah reached the head of the boarding plank Mollie reached out and took Hannah's free hand in her own and gripped it tightly. "Oh, Hannah, I'm so glad to see you!"

The emotional greeting caught Hannah by surprise, and she peered at her friend closely, noting the bruise on her face. "All right now, tell me what happened."

Mollie released Hanna's hand saying, "Come below. I'll tell you the whole wretched story."

The two women went below, and while Hannah laid out her paperwork, Mollie tossed a couple sticks of willow into the still warm range oven and put the teapot on.

"It's such a relief to have this weather change," she said.

"Yes," agreed Hannah. "That grand little rain last week was a real mortgage lifter. We just heard that the prospects for barley as well as western wheat are much improved. The upper lakes grain freights are up a cent and a half from last year."

"We're going to need a good crop and high rates, too. Even then I don't know if we'll make that last note payment."

When the manifests were finished and the papers filed away, Hannah leaned forward. "Now tell me about the trip."

Mollie spoke of working short handed and trying to manage with a boozer and a bully aboard. She told of his continual slacking and disrespect and finally of the assault.

"He hit me so hard I was knocked out for a moment. My head still hurts from hitting the deck. Never have I seen such hatred. It was truly animal rage. I really think he would have killed me if Ben hadn't stopped him. Ben and Mouse and Nate and the ship, too, they saved my life. The *Gazelle* turned the trick when she knocked him on the head with the foresheet block. If there had been a bullet in the gun, I think I would have shot him."

Hannah scowled, "These attacks are more common than you would think. The *Palladium Times* ran a story just a few days ago about a schooner cook who was raped by three of the crew. And Don Burton last year struck his cook so hard she had to be put ashore in Rochester. Yet these vile creatures go right out and ship another female cook, and no one stops them. And then after a rape, they blame us, calling us temptresses, and saying we asked for it!"

"Why? Why do so many men resent us? Why do they want to keep us weak and subservient? We should be able to make our own decisions and control our own bodies."

"They're afraid of us. At least some of them are."

Mollie's brow knitted in question. "I don't see why they should fear us. I guess they have blamed us for bad luck or causing storms at sea for a long time. Women, priests, Finns-they say they're all bad luck aboard ships. Such hogwash."

Hanna replied, "Well, using someone as a scapegoat to divert people from your own weakness or bad behavior is an old game. Why wouldn't an incompetent captain blame his troubles on a Jonah? Or a female cook? Many men resent us, especially if we try to spread our wings and fly out on our own. You know how dangerous it is to be different."

Mollie scowled, "They shackle us to shore or take us in tow like a cut down coal hulk. It's no way to live, and I won't live that way."

"Nor will I! Two hundred years ago, a woman who dared spread her wings was called a witch. They burned witches. And the Church backed them up. To this day, men preachers tell us Eve was born from Adam's rib and sinned by seeking knowledge in the Garden, so we must pay for her sin and be subservient to men."

"I still don't understand. It doesn't make sense," said Mollie. "Adam ate the apple, too. So men are as smart as we are, and they're stronger. Yet, you say they're afraid of us?"

Hannah sighed, "Isiah speaks of these as times of great change. The coming of steam and coal to power huge factories and the railroads that carry the coal and so much other commerce, too, it's all changing everything. He believes the acoustic telegraph and the electric dynamo will soon bring even greater change. There are queer new religions now, like Mormonism and odd ideas like the Second Great Awakening and the notions of the Spiritualists. The unions are gaining strength, and since the war, blacks in the south can vote. There have been huge changes in our cities with the immigrants from Germany and Ireland- it's frightening to many. Men who are cowardly or weak felt threatened even before Susan B. Anthony or Dr. Walker called for our rights. The last thing they want to hear is more women crying for more change."

Mollie looked across the cabin toward her bunk where Reuban was curled up asleep. Cats know how to live, she thought. They go on their way beholden to no one and take care of themselves. A cat will sit in your lap, but only when she wants to, not when you tell her to. I'll never be someone's pet lapdog. Like a cat, I must go my own way. But sometimes it would be nice to be fed and pampered and not worry about money. Sometimes it would be nice to let someone else make the decisions.

But as she sat in the cabin of her own ship, Mollie thought she probably had spent too much time on the water as a girl setting her own course with her Uncle's little fishing boat. I never learned to be a lady. Now I'm too old to become one. I'm like the cat in the story, walking alone and making my own choices. She looked over and met Hannah's gaze.

Hannah sensing her regrets said, "Things are changing for men and women alike. Even nature herself changes, or so Mr. Darwin tells us. You are part of that change. You, your vessel and your crew. Other women are watching. You must stay strong for their sake as well as yours."

Mollie looked away across the cabin, studying the painting of the ship that hung on the bulkhead. It showed the *Gazelle* under full sail, free and joyous as she cut through the waves of a sky blue lake. Too bad life can't always be like that, she thought.

Hanna broke into her thoughts. "I always liked that painting. The artist caught the boat's motion so well. It's not like the usual ship paintings that show the vessel from the side stiff and static."

"That was done by a woman named Linda Connors. She was the daughter of a ship owner in St. Catherines. A lot of people think she's the best ship painter on the lake. *Gazelle's* second owner, Arthur Stevens commissioned it." Seeing Hannah's obvious interest, Mollie continued. "Jamie McPherson of Cat Hollow built the *Gazelle*. She's white oak planked with grown hackmatack knees and elm ceiling. She's one of the strongest two masters on the lake. Jamie built two schooners, one for of each of his sons. Tim McPherson got *Gazelle*, and sailed her with his wife for two years. So she was a family ship back then, too, when that picture was painted."

Mollie and Hanna both gazed at the painting. It showed the *Gazelle* as if seen from the deck of a pursuer. The schooner was depicted sailing along ahead and to windward of the viewer, her graceful transom clearly visible with its antelope leaping over a bit of stylized water. "Will wanted to gold leaf the carving on the transom. I told him she had to make a profit first," Mollie sighed.

Hannah said, "You'll gold leaf that carving yet!"

"I don't know. It's so hard now without Will. Of course, it wasn't easy back when the boat was new either. The McPherson's couldn't keep the *Gazelle* for very long. After the war, freights fell hard. Arthur Stevenson wanted her and paid a good price. He said she was the fastest two master on the lake, and he always made money with her. He looked after her and kept her up. Will only got her after Arthur died. I like to think of her when Tim and his wife were sailing, back when she had a couple on board." Mollie shook her head. "They lasted longer than Will and I did!"

"Something will come along."

"It better come along pretty soon," said Mollie.

Chapter Seventeen

"I can't die but once" H. Tubman

"It's not summer anymore," Mollie said to Nate as she stood beside him at the wheel. She was watching the tug ahead as they towed out. Each year, she thought, sometime late in August summer slips away. It vanishes in a three day rainy spell, or a chilly night, or sometimes it's that first northeaster like we had last week. The birds are so quiet now in the morning. Soon they would begin drifting south. She watched a lone black and orange butterfly fluttering past *Gazelle's* stern, its wings beating with sturdy persistence against the light southerly. Watching it dwindle in the distance, she recalled another sign she had just seen of the season's shortening days- the first bright glow of goldenrod blooming in a vacant lot.

She dreaded the approach of fall, and the gales that would come with it.

"Barley will be coming in soon," offered Nate. "I wonder what the freights will be."

Mollie answered with a sigh, "Whatever they are, we'll do what we can."

She turned forward to survey the main deck where Tommy, a still limping but welcome presence, was helping Mouse ready the mainsail's throat and peak halyards. She was glad the heat had broken, but that cool gray spell last week had turned her thoughts to the fast approaching deadline for their next payment. She left Nate's side to go lean upon the bulwark and gaze moodily down at the passing water. Still nearly a thousand dollars to go. We'll never make it at this rate.

Mouse came bouncing aft. "We're ready to raise sail, Mr. Nate." He called out.

Nate turned the wheel over to Mollie and went forward to lend his muscle on the main halyards. Watching Mouse trip along like a young colt next to Nate, Mollie's mood lifted a bit. Mouse, with his boundless energy and enthusiasm, had been the one bright spot in an otherwise awful week and a half. Lately, the boy taking heed of Ben's warnings about the decline of sail on the lakes, had come up with a new career goal. Now, instead of commanding a four masted Cape Horner, he had decided he would go a-yachting as skipper of some rich toff's schooner yacht. She suspected the sight of the splendid big black hulled schooner *Oriole* from Toronto booming into the river yesterday under full sail, might have influenced him.

"He's a smart lad," she murmured to *Gazelle*.

She thought of the scene on *Gazelle's* deck two days ago after Tommy had come limping aboard, and Ben had told Mouse he must pack his kit and go.

"We can't afford to keep you on now that Tommy's back."

Mouse had looked stricken and blurted out, "I don't wanna go home. Let me stay. I'll work for nothing."

"That wouldn't be fair. Besides your family needs the money."

"They won't have to feed me if I stay here. I can be an apprentice. You can teach me to be a mate. Sometimes apprentices work just for board. Please!"

Ben looked pained. He liked Mouse but couldn't bear the thought of treating the boy or his family unfairly.

Nate offered, "I'll skip next month's pay to keep him on."

At that point Mollie had intervened. "We can pay Mouse five dollars a month as an apprentice, but only if Ben and Nate are willing to teach him." Both the men looked relieved. Nate gave Mouse a gentle shove toward the bow. "Come on, I'll show you how to put a long splice in that dockline."

Ben smiled at Mollie. "We really can use his help. And I know Clancy's family needs the money."

"An extra five or ten dollars isn't going to matter that much to Sloan. And he is good to have aboard."

Days were noticeably shorter now. And today there was an unexpected chill in the air. She remarked upon it to Ben after they had raised sail and begun slowly gliding over the nearly calm water.

"The lake's turned over. We may see some fog with this cold water when we get offshore," he had replied.

At dusk the fog gave way to a light drizzle. The galley range's warmth felt good for a change as she tidied up after supper. The wind held light as the boat, deep laden with coal, ambled along traveling a bit faster than a brisk walk.

The crew settled into the first night watch. Mouse was at the helm, Tommy forward on lookout, while Ben Nate and Mollie were below.

"Call us out if it picks up so we can get the topsails off her. And keep a sharp watch. There'll likely be more fog patches and poor visibility tonight," cautioned Ben. He added to the young helmsman, "Remember when both sidelights you see ahead, port your helm and show your red, and if to your starboard red appear, it's your duty to keep clear."

This prompted Mouse to finish the jingle, "I know, both in safety and in doubt, always keep a sharp lookout."

In the darkness after supper, Tommy settled himself against the pawl post in the bows and eased his sore leg. He thought of Zeb, beached with his burns and wished his friend was aboard. Then he wondered how Katie the pretty yellow haired maid in Charlotte was. I'll probably never get back there to see her. It surely was dark. Perhaps there was a bit of fog about like Ben said there might be. It's as black as the inside of a hat.

Tommy stood up, holding onto the bulwark to keep the weight off his still tender ankle and looked carefully forward. Then he slowly scanned the darkness off to port and starboard. The fine drizzle began again, and Tommy stepped back leaned against the windlass drum and crossed his arms tight against his chest feeling the night's chill. Ben said the lake had turned over so the cold water had come up to the surface. What made it do that? We must be going through a patch of fog or mist on the water. It's so damp and there's no stars visible overhead. Tommy listened and heard only the small sigh of the *Gazelle's* bow wave and subdued creak of her rigging in the quiet night.

His ankle throbbed. He bent down to rub it. Was that something off to port? A sound almost like a small wave breaking? Should I sound the fog horn just in case.

He had just reached for it when he heard the sound again, a kind of a low continuous grumble mixed with an unmistakable hiss and surge of a continuously breaking wave. A ship's bow wave. Abruptly, Tommy saw the dim green glow of a running light frightfully close.

"Mouse! A steamer right on us! Hard a port!"

Seth Baker, second mate of the *Lady of the Lake*, leaned forward slightly as he peered through the rain streaked glass of the pilot house into the darkness. The mist patches lying over the cold water and the light rain unnerved the newly promoted officer. He thought of the collision on Lake Erie only three weeks ago. It had happened on a night exactly like this. The steamer *Alexander MacKenzie* had run down a two master. She had hit the schooner forward tearing away much of its forward rigging. The foremast had stood, though, and the two ships had parted after the *Mackenzie* spoke the schooner and received assurance she wasn't taking on much water. The battered schooner limped into port two days later. But the *Mackenzie,* with thirty five souls aboard, was never seen again.

Somehow, she had been holed, though there had been no indication of distress from her at the time, the schooner captain said. Thirty five men, women and children, every single passenger aboard, had drowned in Lake Erie that night.

Seth clenched his jaws as he tried to penetrate the obscurity beyond his window. He plucked nervously at his close trimmed beard. The *Lady Of The Lake* was the queen of the Ontario Line. The Ontario Line prided itself on safe efficient service. In the twenty years the line had been in business it had never lost a ship. Seth, just promoted last month, wasn't about to have it happen on his watch.

At the instant he heard the bow lookout's shout, he saw it-a faint red sidelight off his starboard bow. "Hard a port! Full astern!" he shouted into the speaking tube as he grabbed the whistle cord. "Dear God, we're going to just miss her," he thought as he yanked on the cord sounding the steamer's whistle in repeated blasts. He felt the steamer shudder as the engine shifted astern. Then unaccountably, he saw the schooner change course and turn towards them. Helplessly, he shouted, "Hold your course!" at the pilothouse window. Then the two ships came together with a heavy crash.

Tommy, still at the bulwark, saw the steamer's bow blacker against the black night, her bow wave dimly illuminated by the *Gazelle's* own sidelight. Frozen with fear, he watched Death approach. Just before impact, he lunged for the forecastle scuttle door a few yards away shouting, "On deck, on deck everybody!" He was pounding on the door when the *Lady Of The Lake* and the *Gazelle* collided with a splintering rumbling impact. The shock of the blow threw him to his knees.

Tommy watched the jib boom bend, then snap. The foremast swayed alarmingly overhead as the heavy cables supporting it were ripped loose from the bowsprit and jib boom. The *Gazelle's* deck did a peculiar little dip beneath him, and the schooner briefly heeled towards the other ship as the steamer now churning furiously astern began pulling away. Then her engines stilled, as her unseen crew began hailing them with shouts in the night.

Ben and Nate came scrambling on deck. Ben seeing the broken jib boom and mangled bowsprit and rigging, shouted aft to Mollie, now also on deck, "Check the well!" Then he called, "Stand clear of the foremast." If the heavy mast and its gear came down, it would kill anyone in its path. Ben sprinted aft to lower the yawl boat.

With three hundred tons of coal in her, she'll go down fast, he thought. Even now a torrent of water must be gushing into the hold through the shattered planking. A minute, maybe two, and she'd be gone.

He saw Mollie working the pump handle with all her strength. Water gushed forth and spilled on deck. Then abruptly came the wheeze of a pump sucking air.

"Nothing!" Mollie shouted. "She's dry."

Ben swerved abruptly from his dash for the yawl. He seized the pump handle and tried it himself. Only the frothy sound of a nearly dry bilge came to his ears.

Mollie cried out, "Where's Tommy?"

Stricken, Ben dropped the pump handle and looked forward. Blinded by the glare of the nearby steamer's lights, he could barely make out the main mast a few feet away. Had Tom gone overboard? He started back towards the bow when he heard Nate shout, "He's here by the windlass, he's ok!"

Ben had just reached the foredeck to see Tommy for himself, when a hail came from the steamer, "Are you taking on water? Do you require assistance?"

Ben looked aft at Mollie still beside the pump. She tried it again. Nothing. Had the steamer somehow missed making a direct hit upon the hull? He looked forward. The foremast still stood. Already Nate and Tom had unshackled the staysail halyard from the sail and taken it to the windlass. Tommy had wrapped a couple turns on the gypsy head with the halyard, and Nate was working the windlass handle to tighten it up for a temporary substitute forestay support.

"I think the mast will stand," he told Mollie who had left the pump and joined him. "Nate, Tommy, we'll get the fore down and set up another halyard." Ben shouted aft, "Mouse, keep her dead before the wind."

Mollie cupped her hands to her mouth and hailed the waiting ship, "Ahoy, the steamer. We are not taking on water. We are alright."

Already the foresail was coming down, and Tommy and Nate were getting another line led forward to further support the wobbling mast.

The steamer crew must have seen this, for the unseen officer called back, "Do you require a tow?"

Mollie shouted back, "No."

"Very well. We shall leave you then. Good luck and Godspeed." With the sound of engine telegraph bells and a rumble of water under her paddlewheels, *The Lady Of The Lake* then pivoted and steamed off into the darkness.

Dawn found the *Gazelle* in mid lake sailing slowly with a light southerly over a calm lake. As her crew surveyed the jury rig and the wreckage up forward, Ben announced, "We're going to Eel Bay. We can make repairs there better than anywhere else. We'll telegraph Conger and tell them their load will be a wee bit delayed."

Mollie nodded. The collision had left her shaken, and in the gray light of early morning she looked upon the cracked heavy hickory timber of the bowsprit and thought what would have happened had the steamer hit *Gazelle* ten feet further back. She glanced down at the deck underfoot and thought of the full hold below. Three hundred tons of coal. Had she been holed with a belly full of coal, *Gazelle* would have gone down like a stone. They might have been feeding the fishes this morning, on the cold dark bottom of the lake. She saw Ben look down, too.

Mollie met Ben's eyes when he looked up and said to him, "I guess Reuban had one life left."

Ben shook his head slowly, "I hope it wasn't his last one."

Nate came over. "Has anyone seen Mouse?"

Mollie's brow creased with pain. "Yes, he's below. Ben you need to go talk to him. He shut himself in the foc'sle, and I couldn't get him to come out."

Ben nodded and moved off, while Tommy limped aft to trim the mainsheet.

Mollie went to the helm. She scanned the unbroken gray clouds overhead and wondered how long the light winds would hold. They couldn't set any sail forward of the damaged mast now, and even raising the foresail would be highly risky in any sort of weather given the jury rigged support for the mast. If it breezed up, *Gazelle* without her foresail and jibs would be all but impossible to manage or steer. Eel Bay was only about ten miles away and dead down wind on this point of sail. If the wind stayed south.

She gripped the wheel a little tighter and looked up again at the sky and at the wind pennant aloft. If it goes more west we won't be able to lay Long Point, Mollie thought. And then there would be nothing under their lee but Stony Point and Mexico Bay. They called it the bay of dead ships for good reason. The lake's east end was no place for a cripple. Mollie breathed a quick silent prayer for the southerly to hold.

Ben, meanwhile, had gone forward. He knocked on the fore hatch door and called out "Mouse. It's me. Open the door." After a long pause, it swung open, just as Ben was raising his hand to knock again. Mouse, his face wet with tears, stood slumped as Ben entered the small space closing the door softly behind him. He settled on his bunk and said, "Now Mouse. We're going to Eel Bay to make repairs. If the winds holds we should be able to nurse her along at three or four knots and be there by noon." Ben paused trying to find the right words as Mouse stared dully at him. Ben drew a breath, sighed and went on, "We had a tough break. But we're going to be ok. No one was hurt and the boat can be mended."

Ben pulled his watch out, opened it, studied it for a moment, then slipped it back into his pocket. "I think it's your watch on deck. " He paused and put a hand on Mouse's shoulder. "We all make mistakes. On the lake mistakes can kill people. I don't know yet just what happened to Will, my brother, but if I'd have gotten that tackle on a minute sooner..."

Mouse looked at him with anguish in his eyes and then, as Ben reached out, the boy leaned into him. Ben drew him close and hugged him fiercely as Mouse began sobbing.

"I thought I was supposed to turn to port, not port the helm."

After a spell, Ben pushed him away gently and said, "Will wanted this boat to make lots of money. I guess we'd better get to work for widow Mollie. And you're on the wheel now."

He got up and went out leaving the door open. A few moments later he saw Mouse heading resolutely for the stern where Mollie had taken over the task of coaxing the crippled schooner homeward.

After being relieved by Mouse, Mollie checked the ship's barometer on her way to the galley. It was up a bit. Soon the clouds would move off, the sun would return, and with it the wind would pick up and go into the west. Just give us two more hours, she thought. We'll make Long Point then. After she had cleared away noon day dinner's dishes, she went on deck and sought out Ben.

"The barometer's rising."

Ben looked to the west and nodded. Mollie followed his gaze and saw a narrow band of pale yellowish light on the horizon.

"When that gets here so will the westerly," said Ben.

The dark line of Long Point lay ahead of the schooner on the horizon, perhaps three miles away. "Another hour, that's all we need. Once we're around the point we can anchor and it won't matter," said Mollie.

"I don't think we're going to get another hour," said Ben. He looked up at the foremast while rubbing his sideburn. After a long pause he said, "I'm going to try the fore. I think she'll stand it. Take the wheel. I'll need all the crew."

Mollie grimaced and stepped aft to relieve Mouse.

The crew had previously cleared away the worst of the snarled mess of rigging forward. Ben's biggest worry was the unsupported topmast. He sent Nate and Mouse aloft to run another line from it down to what remained of the bowsprit to brace the spar. Then every one tailed on and hauled the foresail aloft. With the wind still dead aft, there was little strain on the foremast, and to everyone's relief the schooner's speed picked up noticeably. All eyes turned to the end of Long Point.

Mollie had gone below to change into dry clothes, when she heard a welcome call from Tommy who was forward. "I see the hill. We're almost home."

Mollie hurried up on deck. From the cabin companionway she saw with a rush of relief that they had rounded Long Point. Now the familiar flat topped lump of Dunn's Bluff hard by the entrance of Eel Bay lay just a mile or two away ahead of the schooner and the protective arm of the point was sheltering the crippled schooner from incoming winds and waves.

"Praise God- there's home and safe harbor," she said to Nate who was on the wheel. She allowed herself a smile, the first since the crash.

Nate returned it, saying, "That sure does look good. We're going to be ok now."

Mollie continued aft and stood by the mainsheet block behind Nate. From here she could see the whole deck before her with the mangled twisted wreckage forward and the crew by the windlass readying the ground tackle to anchor. She said a silent prayer of thanks for the gentle weather that had given them the extra hour they needed, and then added a blessing for Jamie McPherson whose stout hull had withstood the hard knock forward and the sudden strain of an unsupported mast.

"This will be our last load of coal for awhile. It'll be barley after this old girl," she told *Gazelle*.

Ashore Uncle John, having been summoned by little Sid Peltier, joined the boy's father, his own brother Robert, and several other townspeople at the head of the harbor to watch the *Gazelle* slowly come to anchor. He'd known there was trouble the moment he'd heard of her sighting. Now as he stood beside Andre he heard the other man murmur, "That ole devil lake."

"Let's get Rob's lugger and go out," he said.

Andre nodded, "Looks like plenty of work to be done."

A half hour later they were standing on the deck with the *Gazelle* crew, all of them studying the shambles up forward. Andre taking in the splintered wood, snarled head gear, and twisted broken hardware, said to the ship, "Well they've clipped your wings now. But not for long. We'll soon have you back at work again."

Uncle John beside the foremast looked aloft, "You did well Ben. I think you could have gone on into Kingston with that jury rig." Seeing Mollie's long face he added, "This is a three day job. We'll have her patched up in no time."

Mollie answered, "We surely didn't need the delay nor the expense right now."

"Expense?" There'll be no talk of that," said Andre turning a scowl upon Mollie. "You think I don' know what it's like to be stuck where you don' want to be? I've been a free man in Canada for twenty three years, and Canada has been good to me. No more 'bout expense now. We talk about that later. Right now, we got to get you back on that lake to catch that wind again."

Mollie taking in his look and the way he stood facing her, his powerful arms folded across his chest, his wide shoulders squared, decided not to argue. She mumbled something about paying later.

Andre answered, "That's right. Later. Right now we got work to do! Right now we need to line this old boat into the dock there and get started."

All other jobs in the yard came to a halt after the *Gazelle* was alongside. She became the top priority. The clang of Andre's hammer in his shop sounded steadily for a whole day as he beat out and shaped new fittings, new bands for jib boom and bowsprit, new shackles and straps, rings, hooks, spikes and bolts. Ben and Uncle John cut, adzed and planed the new jib boom and bowsprit. Andre's oldest boy sailed Uncle Rob's fishing skiff to Picton to purchase new cordage, and the entire crew turned to reeving, splicing, patching, and rigging. They worked hard and long, and after three days the *Gazelle* was ready to go back to work.

Chapter Eighteen

"Don't ever stop. Keep going." Harriet Tubman

"How did you end up here in Eel Bay?" asked Mouse

"It's a long story. You'd be bored," answered Andre.

"No, we want to hear it," said Mouse.

Ben Mollie and Mouse were seated at the kitchen table with Uncle John, while Aunt Sara cleared away dinner in preparation for desert. It had gotten so late that Andre had agreed to eat with them after their final push to finish up the job, his own family having long since had their supper and settled in for the night.

Andre answered, "I was a little younger than you when I came to St. Catherine's and a good man named Rene Peltier took me in and taught me my trade. Like Miss Mollie, I, too, wanted my freedom. And thanks to the bravest woman I ever met, I got it here in Canada.

Mollie perked up a bit. "A woman helped you come to Canada? Who was she?"

"Her name was Harriet Tubman. Have you never heard tell of her? She was the Moses of her people."

Mollie shook her head. "No. I haven't heard of her."

"Well then, You shall hear of her now."

Andre sat back in his chair and reached for his pipe. Uncle John followed suit, firing his corn cob up as Mouse, Ben, and Mollie, looking expectant, waited for a story.

"Harriet Tubman was a small woman and dark complected. She was powerful strong and could walk the legs off a man twice her size. She was a conductor on the underground railroad. More than once she told her passengers 'Keep going. If you want to taste freedom you got to keep going.' I saw her for the first time when I was twelve years old and I owe her my life. This is how it happened."

Andre, then known as Andy Williams, grew up on a plantation on the eastern shore of Maryland, a land not unlike that shoreline he now called home. He lived a half day's walk from the plantation that Harriet Tubman had run away from five years before. His home farm sprawled along the shore of a tributary of the winding slow flowing tidal Choptank River.

Here, young Andy worked on land and water alike. He learned to fish and crab and worked one winter on an oyster drudge boat. When he was eleven, he was hired out to work in a nearby boat yard to learn iron working from a smith there.

One evening, he heard a woman singing outside the cluster of hovels where he and the farm's three other slave families lived. It was a still clear night in September with a touch of frost glittering on the grass. The strong voice, lifted in song, sent a chill down the boy's spine as it rose in plaintive minor key with a quaver not unlike the tremulous cry of a screech owl.

"Dark and thorny is de pathway
where de pilgrim makes his ways.
But beyond dis vale of sorrow
lie de fields of endless days…"

As the song faded, the startled boy turned to ask, "Mama what was--"

"Hisst," she replied holding up a hand as another fragment of song reached them.

"When the good old ship of Zion comes along, be ready, oh be ready to step on board…" The last notes he heard were "farewell, farewell, I'm sorry friends to leave you-"

Then the melody was cut off as the singer had apparently passed behind a building. Andy's mother turned to him. "That's Harriet. She come for her passengers. She come to take 'em north to Canada on the underground railroad."

Wide eyed the boy asked, "When is she leaving?"

"Tonight," said his mother. "And your uncle is going with her."

Andy's heart leaped. Canada. Where the great Queen Victoria would welcome them after they had crossed a wide water. "Mama, I want to go!"

"There are already nine. She dare not take any more this trip."

But Andy had made up his mind. Later that night when he heard his uncle quietly close the door behind him, Andy left his bed, crept across the cabin floor, slipped outside, and followed him under the cold star filled sky to the gathering place.

Here Harriet looked the boy over and asked, "Kin you walk all night?"

Andy looked her straight in the eye, "Yes'm."

Satisfied with his reply and his looks, she said, "There be room for one more. Come along now."

They set out at a brisk pace and traveled over thirty miles that first night. But Andy kept up and even helped a young mother by taking a turn at carrying her baby. Though they grew weary as dawn paled the east, they stepped along, legs aching and feet sore, as Harriet told them "keep goin'." Just as dawn was washing the morning star out of the sky, they reached their first station and were taken to a barn. Here, they ate and rested their throbbing feet, sore legs, and stiff bodies in the hay filled loft. Here, too, young Andy thought that somehow, someday, he would return for his Mother and Father and lead them to freedom.

The next night the fugitives followed a narrow game path through a large tract of forest. Under the tree canopy the intense darkness slowed their pace as they followed their tireless guide. The barely seen closeness of the giant tree trunks and the occasional branch in his path frightened the boy. He was certain that snakes and bears lurked about nearby. Once the wavering eerie call of a screech owl sounded overhead. Surely, this was the spirit of some recently departed soul crying a warning to them. Further on, Andy spotted a strange dim greenish glow beside the path on the forest floor. Foxfire. The witch light. Someone had died nearby recently.

Then in the wee hours of the morning, they heard the baying of the dogs. First in the distance, then louder and closer came the howls, wails, cries and yips of the pack. No one alive could outrun slave catcher dogs. Long legged, lean bodied, and powerful, the big hounds could run all night, and Lord help the child or woman that fell to their jaws. The dogs had killed more than one fugitive after outrunning their masters' control.

"Quick now"- Harriet commanded, "Into the crick!"

The fugitives waded through knee deep water stumbling and sliding over the slick rocks for what felt like hours. But it worked. The hounds lost the scent.

That night they came to a small weathered cabin and were greeted by an gray haired blue eyed woman, in the plain dress of a Quaker. Mrs. Hall had just settled the six men, Andy, Harriet, and the young mother, Minty with her child at the table for a late supper, when a sharp knock sounded. A young black boy stood there- "Quickly you must hide them. The bounty hunters are coming."

Without a word the old woman hurried to the back door followed by the fugitives. Outside she opened the cover of the root cellar, and the fugitives crowded in. She dropped the lid on them, and they stood jammed together in the utter blackness. Moments later, they heard two angry male voices and the higher pitched murmur of Mrs. Hall's replies. The air in the cellar seemed as thick as molasses. It was hard to pull into their lungs. The stuffy darkness pressed against Andy's chest. Minty uttered a small moan, swayed and abruptly dropped her arms with her baby in them. Andy made a grab and caught him, but the child squealed in protest.

They all heard the gruff voice a few yards away over their heads.

"What was that?"

Everyone froze.

Andy cuddled the infant to quiet him.

Mrs. Hall said calmly, "Must be those raccoons out there again. Talkin' about a raid on my hen coop."

The other voice grunted, and they heard feet shuffling away through the grass and leaves.

After that night, the fugitives walked for many more miles, always moving as quickly and silently as possible. They stayed in secret rooms, basements, and once even jammed themselves into a closet so small they took turns sitting down. Once Harriet stopped them as they walked along a river bank saying, "We goin' cross here. Now!" She had heard her "voices" speaking in her head telling of danger close by. No one wanted to wade into that icy cold black river. They balked like stubborn mules. So Harriet went on ahead alone wading into the river, telling them "Come or stay!" The water rose to her waist, to her breast, and then nearly to her chin before the river became shallower again. Shamed into it, the men and Andy and Minty followed.

When at last they made it into Pennsylvania, travel became easier. They now felt safe enough to walk during the day. Near the border with New York, Harriet left them. She turned them over to another guide. They continued on, while she went back for another load of passengers.

"We were safer now, though we could still be taken. At last, we came to our final station, a grand big house in a town called Williamson. Here, the station master told us we would ride a wagon to Pultneyville the next night and be put aboard a ship. It might be Captain Throop's steamer, or it might be another ship. Even the conductor wouldn't know 'til we got there, what ship it would be."

By now, Andre said, it was almost November and too late in the year to use the 'station' at Maxwell Creek, a settlement of free blacks a few miles west of Sodus Bay where several men worked as conductors. There the ships simply stopped in the open lake at the foot of the high bluff to take on their passengers, and the fall weather was now much too unsettled to use that place of escape.

"We were afraid we'd be too late to reach Canada before winter. The bounty hunters often came to the docks looking for runaways. At the last minute we was split up and sent aboard two ships that came into Pultneyville."

Andy and his uncle joined two other men on their night of departure. Under a quarter moon in the frosty blackness, they walked quickly from the house across the road and down onto the dock. Here, they crouched low and crept behind the long pile of stacked cord wood used to fuel the boilers of the steamers. The pile ran most of the length of the dock and was to be loaded aboard Throop's steamer the next day. At the end of the wharf lay their good old ship Zion.

"She was called the *Wide Awake*. She was a two master about the size of your *Gazelle*. But to me she seemed a great ship. Her masts rose like trees into the night. All I could think was Canada, Canada. A man was waiting for us on her deck and he motioned us aboard –quick quick. He hid us in the hold with the barrels of apples and boxes and crates. The next day we shook the lion's paw in Canada."

After that, the boy and his uncle went to St. Catherines where a large settlement of escaped slaves had been established. Here, Andy was taken in by a kindly smith to serve as an apprentice. The smith, Renee Peltier, was himself a recent immigrant who had fled from his village in northern Quebec after a fierce wildfire devastated the region and burned his village to the ground. Peltier knew what it was like to be a stranger in a new land, and he took to the boy and treated him like a son. Andy took the man's name for his own, and soon picked up a good bit of the French tongue as he learned to head a bolt, draw out barstock and rivet two pieces.

As a journeyman smith, he went to work at Shicklunas, the best and one of the busiest yards on all the lake where a number of other ex slaves had found fair treatment and good wages. "We had more than two hundred men in that yard when I was there. No one built a better ship than Louis Shickluna, the Manxman."

Andre created ironwork for the schooners as well as tools for the shipwrights. "I recall in 1858, we stepped a mast and rigged the schooner complete in one evening. Shickluna bet Dave Muir over at the Muir shipyard a thousand dollars that we could do it. And we did it."

After the War, Andy was able to bring his parents to Canada. And while at Shickluna's he met John McIntyre who was working as a joiner. They became good friends. "When your uncle started his yard in Eel Bay, he wrote me to come on out. He wrote you'll like the land and the bay. And he was right. It's fine here, as good as the land by the Choptank. I'm grateful to be a Canadian," Andre laughed. "Even though the winters are colder than on the Chesapeake, I'll never live anywhere else."

Andre re-lit his pipe and then drew on it a time or two before continuing. "I'm not sorry I came here. But I am sorry for the war that happened after I left and powerful glad I wasn't there then. Harriet Tubman fought in that war. She nursed men, white, black, Yankee, and southern soldier men. I have a book at home about her. In it she told of a battle she was in. I remember she said, 'And then we heard the lightning, and that was the guns. And then we heard the thunder, and that was the big guns. And then we heard the rain falling, and that was the drops of blood falling. And when we came to get in the crops, it was dead men that we reaped."

In the silence that followed, Mollie gazed down at the table cloth. Her own life had been sheltered and soft indeed, compared to that of Tubman, ex-slave and battlefield veteran. Mollie had never heard a shot fired in anger. Before this summer, she'd never even been slapped, let alone physically assaulted. And though she'd felt the sting of ridicule and bigotry, being mocked or spat at was nothing compared to what slave girls and women suffered routinely. Women like Tubman had experienced far worse than an attempted rape. They had been beaten, kicked, violated and sometimes left for dead.

Andre pushed back his chair. "I'm wore out. It's time for me to get back to my house and bed."

Uncle John agreed, "Time to douse the lights here, too."

After good nights were exchanged, Andre set off on the short hike up the hill to his house, and Mollie headed for the harbor where she was staying alone aboard the *Gazelle* in her cabin. It was a pleasant early

September night, with a waxing half moon overhead. The soft mild air was filled with the sounds of late summer. The sizzle of grasshoppers in the tall weeds by the road, and the chorus of crickets in the grass underfoot spoke of fall's short days soon to come Several Katydids called incessantly from somewhere around the lilac bushes, as Mollie walked along, soothed by the insect music and the fog horn calls of the harbor's bull frog population. She considered, again, Andre's story and Harriet Tubman's work on behalf of her people. She must be an incredible woman, thought Mollie. She simply could not imagine such courage and pure physical strength. Walking night after night, fording freezing rivers, dodging slave catchers and their dogs, snatching a few hours sleep, always in constant mortal danger as she moved her human cargoes north. And then to go back to the front and work on the battlefield? Even nursing and saving the lives of the very southern soldier men who might have whipped her as a slave? I could never in my life do that.

When Mollie reached the dock and the boarding plank, she paused and stood looking at the *Gazelle,* her decks now silvered by luminous moonlight. Clearly, there was no possibility of having the full amount of the note due to Sloan by the end of the month. But what was it Harriet Tubman had said? "Keep going. Keep going or die."

I will keep going. At least I'll try. I'll go see the banker tomorrow. I'll offer him all that we have now and pledge to have the rest by the end of the year. But what if he refuses? Susan B Anthony's words rang in her memory "Failure is impossible." Mollie stood a little straighter and lifted her gaze upward towards the mastheads dark against the moonlit sky. Then she marched up the boarding plank and stepped aboard saying out loud to her schooner, "We're not licked yet."

The next morning, Mollie and Uncle John borrowed Andre's mule and wagon and headed into Picton to meet with Sloan. The fair morning sky and gentle September sun gave her hope. Mollie looked off at the farm fields beyond the weathered split rail fences as the mule jogged along. Clumps of goldenrod and the occasional proudly defiant six foot thistle decorated the pastures with color. The new grain had headed out, and fields were fast ripening into pale gold. Soon it would be harvest time. She listened to the lilting liquid notes of a bobolink on the wing overhead. He'd be heading south before long. She wondered about the crops to come and their prospects. Maybe Sloan will refuse my offer, but what have we got to lose? Still, she worried. She had heard yesterday at the dinner table that Sloan's health was not good.

She remembered Uncle John saying, "The last time I saw him he had aged ten years- It's the pain you know. He's lost a lot of weight."

Mollie wondered what if Sloan dies before we pay off the loan? Then his son-in-law would inherit his stock in the bank. Jared Kraut was ruthless ambitious and arrogant. She remembered him a few months ago whipping the downed horse in Oswego. She remembered the sneer as he laid on the lash. He had looked like he was enjoying himself. Kraut had broken a strike in Kingston two years ago, sending in his thugs and goons with their clubs and literally breaking the strike by breaking the limbs and skulls of the picket line workers. She recalled there had been gunfire, too, and at least two strikers had been killed. That high and mighty cock of the walk gives no quarter. They say ice water runs in his veins. He'll crush us and smile while he does it.

Ned Sloan sat at his desk reading the Picton Gazette. He had just pressed his hand against his shrunken belly to ease the pain after reading that there was talk again in the U.S. of renewed lumber tariffs on Canadian timber. Reciprocity was about to take another hit. Damn that gut and the Yanks, too, he was thinking when a knock on the door intruded.

He snapped, "Yes, what is it?" at the clerk who had opened the door a crack.

"There's a Mr. John Cressy here to see you." Seeing Sloan's dark face, the clerk added, "He's the shipwright from Eel Bay, and he has Mrs. McIntyre with him."

McIntyre, that was the young widow woman. She had a note for twelve thousand dollars on that two master, that little ten thousand bushel boat. The image of Mollie's face, her icy gray eyes fixed on his as she looked across the table on a May morning came to mind. Her father and this uncle or whatever he was had come around a couple of days later with three thousand dollars. Damn good thing, too. That money had been extremely useful right then with the MacKenzie loan gone bad. What was she doing here now? Her second payment wasn't due for two more weeks. Probably she's come to beg and plead for an extension, he thought, as he told the clerk to send them in.

Uncle John, his hat in hand, and Mollie entered the room, and after Sloan gestured shortly at the two chairs against the wall, they seated themselves. Mollie was taken aback by Sloan's appearance even with forewarning. He had indeed lost weight. The loose skin under his chin flopped like the dewlap of an old milk cow, and his face was pasty and a bit sallow, quite unlike the high color she remembered from a few months ago.

Sloan took their measure noting that Uncle John was perched uneasily on the edge of his chair looking down at his hat and fiddling with it, while the tall sturdy woman sat straight and still returning his look with a steadfast one of her own.

"What do you want?" he addressed Uncle John.

A long silence followed as Uncle John struggled to come up with the persuasive words they needed. Just as it seemed Sloan was about to dismiss them for wasting his time, Mollie broke the tension. "We're here about the note on our ship."

"What of it?"

"We won't be able to make the whole payment due by the end of the month. So I've brought what we have, 1550 dollars. Once the barley trade begins, we're sure we can make up the rest of it."

As she spoke, Sloan recalled something else about the widow McIntyre. A couple of weeks ago, he remembered hearing that her schooner and an American two master had come into Kingston under full sail making a grand finish to a race across the lake. The widow had been at the wheel and had brought her boat right into the dock making a flawless landing under sail. Everyone had talked about it then. She looked different, too, than she had back in May. It wasn't just the sun browned face. There was a surety about her that he didn't recall from their first meeting. Now he saw the light of determination in her eyes.

"Why should I settle for half of the amount that's due me?"

"Because by the end of November we'll pay it all back. If we don't, you can have the ship. This way you may get all that's due before the end of the year. But if you take our ship now, we can't raise any more money for you."

Watching Mollie state her case, Sloan thought of his daughter, Miriam, so frail, delicate, and often these days, now confined to the house. When he had left in the morning Miriam had been seated by a window, pale and slack, as she looked out at the fine day. I wish she had a little of this widow woman's spunk, he thought. That Jared, he dominates her completely.

"Well, you are at least honest about your situation. And it is true that by the time I got a judgment against your ship it would be nearly the end of the shipping season anyway."

"You won't need a writ or a judgment or a sheriff to post it if we don't pay you by December first. I'll sign the papers to transfer ownership that day if we fail to pay you."

Sloan leaned back and looked at Uncle John and then at Mollie who still sat with her chin up and challenge in her eyes. He thought I wish my daughter were here to see this.

"I'll accept your offer of partial payment with the rest paid in full on December first."

"Mr. Sloan, you won't be sorry," she declared.

Then they were all standing, and it was Mollie who shook Ned Sloan's hand with a firm grip. "Barnes out there will draw up the necessary paper," he told them as they all moved to the door.

When he heard them leave the building, he looked out his window and watched them climb into a well used wagon piled with a jumble of what appeared to be sea going gear in the back. He wondered if he would see them again in two months.

As Millie and Uncle John climbed into the wagon, talk was subdued. "Well," said her uncle in law, "at least we have a few more months. If Sloan lives that long. "

Mollie shook her head. "He doesn't look good. That's not gout. I think he must have the cancer eating him up."

"We better hope he makes it through November. If that brute of a son in law takes over he'll squash us like a bug."

Chapter Nineteen

"Trust in God: She will provide." - Emmeline Pankhurst

With a stout new jib boom of spruce and a sturdy bowsprit of good Ontario elm, the *Gazelle* set sail for Kingston to deliver her delayed load of coal. She then headed west on her last run of the season to Dark Harbor. No more pushing, shoving, piling and stacking lumber after this trip. Soon a golden harvest would flow into her hold to be carried to Oswego's grain elevators. From there Oswego's hungry malt houses and breweries would devour, digest and transform the best barley in the world into ales and lagers and stouts to satisfy thirsty tavern goers no longer willing to pay the stiff tax recently imposed upon their whiskey by the temperance movement and the government's need to fund debts left from the war.

Last year, nearly a million bushels had been carried across the lake from Prince Edward County to be stored and processed in Oswego. Beer was big business these days, and barley was literally gold. It was the best chance Mollie had for paying off their debt to Sloan. It was their only chance.

Flying light with a brisk offshore wind and flat water, the *Gazelle* made splendid time as if she were eager to cancel the note as quickly as possible. She hadn't stepped along at such a rate over flat water since the run up Long Reach last May to meet Isiah. The crew were in good spirits with much banter and cheerful talk about trade, vessels and future wealth.

Ben stood by the weather rail, looked aft at the wake, and marveled once again at the canny design work of Jamie McPherson. He said to Nate who was lounging nearby, "I'd like to try building a fishing skiff with that same run and deadrise aft-I think that's her secret. Her hull runs out there differently than most, and I think it makes her easy on the helm while she takes waves on the stern."

Nate observed, "Trim makes a difference, too. I once sailed on the old *Lizzie Morse,* and the only way to get her to go was the loading. You had to put her down an inch or two by the head. But if you tried that with *Gazelle*, why, she'd turn around and look at you."

Ben nodded, "There' so much to making a boat go. If I were building fish skiffs I could try several different models. I'd like to try the *Gazelle's* run on a square stern skiff and see how it would do. I might not carry the beam aft quite as much on a small boat like that. There may never be much call for faster cargo schooners in years to come, but they'll be sailing skiffs and sloop boats for a spell yet."

"Maybe if we do good with barley you'll have money to build one or two this winter," said Nate.

Mouse chimed in, "But why build a fast fish boat? It's the yachties that have money. Let's build a boat to race in the regattas next summer. We'll show the Yanks our stern, then sell her to a rich yachtsman for 3000 dollars."

Ben laughed, "Mouse, you got an idea there. How would you like to be our peddling packman? With that nimble Irish tongue, you'd be a dandy little promoter for our new line of lake yachts."

Mollie said, "Ben better sign you on to work in the shop this winter, Mouse. We probably would be wise to diversify into yacht building in case freights fall again next year."

But even as she bantered with the crew, Mollie looked forward along the main deck of her ship and thought of the uncertain future. She ran her gaze over the stout rig, the tall strong spars, and curved sails overhead, taut with the wind. Beyond them lay the wide free horizon that the schooner's jib boom was pointing the way to. Always now, worry prowled like a wolf in the back of her mind. *I hope I'm here again next year on the deck of my own ship. If we don't get a good crop this year, it'll be the auction block for Gazelle and the beach for me.*

Loading went quickly with the assistance of two extra dockworkers that Mollie was able to hire for three dollars a day. Though it was a high wage, the crew was anxious to make their last run with Isiah's lumber so they could fill the ship's hold with more profitable barley. The cooler weather helped everyone's energy level, but it also turned Mollie's thoughts towards fall's shortening days, stronger colder winds and the ever dwindling days of the season remaining.

Gazelle set sail late in the afternoon for Oswego. She was down to her marks with lumber, and a sweet west wind filled her sails to power her along on a smart reach. After supper Mollie came up to give Ben his usual short break. But on this evening Ben lingered. He had been watching Mouse and Tommy skylarking aloft, scrambling up the ratlins and daring each other to brave the triatic, going hand over hand along the cable between the tops of the masts.

"I'm glad you kept him on, Mollie. He's a good worker and a quick one. He's so keen to learn of sailing and ship keeping with his talk of saltwater packets and clippers and now his yachting notions."

"He seems to have gotten over his mishap with the helm and the steamer."

"Mouse is young. The young are supposed to make mistakes. That's how they learn."

"We all make mistakes, I guess," sighed Mollie. "Like that deck load I insisted we carry. Or like talking Will into boxboards."

Ben looked hard at Mollie and said, "You shouldn't put all the blame on yourself. Will made a few mistakes, too. One was getting up on that deck load and trying to push the boom out against the wind. He knew we were sailing by the lee, but he kept shoving on it instead of waiting until Nate brought her up. Of course, if I'd gotten the preventer on a bit faster..."

Mollie returned Ben's look with a stern one of her own. "Now who's taking the blame. You're right. We shouldn't blame ourselves for everything. Will did know better, but you know how impatient he always was to get things done."

Ben sighed and nodded. "I guess I"ll go catch my forty winks below, while you take the next hour."

With that he moved off forward towards the focsle. Mollie's optimism of a few minutes ago faded with the day's end. Those clouds against the sunset, they had the look and feel of fall, flat, dark and heavy. And the sun goes down so quickly now, she thought, as she watched it sinking towards the sharp gray horizon. The last light edged each large dark cloud with a line of gleaming gold, while the cold blue sky behind the clouds made her think there might be at touch of frost in the valleys on shore tonight.

As the sun hung just over the water horizon, for a few brief moments its low golden rays were caught by the breaking crests of the small waves to the west. Briefly, the light touched the top of each wave, outlining it with molten fire as it had lit the cloud edges above. A vast field of flickering twinkling golden flames arrayed in rows stood out against the dark shadowed troughs of the lake's waves. Mollie, looking west into the dying day, thought the movement of the gilded wave crests reminded her of a field of grain moving in the wind. Then the last of the sun dipped below the water. The magical light died, and the shadows deepened and ran together on the lake surface. She looked over the deck with its stacked lumber and wondered once again, would the barley harvest freights bring in enough to keep the boat?

Late season freights always paid the best. Perhaps if they kept running through November they could earn enough. But then the insurance rates always went up as the weather got worse with more gales, some of them bitter cold with freezing spray, ice, and snow. She thought back to the snowstorm she and Will had been in last year aboard the old *Alma*. It had snowed so hard they had feared they'd pile up ashore before they ever found the harbor. Nothing but opaque whiteness had wrapped around them that day. It muffled the sound of the harbor fog horn, and it had been pure luck that the sky had cleared and the snow stopped a couple miles offshore to reveal the harbor entrance. She also remembered a night last year when the decks had iced up, slick and deadly underfoot. Even the blocks and running gear had frozen. There was no way to trim or reef the sails. Was it worth the risk to push the sailing season through November?

As she was brooding over their prospects, the schooner strayed a bit off course, and Mollie gave her a spoke to bring her up a bit. As she did so, for a moment in the gloom she saw Will's tall figure seemingly standing beside the main mast, feet slightly spaced, braced against the ship's light roll with an easy grace as he faced forward. It was as if he were looking in on his ship and crew to see if all was well. Then the figure turned back into a shadow on the deck.

Mollie lifted her eyes to look aloft where the slow sway of the spars and sails moved against the darkening sky. She felt oddly comforted by the apparition as well as by the familiar fabric of the ship around her, now made whole and strong again. The endless needs and demands of the schooner and the unremitting labor of sailing her had been a salvation and a blessing during these months since Will's death.

Will was gone, but perhaps his spirit truly did ride upon the September wind filling the sails that give his ship movement and a life of her own. He had been absorbed back into the vastness of the sky and the lake. Life and death are partners. One cannot occur without the other.

"We are all going to die someday," Mollie murmured to the ship before her. "You'll become a pile of old timber on the beach. Me, Ben, Reuban, all of us will go back to dust. You can't have life without death. If we didn't die there'd be no room for any new people or ships."

Somehow, the thought that death was universally shared by cats schooners and people was oddly comforting. It made her feel a little less lonely on an early fall evening in the middle of an empty lake as they sailed forward towards a clouded future.

In Oswego the next day with customs cleared and port fees paid, Mollie was delighted to see Hannah coasting down the dock towards them aboard the red velocipede, her file folder secured in a basket mounted on the steering bars. It seemed like a year since she'd last seen Hannah. There was surely so much to tell her.

"Look whose coming," Mollie said to Reuban who was seated on the deckhouse roof surveying the bustle around the deck with disapproval. "I wonder if she'll notice the different jib boom?"

She did, and after the cargo manifests were dealt with and a bank draft had been written out to Mollie, Hannah settled in at the table for tea and demanded the whole story of the collision and subsequent repairs. Mollie related the events and also told her of Andre and his story of how he had come to Canada. This prompted Hanna to volunteer information of her own.

"Harriet Tubman lives over in Auburn now-just a day's journey south and west of here. Isiah has a copy of that book about her you mentioned. I will get it from him and bring it down for you. It is very interesting and was written by a good friend of Aunt Harriet, as they called her, to raise money for her needs. She was virtually destitute after the War. You may know that the government refused to pay her the pension that she was entitled to. Just like Dr. Walker, the men of Congress denied her the small sum of money that was paid to nurses, while men who served in battle as Tubman did, received far more generous payments."

Mollie asked, "Harriet Tubman was on the battlefield?"

Hannah paused, her brows knitted in a frown, and took a sip of tea. She set her cup down and continued. "I can't help but get angry. Yes, she was in battle and under fire. Several times. Harriet Tubman was a true war hero. Some called her "General Tubman". She piloted a gun boat under enemy fire up a river on a raid that freed over 700 slaves. Many of the men she freed signed up with the army to fight for the Union. She worked as an armed scout, and she worked as a nurse as well. She knew

173

more about herbs and "cures" than most of the doctors did and saved many lives with them. Yet, she couldn't collect the pitiful pension she was owed because she was a woman and a Negro, and her service never was officially recognized.

"I suppose she had an especially hard time making her case because she could neither read nor write. But if anyone is deserving of compensation it is she. She is no longer young, yet she continues her charity work and seeks money only to maintain her home and farm for the poor. She turns no person of any color away from her charity."

Mollie shook her head. How could men cheat a woman of such courage, strength, and selfless devotion to the welfare of her people? How could she continue after the war, impoverished herself, yet still working to help the broken and helpless. "How could she live such a hard life and still be so big hearted?" she wondered aloud.

Hannah replied, "She's certainly not naive or foolish. Aunt Harriet, as the citizens of Auburn call her, knows of Susan B. Anthony's work, and she supports it. She has spoken many times on the disgrace of women's inequality and has traveled at her own expense to Washington, Boston and other cities to do so. If anyone understands the need of equal treatment for women under the law and the need for our right to the vote, it is a woman of color such as she."

A silence followed as the two friends reflected upon the service of the woman known to some as General Tubman, and to others as Moses, and the injustice she had suffered since then. She must be as strong as the iron Andre hammers in his smithy, thought Mollie. My problems are nothing compared to what she has dealt with and with the challenges she still faces today.

"All I have to do is worry about paying off Will's note. I guess that isn't much compared to what she's done."

"How much is left to pay?"

"A little over 5400 dollars plus the interest."

Hanna looked off across the cabin, apparently studying the painting of the ship that hung on the aft bulkhead. Then she took a deep breath.

"Dan will be down in New York City this fall. So last month Isiah promoted me. He put me in charge of the Oswego office. He gave me a raise. I'm making a hundred dollars a month now."

Mollie gasped, "Why Hannah, that's more than many lake captains make. That's a great sum of money."

"I have nearly a thousand dollars already saved, and now with my raise in pay I can save a good deal more. Would a thousand dollars along with the barley freights be enough?"

Mollie felt a conflicting surge of emotions as she sucked in a deep breath. Hope flared briefly, followed by a sharp stab of fear that then settled in and knotted her stomach. She didn't want another person to put their well being and future security on the line for her sake. That of Father and Uncle John were already at risk. Yet, another thousand might, just possibly, be enough with good freights to pay off the balance.

While she was debating the pros and cons, Hanna said, "I wouldn't need to be paid back anytime soon. My position and salary are secure." Hannah paused, leaned forward, and continued, "Mollie you must succeed. You have shown people what a woman can do. You have shown them it is not unnatural to be independent and different. But if you fail this fall, the know-it-alls and groaners will use your failure to put down *all* our efforts. Other women in Oswego know about you. They're watching. I just heard that Abigail Potter has been nagging her husband for a yacht. She wants to learn to sail! Arthur Pearson told me Mr. Potter was down at his boatyard looking at the *Cora* and made an offer on the vessel last week."

Seeing Mollie's eyebrows lift in question, she explained, "The *Cora* is a splendid yacht-she's modeled after the New York pilot schooners. She's 80 feet on deck and came up from the coast about five years ago. So you see, you've got to keep going. Who knows, maybe some of the other fine ladies of this town will start to show a little spunk if you make it through the season and pay off that loan."

Mollie sat mulling things over. Hannah's offer surely was tempting. She thought of the arrogant customs official, Captain Burton's sneering contempt, Blake's hatred, and the countless other condescensions and criticisms she had endured since becoming a ship owner. With Hanna's loan plus the higher freights, they might do it. She was giving them a solid chance anyway to pay off the note.

Hannah was still talking, "Women are too often viewed as merely tasty little deserts, sweets to pamper the male appetite. Or the anti's mock us for seeking the vote saying we're mannish and self absorbed. We'll never be respected unless we show them that we are powerful strong and capable. That's why you must keep your ship. To those who say a woman's place is at home, I say it's equally her place to be on the deck of her own vessel as an owner."

Mollie lifted her head, squared her shoulders, and nodded, "I will accept your loan, Hannah. And I'll pay it back with interest if it's the last thing I do. It may take a year or two or three, but I'll do it."

Hannah sat back her face alight. "I know you will. I'll bring you the money first thing tomorrow before you sail."

She was as good as her word appearing on the dock afoot that morning with a draft on her account for one thousand dollars as the crew was getting ready for the tug to take them out. After handing Mollie the envelope, she threw her arms around her friend and hugged her. Mollie returned the heart felt embrace and then Hannah stepped back and moved off towards the boarding plank saying over her shoulder.

"Go. Get your barley. I'll see you at the Northwestern elevator in a few days."

She swung up on her wheel and glided off down on the dock. As she came abreast of the ship's prow, she glanced at the vessel and crew that she now had a financial as well as emotional stake in. She spotted Reuban perched on the rail, staring back at her. She murmured as she passed by, "They say luck is in keeping a good lookout, so keep your eyes open, Reuban. And if you really are a lucky cat, keep those seven toes crossed and tell your ship to sail like she's never sailed before."

A short time later Hannah joined a small group standing beside the small building that housed the waterfront offices of Fitzhugh and Son. The gathering consisted of Mouse's father, Clancy, Andy Doyle, the work gang boss, and Isiah. The men were conferring over the day's tasks, except now in the timeless fashion of waterfronts the world around, they had paused to watch a vessel's departure. The outbound vessel was the *Gazelle,* and each of those who watched her depart on this blue sunlit September morning, were stirred in some way by the sight of the little ship heading out with her crew's high hopes for the beginning of the barley season.

Hannah felt a restless urge of her own as she viewed the trim little two master, the tug on her quarter, moving off down the river towards the entrance. She thought of how movement and change was life itself. Once she had stood by her father's side on the deck of her own family ship as it had gotten underway bound for the open lake. Now the *Gazelle* was setting forth on yet another lake crossing, outbound on the wind road again. That ever shifting shimmering wind road, today sparkling silver in the sun, tomorrow dark and angry, always new, always calling.

It called to Hannah with unusual strength this morning. What awaits her and her crew? Fair winds and a quick passage? Profit and triumph or delays and disaster? Hannah felt a quickened longing for freedom and change. I hope it goes well, she thought. May they have good freights and fair winds.

Andy Doyle, standing next to her, also watched the ship's departure. He spoke to Clancy beside him. "Now there goes a trim little hooker."

"You mean Mrs. McIntyre or her schooner" asked Clancy with a grin.

Doyle laughed, "I speak of the vessel. I went mate four years on salt water, and I'd wager our *Gazelle* there would hold her own against most any two sticker her size on tidal water."

Clancy was still smiling as he replied, "Well, I don't know about her sailing, but I do know she made my son grow up considerable in a month's time. The little runt never used to do a lick of work around the house. Now he brings in the wood, carries out the slops, and doesn't sass me a bit. I remember when I first saw the widow McIntyre after I tried to give her cat a boot into the river. I thought I was pretty tough 'til I tangled with her crew."

After a pause in which all watched the tug taking the hawser out ahead, Clancy added, "They're a loyal lot. They stick together, and I hope they keep my Mouse on. There's a lot yet he can learn from 'em about sailorizing and working with a gang."

Isiah watched the ship and her company as they moved off, nearing the harbor entrance, the details of her structure and those manning her dwindling. He could still make out Mollie in her dark bloomer outfit back aft at the wheel, as two of the crew were taking gaskets off the sails and others were stowing lines, getting ready to raise sail as soon as they cleared the jetties and dropped the tow line. Mollie stood straight and tall, her dark hair in a long braid down her back. Isiah thought, now there goes a worthy level-headed woman. I wish Dan would give her a look instead of making eyes at that silly little Rowena Parker with her two dozen velvet dresses and lace flounces.

It had not been an easy summer for them, yet there went owner and crew still on deck, still underway, heading out for the first barley of the year. Isiah resolved to have Hannah report on their arrival at the elevator.

If the freights aren't satisfactory I could raise their charter rate for the month of October, if they'd go back to hauling lumber. He wondered what the fall season would hold for the ship and crew. Soon the shortening days on the lake would bring the most trying times of the sailing season.

Even though the *Gazelle* and other lumber carriers would be laid up for the winter in a month or so, Isiah was determined to keep several schooners in charter next year. It was far easier to deal face to face with one or two honest ship owners like Mollie or Captain Martin than to do business with the railroads even if they did run year around.

The recent railroad stock shorting and dumping had been severely disruptive to a marketplace in need of honesty and order, and the constant kickbacks and rebates that put the squeeze on small and medium sized operations like Fitzhugh and Son while favoring the big shippers were driving some firms out of business. There was far too much power concentrated in this single industry. The monopolists were much too cozy now with the government. We need balance and competition, thought Isiah. We need ships and canal boats, along with railroads, to carry cargo.

But every year, it seemed another one or two schooners from Oswego's regular trade were lost to fall gales, and few were being built to replace them. The days when Oswego's yards had launched a half dozen ships a season were long gone. It had been several years since Goble's shipyard had built a schooner. Shipping on the lake was unquestionably in decline. And even the stoutest ship and the best crew could have a spot of bad luck, especially in the fall, he thought as he turned to go into the office.

"Say, what's that there?" he heard Clancy asking. He followed the other's gesture pointing skyward.

Two large long necked white birds were flying on powerful wings high overhead. As Isiah looked up, one bird gave voice to a wild clear cry with a sound very like that of a brass bugle. It touched a strange longing within all watchers as they saw the birds swiftly pass over the harbor.

"I think it must be a pair, male and female. They're heading south now," said Isiah.

"I never saw birds like that before," said Doyle.

"They sure do fly. Wish I was goin' with 'em," said Clancy.

They were indeed odd birds, thought Isiah. He'd never seen birds like that with their broad white wings, swift flight and strong voices. And for some reason he was certain the female was in the lead. Heading south, away from November gales and the soon to be iced over waters of the lake.

Chapter Twenty

" nothing is hopeless that is right" Susan B. Anthony

A week later Hannah stood on the wharf watching as Mollie's crew secured their vessel under the chutes of the Northwestern and hastened to knock the hatch cover wedges loose to pull the tarpaulins off the heavy hatch boards. Mouse trotted aft carrying several grain shovels. It wouldn't take long to send this load up into the giant wooden tower looming high above them. Oswego's 450,000 bushel Northwestern was the biggest and most modern elevator on all the lake. Its hundred horsepower steam plant could lift 8000 bushels of grain from a vessel in one hour, so the *Gazelle* would soon be headed back to Kingston for another load.

Mollie hurried down the plank toward her, market basket in hand. "I've got to get to the grocer's, will you walk with me?"

Hannah fell in step beside her. "How was the trip?"

"Oh, excellent. We were over and back in three days with the first load. We had an absolutely glorious run back Monday-made it in steam boat time. Finally, we're having some luck."

Hanna saw the spring in Mollie's step and heard the lift of her voice. "Freights are holding steady," she said. "If this weather lasts, perhaps you'll be back in Kingston by morning and able to make another trip this week.

"If it holds. I don't like the look of that sky, though."

They turned and headed up Second Street to the Chandlery where Mollie would replenish her stores. "We're nearly out of coffee," she laughed as they hurried along. "And we'll need plenty if we keep on at this rate."

By late afternoon the *Gazelle* was gone, already towed out and heading back across the lake for another load, and Hannah was back in the office at work on her accounts. At day's end she locked the door and started for home. She noted the wind vane atop City Hall had swung into the southeast, and the filmy overcast of mid-day cirrus had thickened to form a solid ashy gray cover of cloud over the entire sky. It felt a bit warmer too. Mollie was right. The old lake probably will get dirty tonight, she thought.

Aboard the *Gazelle,* Ben noted the dropping barometer and lowering veil of smoke-like cloud at twilight and said to Mollie as he sat down to supper, "Our good luck with the winds is about to run out. We may not get in by first light after all depending on when it starts to kick up and how strong it comes on."

Mollie at the range dishing up meat pie for the crew replied, "I guess we can't have fair winds every day. But it sure was nice while we did."

Even as she spoke, they both heard the sharp rattle of heavy rain drops on deck and felt the vessel heel slightly to a puff of wind. "No rest for the wicked," sighed Ben as he awaited his supper thinking of the long wet night ahead of him.

By morning *Gazelle* was trudging along under single reefed lowers and only a fore staysail, while the northeaster whined hummed and occasionally howled in her rig. She butted into the short steep seas sending sheets of spray aft as far as the deck house, and occasionally a bit of sold water managed to board her, though with an empty hold she was considerably drier than she would have been with three hundred tons of coal aboard. Still, it was slow wet work, slogging upwind, and the fast crossing of two days ago seemed a distant memory. We won't even get there by noon at this rate, thought Mollie who had put on her own oil skins to stand on deck and peer impatiently into the gray rain and mist ahead. Every day now was precious as the store of time left in the shipping season dwindled. Less than two months remaining until lay up to earn three thousand dollars.

Ben said, "It's starting to flatten out, we're getting under Wolfe Island. I think we could put her around on the other tack now."

Mollie nodded, and after the ship had gone around she went below to strip off her slicker and start a fire for a midday hot dinner now that they weren't bouncing and lurching so much. Perhaps they would still arrive in Kingston in time to get a spot on the wharf, though she doubted it. Ben and Tommy, who were the first watch, had just come below to get their dinner when she heard Mouse's shrill voice on deck shouting, "Ahoy, ahoy, there's a ship out there-I think he's in trouble!"

Everyone made a mad scramble for the deck, Mollie close behind the men. As she joined them at the rail, she saw the rain and mist had cleared off a bit. Less than a mile away, under their lee, a small white two masted schooner lay under bare poles.

Mouse said, "I saw a bright light, It must have been a flare."

The vessel was in obvious difficulty. She was very low in the water, her decks nearly awash. She was laboring heavily, frequently swept by waves, and had nary a stitch of canvas up. Some shreds of her foresail and outer jib still fluttered forlornly in the wind, and her main and other headsails were furled. Mollie could see two of her crew were working the pump handles with all their strength. Ben rapped out a series of orders to reduce sail and change course to run down to her.

"It looks like she's sinking," said Nate who was on the helm. "I wonder what happened to her yawl boat?"

"They lost it, or else someone jumped ship," suggested Ben.

"There's somebody aft," Mouse called back to them from his perch half way up the fore ratlins.

As *Gazelle* approached the disabled two master, Mollie saw the two men abandon their efforts at the pump to go to the rail and shout and wave. Back aft stood two more figures. Nate steered close under her stern, and one of the men cupped his hands to his mouth and shouted, "We're sinking. We've lost the yawl. Can you assist?"

Gazelle swept on past, and Mollie saw that the crew, stooped with fatigue, were going forward, evidently intending to get their gear from the focsle. She also saw that the figure beside the captain was female, and on the schooner's transom she saw that the lake's latest victim was the *Julia* out of Stella Bay.

"They're giving up," she said.

Ben turned to go aft to the yawl boat davits. "Call Tommy. We're going over. You stay hove to close under her lee."

Though they were still well offshore, the slight shelter from Long Point and the Duck Islands had calmed the seas a bit making launching the yawl boat easier than it would have been a few hours ago. But Mollie still worried as she saw the small boat disappear within the troughs and then rise again on the steep short seas as Tommy and Ben rowed over to the wallowing ship.

As the yawl neared the *Julia*, Tommy said, "She looks awful low."

"She's still afloat though. And you don't leave your ship until you have to step up to get into the lifeboat."

Alongside, Tommy scrambled aboard first, followed by Ben who quickly secured the yawl aft where it wouldn't swamp or be smashed against the *Julia*'s side. They could ill afford to lose the only lifeboat available.

The schooner felt bad underfoot. She was heavy and sluggish and slow to rise to the waves with her hold full of water. The slow roll as she staggered and lurched through the waves told Ben it wouldn't be long before she failed to rise. Soon she'd make her last dive to the bottom.

Ben took in the ship and crew at a glance. A youngster about Mouse's age and a grizzled man of about fifty, stood by, both clearly all in from working the pump. Ben saw the older man's hand tremble as he wiped the moisture from his face with his sleeve. The captain nearby was leaning heavily on the deck house. A short sturdy woman, dressed like the rest of the crew in oilskins, stood close beside him.

"I'm John Whitehorse-this is Jessie my wife. That's Henry, my boy, and Mr. Robbins, my mate. We're powerful glad to see you."

"What happened?"

"We were beating up from Frenchmen's Bay with wheat for Oswego. She started leaking about ten o'clock last night. We held her at first, but it got worse a few hours ago. I think the grain swelled and started a plank. Anyways, we tried to lay her off and run for Charlotte, but she was so waterlogged Jessie here couldn't hold her on the jibe. The foresail split and the main gaff broke. We been pumping ever since. I went and dinged up my ankle, too."

"How much is in her?"

"Probably three or four feet now."

Ben moved towards the pump. "Come on Tommy let's see if some new muscle can hold her up."

The two men took hold of the pump handles, and Tommy set a blistering pace. Twenty minutes later, Ben's arms were aching and his heart was pounding when he called a halt. Tommy, his chest heaving, dropped the handle, seized the sounding rod lying on deck, plunged it down the well and pulled it back up. Captain Whitehorse groaned. "You gained about two inches."

Tommy flung the rod down with a curse.

"It's no use. You'll have to take us off."

Ben stared across the water at the *Gazelle* considering the sea state and distance to safe harbor. Captain Whitehorse continued, "We're all in. We worked all night on the pumps before it got worse. My wife, too. If only I hadn'ta bust my anklebone-"

Ben now looked at Henry the youngster who had joined the mate in setting on the tow line's coil by the deck house. "Can you row your Mom across?"

The boy nodded and stood up. "Then get her in. Bring the yawl right back."

Mrs. Whitehorse went below and returned a few minutes later with a small bundle of personal gear and a leather wallet of ship's papers. She was also wearing a cork buoyancy belt. Ben saw it and thought we should have some of those aboard the *Gazelle.*

Captain Whitehorse briefly clasped his wife's hands in his own and said something quietly to her about taking care before giving her a gentle push. She was clearly reluctant to leave. "Come right back," he called out to Henry as the boy prepared to get into the yawl.

They watched them off. Then Captain Whitehorse turned away to look forward at the decks nearly awash now. "Fifteen year we've sailed this boat. She's all I got." He sounded choked.

"Is she insured?" asked Ben.

"The cargo. Not the boat."

Ben glanced quickly at Whitehorse. Seeing tears rolling down his face, Ben turned away from the old man's pain. He again looked off towards the *Gazelle,* hove to a few hundred yards to leeward, riding the chop like a gull sweet and steady. The yawl was nearly there. The weather had cleared some. He could make out a darkening of the gray mist behind *Gazelle.* Land, not much more than an hour's sail away. "We can't be more than five miles from South Bay. It's almost dead down wind. I'm going to try towing you. If we can beach her in behind Waupoos Island we could still save her."

The quick flash of hope in Whitehorse's eyes spurred Ben into immediate motion. He turned to the mate, "Get your heaving line and your hawser out and start working on a messenger. When Henry gets back, I'll take the yawl over and get my crew ready."

It wouldn't be easy Ben thought as he rowed back to the *Gazelle.* He Zeb and Nate would have to haul the *Julia's* heavy tow line over short handed as Tommy's muscle was needed on the *Julia's* pump. He would have to trust Mollie's hand on the helm as she brought the *Gazelle* close to the less maneuverable *Julia* so Tommy could get the light heaving line over. Mollie was up to the job he was certain, but he hoped the sinking schooner's towing hawser was in better shape than her hull. If a heavy line like that breaks under tension someone could get hurt.

Once back on board, he outlined the plan, and the boys carefully laid their own hawser out on deck to bend on to the *Julia's* for extra length after it was hauled aboard and secured. He looked across the water to see Tommy forward aboard the disabled boat with the heaving line in hand. He had taken up his stance and was ready to make the throw. Ben went aft to the wheel and spoke to Mollie.

"Take her by to windward of the *Julia* as close as you can. As soon as we get the messenger belayed, try to luff and slow her down, so we'll have slack to haul the towline in."

Mollie nodded silently and stood by as the crew ran up the outer jibs and slacked the fore sheet off. She then put the helm down and began working the *Gazelle* up to windward of the *Julia*. When she had gotten into position, she bore off to pass about thirty feet from the other vessel. As they surged by, Tommy flung the heaving line over with perfect aim. It landed squarely on the deck, and Nate lunged to make a grab for it. But before Mollie could slow the ship, the line slipped away from him. He cursed as he saw the end flick overboard. Mollie spun the wheel hard up and went around for another pass. This time she took the *Gazelle* so close to the *Julia*, she was afraid the two vessels would foul each other's rigging aloft as they wallowed in the chop. The waterlogged vessel was rolling slowly and heavily, but she just missed snagging *Gazelle's* foremast shrouds with her mast. Only about ten feet of roiled surging water separated the two ships. Mollie, as she steered, firmly pushed away the thought of a chance wave shoving her off course to slam *Gazelle* into the sinking *Julia*. She thought, *Steady as you go,* as she glued her eyes on the water ahead.

Tom shot the messenger and line clean across the deck this time. Nate fell upon it and seized the light line to belay it. Then he, Ben and Zeb worked furiously to haul the heavy tow line over. As they did so, Mollie edged *Gazelle* up into the wind slowing her speed through the water and swinging her stern in towards the *Julia* to lessen the distance and weight of the heavy line even more. A few feet closer and her main boom would have surely fouled the *Julia* possibly dismasting both ships.

With seconds to spare, Ben Nate and Zeb got the hawser aboard and on the bitts before the *Julia* drifted too far to leeward.

A half hour later, Tommy now working with Nate, was back at the *Julia's* pump, and the little schooner was under tow with her crippled captain on the wheel. The pace was agonizingly slow, but with scarcely five miles to the shelter of Waupoos Island, the boys were sure they could keep her afloat for another hour or two. Henry and Mr. Robbins, the mate, after a hot drink and a bit of chow aboard the *Gazelle,* were also back aboard and standing ready for another turn at the pumps to relieve Tom and Nate.

Ben, aboard the *Gazelle,* was watching the towing bridle off the stern and using all his sailor skills to coax a bit more power out of the main and foresail with Zeb Mollie and Mouse's help. They were moving well now, though. Slow but sure. As he had left the *Julia* after dropping Nate off to help with the pump, he had clapped her captain on the shoulder saying, "If we beach her at Waupoos you'll be right around the corner from Cressy's shipyard. We can fix her up for you in no time after you get her pumped out."

And the drooping gray faced man Ben had seen upon first boarding now stood as straight as his ankle would allow and grinned back, "I'll get her down to your yard if I have to carry her."

Dusk found both vessels safe in the lee of the island, the *Julia* lightly grounded and already apparently leaking less in the quiet water. Her crew had joined the *Gazelle's* company for dinner, filling the main cabin. The boys sat on foot lockers to eat making room at the table for their guests. Mollie's stew and fresh hot corn bread had renewed their energy reserves, and now, as Mollie and Jessie Whitehorse attacked the dishes, the men sat back to fire up their pipes, relishing the warm cabin and full stomachs.

Whitehorse spoke with a sigh, "Well, I guess our season's finished. We'll have to take out another note to get her fixed up to rate for insurance again. We just got our last note paid off hardly six months ago."

Ben nodded. "We're in the same pickle, we've got one to pay off now-3500 dollars.

"When's yours due?"

"The end of November."

Whitehorse whistled low in sympathy. "You got to do some hustling to pay that off."

At the sink, his wife said to Mollie beside her, "We've cost you two days delay at least."

Mollie shook her head, "It's no matter."

186

John Whitehorse spoke to Ben, "I know you already refused once, but I have to ask why you don't claim salvage?"

Ben seemed absorbed in the checked pattern of the table cloth, studying it with deep interest, so Mollie turned around and spoke, "Because next time it could be us that's in trouble. And what would be the good of putting a claim in on your *Julia* anyway? If we don't get our note paid off, then the banker would go after you, too, and we'd both be dragged down."

John Whitehorse shook his head, "We're powerful grateful to you."

Ben now looking up from the table said with a smile, "Oh, don't worry about us. You go get that mortgage, and Uncle John and I will take it all from you this winter at the shipyard. So we'll manage one way or another."

Jessie Whitehorse and Mollie, having finished clean up, now joined the table, each sitting on a chair vacated by Nate and Mr. Robbins, the mate, who moved to the lockers. The captain's wife still looked troubled as she said to Mollie, "I know how hard it is. We lost our house. It burned last year, so the *Julia* has been our home since then. I really don't know what we would have done if she'd gone down. You and your husband have done us a great service."

Ben's smile faded, and he coughed on some pipe smoke that had apparently gone down wrong. Jessie Whitehorse looked at Mollie in question.

"Ben's my brother in law. We lost Captain Will, my husband, last spring."

Ben got up and broke the awkward silence. "I'm tuckered-time to hit the bunk. No anchor watch. We'll take the night off this time."

As Mollie went to the companionway with the other women, Jessie turned and took Mollie's hand in both hers and said, "I don't know how, but we'll re- pay your good work." Then she turned and hurried up the steps after her hobbling spouse.

The winds were light and westerly the next day, well suited for coaxing the soggy *Julia* down into Eel Bay. After seeing them started on their way, the crew went to work at the windlass to raise *Gazelle's* own anchor. She then ran off wing and wing out of South Bay and around Amherst Island to Kingston. She came to anchor once again in the city harbor late in the afternoon to await her turn at the elevator the next day.

"Look there," called Tommy after the ship had drifted back on her chain. "It's the *Black Oak.*"

"That's the ship you beat in the race wasn't it?"asked Mouse.

"Yes, and if you see her captain anywhere ashore, stay away from him. He's a mean devil, and he likes us even less now. He'll beat the stuffing out of you if he gets half a chance."

Ashore in the deepening shadows of twilight, two men stood on the wharf in front of the now silent elevator. One was Burton, recently arrived light to load grain, the other a tall red haired Irishmen, Red Connors. Burton's *Black Oak* had just warped in to the elevator to be loaded at first light. He stood beside his old shipmate, a fellow hell raiser from their days of stone hooking and a bit of casual smuggling on the side with a little schooner scow they had owned together. Connors now ran the lifting machinery of the elevator. He went home to wife and bed each night, usually with a stop at a tavern enroute.

"Come on, Let's get on up to the Pump Room. I could use a bit of applejack. It's dusty work here."

Burton was glaring across the water. Even in the dimming light, the *Gazelle's* trim profile and rounded stern as she rode at anchor were unmistakable. Following his gaze out across the water Connors sniggered.

"Ah, your favorite girl friend. She got in this afternoon. The widow whipped your ass last month didn't she?"

Burton spat some excess tobacco juice on the dock. "That she witch and her kid brother captain. Strewing lumber all over the lake-the way she goes around on deck showing her leg in them pant'loons pulling and hauling. A whore has more pride than that. It shouldn't be allowed. Before you know it there'll be women sailors and mates working the deck and taking men's jobs. She belongs ashore scrubbing floors."

"Well, she might be ashore for good pretty soon."

"Why? Who says that?"

"My wife. She heard it from her half sister whose mixed up some ways with banker Sloan's family. I guess the widow McIntyre didn't quite make her last payment. She bargained with the old goat for an extension, but if she misses again, Sloan gets her boat."

Burton stopped glaring at the distant schooner and turned to meet his friend's smirk. "You don't say. Now that's interesting. Hey, let's go get that drink you was groaning about."

The two men headed up the street a short block to the Pump Room tavern for a bit of refreshment. Once settled at a table, Connors with his applejack and Burton with a whiskey, Connors renewed his chronic complaints about the state of his life and finances since coming ashore to work at the elevator.

"I asked the boss for a raise, and the bastard laughed at me and said I'd been sick so often that I ought to take a cut instead. He don't know what a hot dirty job it is shifting grain up in that tower."

"Your problem is you gotta get better at the cards. I heard about that game you was in with Poker Jane last week. An' I heard you got skinned too!"

"That little tart. She had me all right. And my old woman had me, too. The bitch gave me holy hell for it, so you're not the only one with woman problems. They're stupid but they're sneaky, too."

The two men finished their drinks in a morose silence, and each called for another. Burton asked, "Did you hear by chance how much the witch owes Sloan?"

"Back in September it was 3500 dollars."

Burton grunted. "How many times has she been to the elevator?"

"She got in three times last week, but this is the first I seen her this week."

Burton sipped his whiskey thoughtfully. "That little northeaster must have scared her. They were probably afraid to poke their nose out into it and stayed in Oswego. I wonder if we could delay widow Molly a bit more?"

Connors saw where the conversation was headed. "A day here, a day there and she runs out of days. Yeah, I bet could arrange a breakdown. They owe me time anyway for working my butt off."

"Well, wait 'til she's at the elevator, ok?"

"They 'll be there by noon. I'll just drop an iron down on the chain- she'll jam up and crunch. No more grain. She usually breaks, and that's a good half day to fix.

Burton nodded. "That'll work. With a bit of luck then we'll get that southerly I feel coming on, and they'll lose another day getting to Oswego after they do load."

The two men laughed, and Connors raised his glass and drained it in a toast to high flying whores and the knock down of same. Then he remarked as he slouched back in his chair, "I'm sick of this shore life. I'd like to get back out on the lake again. I'd guess if a boat was to be for sale in December to pay off a note the price might be pretty fair. And whatever you think of her owner, the *Gazelle* is a handy little packet."

Burton smiled slowly, "Sloan isn't going to want to look after a schooner all winter. He'll let her go cheap."

This thought called for another round and further discussion. It was very late indeed when Connor's wife heard him stumble in the door of their cottage.

The next day began clear dry and warm, a fine early fall morning of gentle winds and blue skies. When space opened up, the boys willingly kedged the *Gazelle* into the wharf and then lounged about the decks, while Ben and Nate puttered around with small ship keeping tasks. Shortly after noon dinner, it was their turn to warp up to the chutes. Mollie watched from back aft as the golden river began flowing down into the hold with a whispering rush. All was well, though she wondered where Reuban was. He usually hung around the deck near the hatch in case a dislodged mouse dropped down out of the chute and landed near him. It wasn't like him to hide out below, and she was certain he was aboard somewhere.

She did not see Connors quietly slip inside the elevator with a short pry bar in one hand. No one saw him climb the ladder in the dusty tower beside the continuous chain that lifted the scoops of grain up to the weigh scale bin. No one saw him lean out and drop the iron down onto the driving wheel at the bottom of the chamber. And only Connors heard the short sharp metallic sound as the chain jammed. It was very nearly the last thing he heard before he died.

Down on *Gazelle's* deck and on board the other schooners waiting their loads, the crews heard a dull heavy kawumph. It was immediately followed by a second loud sharp explosion. Mollie back aft, still looking for the cat, turned towards shore. Astonished, she watched the entire north wall of the wooden elevator building falling outwards. Dust billowed out from the structure as the remains of the roof crumpled inwards. Men shouted, and some one screamed, a cry that was abruptly cut off.

Then she heard Ben's warning, "Watch it!"

A large piece of roofing landed with a solid thump on the deck house a few feet away from her. A scattering of smaller bits of shingle and wood rained down clattering around them. A growing pall of dust and pale smoke continued to rise above the shattered tower. Mollie stared in horror at the elevator ruin.

"Dear God. What happened?"

"Dust explosion. There must have been a spark somewhere."

Mollie stared at the wreckage. The darkening cloud of dust over the shattered elevator spread across the sky like a mourning cloak. Death had reached out and touched the waterfront once again. And how, Mollie wondered, will the grain carriers possibly load now?

Chapter Twenty one

"Nothing strengthens the judgement and quickens the conscience like individual responsibility" E. C. Stanton

Mollie leaned against the bulwark feeling the morning sun like a warm shawl upon her shoulders. She watched the grain flowing down the narrow chute into the hold.

"Looks like a stream of gold," she said to Ben.

"It is gold, gold to pay off the bank."

"I do prefer barley cargoes to coal."

Ben nodded, "Coal's a chore to be sure. Hard on the ship, too."

"It's dirty. Coal dust everywhere. It lies heavy in the hold. You look at those sharp black rocks and think of people dying in the coal mines. Remember those strikes last year in Pennsylvania?"

"People died in those strikes, too. Yep, coal is dark. But it pays."

Mollie frowned as she watched the grain whispering down the chute. "It doesn't pay enough. Barley comes from farm fields, sunlight, and rain. Barley smells good, at least when it's growing. I think of birds and summer daisies and buttercups in the meadow when I smell barley."

"And beer," said Ben.

"Yes, and good ale, too. I like the smell of toasted barley from the malt houses. Not that it isn't a lot of work to plant and reap and thrash it out and get it to the elevator." She sighed. "And accidents happen there, too. That explosion, last week-that was so odd."

"It happens, though. There was a big 'un in Buffalo a couple years ago. You gotta watch that dust. One spark and up she goes."

Mollie turned away. Her shoulders slumped as she looked off across the little harbor of Green's Bay. "Sometimes it seems like you can't get away from it. Everywhere you turn- bad luck and loss and death."

Ben grunted and moved off to the deck box to lend a hand where Mouse was getting the towline out to repair a chafed spot.The whispering stream of grain began to dwindle, became a trickle, and then ceased. Mollie looked up at the small tower and scowled. Tommy and Zeb emerged from the hold where they had been leveling the grain. Ben, who was renewing a serving to protect the towline with Mouse's assistance, looked up.

"How much have we got now?" he asked.

"Maybe two thousand bushels," answered Tommy.

Ben sighed, and Mollie groaned. At this rate it would take a week to get a load. But what choice did they have? With the big elevator in Kingston totally destroyed by the explosion, the jam up at the remaining elevators there would have been intolerable. They would have waited at least a week before *Gazelle* could even get to one for a load. The crew had agreed with her decision to go down into South Bay and the Bay of Quinte to tramp around from one tiny bay port to another collecting grain from each small elevator.

At one port, they had stripped off a jib and laid it out on a hill side and shot the wagon loads of grain down onto the deck and into the hold. A thousand bushels here, two thousand there, slow but sure. At least they weren't just sitting around. Soon, wagons from nearby farms would be rolling in with more grain for the little single chute elevator serving Green's Bay. By dusk there would be another five hundred bushels under *Gazelle's* decks. But it was slow going, filling a schooner one wagon load at a time.

Ben seated nearby saw Mollie's long face as she leaned upon one elbow propped upon the rail. He decided it was time for action and put down his ball of tarred twine.

"What do you say to taking a little sail with the yawl? The boys can deal with loading and trimming. We've got three and a half good boys here," said Ben with a wink at Mouse beside him. "We'll put Nate in charge. We could sail down to Alice Baird's. It's been an age since we saw her."

Mollie stood up, her face brightening. "Well, why not? We could take a picnic along. I haven't seen Alice since fitting out."

Mouse asked, "Who's Alice Baird?"

"She's the wise old woman of South Bay," Ben told him. "She's a peach. Alice Baird is a widow lady that can swing a scythe and pull an oar as well as any man on the north shore. She fishes, too. She's got her husband's skiff the *Mary Ellis*."

Mollie added, "She's strong as a horse. She's as tall as I am but built like a tug boat. Her husband died twenty years ago, washed off a schooner on Lake Michigan. She never remarried and lives alone on a little farm about half way from here to Eel Bay."

Tommy chimed in, "She doesn't live alone if you count the animals. She's got about five dogs and I don't know how many cats."

"Don't forget Calliope," laughed Ben. "Calliope the goose. Alice takes her along in the fish boat, and she sleeps in the house up on Alice's dresser every night."

The thought of seeing hearty Alice Baird lifted Mollie's mood immediately and Ben, observing this, got up and said, "Come on Tommy. Let's get the yawl down. The owner and captain of the *Gazelle* are taking the day off."

Ten minutes later, the boys watched the yawl pull away and grow small in the distance.

Nate said, "They deserve a day off. It's been a rough week."

"You guys were pretty amazing with that rescue," said Mouse.

"Yea, that was a pretty close call. Another hour and the *Julia* would have been a winter home for the fishes."

Tommy spoke, "You know last week I met a guy at the Great Laker Tavern, he was a mate on a big schooner down on salt water before he came up here. He told me he'd never sail on the lake again after this season."

Mouse asked, "Why not?"

"Too dangerous. See, the ocean has hurricanes and huge waves, but it also has sea room."

"What's that?"

"Out on the ocean you got lots of miles between you and the hard stuff. You can heave to and drift or run with the storm under bare poles for days. Here, you're never more than a day's sail from piling up on a lee shore."

Nate added, "And we can get twenty foot waves here."

Mouse asked, "Have you ever seen one?"

"No, but I know people who have. And the waves on the lakes are so close together that they'll swamp a ship. It's not like the ocean. Sometimes, you have to bust the bulwarks out of her to free the deck. Too much water and she can't rise..."

Tommy nodded, "That mate, he said freshwater is heavy. It falls like lead on a deck. Salt water has more lift to keep a ship on top of the waves."

The boys fell silent again leaning against the house in the sunshine as they watched the yawl dwindle in the distance.

The air this early October day was as sweet and clear as a glass of golden wine. The distant low land of Long Point off to port lay softened by a light blue haze. Mollie thought, as they sailed along over the lightly rippled water, that these sunny days of autumn were especially sweet because there were so few left before winter.

"Alice has always amazed me the way she manages alone. Not many women live like that, all on their own without a man."

Ben laughed, "Maybe you'd enjoy not having five hungry crew to feed and clean up after all the time."

Mollie replied, "I do admire her. But I don't envy her. I think it must be hard not having someone around to talk things over with."

"Well, her son does live right over in Soup Harbor."

"Yes, but he's a good two hours away. She's mostly alone. I've never been alone like that for more than a day or two."

"I guess I never have either. I don't mind working by myself, but it's good to have the other fellows around in the yard. I don't believe I'd care for it. Besides, I like your cooking a lot better than what I can manage."

The little yawl boat moved along smartly though the wind off the land was scarcely strong enough to flap laundry hung on a line.

Ben asked, "Do you think you'll ever marry again?"

Mollie shook her head. "It's too soon to even think about such things." Then she glanced at Ben back at the tiller and wondered *why did he ask me that?*

Well before noon, they made out the widow's small white washed cottage and her unpainted barn. Ben offered Mollie the tiller for the rest of the trip, but she declined. "I don't mind just going along for the ride. It's nice to just sit for a change and not worry about anything."

Ben stretched in a comfortable slouch against the weather side of the boat agreed. "I'm a little tired of looking down into the hold at that puny pile of grain myself."

"Maybe we should go back and get in line at Kingston and finish our load there," said Mollie.

Alice Baird was working on the shore at the mouth of the small creek that ran through her fields to enter the bay where it formed a tiny harbor. She left off scrubbing out her fish boat, hitched up her skirts, kicked her boots off, and waded barefoot out to take their painter calling out a hearty greeting over the dogs' racket. Surrounded by an enthusiastic and vocal trio of dogs of various sizes and shapes along with one large white screeching goose, she and Ben pulled the yawl up alongside the fishing boat and secured her to a wooden stake pounded into the ground.

Alice then turned to admonish the pack. "That's enough Nero, Syb, Venus, Calliope! Now it's our turn to talk. Mollie, Ben McIntyre-Lordy it's good to see you. Mollie what in blazes is that outfit you have there?"

"It's my bloomer. I saw a woman in Oswego with something similar and copied it. I can work on deck so much easier with it."

"Leave me look at that. You always were a smart thing with a needle." Alice peered closely at Mollie's figure, turned her around once, felt the cloth and said,"Looks sensible. Maybe I'll make one."

"You'll never wear your skirts again in your skiff or in the barn either," said Mollie.

As the two women talked, Ben examined the *Mary Ellis* a sturdy Mackinaw boat. She was a double ender about 25 feet long with two oiled pine masts, a nearly plumb stem, a short bowsprit and a single jib. He had always admired the boat, built by Alice's grandfather nearly thirty years ago. The builder was said to have done a bit of smuggling in his younger days, and the *Mary Ellis* was a smart sailor. Last winter he and Uncle John had put a new keel in her, and he remembered thinking at the time that the hull was a powerful as well as fast model of her type-probably as good a sea boat as any now fishing the lake.

"How's the boat doing?"

"Oh fine. I'm just cleaning the muck up from a little set I put out just to see what was out there."

"Won't be long before the ciscoes start coming in," said Mollie.

Alice nodded, "The year just keeps flying by. I've still got to put my garden to bed and pull my beans and stook the corn. We had a light frost last week."

As if to add emphasis to her words, Calliope, the white goose, suddenly started screeching and honking and flapping her wings. Alice looked up, and Mollie and Ben followed her gaze. Far overhead, no bigger than gnats against the clear blue sky a long wavy line of wild geese beat steadily south stitching a trail across the sky.

Alice remarked, "I heard them last night, too, flying over. Likely some cold weather coming along chasing them south. My bones feel like rain on the way."

"I hope not. We're up in Green's Bay trying to load barley." said Mollie.

Alice tossed her scrub brush into the *Mary Ellis*. "Let's go up to the house. It's nearly dinner time. You are staying aren't you?"

They assured her they were, Mollie drawing forth her own basket of provisions.

"We brought you some New York apples."

The three friends made their way up a well trod path to the house walking past the split rail fence of the pasture where a roan cow and her well grown calf along with a small flock of sheep were grazing. Mollie noting the sturdy fence and tidy flowerbed still bright with color in its sheltered nook by the door wondered how Alice found time to look after her farm and still work her nets and trotlines, too.

Alice and Mollie set out a simple dinner of cold sliced ham, cheese and bread from the picnic hamper, while the pot for a bit of late sweet corn came to a boil.

"I've got fish chowder here and some brown betty for desert, too," said Alice. "It's so grand to have company. I would have fixed a chicken if I'd known you were coming."

The company made short work of their food. Once the plates were pushed aside, they settled back to exchange news. They spoke of the rescue of the *Julia*, and of the warehouse fire, the elevator explosion, and other set backs. Alice shook her head and pursed her lips in sympathy upon hearing of the squall and the damaged bulwark and lost load.

"Makes a body grateful for being stuck here in this little backwater."

Mollie asked, "How has the fishing been? There was a big die off in the Oswego river and out in the lake near the land, too, a month or so ago."

Alice replied, "It hasn't been the best. I've certainly seen better. Ben's Uncle Rob told me it's those steamers and the new nets they're using. You know we have three steamers now fishing the bay. He says they put out sets a mile long, and the nets are small mesh, too."

"We saw one of them on our way in," said Mollie.

"First the steamers steal our trade in lumber and grain, now they take your fish," said Ben.

"I don't think it's all the steamers doing," answered Alice as she started dishing up the dessert. "I believe some of it is the rivers, like you saw in Oswego, Mollie. They're dirty and it's killing the fish."

Mollie nodded. "This summer there were days you could smell the river a half mile out. The city and starch factory filth get pretty bad."

"It's the same in Kingston. More factories and more filth every year. Eventually it makes a difference here in the open lake. And another thing, the fish are different. I've never seen so many of those shadines. Your uncle Rob calls them alewives. I think they're chasing the ciscoes off."

"Are they good to eat?" asked Ben.

"They're miserable bony creatures, so oily you can't stand 'em. Hog food, I'd call 'em."

Mollie said, "Isiah Fitzhugh in Oswego was telling us about some new kind of fish the government was bringing to Great Sodus Bay, carp from Europe. He wondered if they might help the fishery."

"I've heard 'bout them, too. They grow to twenty pounds, and they say you can feed 'em on corn. We'll see how they do. I guess they're pretty hardy and that could help us out some," said Alice thoughtfully.

"They better be. Remember what we saw after that big gully washer last month in Oswego?" Ben said with a laugh recalling the dead calf and other assorted unsavory debris that had floated past the *Gazelle* that afternoon.

Mollie passed Ben's serving of dessert over to him with a slight frown and said, "Lets talk about something else."

Alice laughed and Ben said, "Good enough. Alice give us a story or two about Captain Ellis will you?"

Alice pulled out her pipe, and Ben followed suit, as Mollie got up to clear the table. She asked, "Who is Captain Ellis?"

"He's my Ma's father and a seafarer from way back. He sailed salt water for near fifty years. He's swallowed the anchor now and stays ashore, but he's still telling tales," answered Alice.

After a pause for set up and ignition, Alice puffed away on her pipe before continuing. "I shall tell you now about an amazing woman Captain Ellis encountered, a woman who saved hundreds of sailor men from certain death. A business woman who is now wealthy. You recall those flares that led you to the *Julia*? Well, I will tell how those flares came to be."

Chapter Twenty two

*"The frauds that were practiced upon me, almost disheartened me; but …
I treasured up each little step that was made in the right direction-"* Martha
Coston.

"Captain Ellis met the inventor of those signals, a woman, named
Martha Coston."

"A woman invented those flares?" asked Mollie

"Indeed she did. She was a woman of good family and married a fine
smart young navy man. He got the idea to create night signals using
various chemicals to color flares to communicate among navy ships. He
worked for years to create the signals, and the chemicals made him so sick
he died.

"So there was his wife, Martha, with two young children and a little
baby and hardly a dollar to her name. She was that desperate. And scarce
a week or two later her baby died. And then her own Mother passed. How
dire a lee shore she was on. No husband, no mother, on her own with two
boys still to feed. But she remembered her husband's papers with his plans
for those signals. She found his formula and his scheme that called for
using three colors in combination to send messages. So she decided to
finish the work he started and sell those signals to the Navy.

"She found a fireworks maker to formulate the signals according to Mr.
Coston's recipe. But then she needed a patent to protect the formula.
What a struggle she had to get anyone to listen to her. Sometimes, she
pretended in her letters to be a man so her letters would be read. It took
many months before she got a patent. At last, the navy offered a trifling
payment for her invention. Coston's signals were used during your War
with the South and helped the navy take the largest fort in the
Confederacy.

"After the war, Martha Coston traveled overseas alone with her two
little boys to offer the patent to the British. Of course, they tried to rob
her. They told her an Englishman had invented the signals. They said a
woman could not possibly have done this. Her patent must be a fake.
When they did finally make her an offer, they cheated her disgracefully
even though her flares were better than any of the others they tested."

Mollie sniffed, "Sounds typical!"

"The French weren't any better. They held her up for months. They bought a few of her flares and tried to figure out her formula. They couldn't do it, though. Eventually they had to pay her. The Italians held her up for nearly a year while they tried to cheat her. But she learned. She learned how to out fox the men at their own game.

"She spent years in Europe traveling around to Navy departments putting up with constant fraud, lies and disrespect. Captain Ellis said she told him she only kept on because she wished to prevent wives of sailors from becoming widows like herself. She didn't want to see their children with no other father than the wise and all merciful One above us all. Well, every Life Saving Station has her signals now. Her invention has saved the lives of hundreds of sailor men."

Ben nodded, "The crew of the *Julia* was lucky she did keep at it. There'd be four more dead mariners on the bottom today without her work."

"I remember Captain Ellis saying she told him, "Chivalry from men vanishes like dew before the summer sun when one of us comes into competition with them.""

Mollie laughed, "That's for sure."

"She had the last laugh, though. She has made tens of thousands of dollars from the signals."

Ben was packing his pipe again settling back to digest a bit before they started back to the *Gazelle*. Mollie started to get up, but Alice waved her back into her chair. "The dishes will keep. I'll get them later. I don't get a chance to talk with company much these days."

"What type of vessel did Captain Ellis sail on?" asked Mollie.

"He sailed aboard a three master that took a load of lumber from Michigan over to England. He liked it there and stayed a few years. Captain Ellis met Martha Coston when he was running a ferry across the English Channel that she sailed on. I recall he told of an odd dream she had that she shared with him- a vision of our dear Lord Jesus who warned her of deceit by a man she trusted. Her vision gave her the wit to avoid being cheated." After a pause Alice added, "I always thought you should listen to your hunches. There are things that happen that are beyond our understanding and it's wise to remember that."

Ben nodded and said, "Well, odd things happen right here on this lake. Did you hear about the black dog?"

Alice shook her head.

"That happened was last fall. The schooner *Jenkins* was towing through the Welland with grain for Oswego. A sailor jumped ship there. He said he'd seen a black dog come aboard while they were sailing on Lake Erie. It climbed over the rail, walked across the deck, and disappeared over the other side. He said it was a sign, a warning that the ship was going to sink. So he packed his kit and left."

"Well, did she?" asked Alice.

"Not a week later the yawl boat was found near Nine Mile Point hardly an hour from Oswego. There wasn't any other wreckage and no survivors. She must have gone down fast. There was a farmer nearby who said he found a black dog on the beach, though."

In the silence that followed Mollie pushed a bit of desert around her dish. She didn't put much stock in signs superstitions and ghost stories. But she did know that luck and chance were always part of a lake sailor's life. She hadn't forgotten the collision and the harbor tug's exploding boiler a few months ago in Oswego. Nor had she forgotten the squall and the lost deck load.

She said, "I know you should listen to hunches and that luck happens. But our own actions and choices make a difference, too. Martha Coston earned her money. She wasn't just lucky. She was smart. She waited months to see the right person sometimes. And what about our neighbor Moses Dulmadge? Wasn't that his own fault?"

"That was just last fall, too," said Ben thoughtfully.

"Oh, poor Moses," said Alice with a sigh. "Poor foolish young Moses, so strong and bold – gone just a year now."

"And so dead," said Ben.

"But it was his own fault," Mollie persisted. "He shouldn't have rowed over to the *Olivia* with it blowing so hard that night. He wouldn't have been driven offshore and frozen to death if he'd stayed on his own ship instead of going visiting."

Alice sat back shaking her head. "But it was luck that you spotted the *Julia*."

"Yes, it was luck, and also Coston's signals," replied Mollie.

Looking out the window at the serene blue waters of South Bay, Mollie saw a sudden picture in her mind's eye of the cemetery where Will's grave should have been, a place now green and peaceful with its gnarled old locust trees and dark cedars. A few rows away from the McIntyre plot stood the stone of Moses Dalmadge, the farm lad who had drifted across thirty miles of open lake in his yawl boat on a bitter cold Halloween night one year ago. He had been found by the keeper in front of the Stony Point Light the next morning. The boy's body was still lashed to the thwart, and one oar was floating near by in the slush ice.

Her own Will had gone to his grave after a chance wind shift and a flying jibe. Young Moses had deliberately dared the lake when he took his yawl boat out into the storm. And Will had been up there on the deck load by his own choice shoving on the boom. The lake rarely forgives mistakes.

She pulled herself back into the present to look out the window at the lowering sun and said reluctantly, "We should be going on back to the *Gazelle*."

Alice pushed her chair back and stood. "Let me pack some things in your basket to take along."

They bid Alice farewell promising to visit her again as soon as the schooner was laid up for the winter. Alice sent them off with a hug for Mollie and a full basket of provisions for the boys.

As they sailed along, Mollie thought about Martha Coston, ghost dogs, Moses and Will. Martha Coston had truly shaped the course she sailed through life. Yet luck and fate played a part, too. A wind shift of a point or two could mean the difference between making port or not. The *Julia* had started a seam and nearly sank. If she had lasted another hour, she would have been safe under the land. And if Mouse hadn't seen those signals? She would have gone down for sure.

No matter how prepared or careful you were, luck was a factor. If that steamer had hit us ten feet further aft, we would never have made it to the yawl boat before the *Gazelle* went down. And that explosion at the elevator right as the harvest began- that was bad luck to be sure.

Maybe our luck has run out. If so, why fight it? Taking chances with the late season lake is foolish. Perhaps she could work for Father on the *Anowa*. Somehow she'd pay everyone back. It took Susan B. Anthony seven years to repay her debts, but she had done it. Yet the idea of quitting made her jaw tighten in frustration. What had Susan B. Anthony said? "Failure is impossible." She'd lost her treasured newspaper, her platform for making her voice heard, yet she had kept on. She found other ways to fight for suffrage. And Coston had been swindled and cheated yet she, too, kept going. Just like Harriet Tubman.

The most important thing, though, was the family. And staying alive. You can always start over like Anthony, even if you lose everything. But not if you're dead. And you don't want to take the family to the bottom of the lake with you. If we quit now, maybe she could go back to Sodus Bay and work with her father. If we sold the *Gazelle*, Ben would go back to the back to the boat shop.

She was about to share her thoughts with Ben when he interrupted them with, "It's clouding up over in the west. I bet we do get that rain Alice spoke of."

Mollie looked off towards the bank of gray stratus slowly rising above the horizon. More delays. The farmers couldn't bring their grain in during wet weather. One less cargo. One less freight payment. Maybe it really was fate. Seeing Mollie's dark face and hoping to take her mind off the oncoming weather Ben offered small talk.

"It's good we went down to see Alice. I was glad to see her boat was holding up."

Mollie answered, "I hadn't been down there for over a year. I remember when Will took me to her place not long after we were married. He wanted me to meet her."

"She's been a special neighbor to the McIntyre's for a long time," said Ben. "Uncle John wouldn't take cash for the boat repairs. He agreed to a barrel of salted ciscoes. But all summer she stopped by with fruit from her orchard, too." Ben flashed a quick smile at Mollie. "Sometimes you remind me a little of her, the way you stand up on your own two legs and keep going."

Mollie, still thinking of quitting, did not answer.

Ben eased the sheet of the sail hoping to catch more of the softening wind that was dying with the day. Then he asked, "How did you meet Will? I never really heard much about it from him."

Mollie shifted the picnic basket to free up space for her cramped legs and settled into a more comfortable position. Here was a pleasant memory of the past, something she'd much rather think about than the future.

"We met in Sodus Bay. Will's ship was waiting to load coal at the trestle. It was the end of the summer, and I was at home helping Aunt Anna. I had gone with Father earlier as cook, but he didn't want me along in the fall, so he had hired a cook. Freights were low and wages were, too, that year. There were plenty of men on the beach looking for work, so he

203

found a cook quick enough. Father had bought me a nice double ender from the St. Lawrence to sail on the bay. I used to row or sail over from the farm and sell eggs and fresh bread to the boats along the trestle, and that's how I met your brother.

"I saw him standing by the rail. He was so fine looking with the sun on that red hair of his. I couldn't help but stare at him. Then he looked over at me. He hailed me, and I sailed over and came alongside the wharf where he took my painter. I remember he complemented me on my boat handling. You steer those skiffs with your weight, you know. It's a bit of a trick, and I thought it great fun to sail around without a rudder. Anyway, we started talking, and he invited me aboard and showed me around. I thought he was the finest thing. I set my cap for him after that. Every time he was in at the trestle that fall, I was there to keep company with him. The following spring he was back, and we decided to marry. Will was so keen, so confident and sure. And the next year he was captain of his own ship. For two months."

A flight of geese passed over low and noisy as they sought a spot to settle for the night. "They sound almost like people calling back and forth. They sound sad now that it's fall," she said.

Ben sighed, "Will was a first class sailor. He was a natural. He always seemed to know what to do."

Mollie shifted her eyes from the geese to look at Ben. "Well, you don't do that badly in a jam. Look how that *Julia* tow turned out."

Ben frowned up at the now limp sail overhead. "Luck and a good crew that was. Say speaking of crew, I think we're going to need an ash breeze to get ourselves back before dark."

Mollie reached for the oars. "I'll take a turn. You can steer for a spell. Guess we're not such smart sailors, letting the wind die on us for that second helping of dessert." They both smiled at the memory of Alice's table with her hearty presence three expectant dogs and one bright eyed goose underfoot watching for a stray crumb.

"That dessert did set us down on our lines," agreed Ben.

The sun had slipped behind the oncoming clouds, and the colors of the day were giving away quickly to shadows and the gray shapes of near night as they came alongside the *Gazelle*. A warm glow of yellow light from her deck house ports told of life below. The boys had probably started the range and were playing cards in the main cabin while they waited for their supper.

As they came alongside, she looked up at the tall masts against the darkening sky.

"Here's good old *Gazelle* waiting for us," said Ben.

Mollie felt a stab of sorrow at the thought of quitting. Trying to sound bright she answered, "With her crew waiting for the cook. We'll see how they like this smoked fish Alice gave us."

Ben secured the yawl and climbed up on deck. For a brief moment, Mollie stood in the yawl looking at the familiar vessel she was about to board. She thought how good it felt to be 'home' and how much she would miss the close knit little world of the *Gazelle* if they failed to make the next payment to Sloan. Cheerful Alice keeping her farm up with just her flock of pets for company was an inspiration, but Mollie was glad to have her five boys to cook for and eat with. She gripped the rail and hauled herself up using a scupper for a step.

Chapter Twenty three

Mens Rights are nothing more. Women's rights are nothing less. S. B. Anthony

Rain pattered on the deckhouse top and rattled against Mollie's southwester. It ran down the mainsail and drained off the end of the boom in a steady stream. The sodden canvas overhead occasionally slatted sending more water splattering onto the decks below. The wet seeped up Mollie's arms and crept down her neck in a relentless spreading chill. She wiped the water out of her eyes as she peered at the rain streaked binnacle glass barely able to make out the dimly lit compass card. Fall rain. Steady, soaking, raw, it streamed along the deck and flowed steadily out of the scuppers. If there were any deck leaks, they'd find out about them tonight, she thought. At least it's not snow. Yet. But it was plenty cold. She only had to mind the helm for the short dog watch after supper to give the crew a little help. But even two hours was a long time on a dirty night like this.

After a day and a half of sitting at Green's Bay by the little elevator in the steady drenching rain, Mollie had decided to sail for Kingston and wait there to finish their load. The farmers would need at least one good day of drying sun before they could bring any more grain to the elevator. So off the Kingston the *Gazelle* went, departing in the rain, and now sailing in the rain, carrying scarcely two feet more draft with the barley she had accumulated after lying for four days in the little port.

Dimly through the gathering night Mollie could see the steady constant flash of the lighted beacon marking the south end of Simco Island and the harbor approaches. Before long they would be anchored to wait some more. First week in October. It was difficult to imagine how they could possibly make 2500 dollars between now and the close of navigation scarcely six weeks from today. After mid November few underwriters would issue insurance on a cargo or on the vessel carrying it.

The whole crew had been subdued with little talk or banter as they had worked their way out of South Bay against the light easterly wind and the unrelenting rain. They all knew there would be more weather delays as November approached and that the possibility of making the next mortgage payment was slipping away.

Three hours later in the early October darkness the *Gazelle's* anchor went down with a rattle of chain. The crew furled sails, lit a riding light, pumped the bilge, and went off to bed. Gloom hung over the ship as heavy and palpable as the overcast and light drizzle as they set their windlass brakes and secured for the night.

Mollie, already below in her cabin, cradled Reuban in her arms. She sat on the edge of her bunk comforted by his soft warmth as she gazed at Will's photo on the bulkhead. How different would things be, she wondered, were he still here. Would they have faced default? And if so, would they have argued and fought over it? She remembered with a pang of guilt how she had harangued Will about the manifest and other papers that last night he had been alive. It hadn't been easy since then, though they had given it their best. Once again her thoughts ran in a well worn groove- what would they do if Sloan foreclosed? What sort of future awaited a widow ashore without Will?

"Do you miss him?" she asked Reuban.

The yellow green eyes looked back half closed, contented and sleepy. Reuban seemed to say, "As long as I'm dry and safe and have someone to love me, I'm happy."

The next morning Mollie and Ben stood on deck surveying the line up of shipping at the Eastern King elevator. The harbor was thick with masts and jammed with schooners. Over a dozen vessels lay on the wharf rafted two and three abreast, while a half dozen more rode at anchor around the *Gazelle*.

"Looks like at least two days before we can load, or maybe longer," said Ben.

Mollie's fingers drummed against her thigh as she stared at the rafted barley carriers. Despair heavier than a full load of coal settled on her shoulders. We're finished. Might as well go back to Eel Bay now, she thought. Just lie down and die. There's no way we can make enough runs with delays like this on each trip.

She was about to suggest to Ben that they give it up. It was crazy to risk the lake in November when default was a certainty. Why tempt Fate and the fall gales? Their efforts to keep the ship's finances afloat were clearly doomed. Might as well just lay her up and go ashore. Their luck had run out. She noticed a schooner's yawl boat with two men aboard approaching under oars.

Ben said with a slight smile, "That's Joe Summer. I'd recognize that black bearded old scoundrel anywhere. He's master of the *Tigress*. That's the three master in line next to load on the wharf there by the elevator.

Summer hailed them his deep voice ringing clear over the water. "Mollie McIntyre, Ben! Pass us a line and get your yawl boat over to tow in. You're next to load."

Mollie frowned in puzzlement while Ben rubbed his sideburn. They exchanged quizzical looks, Mollie shaking her head. As they hesitated, Summer added, "We heard about the *Julia*. You come on in and raft on me. When the *Katie S* is finished, you go get the rest of your load."

Ben still looking perplexed seemed about to object or perhaps ask a question, but Mollie gave him a nudge in the ribs. "Let's not argue!"

He glanced at her again, nodded once, and then turned with a grin and a wave and called back, "Aye aye Captain Joe. And thank ye greatly!"

By noonday dinner the *Gazelle* was bound for Oswego with a full ten thousand bushels under her hatches. And the brisk clearing westerly that had come sweeping in with a welcome blue sky and sun after two soggy days took her across to Oswego before supper time. As she entered the harbor behind the tug and passed near the Northwestern elevator, Mouse called out from the foredeck, "I think they want us over there."

Following his gesture Mollie saw several men on the wharf by the elevator waving and pointing. She also saw other men on the schooner just aft of the vessel under the chutes doing the same. Someone tooted a horn, and ahead of them the tug slowed. As they glided up close astern the tug's mate called back, "You're to go there, I guess," and a few minutes later that's where *Gazelle* lay. Next in line to unload.

The *Julia* again. The whole harbor, it seemed, had heard of the rescue. Apparently word had also gotten around about *Gazelle's* remaining mortgage balance and due date, too, much to Mollie's chagrin. She suspected Hannah might have played a part in this. Well, after all, it was a matter of public record, and there was nothing shameful about it. At least half the vessels in this harbor were probably carrying mortgages.

A week later with two more runs completed and another three hundred dollars salted away, the lake decided that Mollie and her crew needed a taste of times to come. The schooner had set out around noon with a fresh westerly and once clear of the Ducks and out in the main part of the lake, the ship and crew found things getting pretty lively. After a solid gust with real authority had put the *Gazelle's* lee scuppers under, Ben decided to call out the watch below to shorten sail.

Responding to the all hands on deck call, Mollie hurried up from the cabin. Once topside she looked to windward and was startled by the wind's strength and the noticeable drop in the temperature from the morning's mild air. Now the near gale played upon the lines and stays of the ship's rig with a hearty roar overhead, while the snarl of breaking waves close aboard sounded a harsh counter point.

"Got to get the outer jib in and put a reef in the main," said Ben. "Will you take the wheel?"

Mollie nodded and moved quickly to replace Nate. Ben sent him forward to help Tommy lower the jib and jib topsail and lash them down. Zach, Mouse and Ben would reef the main.

The schooner was tearing along on a close reach, and Mollie braced herself against the hard pull of the wheel. *Gazelle* had plenty of helm all right. Too much for comfort. The lee scuppers were flowing with water at times filling the deck half way to the hatch covers. Up forward Mollie heard the sharp rifle shot sounds of the jibs flogging as sheets were slacked and the halyards released. She peered forward anxiously as the fast building close spaced steep waves burst over the lee bow in a welter of white. Nate and Tommy worked for what seemed a long time to lash down the jibs as they stood on the chains below the jib boom drenched by spray. When the ship pitched her bows down into the waves, solid water rose up to their waists. She gripped the wheel tighter and worried each time the jib boom dipped. The boys were experienced, but the water was cold, and the ship was moving fast. If a man lost his grip out there and fell, the schooner would run him over instantly.

After what seemed like an hour, the headsails were secured. Now without the sail forward to balance the ship, steering was even harder. Mollie's arms ached with the strain. Ben motioned for her to head up into the wind a couple of points as he and the two less experienced crew stood by the halyards. She saw Ben saying something to Mouse, probably cautioning him about keeping a turn of line on the pin to check the sail's descent before he moved toward the reef tackle. Mollie had seen a sail once come down out of control-the heavy gaff and sail had pulled the halyard through the mate's hands and flayed the skin right off them. You didn't want a big spar like that thrashing around up there either. Sails tore apart and gaff jaws broke when that happened.

Mouse and Zach did well, but she was relieved when the reef was in and the mainsail safely set again. Ben came aft water running off him as if he'd been swimming.

"How's she doing?"

"Much easier steering now," answered Mollie taking one hand off the wheel to show she no longer needed all her strength to keep on course.

"I'm going to leave the fore up for now. The faster we get across, the quicker we'll get into Oswego. Maybe that way, we'll be there before she kicks up too much more."

Mollie agreed. Already she could see the south shore as a thin dark line that was beginning to appear over an increasing span of horizon ahead. They would be at Oswego in two hours at this rate.

Oswego in a strong west wind was dangerous. With nearly two hundred miles of open water to windward, its entrance saw some of the biggest seas anywhere on Lake Ontario each fall when westerly gales blew. Those waves slammed into the stone jetties and then bounced off reflecting back into the lake to create a confused chaos of steep sharp edged seas, some of them the size of a house. Aggravating the backwash was the current from the river. After fall rains, its flow sometimes ran hard out through the entrance. When the seas felt the current, they suddenly steepened and grew. And then there was the bar, that shoal over which the waves tripped and fell with such lethal force. It seemed like in the last few years at least one or two ships were wrecked there every season. Oswego, the deadliest port on the lake, had killed Will and Ben's father. It would surely kill again this fall.

After Nate came aft to resume his place at the wheel, Mollie stayed on deck. They were clipping along, but with the reduced sail the ship was behaving well. She looked downwind off to the east uneasily. They might be able turn around and slog back toward Kingston or maybe try for the mouth of the St. Lawrence if Oswego looked too rough, but there was no other south shore alternative with a west wind. And the decision must be made now while they were still offshore.

"Nothing but Mexico Bay if we can't get in," she said to Ben.

"Mexico Bay and a hard sand shore," he agreed.

Nothing was said about turning back. As they neared Oswego harbor's entrance, the sight of the white smother of foam bursting up from the jetties made her grip the rail tightly. But Ben standing next to Nate, the best steersman of the crew, said "It doesn't look bad yet. We can do her."

The moment *Gazelle* got her nose into the harbor the little *James Moray* was there to take her hawser. The tug snatched her in, and a tired wet relieved crew made fast by the elevator to unload, five hours after leaving Kingston. Fast sailing, for certain, but no one was sorry it was over.

That evening at supper, the wind increased in strength. It rattled blocks and slatted lines and keened and moaned in *Gazelle's* rigging. It's the first full fall gale of the season, thought Mollie. Not the last though. At times the ship trembled with the wind's force aloft, and the dock lines creaked loudly.

Feeling the vessel shiver during the gusts, Tommy turned to ask his friend, "What did you think of that little romp?" Tommy was an old salt now, with this summer plus a whole season behind him last year as cabin boy with Will on the *Alma*.

Zach shook his head, "I didn't think much of it."

"How about you, Mouse?"

"I guess it was all right. It wasn't Cape Horn or anything."

Tommy replied, "It wasn't very cold either. Just you wait 'til next month when your hands are numb and your feet are soaking wet and it's black as a hole while you're trying to find the right line to pull. That's why the pay for deckhands goes up three dollars a month in November."

"Well, it beats being home getting kicked around by my old man. I'll stick it out right here. And I don't need a raise neither. We gotta get that note paid off."

"How much more do we need?" Tommy asked Mollie.

She sighed, "Too much I'm afraid. About two thousand dollars."

"We'll do her," said Mouse. "A dozen trips. We'll whip that debt, you wait."

After supper, the boys and Ben decided a short tack up to the Great Laker for a tankard or two of ale was in order. Mouse, after a gentle reminder from his ship owner, decided reluctantly to hike over the bridge to his family's house on the east side to see his Mom for an hour or two. He was emphatic that he would not spend the night with his family. Having had his own bunk on the *Gazelle*, he was now above sharing a bed with a younger brother.

Mollie's arms still ached from hanging on to the wheel that afternoon, and her eye lids kept trying to close, so after reading for a few minutes by her bunk she turned out her lamp and gratefully climbed into bed. In the darkness the wind continued to blow at near gale force. She lay still listening to its moans and shrills overhead in the rig and wondered what the next few weeks would bring. Despite Mouse's optimism, the possibility of making a dozen more trips was far from certain. Would they scatter then, each off to his or her own life? Tommy will ship on another schooner she was certain. Nate might join Ben in the boatyard if there was enough work. And Zach, he'll head back to the family farm as quick as he can get there. I wish I had five more like Mouse, she thought. When his strength matched his spunk he'd be a grand one to have on deck. He'll find another ship for sure. He's never going back to the docks or to factory work.

She would miss them. She would miss the cheerful banter at meal time, and she'd miss the strength she drew from them as they worked the ship together. Never had a single one questioned her decision to hang onto Will's dream. They were proud of their ship. Will's dream was hers now. And theirs. Giving up the *Gazelle* was going to be like cutting her arm off. As she lay there in her bunk, she drew a long breath trying to relax her tense muscles and turn her thoughts from defeat. She would miss the swing of the deck underfoot and the feel of the free wind blowing past. Going as cook with Father wouldn't be the same as being owner of her own vessel. She was in control of her destiny (at least a bit) now, and she didn't want to give that up. And then there was all the money she owed to Hannah and Father and Uncle John. At a cook's wage it would take forever to pay them back. *Gazelle* could earn it in one more season if the freights held up.

She finally drifted off to sleep as she tried to count up exactly how much they had put away towards the debt. When she awoke with morning light she could still hear the wind, and the lake, too, booming and bellowing outside. They'd make no money this day. They were wind bound in port.

Chapter Twenty four

"There will never be a new world order until women are a part of it."
Alice Paul

In the afternoon, Mollie decided to walk up to the top of the hill west of the harbor to look at the lake. When she reached the heights and stood looking towards Canada, she could see the water was still very angry. The wind pushed and shoved her around up there on the heights, and the waves rolled in from the west crashing ashore in endless procession. Spindrift and foam streaked the steel gray water with white. Often the seas crashed clean over the harbor breakwater in a smother of foam and spray. Low shreds of clouds scudded overhead, and the dark horizon was jagged with rollers. The air was downright sharp, she thought, as she drew her cape around her more tightly. Tomorrow it would be settled enough to leave. But today she was content to be in port.

Buffeted by the northwest wind, Mollie scanned the expanse of savage water. On days like these, when seen from safe ashore, the lake had a majesty to it. Here, with her feet planted safely on solid ground she loved to see it so powerful and unfettered. A gull streaked past overhead, its wings set, and she followed it with her eyes, envying its casual mastery of the tempest. To be a gull free and swift high in the sky would be a fine thing. But it would be heavy going out there for the *Gazelle* today. It was a good day to be in port.

She was about to start back down the hill when her eye caught an irregularity breaking the lake's horizon. There was something there. A bird? A seventh wave bigger than all others? It was the rigging of a vessel. She squinted against the wind seeking details. The vessel was a three master, scudding along with just a scrap of sail. After a minute or two as she watched, she could pick out the double reefed main and fore, no mizzen and a fore staysail. The vessel was moving quickly running before the wind. After a few more minutes, Mollie could see the plumb stem and steeved bowsprit of a schooner sized to fit the Welland Canal locks and a white painted hull. As the vessel neared, she watched it dropping into the trough, its hull disappearing among the big seas, then rising again. Those are twelve footers at least, out there or maybe bigger. That steeply steeved jib boom looked familiar. Could it be the *Anowa*? Then she saw the schooner take a heavy roll, showing the lead colored bottom.

"Father!" she gasped aloud.

Mollie turned and ran down the hill back to harbor and the *Gazelle* as fast as the shore going skirt around her legs would allow. As she ran, she thought of the channel entrance where so many ships and crews had died, right on Oswego's doorstep. And there was nothing that anyone could do to help.

Ben and the boys tumbled out from below at her breathless hail. They joined her hurrying down the wharf to get a clear view of the entrance. Here, they saw the old canaller's mastheads swinging in wide arcs against the sky as she neared the entrance. Ben put an arm around Mollie and drew her close.

Only a few hundred yards now before the *Anowa* had to jibe over and shoot into the narrow opening between the jetties. It was too rough for the small tug *James Moray* to risk going out into the lake after her. The tug waited with steam up just inside the entrance. Mollie put a fist up against her mouth. Behind her Tommy fretted about the *Morgan's* absence. The big tug had been called out to Sodus Bay yesterday to pull a schooner off the beach there. Then it had been too rough to get back to Oswego. Captain Thomas would have to sail in through the entrance unaided.

Just off the entrance the foresail jibed over, then the main. The vessel altered course swinging around almost broadside to the steep seas. Mollie heard Tommy's breathless curse as the *Anowa* staggered a few yards outside the entrance and lurched heavily towards the lee jetty. Ben's arm tightened around her but she didn't feel it. She shivered with the cold. And dread. A freak sharp peaked wave came up behind the ship looming above her stern. Mollie expected to see it topple and crash onto the deck, washing the man away from the wheel. With no one on the helm, the schooner would be doomed. The next wave would slam the *Anowa* into the stone jetty cracking the old hull like an egg.

Not again, she thought. *Please, not more men's bodies battered against the rocks. Not Father.* After so many years of sailing all the lakes, to die on Oswego's doorstep? Duncan's death and the loss of so many others flashed through her mind.

But the old canaller still had some fight in her. She lifted to the big wave and rode it down half the length of the channel. She swept over the bar with white broken water foaming alongside, and settled into the trough ready for the next wave. Luckily though even steeper, it was far smaller. Instead of smashing down on her decks, it broke just astern and shoved her the rest of the way to safety where the *James Moray* hovered ready to snatch her into the calm harbor.

When the *Anowa* came into the landing next to the elevator with her cargo of western wheat from Buffalo, the *Gazelle*'s entire crew waited to take her lines. Nate, Tommy and Ben caught the heaving lines, pulled the dock lines in and secured them. As soon as Mollie saw the boarding plank laid in place, she sprinted up it and into her father's arms as he stood by the rail. After a long embrace, she stepped back to look at Captain Tom.

He's aged ten years since I saw him in July, she thought.

"I didn't expect such a welcoming committee but it's good to see you all," said the *Anowa's* captain, and he put his hands on Mollie's shoulders and gave her a gentle shake. "I trust your vessel was safe in port this past day or two young lady."

Ben had now joined them and he grinned, "Yes sir, Captain Thomas. *Gazelle* was snug as a bug in port since yesterday. When did you leave the canal and how was it?"

"Well, it picked up yesterday evening a couple hours after we left. So we just shortened her right down and loafed along easy all night. I figured if it got real bad we could always run her on up to Kingston. But about off Sodus Bay it started dropping down a little so I figured we'd be ok to go on into Oswego. I didn't figure on not having a tug out there, though." He laughed. "But we muddled through. I've got a good crew and old *Anowa's* been in here so often she could probably find her own way in without a helmsman."

Mollie said, "When you get squared away here, come over and have supper with us. I have pie left from dinner.

"I would be right pleased to do that. I guess it's too late to start unloading here now so I'll be along directly."

Mollie and Ben went back down the gang plank to rejoin the boys and all the ship's company headed back to *Gazelle*. As she walked along, Mollie thought how drawn and aged Father had looked. Clearly his all nighter on the lake had taken its toll. Few lake captains lasted in the trade much past fifty. She knew Father was well into his fifties now.

Mollie had fired up the stove and baked several apple pies and some muffins as well, for noon day dinner in port, so there were still two pies left. That, along with sliced cold beef from the good roast they had enjoyed for their dinner, made an excellent evening meal. Captain Thomas ate heartily, for there hadn't been much grub aboard the storm tossed *Anowa* for the last day or so. When he was finished and pushed his plate back with a contented sigh, he said "If you do give up being a ship owner there's surely a job in the galley next season for you somewhere."

Mouse asked, "What was it like out there Captain Thomas?"

Mollie's father settled back in his chair as Mollie poured him a cup of coffee. He looked over at Mouse and said, "It got pretty dang brisk for awhile last night. I heard that in Chicago when this went through it went from 65 and sunny to snow and blowing hard in fifteen minutes. It wasn't that cold out on the lake here, but it might have been in the 40's. It came on strong after about ten o'clock or so. That's when we took the second reef in, after the seas started washing over the rail."

He addressed his next comment to Mollie with a sigh, "I'm not as young as I used to be. These all night affairs do make a man feel his years."

He sipped his coffee and then asked, "Did you hear about the *Alpena?* Up on Lake Michigan?"

Ben and Mollie both shook their heads. Captain Thomas said soberly, "We got word via the telegraph in Buffalo. She went down, with over a hundred passengers aboard. They were all lost. She was a wooden side wheeler. She was fourteen years old and sailed out of Grand Haven on Friday. It was as mild and sunny as you could want, but that night it came on hard out of the southwest blowing a whole gale.

"She was sighted the next morning laying on her beam ends adrift. My guess is she rolled so badly in those seas that one paddlewheel came out long enough for the strain to snap her shaft. Anyway, after that, no one saw her again. A lot of wreckage came ashore near Holland along with thousands of apples. They say there was wreckage strewed for fifty miles. They knew it was from her because of the apples and because the piano from her saloon came ashore. So she must have gone down off there somewhere. Not a one of the crew and passengers aboard her survived."

A heavy silence fell over the table. Then Captain Thomas said as he gazed down at his empty dinner plate, "You know I've been thinking. Maybe this will be my last year." He looked up at Mollie and said, "I've sailed the lakes for twenty five seasons as captain and I've never lost a ship or a man. I'd like to quit while I can still say that."

Mollie, seeing his face etched with fatigue, thought he is almost sixty. It came to her as a bit of a shock. She'd rarely thought of her father as being old, for he moved easily and quickly about on deck and never complained of aches or rheumatism. Captain Thomas had started sailing on his own father's ship when he was thirteen. He had been a mate by the time he was twenty and a captain a few years later. It was hard to imagine him without a deck under his feet.

Captain Thomas evidently saw in Mollie's face some of the surprise she was feeling for he offered an explanation. "Truth to tell Mollie it's not just old age and low freights. My partner Horace Winfield is retiring. He sold his shares in the ship to a big company out of Cleveland. He was the majority partner, but he always let me run the ship as I saw fit. But if I have to answer to a board of directors, well, I'm too old a sea dog to jump at their say so. I can't see working as a wage slave for anyone. Times are changing anyway, with the unions trying to push up seamen's pay and the steamers and railroads now taking our freight. You're better off with a family ship. And you can get *Gazelle* into harbors like Belleville and Napanee and Dark Harbor where the big steamers can't go."

"What would you do ashore?"

"Well, there's that orchard your uncle and I set out back on the farm. Those trees are staring to bear nicely now. He says we picked five hundred bushels last year. I might just go back and take up apple farming. I think one could make a tidy living off that orchard." He paused and looked at Mollie with concern in his eyes. "The only thing is, if I do go on the beach, I won't be able to give you a job as cook if you were to need it next year."

Mollie met his eyes. "Oh Father, don't worry about that. I'll keep the ship. And if I don't, well, I'll find a job on some other schooner somewhere."

"I suppose you could," said Captain Thomas, "though times are so slow it may not be easy to take a man's job next season. And I hate to think of you ending up on a boat with a captain like Burton."

Mollie thought of Hannah's experience. Such attacks and assaults were far from rare. Just last year there had been an incident on the upper lakes. A schooner had run aground because the mate had been down below fooling with the cook. It had prompted another round of newspaper editorials calling once again for a ban on female cooks.

"If anyone tries to have their way with me, I'll give them a good fight. And I won't ship with anyone that expects me to wear skirts aboard. If I can't wear my bloomer gear, then I won't cook. That ought to weed out the worst of the skirt chasers."

Captain Thomas laughed. "Maybe you're right. Assuming you can find a captain that tolerates your bloomers, you'll probably manage."

But even as Millie tried to sound cheerful, she felt a clutch of foreboding in the pit of her stomach. What if the ship owners got together and did ban female cooks? Or if she managed to find a job, what if she got stuck on some boat fifty miles from shore with another Joe Blake? Remembering Blake's powerful grip, she knew the odds of successful resistance were nil. She had to make a living somehow, though. Better to risk a chance of rape aboard ship then to end up like those bent figures she saw shuffling down the streets in early morning on their way to work as washer women or scullery maids. Ashore she might end up in a factory in Oswego or Auburn working fourteen hour days six days a week, for a few years before her lungs were ruined by consumption or she was caught in the machinery and permanently crippled. Or killed. And when you couldn't work any longer, there was only the county poor farm.

She had to keep the ship.

Chapter Twenty five

"Knowing what must be done does away with fear." - Rosa Parks

The next day brought more unwelcome news. It had dawned dull and cool with low clouds and a light raw northerly wind. With the calmer conditions, the crew lost no time after breakfast in preparing to get underway. But after the boys had pulled the sail covers off, Ben discovered a crack in the fore gaff near the jaws.

"It must have happened when we were reefing Tuesday. We'll have to repair this," he said.

Mollie thinking of more heavy weather to come nodded. No argument here. They would be badly crippled without the foresail if another stiff wind were to come up and break the gaff.

"I'll go see if Hannah can help us get some spar wood for a new one. No sense in making a half way job this time of year."

The gales of November would test their vessel to the utmost. Delay or not, repairs must be made. The *Gazelle* must be as strong and fit as possible for the season's last weeks, and every detail counted. Mollie hurried off to the office building.

She opened the door to find Hannah and male worker beside her at her desk. The man beside Hannah turned and greeted her with a smile as his dark eyes danced with pleasure.

"Mrs. McIntyre, how grand to see you again."

"Dan. You're back."

"Thank goodness. They can have that life down there in Gotham. I'm glad to be back here in Oswego. But what brings you into our grand quarters so early and in such haste?"

Mollie explained the need for a new fore gaff, and Dan said, "I know exactly where to get some good spar grade spruce. I'll have the dockers to fetch it down to you immediately." With that he donned his hat, swept up his cape and hastened off.

Hannah smiled, "Looks like he hasn't lost interest in the welfare of the *Gazelle* and her owner."

Mollie returned Hannah's grin with grimace. Hannah persisted, "You could do a lot worse than the boss's son."

"Oh, Hannah, I don't even want to think about getting involved with another man. Not now anyway!"

Hannah nodded, "I know. It's nice to answer only to yourself. Still Dan is not a bad sort."

But Mollie shook her head. "I've got to get back and tell Ben about the spar."

Hannah watched out the window seeing her go with hurried steps down the wharf. Only a little more than a month left now before her last payment.

Mouse was still sweeping the chips off the deck as the ship towed out late that afternoon. The wind sock up at the mainmast truck hung limp, as he dumped the scraps overboard. Mollie watched the dull gray water ripple astern. It would be a slow passage this night. It was now late October with only a few weeks left before the close of navigation. They had worked hard, prodigiously hard since April, trimming, moving and lifting hundreds of tons of lumber, grain, and coal by muscle power. Though *Gazelle* had merely sailed back and forth across the lake between the U.S. and Canada with no single trip being much over a hundred and fifty miles, she had carried thousands of tons of cargo, traveling a total distance greater than across the Atlantic. Her stiff heavy canvas sails had been raised, trimmed, lowered and furled, her gear had been shifted, lugged, toted, and hauled, her bilges had been pumped, and her anchors weighed all entirely by man boy and occasionally woman power. Mollie couldn't even guess how many bushels of potatoes she had peeled or how many barrels of flour had been transformed into dough to be kneaded formed and baked to fuel those muscles. Today, under the cloak of low iron colored cloud, she felt the months of labor deep in her bones.

But when Ben signaled for help in raising the mainsail, a job for all hands, she stepped to the wheel to steer as Nate went forward to the main mast. Once fore and main were set and the towline cast off, the slight ripple of water under the counter quieted as the ship coasted slowly to a stop. The lake had flattened utterly from the gales of two days ago. Today it lay like glass around them as they sat becalmed while dusk gathered.

Ben sent Mouse and Tommy aloft to cast off the gaskets on the topsails, and he and Zeb and Nate ran the jibs up. *Gazelle* sat on her reflection upon the mirror like water as the early dusk of nearly November settled upon her. The dull weather and lack of wind further dampened Mollie's own spirits already subdued from the news of her father's retirement. Ben came back to join her on the after deck as she served out the brief after dinner dog watch on the helm.

"That was tough news yesterday about the *Alpena*. Were you surprised that Captain Thomas is thinking of going ashore?"

"I was," answered Mollie. "But I don't blame him for it. He is nearly sixty."

Looking away from the ship before her, Mollie met Ben's eyes and said, "It's hard work being a captain."

Ben answered with a grin, "Not on this ship with this crew. Why things practically run themselves."

Mollie taking in the dark smudges under Ben's eyes and the deeply furrowed lines of his face said, "Well, you look closer to forty than twenty after just one summer at it."

Ben gazed up at the main topsail with studied nonchalance. "It's that ship owner. Any captain will tell you how hard it is to have a ship owner looking over their shoulder all the time."

Mollie swatted his arm. "Why, I never tell you to do anything you wouldn't do anyway. Not after that squall!"

Ben raised his arms as if to fend off an attack, then dropped them with a laugh as he saw Mollie's smile. He grinned at having cheered up his ship owner at least briefly. Then in a more serious tone he said, "So you think we'll all be retired from the lake after next month?"

Mollie leaned against the wheel box and gazed out at the calm lake. "Probably. I don't see any way we're going to make a dozen trips between now and the close. I've tried to figure every possible savings. Even if we dropped our insurance it looks hopeless."

"We can't to do that. The ship's mortgaged to Sloan."

"It wouldn't be enough anyway. All we can do is carry on and hope we can talk Sloan into another extension assuming he's in shape to do so."

Ben offered, "Well, you charmed him into one. Maybe he's good for another."

Mollie frowned, "I think we've gotten all the slack he's going to give us. And Heaven help us if his son in law takes charge. But we shall try our best to keep going."

A light northerly wind came up at the end of Mollie's brief turn at the wheel and stirred the *Gazelle* into moving again. But the night was dark with overcast skies and a haze low over the water that cut visibility down to a couple of miles. Ben cautioned the crew to keep a sharp lookout, a warning they scarcely needed. No one had forgotten their encounter with the *Lady Of The Lake* on a night much like this.

The wind stayed light as *Gazelle* crept along slowly close hauled making a couple of knots. Mouse and Nate came on watch at midnight, and a few minutes later a light mist began prickling their faces as tiny droplets formed on their wool jackets. Nate had the wheel while Mouse, remembering the moment he had turned the helm the wrong direction on a dark night much like this one, stood forward, scanning the blackness and listening. Ben was also prowling the deck after three hours in his bunk. He didn't like the feel of the air, the flat lake notwithstanding.

He, too, was remembering the collision. Fog was a curse to be sure. There had been that wreck just a couple weeks ago when the steamer *Ocean Foam* had run down the little two master *Sea Bird* off Charlotte. It had happened a day or two after their own collision, and the schooner, struck amidships, had gone down in minutes taking two of her crew members with her. One of them was the cook, trapped below in her cabin.

Mouse called aft, "Mr. Ben, what's that over there to port? Could it be a light?"

Ben looked off to see a dim orange glow in the mist. A lurch of fear roiled his stomach. He gripped the forward mainmast shroud tightly as he strained to see through the darkness. "Nate, helm down. Bring her about. Come on Mouse. We'll shift those jibs."

Mouse following him forward was asking why they were turning towards the glow when they all heard the first whistle blast.

Full throated, unexpectedly close, a steamer was crying in desperate distress. Fire! Fire! Ship afire! For perhaps a minute the repeated pleas of the hooting whistle continued. Then there sounded a long last wail as the steersman tied down the whistle and left the wheel house.

"On deck all hands!" shouted Ben.

Fire, the absolute worst thing a captain or crew had to ever face aboard a wooden ship. A stray spark landing on the upper deck, a ship filled with passengers, each with their own oil lamps and candles in their cabins, a mishap firing the boilers, or in the galley, even a stray ash from a pipe or cigar, could destroy a vessel in minutes. Not only the hull but almost everything in it was flammable.

Gazelle steadied on her new course and crept toward the strengthening orange glow. Then the drizzle stopped and the mist shifted. No more than a half mile away lay the burning steamer. As *Gazelle's* crew stared with horror, they heard a dull thud. A fountain of flame sparks and debris shot upward from the burning ship. A boiler had gone. She wouldn't stay afloat long now.

She was a small side wheeler about 150 feet or so, and brilliant tongues of flame now leaped twenty feet or more into the air. They had already engulfed the pilot house and much of her topsides. When Mollie joined Ben and Mouse at the rail, she saw the ravenous flames were fast devouring the ship's upper works. The *Gazelle* was closing at a snail's pace as her sails filled with the light wind. Mollie pictured conditions below decks, each stateroom now a furnace, each hall and passage a flue of fire. The leaping flames pushed the night back, and the dying steamer lay in a circle of fire lit water. The crackle and whip snap of incineration sounded over the hum and low roar of flame pouring out of hatches, pilot house windows, and ports.

"Dear God, can't we go any faster? What can we do?"

Ben said, "We'll get the yawl down. You, Mollie, take the wheel. Sail right by her. When you get close throw every board and keg and deck box we've got for them in the water."

A throng of passengers and crew members crowded the aft end of the hurricane deck where the flames had not yet reached. The *Gazelle* was close enough for her crew to see two men silhouetted against the flame trying to launch a boat. The tackles started, halted, and then jammed in the pulleys. The empty boat dropped unevenly, hitting the water on its side. It filled immediately. Some of the passengers began leaping into the water. A dozen or more plunged down from the upper deck. Several men and one woman, clutching an infant, clung to the wheel guards just above the lake's calm surface. Heads bobbed in the water ahead of the schooner. Some of the passengers struggled and thrashed in the icy lake.

While Ben and Tommy lowered the yawl, Mollie steered directly towards the blaze. They drew close enough to feel heat from the burning ship as it lit *Gazelle's* decks casting dim shadows that jumped and flickered. Mollie and the boys flung gear, wooden buckets, planks and even the stovewood box from the galley into the lake for the passengers to grab. They then hove the ship to for lowering the yawl.

Ben and Tommy leaped down into the boat and pulled hard for the steamer. Mollie put the helm up as Ben had directed her to and set the ship to slowly sailing back and forth to windward staying as close to the burning steamer as they dared. For one eerie moment the ship's whistle sounded again in a low breathy sigh as if the steamer were moaning in its last agony. The flames had heated the remaining boiler enough to drive a last whisp of steam through the tied down whistle. A breath of wind moved across their decks and briefly bent the flames downward. The fire responded by busting forth with terrible ferocity, leaping as high as *Gazelle's* mastheads. Several pieces of fire the size of blankets broke off from the main blaze and flew upwards into the darkness.

"She'll go soon now," murmured Nate beside her.

A hail sounded off *Gazelle's* quarter, and black against the reflected flames in the water Mollie saw a ship's boat a few yards away riding low in the water packed with people. She put the schooner up into the wind to stop, and as the boat came alongside, Nate caught the painter and made it fast. Mollie sent Zeb and Mouse forward to lower the jibs and back the staysail. She slipped a lash on the wheel and hurried to the rail.

A young man scrambled over the side. He was hatless barefoot and without a jacket. "We've a burned man aboard. He's unconscious, and the mate's injured."

Several other passengers also climbed aboard with help from Nate and Mollie to make room in the lifeboat for the transfer of the injured. Among the passengers was a young woman clad only in a night dress. Despite her disheveled appearance, she spoke calmly to Mollie. "Mr. Burrell, the mate, is in terrible pain and can hardly move. We've several people who were pulled from the water. They must be made dry and warm. Can I assist?"

"Take them back there into my cabin. Mr. Burrell, too," Mollie said pointing to the deckhouse. "I'll go start the stove. You can put the unconscious man in my bunk that's made up."

A second older woman, who had also made her way onto the deck unaided, came forward. She, too, was clad only in night clothes, her long gray hair hanging in braids. But like the younger woman, she stood straight and steady as she spoke with a heavy accent. "Show me der stove. I vill start fire."

Mollie led the two women aft to the cabin door saying to the younger one, "The blankets and bedding are in the long lockers by the bunks."

As she led them down the steps, she hesitated for an indecisive moment. What should she do first? There were so many in need, where to start?

The older woman said with a gesture towards the other female passenger, "I'm Helga. I am cook for Miss Flowers."

224

Mollie pointed out the wood dumped beside the stove. "If you could heat water, we'll get the people dried out and give them hot drinks."

Later, looking back on that dreadful long night, Mollie recalled isolated incidents that stood out in the mind's eye with great clarity almost like photographic images amidst the blur of horror. One was of the dark haired young passenger, Diana Flowers, working with Helga to bundle another older woman shuddering with the cold into dry blankets as they settled her beside the stove. She remembered Ben and Tommy coming alongside in the yawl with scarcely six inches of freeboard and seven passengers crammed aboard, among them a young mother clutching an infant. Seared into Mollie's memory was the sight of a male passenger leaping off the upper deck, his clothes afire, to plunge into the black water and disappear. And she would long recall the sight of a man in the water a few yards from the ship hanging onto a plank with one hand and holding a woman by her hair to keep her face from slipping under. Just as the yawl reached them, the man let go of the plank and vanished.

One female passenger nearly drove Mollie from the cabin with her hysterical shrieks and cries for her missing husband. Diana got her settled on a chair near the stove, but her incessant whimpering and sobbing were clearly unnerving the other survivors. As Mollie gritted her teeth trying to ignore the woman, she spotted Reuban who had emerged from behind a chest. She went over and picked him up and whispered, "I need your help." Reuban settled trustingly in her arms. He loved being held, and he beamed as only a contented cat can. She carried him over to the grieving passenger and placed him gently on her lap thinking, "If she hates cats or loves them, either way hopefully she'll shut up for a moment."

The woman who had been sitting hunched and weeping with her arms tightly folded across her chest, straightened, looked at the cat and then up at Mollie. She placed one arm around Reuban and began to stroke him with the other hand. Reuban immediately decided the lap was satisfactory, settled, and began to purr. After a loud sniffle, the woman said softly, "You look like my Marmalade."

Mollie moved off anxious to deal with something besides consoling the bereaved, something like making tea or finding a blanket.All together nearly three dozen passengers and crew members were pulled from the water or plucked off the burning wreck that night. The soaked exhausted shivering castaways were dried and warmed, and the crew dug deep into their own sea chests to hand out what spare clothing they had. Helga and

Diana Flowers worked alongside Mollie dealing with the most acute needs. Gradually, as night gave way to morning's wee hours, the now packed cabin quieted. As Mollie was helping Helga hang some soaked garments to dry behind the range, Diana came up and touched her softly on the shoulder.

"Can you come look at this man? We must do something."

Mollie followed her to the side of the burned stoker lying in her bunk. When she saw the man's torso, bile backed up in her throat, and she nearly gagged. She had never seen anything like this. Most of his shirt had been burned off, and the flames had seared his left side so deeply that in places the flesh resembled cooked meat. Oozing fluid lay over the red and black patchwork of his flesh. His left forearm and hand were charred, and before she looked quickly away to keep her heaving stomach's contents in place, Mollie saw a fleeting impression of exposed bone showing at the tips of two fingers.

Oddly, except for a bit of soot and grime, the man's face was unmarked. It was very pale as he lay there, his chest rising and falling in rapid shallow gasping breaths.

Dianna whispered, "feel his brow."

Mollie touched the man gently and pulled away quickly. He was cold. Death had laid its hand upon him already. But at her touch his eyes opened. They were gray, much like Ben's but clouded with pain. "Bring the laudanum, it's there, Mollie said to Diana gesturing at the small foot locker that contained the ship's medical supplies.

She measured out a large dose of the drug and put it to the dying man's lips. She hardly dared touch him as she lifted his head slightly, fearing the agony this movement must cause him. However, he swallowed the opiate and closed his eyes. As she laid his head down carefully, Mollie looked over at Diana who silently shook her own head. Sickened by the sight of the scorched flesh and feeling utterly helpless in the face of such suffering, Mollie wanted to wail in grief and bolt from the cabin. She whispered to Diana that she would try to tend to Mr. Burrell's broken arm now. Diana nodded. Relieved to be dismissed, Mollie walked off hurriedly, but Diana stayed by the stoker and clasped his unburned hand gently until he slipped away into unconsciousness.

Chapter Twenty six

"then I will speak upon the ashes..." Sojourner Truth

An hour after the burning remains of the steamer had settled beneath the water, the schooner *Frank Merrill* arrived. She, too, had seen the flames and used the light wind to hurry best as possible to the scene. She took up the search for any survivors still clinging to wreckage in the water, and Ben and Mollie fearing for the injured and burned among their company, decided to make for Oswego, the nearest port.

All through the night, the women worked with the survivors, while Ben and the boys set every bit of sail they had in the light breeze to urge the ship along. By the time dawn began to pale the east, the stoker had died. Nate and Tommy carried the body on deck and laid him out on the fore hatch shrouded from the view of the other passengers by a piece of old canvas. Ben told Mollie as they stood watching the morning light glint off the calm lake waters while the wink of the Oswego light off the jib boom faded into day, "We're lucky to have lost only one."

Mr. Burrell joined them as the smell of bacon began to perfume the damp cool morning. Despite the sleepless night, the pain of his burns and his splinted arm, he managed a shaky grin. "Helga's cooking up your entire ship's supply of bacon and eggs down there."

There's a lot of mouths to feed," answered Mollie. I'd best go help her."

"No. You sit, Mrs. McIntyre. She's got three other passengers helping her. You've done enough."

Ben looking him over asked, "How's that arm of yours?"

"Fine as long as Mrs. McIntyre keeps the laudanum flowing."

Mollie sitting on a deck box patted its surface beside her. "Please Mr. Burrell, take your ease. We're still several hours out with this light wind."

They sat in silence for a few minutes watching the pale silver disk of the morning sun struggle to burn through the low clouds. Slowly its reluctant light revealed the deck before them. The group took comfort in the normalcy of the well kept vessel around them and her slow but steady progress toward the harbor.

Burrell looking aloft at the topsails overhead said, "I started out in a boat about like this back in '66. I should have stayed with her. I don't ever want to go in steam again."

Mollie asked, "Do you know what started the fire?"

Burrell shook his head. "It didn't start in the engine room. The Chief didn't make it up on deck, but I saw one of the black gang before we jumped. He said our alarm was the first they knew of it."

Mollie shook her head slowly, "At least nine dead."

"There could have been thirty more if you hadn't come along when you did."

Ben asked, "Did you see what happened to the captain?"

Burrell 's face darkened. "The last I saw of Captain Winters he was launching a boat with two seamen and making a botch of it. I expect he's ashore right now making up a good story."

Mollie asked, "What kind of a story?"

Burrell growled, "An imaginary one. Captain Winter's is a drunk. I saw him nip at his flask at least three times on my watch. The second mate saw it, too. I spoke to Winters of it not an hour before the fire, and he got his back up and dismissed me from the bridge. He's probably ashore right now doing some fast talking."

No one said anything for a while after that. They sat listening to the quiet murmur of the water alongside and the soft creak of the sheet as the fore boom moved nearby, each busy with his or her own thoughts. One that kept returning to Mollie's mind though she consciously tried to forget it was of a woman leaping into the water and disappearing almost immediately, entangled and drawn down by her heavy clothing. Ben and Tommy in the yawl boat had seen her, too. They had pulled for the spot and found a life preserver. When Tommy picked it out of the water, the straps were still tightly knotted. She had slipped out of it after she hit the water. It was one of the few life preservers any of them had seen that night.

Ben must have been thinking of it, too, because he asked Burrell, "You wouldn't know when your last life preserver inspection took place would you?"

Burrell responded with a short sharp laugh, "Inspection? If you could call it that-yes, it was last month. And what a worthless load of trash was foisted on us, too."

"What do you mean?" asked Mollie.

"I mean that Captain Winter's son-in-law supplied them jackets, and his cousin did the inspection. They were Leduc's Tule Life Preservers and they're junk! After fifteen minutes in the water, the reeds soak up so much they weigh thirty pounds. Winter's son-in-law replaced the cork life preservers with those things saying they were "modern". Well, if modern means cheap then they were. You could see how poorly the baggy things fit."

Mollie nodded frowning, as she remembered a couple of the passengers coming aboard wearing the life preservers.

Ben caught her eye. "I think we ought to put one of those life preservers aside. Somebody might want to take a look at it when we get to shore."

Mollie got up. "I'll go do it now."

Four hours later Hannah looked out the window by her desk and saw the *Gazelle*. She to jumped to her feet exclaiming, "It's Mollie back already! There must be something wrong."

Dan peering out beside her said, "Her flag is at half mast."

"Perhaps there's been an accident. Should we get a doctor?"

Dan was already on his way out of the office, and after a moment of indecision Hannah followed him. She joined Dan, Clancy the longshoreman, and Andy Doyle the crew boss at the company wharf where the tug was bringing the schooner in.

"Looks like trouble," said Clancy.

"Looks like there was a wreck," said Andy. "There's twenty people aboard back there aft, and I'd say that's a stiff laid out on the hatch."

The heaving lines dropped before them, and Clancy Dan and Andy each grabbed a line and started hauling in the heavy dock lines as the tug nudged the ship into the wharf.

"I'll go get the harbor master and Isiah," said Hanna, and she jogged off to fetch her wheel.

Within a half hour word had gone around the harbor, and a flock of chattering quacking idlers had congregated on the Fitzhugh wharf. Andy Doyle appointed Clancy and another stevedore to keep the gawkers off the *Gazelle*, though they were unable to stop two reporters who slipped like ferrets through the throng and got themselves aboard to pepper the crew and survivors with questions. The agent for the Ontario Steamship Company arrived on a lathered horse, followed a short while later by an underwriter's representative. The *Gazelle's* main cabin became an impromptu and noisy hearing room as reporters shouted questions and various officials interrogated Ben, Mollie, Burrell, and some of the surviving male passengers. Then word came that the schooner *Lake's Queen* had just towed in with one of the steamer's lifeboats and more survivors, among them Captain Winters. The official folk promptly departed, heading for the schooner's berth and taking most of the onlookers with them.

The throng of strangers on *Gazelle's* decks thinned, and the confusion and clamor diminished. Thanks largely to Hannah's efforts, the survivors were given accommodations ashore and messages were sent by wire to families and concerned parties. The Canaler Chief Hotel sent word down that anyone needing a room for the night would have one for free. Not to be outdone, the Great Laker Restaurant sent a boy down to match it with an offer for dinner on the house.

By late afternoon nearly everyone had gone ashore. But as things were settling down, and Mollie and Ben were thinking the ordeal was nearly over, Isiah Fitzhugh came aboard looking sober.

"The underwriter wants to meet with you again tomorrow. He's been interviewing both Captain Winters and the mate. The coroner, Jonas Dutton, also will be convening an inquest tomorrow, and he, too, wishes to speak to you on this matter."

Mollie nodded, "Of course, we'll stay."

Ben said, "I've got a thing or two I'd like to tell them. And a life preserver that they should see."

"Very well. Dutton has promised to begin early as possible so you can leave after that."

Mollie replied, "There's no hurry. We'll need part of a day to get ourselves squared away and some of our provisions need restocking, too."

Breakfast had been stowed, the galley tidied and the debris and disorder on deck largely cleared away by the time the coroner, Isiah, the underwriter and several clerks and officials came filing aboard grim faced. Ben, Mollie and the cousins sat down with them around the crowded table leaving Zeb and Mouse free to go. The two youngest crew members headed ashore and split up. Zeb went off to explore the waterfront, and Mouse headed for the bridge to cross to the east side and visit his Mum. Or so he said.

As he strolled along enjoying his morning of freedom on a cool sunny late October day, he peered down into the river. He watched two gulls squabbling over something long deceased floating a few yards offshore.

He threw an experimental rock at the pale gray carcass the birds were arguing over. It struck with a satisfying soggy smack knocking a bit of decay off it. Mouse started pitching more rocks at the corpse with a vague idea of knocking it to pieces to make it disappear. The poor old river was disgusting enough without that bloated stinking thing in it.

He noticed a man with a well cut frock coat, silk vest, polished shoes and a top hat strolling along the wharf headed towards the *Gazelle*. Now what was that dandy doing there looking at the ship? Mouse noted the close set eyes and slight sneer on the young man's face and didn't like what he saw. Mouse casually backtracked still studying the murky water as if seeing something of great interest. Yes, the gent was definitely looking the *Gazelle* over.

Mouse said, "That's the ship that rescued those people from the steamer *Naiad*. Did you hear about it?"

"Ah," the man replied, "So this is the heroic crew's vessel. She looks stout and sturdy." Noticing Mouse's puzzled look he gestured over the river towards the Northeastern coal trestle. "That's my steamer, the *Miriam*. This vessel should serve very well as a consort to her."

"But the *Gazelle* belongs to Mrs. Mollie."

"Not after December first she won't. My father-in-law holds the note on her, and from what I hear Mrs. Mollie is nowhere close to paying it off. No, I'll be buying her then for the balance of the note. If I don't inherit first. She'll be very useful as a coal hulk."

With that the man sauntered off along the wharf, his head in the air whistling a verse of The Red Iron Ore softly.

"I'm glad that's over. I don't think I could have answered one more question," said Mollie at the evening meal.

"And I'm glad you set that preserver aside," answered Ben. "Whoever inspected those should be jailed for murder. For a few dollars saved eight people died."

"Did you see the steamer company man's face after you dropped it in the harbor and then pulled it out again?" asked Tommy. "He looked like he was going to bash someone. Why did it get so soggy and heavy so fast? What's a tule anyway?"

Ben answered, "Tule is a type of reed. It doesn't grow around here. It's hollow and air filled, but it soaks up water just like straw does."

Tommy said, "It's little wonder that woman slipped out of hers after she jumped in. Those baggy things full of reeds were so sloppy and slack."

Mollie reached for a piece of Johnny cake and considered the events of the day. Of all the questions, the droning, and the endless babble of words she had heard, she recalled most vividly the testimony of a passenger who pushed his way through the bystanders to speak to the coroner. He was young, dressed in some of Nate and Tommy's oversized ill fitting spare clothes, and his singed hair and face marked with a red burn stood out. With great vehemence he had insisted on speaking. He and his father had been traveling together aboard the steamer, heading home to Rochester, he said.

His father had awakened him in his stateroom by shouting and pounding on his cabin door. They had fled pursued by the inferno to the hurricane deck. The young man had choked with emotion as he spoke to the coroner of his last conversation with his father just before they had jumped into the lake.

"He told me at the Captain's poker game a quarrel broke out. Captain Winter stood suddenly and he or someone else knocked a lamp over. The table top was aflame in an instant. He said they tried to beat it out, but in a moment it spread around everywhere..."

Those, he told the silent listeners in the crowded room, were his father's last words. Moments later, they had leaped overboard together. The older man never surfaced.

Ben turned to Nate. "Tomorrow we're going to have a fire drill. And I want you to take all our life preservers out of the locker and check every one. Look for rat damage, chewed straps, or anything else. I want to know all is in order with them and that they're stowed where we can get them in a hurry.

"What kind of life preservers are they?" asked Mouse.

"They're cork block. Just like Mrs. White had on that day on the *Julia*."

Ben looked around the table. Everyone sat up a little, even Mollie under his grim gaze.

"I know we just got them a little while ago. But we should pull them out and look them over anyway. We should check them a couple times a season. And we're going to do an abandon ship drill, too. After we get underway tomorrow, I want everyone on deck by the main mast for it at my signal. We'll heave to and you'll all put on a life preserver properly. Unless it's rough we'll lower the yawl boat, too."

"I wonder how high she would ride with all of us aboard?" said Mollie thinking of the boat load of passengers Ben had rescued.

"A good question. Perhaps before we tow out we could put her over her in the river and find out how she looks with us all in her."

Nate spoke up, "Mollie and Mouse and me together weigh less than that one man you had in there last night. She'll take us all. She's McIntyre made."

Ben sat back and gave Nate a quick smile. "I'm sure you're right. But let's test her anyway. It would be interesting to check her freeboard."

"We'll toss Mouse overboard if we're too low," said Tommy giving Mouse a gentle poke.

To Mollie's surprise Mouse didn't respond with his usual vigor and quick tongue. Indeed, he had been unusually quiet at dinner. Perhaps he, too, had been affected by the sights and memories of the burning steamer. Though he was still full of energy, the last few days had left their mark on him.

As Mollie settled in to her bunk after supper, she was grateful for a quiet night in port. She had been so fatigued the day before she had been barely able to speak, let alone do any work by day's end. And last night as tired as she was, she had been plagued by terrible dreams. The last one that had awakened her, had her surrounded by flames. She heard screams and moans, and Ben and her father had been there, trying to pull someone through a burning door. She had seen it was Will, and his face was white like the dead stoker's. Then Ben's clothes had caught fire, and she had tried shout and warn him. But her throat had closed up and all she could was gasp.

All day the dream had stayed with her like a fit of the blues. Perhaps tonight would be better. Reuban hopped up on the bunk, looked at her with half closed eyes and purred. She gazed at the painting of the *Gazelle* on the bulkhead and wondered what kind of person could possibly betray his ship crew and passengers as Captain Winter had?

"People are so hard to understand," she said to the cat. Money was important to be sure, but it wasn't worth people's lives. Unlike a ship made of wood, people gave no hint of their soundness or inner scantlings. Some, when struck by adversity's iron maul resisted it like a tough piece of elm. But others lacking the interlocked grain of toughness fell apart as easily as straight grained pine.

"Like that woman you sat with Reuban. Why did she turn all hysterical while Diana Flowers pitched in as if she'd been through all of it before?"

Right now Mollie didn't feel very resilient. She felt splintered and split. She picked up Reuban and held him to her breast. She was exhausted. Twenty four hours of pure hell lay astern. She could not forget the sight of flailing thrashing drowning passengers in the black water that they had failed to reach in time. Their thin choked cries for help haunted her, still.

Chapter Twenty seven

"Life is a hard battle anyway"- Sojourner Truth

Mollie Ben and the boys ate breakfast as the wind whined and whimpered through the rig overhead. The October air had an edge to it, and the ship's company welcomed the stove's warmth as they sat at the table. There was little of the cheerful banter that usually prevailed on the rare occasions when the whole crew was able to eat together. Despite the flashes of light on the cabin sole as the sun ducked in and out of the wind driven clouds, the mood was somber. A stronger gust clattered the blocks overhead in the ship's rigging. Ben looked up.

"Blowing a small gale," he murmured to no one in particular.

Mollie pushed her plate of sausage and eggs away and said, "Let's go to Eel Bay."

Everyone at the table stopped eating and stared at her. She in turn looked over at Ben who was sitting gazing at her with a puzzled look.

"I can't do it. I can't abide it any more. And it's no use either. We can't possibly make the next payment."

A shadow of emotion flickered across Ben's face. Doubt? Disagreement? She saw pain in his eyes. Then he nodded slowly and dropped his head to stare at his empty plate.

"I know," he mumbled. "I can't stop thinking about that man who was on fire when he jumped."

Mollie had seen him, too. And heard him. The last sound he had ever made, a long rising shriek, like a loon's howl, abruptly cut off by the lake's waters, still rang in her ears.

Ben pushed his chair back. "Very well, we'll skip the life boat drill in the harbor. Strike the fly for the tug and we'll go."

Mollie got up to clear the table. "I must see Hannah before we leave."

Ben answered, "We'll get stowed and ready."

Mollie didn't notice when Mouse slipped quietly up the companionway. But Ben caught him coming out from the focsl with his kit a few minutes later. "Hold on there. You can't leave without paying off."

Mouse stared down at the deck and kicked at a butt in the planking. "I don't need any money, Mr. Ben."

"Well, you can't leave without saying goodbye at least," said Ben, and he held a hand out. Mouse shook it solemnly. Ben added, "You've been a fine shipmate. I'd sail anywhere with you at the helm."

Mouse looked up his face twisted with misery. "I wish I could stay. Captain Ben, will that man really turn the *Gazelle* into a coal hulk?"

"What man was that, Mouse?"

"He was standing right over there yesterday morning. He said he would be buying her from his father in law in December if the old man didn't die first."

Ben made a fist and pressed it against his chin. Jared Kraut, the ice man, merciless and brutal. Then he sat down on the hatch cover and fished for his pipe.

"I guess maybe that could happen. It's his right to do so if he purchases the ship." Ben looked up at the fore topmast cross trees. "Seems a shame though. She's got plenty of life left in her."

Mouse stood beside him studying the deck.

"Let's not say anything to Mrs. Mollie about that ok?"

Mouse nodded, "I'm going ashore right now."

"Go find yourself another ship, Mouse. You're a good sailor and someday you'll be a great one."

Mouse picked up his kit, glanced aft to see if anyone was there, and hurried down the plank without another look back. Ben watched him go. Reuban came sauntering down the deck to rub against Ben's legs. Then he jumped up to sit beside Ben on the hatch. Ben caressed the cat and said, "Well, Reuban, looks like we'll all be ashore after today. I guess you and I will be going back to the boat shop. I sure wish we could keep the ship going somehow, though."

A few minutes after Mouse had slipped ashore, Mollie hurried down the boarding plank. She was still remembering the looks on the faces of the crew at breakfast upon hearing of Mouse's departure. Nate had looked about ready to cry when he'd shaken Mouse's hand. And Tommy, trying to put up a good front, had told Mouse send for me when you get that yacht command. I'll look after the owner's daughters.

The first parting- soon everyone would scatter, and she would be alone.

The October wind plucked at Mollie's cape as catspaws scampered across the river darkening the water and ruffling the surface with miniature white caps on the wider harbor beyond. At the dockside office, she heard the growl of the lake against the breakwaters. It was starting to kick up. It would probably be a wet ride home. Hannah was at her desk, and Mollie closed the door quickly behind her to keep the wind from blowing her paperwork around. She was relieved to see Hannah was alone.

Following her look at the empty desk, Hannah said, "Dan is over at Rathbun's settling our week's orders with them. Are you about to head out?"

Mollie sat on Dan's stool and worried a loose button on her cape for a moment. Then she looked at Hannah and said, "We're going to Eel Bay."

Hannah laid her pen down and remained silent.

"I'll pay you back somehow. I can't keep on anymore."

"The *Naiad?*"

Mollie nodded and drew a deep breath. "The collision, the elevator explosion- they were bad. But that fire, the way those people died... I feel like we've been warned three times."

Hannah gazed out the window at the water beyond. The wind outside whined around the edges the little building. They both listened to it and to the sullen grumble of the lake gnawing on the stone shore nearby.

"I guess we should be getting underway," said Mollie, and she stood up.

Hannah got off her stool, came over and embraced her friend and said quietly, "May you have a safe journey. And stay in touch. I want to hear from you, and if I don't I'll come looking for you over in Canada."

"I'll write after we turn the ship over to Sloan."

Hannah was still holding Mollie's hands. She gave them a gentle squeeze. "Say goodbye to the crew for me. And to the *Gazelle,* too."

Mollie didn't answer. She just nodded, her eyes bright with unshed tears. She turned away abruptly to open the door and go out. Hannah stepped to the doorway and watched her stride off down the dock.

A half hour later they were bringing the dock lines in to stow. They passed their hawser to the tug and drew away from the dock. The good byes had been said, the last embraces given and released. Perhaps some of the ship's company would return to Oswego and the Fitzhugh and Sons Wholesale and Forwarding wharf. Somehow, Mollie resolved that she would. She had to see Hannah again.

Mollie stood at the rail and looked across the widening gap of gray water at the small group gathered to see them off. Dan, Hannah, Clancy, and beside him the sturdy bulk of his boss Michael Doyle stood watching them leave. The thought flashed through her mind of how wrong first impressions could be. She had sadly misjudged the two dock workers just as they had misread her. Clancy, the drunken lout who had once tried to kick Reuban into the river, now stood with tears running down his face. She regretted keenly not being able to bid Isiah farewell. He was off downstate, and she thought, I must write to him and explain somehow. Would he be disappointed at her decision to give up? She forced her gaze, blurred now with tears, away from her friends and looked up the river. Was Mouse somewhere out there watching his old shipmates cast off?

The figures on shore diminished in detail as the tug drew the schooner away from shore, yet still they remained clustered and watching. Once the *Gazelle* moved out into the river, she ceased to be of the land. Now separate and distinct upon the lake's expanse, she assumed her own life. She was the focal point of all the crew's activity as she began yet another voyage. And though this was perhaps her final trip with this crew and owner, the need to begin anew the task of passage making over powered leave taking regrets and shore going concerns. The journey lay before them. Each passage was another little life to be lived. They must look ahead now to the future and their destination, as *Gazelle* pointed the way with her jib boom. It was time to set sail.

The boys under Ben's direction tied in a single reef in both main and fore, and Mollie watching the spray splashing white up on the jetties, thought it would be a wet thrash ahead with this brisk northwester until they got under the lee of South Point on the Canadian shore. A long day pounding across the lake was in store. Once clear of the jetties, the *Gazelle,* still in tow, began to nod in acknowledgement to the waves as the tug turned upwind.

While Mollie manned the helm the boys all pitched in on the halyards to raise first the main then the foresail and finally the headsails, working together as they had so many times. When they dropped the towline and fell off, the sails filled and the *Gazelle* came alive. She leaned to the wind and began to power along close hauled butting through the waves.

Ben on the main deck helping the crew secure for the crossing, felt the familiar lift and dip of the vessel and wished she wasn't about to be turned into a coal hulk. Jamie McPherson's fine little vessel should finish out her days with more dignity than that. He hoped Mollie wouldn't get cut down, too, to become a mere consort, though it certainly seemed possible. It would be good to work with Uncle John again at the yard, but it had been a grand ride this past season. He had no regrets about being Captain now and would not soon forget it. Nor would he soon forget Mollie.

Ben shook his head saying, "Rotten luck."

"What's that?" asked Nate

"Oh, the elevator explosion, the fire, all the delays. We might have made it without the delays."

Nate said, "I wonder what Mollie will do?"

"I suppose she'll go back to Sodus Bay where her Aunt and Uncle are. I can't see her working in a factory. I hope she doesn't marry Dan Fitzhugh and try to be one of Oswego's 'Three Hundred'."

Nate snorted, "Not much chance of that I'd say."

Mollie held a course for Long Point watching the spray come over the windward bow as the schooner pitched into the building seas. A deep sadness settled heavily upon her. After today she would never again sail this ship, her ship. For one brief season they had given it their best, and they had failed. Although she knew it was illogical, Mollie felt that she had let the crew and the *Gazelle* down. She murmured out loud to the schooner, "I'm sorry. We tried but it wasn't good enough. It wasn't your fault." She refused to think what the future held after this last voyage.

Up forward she noticed that Tommy had paused by the pin rail to look out over the water. He called out to her and pointed. She turned to see a second tug had cleared the harbor entrance even as the one ahead that had towed them out was heading back in. The outbound tug was running wide open with a smother of white at the bows and a cloud of black coal smoke boiling out of her stack. Occasionally spray and some solid water swept clean over her foredeck. That looks like the little *James Moray*, she thought. She's making heavy weather of it, too. What's she doing out here with it this rough?

Ben came aft after stowing the tow hawser, and when she pointed the tug out he peered at the distant vessel. The tug had changed course and was now steering at an angle as if its captain sought to intercept them. But *Gazelle,* charging along light and under full sail, was clearly outpacing the little vessel and pulling ahead. The tug was staggering along battered by the waves that occasionally sent spray right over her wheel house.

"That looks like the *Moray*. I wonder what he's up to?" said Ben.

As he spoke a spurt of white steam appeared above the pilothouse. Then a second, third and fourth appeared.

"He's blowing his whistle," called Tommy. Faintly now the sound came to Mollie's ears, too.

"I think he's trying to catch us," said Mollie.

Ben looked puzzled. Then he moved behind Mollie to the mainsheet and let it out calling, "Nate, slack the foresheet."

Mollie with no further prompting put the helm up and the schooner obediently fell off onto a reach, a heading that put her on a collision course with the hard charging little tug. The crew stood silent as they converged, The *Gazelle* romping along with started sheets taking the white crested waves on the beam, Mollie still on the wheel.

At their course change, the *Moray* had stopped blowing its whistle. As the two ships closed, the tug slowed and a man emerged from the pilot house and began waving using his hat as a flag. Mollie saw Dan's broad shoulders and dark hair. She edged the *Gazelle* a little closer to the wind to slow the ship down.

Dan was shouting and repeatedly pointing towards the shore.

"I think he wants us to go back," said Ben sounding puzzled.

"Why?" said Mollie. "I paid all our bills."

The *Moray* came on toward them, also slowing a bit closing up under their lee. Over the noise of the two ships' surge and rush through the water they heard Dan shout something about -important-must turn back- and.... then something else Mollie couldn't catch.

Tommy came leaping aft from his vantage by the forward shrouds. "There's a reward! We have to go back. It's money- from one of the *Naiad* passengers!"

A half hour later, the ship was again secured at Fitzhugh's wharf as Dan came hustling up the boarding plank. He held a piece of paper in one hand, a flimsy from the telegraph office, that he thrust at Ben as soon as he had reached the deck. Ben studied it briefly, then handed it to Mollie his eyes wide, his jaw slack.

Mollie took the paper and read:

To Mollie McIntyre owner of the schooner Gazelle. Please accept my deepest gratitude for the rescue of my daughter Diana. Stop. I have deposited a draft for one thousand dollars with the bank of Oswego for your use and an additional five hundred dollars to be given to your captain and crew. Stop. Best of luck. Douglas Flowers

Mollie stared frozen at the flimsy in her hand. She heard nothing around her and no longer felt the wind. It was as if she were an insect under the transparent cover of a glass fly trap caught in an airless space. It couldn't be true. After months of struggle to hold on, to bear up, isolated, mocked, assaulted, alone except for Ben and the boys, was such a twist of fate possible? Surely this was some sort of cruel hoax. It had to be a dream from which she would awake. How could life possibly pivot so suddenly and completely to take another direction?

Dan was saying something about Diana Flowers.

"The girl with the cook?" she asked.

"Her father is the president of Rochester's biggest bank. The telegraph came just as you were towing out. Congratulations!"

Mollie still stood befuddled. She looked over at Ben. He grinned back, and the joy on his face was a sudden flash of light through dark clouds. It must be true then. Ben was happy. Somehow it was really so. With a rising tide of euphoria Mollie stuffed the flimsy into the pocket of her bloomer and shouted, "Someone go get Mouse! Zeb, get my basket. You come with me. We're going up town and buy the biggest fattest turkey I can find. We're going to have Thanksgiving dinner three weeks early!"

It had been a splendid dinner. Oyster stew, roast turkey with chestnut stuffing and cranberry sauce, mashed potatoes and turnips and a pumpkin and an apple pie had all been demolished by mid afternoon. Mollie and Hannah had wrought a miracle in that small galley Dan declared at dinner's end. No one else offered anything more than a grunt or a groan of agreement.

Dan had brought along three bottles of Madeira which he said would help their digestion. Mouse and Zeb sipped at a glass cautiously, while Tommy and Nate with the conservatism of the young decided to refrain as did Hannah who had temperance sympathies. Ben and Mollie joined Dan in a glass and then in another. After reaching for the bottle a third time, Ben sat back with his wine and announced, "This fruit juice is downright tasty."

"You'll be thinking otherwise tomorrow when you wake up," Hannah told him as she got up to put the teapot on.

241

Zeb looking flushed from his experiment with Portugal's finest and also emboldened by it now ventured to speak, "Mrs. Mollie how will we be paid our five hundred dollar reward?"

Mollie considered the question for a moment and said, "Well, I suppose I'll go cash the draft on the bank and divide it among you- one hundred each. I guess that's the fairest thing to do. What do you think, Captain Ben?"

Ben had just finished his third glass of Madeira. He now directed a look at Mollie with almost disturbing intensity. Ben lifted his chin a bit and said, "I want my share to go to the ship."

Mouse and Nate immediately chimed in, "Me too."

"Yes, that's what I want."

Zeb, swept up by the current of popular opinion and Madeira clapped a hand on the table. "Mine for the *Gazelle,* also."

Tommy with slightly wrinkled brow decided it best to follow the tide. "I agree. I want a job next year, and if you still have the *Gazelle,* I'll still have a job."

"Here, here," said Dan raising his glass. Ben and Zeb promptly followed suit lifting and emptying theirs.

Mollie looked around the table, lit now in the late afternoon gloom by the soft glow of the oil lamp overhead. She felt not just the pleasant warmth of the galley range but something more, that from a crew unified behind her. A combination of Madeira and gratitude brought a choke to her voice as she said, "You're all silly with wine. I can't take your money."

A clamor of dissent rose from around the table, shouting her down.

"Very well. I accept."

Now Dan spoke up, "Speaking of money Sandy Parsons told me there's wheat up in Toronto to deliver here. They've had a good crop out west and are anxious to move it as there's little storage space room left at the elevators. They're offering six cents a bushel he told me."

Ben and Mollie exchanged quick looks. "With the money from the *Naid* two trips in two weeks would do it," said Mollie.

"Two trips in two weeks from Toronto? No problem," said Tommy. "We have until the 15th to pay Sloan don't we?"

Ben was quiet but with the eyes of Mollie Hannah and Dan upon him he said, "With a bit of decent weather, yes, we should be able to do it."

"We're this close- we have to do it," said Mollie and the rest of the crew nodded and murmured agreement.

"When would you leave?" asked Hannah.

"Why, I think we should go tomorrow," said Mollie

Dan set his empty glass down and reached for the bottle. "I thought sailing on a Friday was bad luck. And tomorrow is All Hallow's Eve, too."

Hannah chimed in, "Don't you remember what happened a year ago on Halloween night?"

Mollie nodded, "Moses Dalmadge."

A shadow seemed to pass over the company around the table. All remembered the end of the lad whose family were neighbors and friends of the McIntyres of Eel Bay.

Dan sighed, "I recall when Captain Walters brought Moses down here from Stony Point to take him back to South Bay aboard his schooner. He drove up to Henderson Harbor and picked up the coffin. There must have been sixty schooners weathered in here then. When the wind finally dropped, they all left that morning with the *Sea Bird* at the fore, her flag at half mast, the coffin on her deck. They all sailed behind her, everyone American and Canadian alike with colors half masted."

The ship's company sat silent in the quiet of the cabin with the soft creak of the dock lines and the occasional hoot of a steam whistle or a stevedore's shout from outside as the early dusk of autumn crept out from the cabin's corners and darkened the shadows. At length Mollie broke the silence, "Well perhaps that superstition about sailing on a Friday only holds on salt water. We sail on Fridays all the time here on the lakes."

She got up to begin clearing the table but Hannah waved her down. "I'll clear. You had best take your rest while you can."

Mollie sat back and looked over at Dan who promptly pushed the bottle over to her. She didn't notice Ben's slight frown nor the tug at his sideburn when she refilled her glass.

"When is Isiah coming back?"she asked intending to steer the ship's company away from more musing upon Moses.

Dan shrugged, "Dunno, maybe next week. Maybe next month," and he swirled his half empty glass of wine around.

Hannah turned from the sink. "Isiah has his hands full right now. He's in a battle with Ray Gold and his gang down in New York City."

Mouse asked, "What's the fight about?"

"He went down to help Jim Mills fight off a take over of his road, the Southern Central."

Mouse asked, "Why does he need to do that?"

"We use that line a lot to ship lumber to Philadelphia and other coast cities. The Southern Central is an excellent road. Mill's line has a low accident rate and fine equipment and he treats his workers very well. 'Work, hard work, intelligent work, and then some more work' that's his motto. And like Isiah, he believes that his business will prosper if his customers prosper. He's the very opposite of Ray Gold who simply raids and pillages. Gold and his cronies ganged up on Vanderpost three years ago and by watering stock took control of that road. They gutted it, siphoned away profits, and left it with broken down engines, loose rails and washed out grades. Gold is little more than a thug dressed up as a businessman."

Dan sighed, "I wish Father had stayed home. Ray Gold will chew him up along with Jim Mills and spit out the pieces, and we'll go bankrupt along with Mills."

Hannah who had turned back to the sink of dishes now stopped and turned around to glare at Dan. She snapped, "You could be a little more involved, Dan Fitzhugh. Your father is making a stand against greed and selfishness. He's standing by a business partner with integrity while you sit here and drink Madeira all afternoon!"

Mouse asked, "What if Mr. Fitzhugh and his friend lose?"

"Then Fitzhugh and sons is sold, and we're all out of the lumber business," Hannah answered.

The last bottle stood empty on the table. Dan shoved his chair back with a noisy scrape. "I guess I should get back to the office and close up."

A chill was creeping into the cabin along with the night. Ben decided he would go fire up the little pot belly stove in the crew's quarters. The idea of an early bunk sounded attractive to several of the Madeira drinkers who got up and followed Ben forward. Mollie cleared the last of the meal and silently helped Hannah wash up. The thought of Isiah their stalwart friend (and source of steady charters) being in financial difficulty worried Mollie more than she cared to admit. Yes, they had wheat to finish this season out, but if Isiah should go under, what of next year? And what would happen to Hannah and to the teamsters and stevedores and other men and their families who depended on Fitzhugh's lumber for their pay?

She followed Hannah upon deck and bid her good night. After a festive start, the gathering had ended sharply quieter.

"So you'll leave tomorrow?" asked Hannah as she stood by the boarding plank.

"Yes, we'll sail for Toronto at dawn."

"Be careful. It's late now. Things happen in November."

Mollie nodded and something besides the dank air from the river chilled her as she watched Hannah's figure fade into the obscurity of Halloween night. Perhaps a restless spirit or two was out and about pacing the docks, she thought. Did the ghost of Moses walk the waterfront? Or that of a poor drowned Oswego sailor from the *Jenkins?* For a moment she almost fancied she saw a dim figure standing aft by the wheel. Was it Will? Or was it some other sailor man's shade standing by to steer a schooner clear of danger ahead?

Chapter Twenty eight

"Trust in God: She will provide" - Emmeline Pankhurst

The *Gazelle* did not leave port the next day. When Mollie awoke in early morning darkness, she heard the lake bellowing like a mad bull as the waves crashed over the stone breakwater. And she heard the repeated scream of a tug's whistle blowing for the Life Savers. Along with several dozen other people, she watched the schooner *Tranchemontague* pound to pieces after striking the east pier at the harbor entrance. The schooner's crew had tried to sail in, and their vessel had been thrown against the breakwater by the backwash. One man, swept off the ship's deck, made it ashore alive, and the Life Savers took off the rest of the crew with the breeches buoy, but within hours the schooner was a complete loss.

When the *Gazelle* towed out on Saturday morning, the wreck's timbers lay broken and strewn about the beach in front of Fort Ontario. A few shreds of canvas from her sails fluttered from tree branches along the shore where they had snagged after being ripped from her spars by the wind. In the backwaters of the harbor, patches of waterlogged rye grain still floated. The *Gazelle* crew was edgy as Tommy, Nate, Ben, Zeb and Mouse took hold of throat and peak halyards and began raising the main.

But no one expected what happened next.

"Watch it!" Ben roared from back aft by the wheel.

With a crash, the heavy gaff and the massive throat halyard block came down on deck.

"Jehosaphat!" yelped Nate as Tommy and Zeb staggered back against the bulwark.

"Where's Mouse," cried Mollie seeing the tangle of gear, canvas, and the unshipped spar lying like a log on deck.

"Here. I'm Ok!" called the boy from up by the mainmast.

Ben shook his head. "Nate, signal the tug to take us back in."

Up ahead the *Morray* put her helm over and back into port the *Gazelle* went to drop anchor inside the west pier and sort the mess out.

"What happened?" asked Mollie joining the group by the main mast after they had the anchor down.

"The strap fitting on the throat halyard block broke," said Ben. "We don't have a spare either. We'll have to take it ashore and have it mended."

Mollie stared at the fractured hardware. It was odd, a failure like that. Mollie had never seen a piece of iron simply break. This was very queer indeed. She didn't like it. Was this another warning? She tipped her head back and peered up the main mast towards the furled topsail, the cross trees and the topmast. What else up there was getting ready to let loose?

Ben must have been thinking the same thing. He told Nate, "While I'm at the smith's shop with this, you and Mouse and Tommy go aloft and look sharp at things up there. Go over it all. We don't want anything going adrift this time of year."

The memory of the *Tranchemontague's* broken bones on the beach hung over them. A torn sail, a gaff jaw jumping the mast, a chafed halyard, even an unsecured shackle pin-any of them could land *Gazelle* on a rocky shore, too.

Two more trips. Two more weeks. That's all we need, Mollie told herself. Then we'll have enough money. Then we'll lay up and be done with the lake.

The run up the length of the lake to Toronto was uneventful. By supper time when Mollie gave Ben his usual two hour break from the deck, they were well along with a gusty south wind, and she expected to sight Toronto harbor's light over their jib boom before daybreak. The chill of early November's twilight seeped into her bones as she stood at the helm. She said to Ben after she had taken the helm, "It gets dark so early now."

The clank and creak of the pump sounded from up forward as the new watch checked the bilges. Both Ben and Mollie listened to the splash of bilge water brought up on deck. The clunk and gurgle of the pump at work continued for several minutes. Then the snore and wheeze of air in the pump well sounded.

"That's odd" said Ben. "She usually takes about twenty pulls. That was more like forty."

"First the block letting go, now a leak. Maybe the *Tranchemontague* shook her up," said Mollie trying to sound light hearted.

Ben wasn't buying it. She saw him frowning as he stood looking forward, turning things over in his mind. Had they forgotten to pump the bilge in the morning? Or was there a leak?

Mollie continued, "I guess I wouldn't blame her either. It's not a pretty thing to see someone's livelihood and home smashed into staves. At least the crew got off. Is that the first wreck you've seen?"

Ben nodded, "Yes, and it must have been almost exactly where Father's ship went on the beach."

A chill crawled up Mollie's spine. She rubbed a thumb over the two grooves cut around the king spokes wooden grip. Ben's father hadn't been like Will. He had sailed for many years as captain and had never lost a man or a ship. He had been careful and methodical. More like Ben. But the lake had won in the end.

"As soon as we make these last two runs we're homeward bound."

Ben nodded again. He was still thinking about the wreck. He remembered how the biggest waves had surged right over the hulk. Others had smashed against the ship's side, throwing spray half way up the masts. Within an hour of driving ashore, the wreck's two spars were already canted at different angles as she lay with her back broken. What had cousin Annie said of Father's ship when it had gone ashore? You could hear, even over the surf's thunder, the big timbers cracking and the spikes pulling through the wood when she lifted and dropped on the rock ledges. It was like a living thing crying out in agony.

Ben's father had been proud of Will when he had been taken on for his first position as mate aboard the *Alma*. So even though Ben would have preferred to stay ashore and work in the shipyard, he had followed in his older brother's wake and begun crewing aboard various bay boats. After Father's ship was wrecked, Ben had wondered why he had made that last late season trip. Why hadn't he come home like their neighbors had after the middle of November? It seemed like they could have gotten by somehow even if they had lost the ship to foreclosure.

Now, after a season in the *Gazelle* as captain, he had a notion as to why Father had kept on. It gets in your blood, he thought. It's not just the money. It was the idea of failing- letting your ship and your crew down. Thinking about the *Gazelle* and her crew his heart swelled with a mix of pride and concern. They had done splendidly this season. The possibility of a new leak bothered him. Not only for their own safety, but for the sake of his vessel.

As he continued to gaze forward into the darkness, he said, "I never realized what a pull this being a captain has on you. You can't think about yourself. You don't have time. It's always the ship. And after that it's the crew. If they don't do their job, the ship can't do hers."

Mollie nodded.

Ben continued, "I never understood why my Dad didn't jump into the yawl with the rest of the crew five years ago. Now I can see how hard it would be to leave your ship knowing there was nothing more to do. It'd be bad, maybe like losing a part of yourself. So he waited a little too long." Ben rubbed his wind chilled face and went on, "Do you remember that old man who lived all alone in that little cabin up on the Owl's Nest Road?"

Mollie looked over, "You mean Mr. Dawson? The captain who lost the *Seneca* and came ashore in '76?"

"Yes, that's him. He died didn't he?"

Mollie checked a slight swing of the vessel with the helm as a wave nudged her off course, and then said, "Why, that was two years ago. They say he took laudanum and killed himself. What made you think of him just now?"

Ben shrugged. "I don't know. I'm going to turn in now. Call me when the hour's up."

Down on deck by the foremast, the crew was sitting talking quietly before the dog watch ended and the off watch went to their bunks. Nate was whittling, Mouse had a bit of marlin he was trying to make into some fancy work for a bellrope, while Zeb watched.

Tommy spoke up, "Did you see that big rat last night? He must have been a foot long not including his tail."

"Maybe that one's too big for Reuban," offered Zeb.

"Reuban could take him. He just doesn't want to. He's waiting for the rats to get fat and juicy on that load of wheat we're going to get."

"I don't mind a rat as long as he stays out of the focsle," said Nate. But I do hate bedbugs."

Tommy said, "There was so many bugs in the old *Buffalo City*-we used to have bed bug races- if we could have gotten them all to pull together on a halyard I bet they would have been able to raise the main for us."

Nate shuddered, "Ugh. I'm glad I'm on a family ship with a woman cook. I'm never going to sail on anything else again if I can help it."

Tommy nodded, "You fellows don't know how lucky you are to be on this boat. We ate salt junk and beans and beans and salt junk all week every day on the *Buffalo City*. Not like you get here- no pies, no fresh bread, not even a decent breakfast." He laughed, adding, "The cook we had, he used to spit in the fry pan to lubricate the eggs."

Mouse answered, "Well, I've never sailed on no other boat, but you don't need to tell me how good the food is here. Back home it's potatoes potatoes and potatoes three times a day."

After a pause broken only by the comforting rumble of the *Gazelle's* bow wave a few feet away, Nate said, "I sure hope we make it. I want to ship out with the *Gazelle* next year."

"We'll do her," said Mouse. "We got the best boat, skipper, and owner on the lake."

An hour later Mollie left the wheel to Ben and went below, glad to climb under her quilt and heavy wool blanket to escape the chill November night. Though tired, she lay awake for nearly an hour thinking about the dwindling days ahead. Completing two more runs by November 15 was no certain thing. It could only be done without any more breakdowns and with good weather. One thing was certain though, never had a ship had a better crew- they'd been troopers. They'd overlooked her mistakes and stood by her, and they'd all done their best. She had no idea how she could pay back Uncle John and Father and Hannah if she lost the ship. What possible job could she find ashore at a wage good enough to put anything by. Trade was so slow now. Men were being laid off all over. What chance would she have to find a job at a living wage?

She finally drifted off to sleep lulled by the gentle roll of the vessel and the occasional quiet creak of the timbers that cradled her.

At Adamson's elevator in Toronto, the load was shot in within a few hours. The boys hustled and had the wheat trimmed and the hatch covers battened down and covered with tarpaulins by early afternoon. The *Gazelle* got underway again under full sail just a few hours after arriving empty. The day was oddly mild for November, and the wind was still south though it had fallen light as they cleared the harbor to sail back down the length of the lake to Oswego. As they worked the ship down the channel to the open lake under a low solid gray sky, Mollie noticed a large gathering of gulls perched on the shore near the entrance jetty.

Ben noticed them, too. "They think there's weather coming," he remarked.

Mollie looking at the clustered birds thought how the oddly loud the hoot of a passing train ashore just now had seemed. And she remembered that Reuban had been unusually restless after dinner. "I saw Reuban up on deck a little while ago. He almost never comes up here when we're getting underway from the dock."

Ben looked up at the low overcast of cloud, scanning it for motion.

"Has anyone cut their fingernails lately?"

Mollie didn't smile at the old superstition as she shook her head.

Despite the calm and mild temperatures, Mollie remained uneasy as she washed up and tidied the galley after supper. When she went on deck to give Ben his brief evening break she confided her feelings. "It feels funny. The water's oily and it's too quiet. There's weather brewing."

He answered, "The barometer's down. We're in for a blow for sure."

After she took over to give him his break, Ben went forward and prowled around the deck looking things over instead of going to his bunk. They were jogging along still under full sail with perhaps a five knot breeze. After a turn around the ship, Ben paced aft and stood by Mollie as he rubbed his starboard sideburn.

"I'm going to have the boys rig life lines on deck. And I think I'll take those topsails in before it gets dark. I know we need to make time but…"

Mollie nodded. "I know. There's something in the air."

A light drizzle began to fall, just heavy enough the wet things down and be annoying. After Mouse and Tommy had gone aloft and secured the light sails and her watch was over, she gladly gave the wheel to Ben and turned in all standing in her bloomer outfit. She felt she wouldn't be in her bunk for long.

She lay looking up at the cabin beams in the dim light feeling the close air. The hanging lamp over the table swung slowly back and forth. November storms were some of the worst. Ben and Will's father had died in a November blow. As had a dozen other vessels at Oswego's doorstep. Back in '76 she remembered a November storm that had wrecked at least three ships. And one year two schooners had been beached at Oswego in a single storm.

She listened to the quiet creak of the ship's timbers as the schooner rolled gently along. That swell hadn't been there when she had left the deck. It'll go into the west soon. It's going to come on strong then. Should we run for Charlotte?

Despite her unease, sleep came and with it dreams vivid and disturbing. She was back in Oswego on the waterfront. Will was waiting. *I must hurry before he leaves. But where is he? Why can't I find him?* She could barely move her legs, as if she were wading in thick molasses. She could hardly pick up one foot and set it ahead of the other. She saw the distant masts of the *Gazelle.* The ship lay at the end of a huge empty wharf that stretched before her larger than a farm field. She was so tired and weak. Her feet dragged. *It's too far. I can't make it.* Then her legs gave out. She collapsed onto the ground weeping. *I can't, I can't do it. Oh please Will, Don't leave. Please wait for me.*

Then a tall woman dressed in a plain Quaker dress, her face oddly luminous in the dim light, reached down and gently pulled her to her feet. "Ben sent me. Come along. You must not give up." But when Mollie reached the *Gazelle,* no one was there. Her decks lay empty before her. A horrible desolation washed over her as she stood alone by the wheel.

She awoke then and lay with tears seeping down her face, still feeling the intense loneliness of the dream. She threw back the blankets and sat up. The ship's roll was heavier now. She wanted someone, anyone. She needed to see another living being. Even Reuban would do. As she reached for her oil cloth jacket on its hook nearby, she heard the hollow moan of a bit of wind passing through the ship's rigging. Here it comes, she thought. She wrestled on her jacket quickly in the darkness.

On deck the rain had stopped, But the blackness was almost tangible. Ben's sturdy bulk stood a few feet from Nate who was steering. "I was just about to turn out the off watch." said Ben. "Did you hear it?"

Mollie opened her mouth to ask "hear what" when a deep rumble sounded off to the west. Fear crawled down her spine and settled in a hard ball in her stomach. November thunder. A winter squall lurked out there somewhere in the darkness. It was stalking them. Soon, perhaps within minutes, it would be on them. And then the main act would follow. The old widow maker would be sweeping the decks tonight.

Chapter Twenty nine

"The best protection any woman can have is courage " E Stanton

The witch of November some called the intense fall storms that screamed in the rigging overhead bringing in snow, ice and frost from the far north. Sometimes winds on the open lake blew with hurricane strength. Time and luck were about to run out this night for all mariners still abroad on Ontario's waters, trying to get their last trips in. At this very moment on Lake Erie, a hundred miles to the west, men were struggling on freezing decks as the waves leaped like wolves upon their ships to drag hard driven vessels down. Schooners would die tonight on both Erie and Ontario-ships and men and a few women, too.

Ben cupped his hands to his mouth and roared, "All hands, all hands on deck. Lively now, lively." Then he said, "Mollie, take the wheel-Nate come along, we'll squat the main. Hurry."

Ben and Nate ran off into the gloom leaving Mollie with the dim binnacle light to steer by as she gripped the familiar helm. In the November night the palms of her hands were sweating. Then a brilliant flash of lightning split the night sky overhead followed by a deafening thunderous crack and crash.

Up forward, hidden by darkness, the boys hauled down the jibs and pulled the fore and main down to the second reef bands. They had partly secured the two big sails, when the first hard gust hit. Mollie, on the wheel, was shocked by the sudden drop of temperature and the savagery of the wind. Ice pellets stung her face before she turned away to leeward. Another flash, this one an eerie greenish color, followed by oddly muffled thunder, lit the decks. She'd been in more than a dozen squalls and gales upon the lake, but none like this.

Then the full strength of the gale slammed into the sails. *Gazelle* reeled and staggered before it putting her lee rail under. Mollie had never heard wind shriek like this in the rigging overhead. It was far stronger than the summer squall that had taken their deck load. Mollie strained against the hard pull of the wheel. The ship leaned even further, solid water now well up the side of the cabin. Hard up hard up. She thought. I've got to get her off before it, She jammed one foot against the housing to keep from sliding down the steeply angled deck and pulled against the wheel with all her strength. She heard the loud thunder of an unsecured jib broken loose from its lashings. *This is bad. This isn't going to be over in forty minutes. This is just the beginning,* she thought. Would the masts stand it?

But now the schooner was beginning to answer the wheel that Mollie had jammed hard over. Slowly she was paying off to run before it. As the *Gazelle* leveled her decks, Mollie peered into the spray and darkness forward. Was anyone left up there? Had they all slid overboard with the knockdown? With a gasp of relief she heard Ben shouting commands as the racket of a flogging sail subsided. They were still at it. The crew was working together. The hard knot of fear in Mollie's stomach loosened a bit.

It took Tommy and Zeb ten minutes or more to lash down the jibs out on the jib boom and bowsprit. By the time they finished and had crawled back onto the deck, the seas had built to eight feet. Already the breaking wave tops were beginning to board the ship over her bulwarks.

Ben joined Mollie and braced himself in the lee of the deck house. "We'll run along the south shore and see how it goes," he shouted over the roar of the storm and the hard rattle of icy sleet on deck. Nate took the wheel back, and Mollie moved over to stand beside Ben. She gripped the lifeline they had rigged earlier.

Ben shouted into her ear, "Maybe we can get in at Charlotte. We may have to take the main down, but right now I'd like to leave it in case we need to come up on the wind and try for Kingston."

The wind was still southwest, but both Mollie and Ben knew it would eventually swing west and then north. Mollie, feeling the ship beginning to labor, thought of Oswego's narrow rock flanked harbor entrance. By the time they reached it, there'll be fifteen footers out here, she thought. It would be better to forget even trying for Oswego even if it meant not getting the cargo to port. They should work offshore for some sea room before the shift north and head down the lake for Kingston. If the shift came before they got under the Canadian shore, they could make for the mouth of the St. Lawrence and Cape Vincent.

As she debated saying anything to Ben, who was, after all the captain, a heavy gust from the west slammed into them knocking the ship down so her rail went under again, even with just a bit of sail up. The wind hardened, so that it was difficult to even stand against it.

"It must be blowing fifty," she shouted but Ben standing a few feet away couldn't hear her.

The wind raised a deep throated roar as it passed through the *Gazelle's* rigging, a bass bellow overlain by shrill whistles and higher pitched shrieks. And with it came waves, building with astounding speed. Huge waves, bigger than Mollie had ever seen loomed out of the darkness along side. Sometimes they broke and toppled with a crash like thunder as the ship ran before them. When a big wave broke against the schooner's oak sides or fell upon the stout pine deck, the *Gazelle* trembled with the impact. No need to discuss Charlotte or Oswego now. They were both out of the question.

They must run before it, run for Kingston and hope for the best. At all costs they must keep her up on the wind and avoid the deadly trap of Mexico Bay. There wasn't a ship afloat that could get back out of there in a wind like this. If the wind shifted north before they got down to Long Point, they wouldn't have a hope in hell of getting through this.

Nate came aft to take the now heavy helm. Mollie retreated to the slightly elevated after deck and clung to one of the yawl boat davits, while Nate wrestled with the wheel keeping the ship before the wind. She saw that the wind shift from southwest to west had set up a vicious cross sea. Now and then, two or three waves seemed to combine forces with each other, rising up to create a house sized hill of water like nothing she'd ever seen. Standing by with nothing to do but watch the rampaging water, time crawled. Ten minutes felt like an hour, and as she watched, more and more solid water came on deck and surged back and forth as the waves built. They might have to knock the bulwarks out of the ship to free the deck up. There were tons of water weighing, pushing, forcing *Gazelle* down, keeping her from rising to the next wave. She couldn't take this much longer. Then a white crested monster struck them squarely.

Mollie saw it coming- a monster looming above the big rollers around it. As she looked up at the massive breaking crest, she thought that has to be twenty feet high. We'll never get over that one. The *Gazelle* lifted to it. But burdened with the cargo of wheat in her hold, the schooner couldn't quite rise clear of the curling breaker at the top. As she lurched and staggered under its assault and heeled sharply, a flood of ice cold water poured over her quarter and her weather side, completely filling her decks rail to rail. The ship shuddered under the strain and struggled to rise and shed the tons of water from her deck. Mollie heard a shrill scream. She groped along the life line in thigh deep water and glimpsed Ben in the darkness lunging across the deck to leeward. Or was he being carried with the surge of water?

She peered into the confusion of spray, now mixed with snow blowing horizontally across the deck, trying to see through the gloom. The now bitter wind brought tears to her eyes. Then she glimpsed Tommy plunging aft through the water with Mouse gripped under one arm. Tommy thrust the limp body at her and gasped something about Ben as he turned and staggered back forward into the darkness.

Mollie felt the body clutched tightly in her arms spasm as Mouse coughed. Well, he was alive at any rate. Still hugging him hard against her with one arm, she slowly worked aft clinging to the lifeline with her other hand to make her way towards the slightly drier after deck. Mouse suddenly found his feet and reached for the line. He was still coughing and retching, as together they retreated to the scant shelter of the deck house. Then Tommy lurched out of the darkness half dragging half carrying Ben.

"He's hurt," gasped Tommy as he eased Ben down onto the deck beside them. Ben sat leaning against the deck house one arm held tight against his side by the other.

"What happened?"

"Mouse going overboard," Ben spoke in short phrases punctuated by gasps, "I grabbed him-think I pulled my shoulder out-"

"Oh, dear God," thought Mollie. *What am I going to do?*" Icy fear, colder than the wind that now froze her skin, stabbed deep. Panic fluttered and beat itself against her will. Without Ben they were lost. She shuddered with cold and dread. For an instant there was nothing in her mind but roaring wind, seething spray, and ocean of black water as panic threatened to overwhelm her.

Ben lurched to his feet, his face pale with pain, as he held his left arm tight against his body. "I'm ok. Get some small stuff- lash me to that ring bolt-I can't hold on now." He staggered over to the attachment point and dropped onto the deck.

Mollie drew a deep breath. *Steady,* she told herself as panic surged again, and her throat tightened. Steady. We'll make it. We'll do it. She pushed the panic down and concentrated on the task before her. Take care of Ben.

Tommy brought a length of twine, and at Mollie's direction wrapped it around Ben's body several times to pinion the injured arm tightly. Then he doubled the line through the ring bolt as directed. Ben braced himself with a groan against the plunging schooner's lurches and rolls and cursed.

Mouse crouched near by, suddenly sprang up and shouted, "Now Zeb-run for it!"

Looking forward, Mollie saw a dark shape clinging to the windward ratlines of the main mast. Zeb, who had jumped aloft when the wave hit, had stayed there clinging fearfully. At Mouse's shout, he dropped to the deck and bolted aft to join the huddle of crew by the deck house.

With everyone accounted for and hanging on to hand holds on the after deck, Mollie now turned her attention to Nate at the helm and by association to the ship herself.

She moved aft carefully going from grip to grip to brace herself beside Nate and shouted in his ear, "How is she doing?"

Nate looked like he had his hands full. As another big wave hit, he rolled the wheel one way, then the other. The ship rose, lurched, and skidded before settling into the trough after the sea passed under. He answered, "I think we should take the main off her. There's a bit of a lull right now."

Though spray and spume still flew off the waves, the sleet and snow had cleared for the moment. Mollie could see the close spaced sharp edged huge waves slamming, bashing, hammering relentlessly at the *Gazelle's* hull seeking the slightest weakness in her defenses. She wondered about the water level the bilge. No way anyone could stand on the main deck to work the pump now. Occasionally when she lifted to a big wave, the schooner speared her jib boom deep into the back of the just passed sea under her bows. Watching the ship, Mollie realized that the biggest seas were now easily twenty feet high. They would continue to grow as the ship ran further east down the lake. Her eye caught movement forward. She saw the flutter of a bit of canvas. She forced the stifling fear back. The task. Think of the task. Not the fear. She tried to sound calm as she said, "That outer jib is coming adrift."

Another shock and shudder as a heavy one hit. *Gazelle* tilted her bow upward again as the wave slid under her. As she did so, her long jib boom angled high into the air, and the outer jib suddenly billowed up and flogged heavily. The entire rig shook.

"That'll take the sticks right out of her, if it doesn't shred," said Mollie. "We've got to secure it."

Tommie punched Zeb, "C'mon bud. Let's go."

The night was clear enough now to see as far as the foredeck, and Mollie watched with ice in her gut as the two youths crawled slowly out onto the steeply angled jib boom. Poor Zeb, she thought. He'd never leave the farm after this trip. If we survive.

They had to move out almost to the very tip of the spar that was now sweeping a forty foot arc through the air. Mouse went forward, too. He stayed on deck and hauled hard on the down haul that held the halyard block tight next to the sail. He then re- secured it. Another huge wave shoved *Gazelle* forward and drove her bows downward. Tommie and Zeb, out on the spar, disappeared, completely submerged, and Mollie felt a clutch of her stomach. Surely they had gone, plucked off the spar by the rush of water, snatched away to drown.

As *Gazelle* lifted her bows, she saw two shapes huddled, both still clinging to the jib boom. She also saw Zeb raise one arm make a grab for the sail as it billowed out again. Then she saw him suddenly lunge across the jib boom. She heard Ben's groan behind her. Tommy had slumped across the jib boom. Zeb somehow had a hold of him with both arms, his legs wrapped around the spar beneath them. She couldn't believe he was able to hang on as Mouse scrambled like a monkey out the length of the bowsprit and jib boom to the two huddled figures. The sail caught the wind and flogged again, nearly knocking the two boys off the bowsprit. Then she saw Zeb somehow hauling Tommy aft. And little ninety pound Mouse had got a lash on that writhing wind wild piece of canvas to subdue it.

Mollie looked quickly over at Ben who told her, "Go on-I'm all right."

Mollie's legs trembled as she worked slowly forward waiting by the deck house to time her dash for a moment when the main deck was clear of rushing water. Then she ran for the bow. Zeb, white faced, shivering, and soaking wet, had made it off the bowsprit and had jammed himself between the windless and the fore scuttle hatch. He still had both arms around Tommy. "The clew iron hit him. He's bleeding, Miz Mollie. What'll we do? He's out cold."

"Take his arms. We'll get him below. I'll take his legs."

Mollie glanced at the cut and saw that it was high on his forehead just at the hairline. Both Zeb and Mollie felt the sudden swoop and lift upward of the bow as the *Gazelle* rode down the backside of another enormous wave. "Quick now, before another big one hits," she said as she seized Tommy's ankles.

With the strength that desperate urgency gives, they dragged and lifted Tommy's limp form aft and wrestled him down the narrow scuttle entrance and steep short companion way and laid him on the focsle floor. Zeb fumbled in the darkness to extract a match from the tin and light the bulkhead lamp, as the waves thumped and thudded and crashed outside. The ship's timbers creaked and groaned loudly around them. It seemed an eternity before the lamp's glow chased the darkness away from the small space that plunged, swooped, tilted, and swung them about doing its best to throw them around like peas in a box.

Mollie braced against the bunk and crouched over Tommy to examine the injury. "He's out all right. But he's still breathing." She felt for a pulse on the side of his neck and found it, steady and strong. Already the blood flow was slowing. There wasn't too much fresh blood running down his face.

"I think he's going to be all right, Zeb. Perhaps his watch cap helped cushion his head. Get some of that bedding."

There wasn't much they could do for Tommy now. She and Zeb stuffed the tick, blankets and several pillows around the inert body to wedge it in place on the cabin sole between the bunks. They covered the soaked youth with another heavy wool blanket tucked around him.

"Come on, Zeb. They need us on deck."

After a cautious emergence from the scuttle and another wait for the decks to drain clear, Mollie and Zeb bolted aft. As they staggered from one hand hold to another, Mollie realized a dim gray dawn was beginning to lighten the sky. She almost wished it was still dark. The size of the seas around them nearly took her breath away. She hadn't thought the lake could ever kick up like this.

Back aft she hunched down beside Ben who was sitting, his jaws clenched against the pain, as he braced against the lurches of the ship. The snow had stopped, but it was now bitterly cold. The wind cut like a knife right through Mollie's heavy wool wrap and her oil skins. Already a sheen of ice gleamed in the dim light of dawn on the masts and bulwark caps where spray was beginning to freeze. Soon the decks and rigging would be a glaze of ice. The lines and sails would become unmanageable encased in crystalline rock hard ice.

Mollie spoke, "We've got to get the main off her."

Ben replied his voice tight, "Take the wheel. The boys will have to haul the gaff right down hard. Lash everything. Jibe over. Sweat up boom tackles. Run for Kingston."

Mollie nodded and stood up. She moved over beside Nate at the wheel. He was their best helmsman. But without Tommy, Nate's strength and skill were crucial to the jibe. As was her helmsmanship.

She spoke to the crew, "Nate, you, Zeb and Mouse have to get the main off her. Set up the mainsheet and boom tackles hard and be sure you lash everything really well. If the sail gets loose it'll go to ribbons and take the gaff and boom and maybe the mast with it."

They all knew what would happen if the main boom were to start flailing around the deck. The spar was forty feet long and with its rigging it weighed nearly a ton. If it started swinging around wild, it could strike and break the wire rigging that held up the mast. And with no mast and no sail back aft to control the schooner, they would be headed straight downwind for Mexico Bay.

"After that, I'll take the wheel for the jibe. Nate, you're on the preventer. Zeb and Mouse will be on the sheet. Watch me, and I'll signal you when to shift her over."

Nate waited until several big seas had passed under them before stepping aside from the wheel during the brief comparative calm that followed. Mollie shivering with cold and tension moved to his place. Nate stood by for a moment in case she needed help. The heavy crash and roar of a breaking crest just astern warned Mollie of another big wave's approach, and her grip on the wheel spokes tightened with her fear as she braced for it.

The stern lifted. The top of the wave washed over the stern rail drenching them up to their knees in froth. She waited and braced for a sudden swerve as the ship staggered under the blow. It never came. Instead the *Gazelle* ran true, holding on to her course and shrugging off the wave's impact. Mollie's sudden relief came almost as a physical sensation quenching the panic that had been struggling to take control of her. *I can do this,* she thought. She gave Nate a quick nod.

Nate acknowledged, "She runs easy. You'll be ok."

He started forward taking the two younger crew with him to set up the main boom tackles. Mollie looked quickly aloft at the head of the double reefed main, the gaff swinging wild arcs dim against the early morning sky. Getting that down was not going to be any picnic, she thought. And they couldn't afford to lose any more crew power to another accident.

With Ben's coaching after the boom was secured, she edged carefully up a bit into the wind with Zeb and Mouse on the halyards and Nate hauling on the downhaul for the luff. They got the mainsail heavy and stiff with frozen spray squatted right down. Once Mollie saw Zeb slip and sprawl on the icy deck. He flung his arms out desperate for a hand hold against the glaze. Nate grabbed him by the collar of his jacket before he slid to leeward, and he staggered to his feet. They lashed the gaff and sail down hard. It seemed to take forever, Mollie thought, as she watched the boys tie off lashings and lines with their numbed fumbling freezing fingers. And all the while the ship charged down wind eating up the distance heading for Mexico Bay. How much longer before it would be too late for the jibe?

When at last the sail was secured, Mollie fell off and resumed her course. Now the jibe. With no time to lose. Again a wave of fear clutched at her. One false move or mistimed action and they'd lose the rig. And they had to do it now. Soon they would be too far down the lake to run for Kingston. Then there was nothing ahead but lake's death trap. In an hour or less they would drive on to the widow maker's waiting wave washed lee shore to be smashed to pieces.

"It's now or never," gasped Ben,

She nodded.

He said, "I'll watch aft. When it looks like a good break coming, I'll sing out."

Mollie nodded again as she steered.

She saw Nate taking up his post at the critical preventer while the two boys began hauling in the foresheet. When the wind caught the boom and slammed it to the other side, it would be largely up to Nate to check the worst of the impact with his line. If the sail came over too hard or quickly, it could carry away or break the spars. And if either the boom or gaff broke or came unshipped, they'd lose the foresail and with it their ability to maneuver or steer.

It was slow going for Zeb and Mouse without Tommy's strong arms to pull the foresheet in. It seemed to take them forever before the sail was hauled in near amidships and ready. Ben had gotten to his feet and wedged himself against the back of the cabin as he looked aft. When would this wind ever drop, thought Mollie, as the *Gazelle* rode down the back of another wave the size of a small hill. Gusts shrieked and roared like demented wild creatures in the rig overhead.

"There's a big one coming. After this one we'll go," Ben shouted.

Mollie braced her feet a bit farther apart and said to the *Gazelle* "steady old girl." The words spoken aloud helped release some of her own tension. She concentrated on steering, no longer feeling the bite of the wind or hearing its rage though the rigging. Then the wave hit. The ship staggered under its assault and rolled her rail down. Mollie glimpsed a welter of green and white water pouring over the rail amidships. It rushed in a foaming torrent across the deck. The crew by the foremast braced themselves against the thigh deep flood that tried to tear them from their posts. She saw Nate's eyes riveted on her. She wrestled with the wheel to keep the course straight. Then *Gazelle* settled into the trough.

"Now!" Ben commanded.

Mollie dipped her head in a deep nod to Nate and began edging the ship off the wind. The boom slammed over. Nate checked and eased his line. Mollie countered the sudden surge of force as the sail shifted. Nate and the boys were continuing to ease the boom off, the youngsters taking up on the lee preventer. It was done. It was over. They were under control. Mollie drew in a quick breath through clenched teeth. She edged upwind a bit more so as to again take the seas on the quarter.

"We did it!" Mollie shouted out to the boys. "Good old *Gazelle*!"

Ben still looking aft sagged against the deck house in relief. "Well done," he said quietly.

Mollie dared now look ahead at the foam streaked backs of the wind cut waves leaping and tumbling, the spume smoking off their crests as they raged on down the lake.

"If you steer north nor'east that should take us up past the Ducks," Ben told her.

Mollie brought the *Gazelle* up another point. Now, with the schooner on more of a reach, the wind was really whistling. It seared her face and numbed her hands and fingers locked tightly on the wheel spokes. But at this speed in less than two hours they'd be under the lee of Long Point sheltered from the worst seas and the build up of ice. By the time the wind worked around north, they'd be snug at anchor in Kingston or at least under some lee out of the giant waves and near safe shelter.

Relief made her feel almost giddy as she spared a glance from the compass towards Ben. He managed a crooked grin, "Nice work," he called. "We stay right side up for another couple hours, and we just might make it."

Chapter Thirty

"All men and woman are created equal" E.C.Stanton

In the early dusk of November, the *Gazelle* came to anchor off Kingston. The exhausted crew let the anchor chain run, set the windlass brakes, and after a brief supper of cold beans and cornmeal mush, stumbled off to bed.

The next morning, Nate went ashore with the yawl boat in search of a doctor. After seeing him off, Mollie went forward with food for Tommy. She found him awake and dressed. He was still wobbly, and he looked decidedly battered with his hair matted with dried blood and a large dark bruise on one cheekbone. She set the plate and mug of coffee down by his bunk and seated herself on a locker nearby. Tommy sat on the edge of his bunk and began to eat.

"How's your head?" she asked.

"Hurts like hell- 'cuse me, like blazes."

"Nate's gone for the doctor for Ben. I'm sure the doc will do something for you, too."

"Did we make Kingston?"

Mollie nodded, "About supper time. You were still out."

Tommy put the fork down, bowed his head, and to Mollie's surprise she saw tears running down his face. Alarmed, she wondered had the bump on his head brought this on?

"I'm sorry I fouled up," choked Tommy, and he sat looking down at his plate while tears dropped into his fresh fried eggs and bacon.

"Tommy, we're all right. We're safe."

Tommy looked up and answered "We're finished aren't we, Miss Mollie. It's Monday. And the loan is due next Friday isn't it?"

She looked away from his anguish. Her gaze traveled around the empty focsle, the overhead and ceiling neat and clean with white paint, the little stove now purring with a morning fire. On the aft bulkhead, someone had tacked up a sketch of the *Gazelle* made by Nate. It showed her under full sail with a bone in her teeth and another two master, undoubtedly the *Black Oak,* far astern. The morning light from the deck prism glass overhead showed the heavy beams, the massive knees and timbers, and the empty two tiered bunks. The small space was orderly, safe, warm and blessedly quiet and still. After a night of the ship standing on her head trying to do somersaults and rollovers, it was a wonder just to sit here. She wished she could stay here all day. Quite likely after this week, she would never see this place again.

"I guess we are done. But we're all going home now. Home to Eel Bay. Maybe we're done, but don't worry about it now, Tommy. Just eat your breakfast. And don't blame yourself. Everyone did their absolute best. We came through, and that's all that matters."

She got up to go. "You lay up and rest today. We're staying right here at anchor while we straighten things out. I've got to go see how Ben is."

Tommy resumed eating, and Mollie went quietly up the short companionway and onto the deck.

A few hours later, Mollie opened the companionway door just as Doctor Wayne gave Ben another dose of "painkiller" from the bottle of whiskey they kept aboard tucked away in the bottom drawer of the ship's desk. Though his face was pale as he sat in the main cabin at the dinner table with his arm now in a sling, Ben was obviously relieved to have his shoulder back in place. He and the doctor paused in their talk as she came in and sat down beside Ben.

"Doc says at least seven ships are on the beach," Ben told her.

Dr. Wayne said, "They're saying it hit sixty knots or more, and some are saying it was the worst gale in thirty years. The water rose four feet in the St. Lawrence from the wind surge. Last night, the *Baltic* came in without a stitch on her, and the *Norway* capsized out near the Ducks and lost her spars and not a man found aboard her."

Mollie looked over at Ben and said, "I guess we did all right. We only lost one sail and about a quarter of our grain was wetted by deck leaks."

The Doctor nodded. "The *Wood Duck's* ashore at Oswego, the *Wave Crest's* scuttled at Frenchman's Bay and the *Belle Sheridan* is in pieces up at Presquile. Only one man came off her alive. Her wreckage was spread all the way to Wicked Point- not a piece bigger than three feet long." The doctor lowered his voice and added, "They say a human heart was picked up off the beach."

Mollie had kept a tight rein on her emotions over the last two days. But now, she quailed inwardly while carefully keeping her face impassive. The memory of the huge gray seas rising up behind them, the ship stabbing her jib boom deep into the backs of the waves, the burn of the bitter wind

265

on bare flesh, and the unearthly din of the gale screaming in the rigging, flashed through her mind. How could anyone live more than a minute in the lake under such conditions-a lake so angry that its surf literally tore a body apart.

Dr. Wayne was still talking, "The steamer *Zeeland*'s missing, too. She may have gone as well."

It had been no ordinary November gale. Over a dozen ships were known to have been wrecked or sunk. "Have you had any word of the *Anowa*? That's my father's boat."

Dr. Wayne shook his head, "No Ma'm. But a lot of ships are overdue. She might still be at anchor somewhere making repairs- maybe she's under Long Point or up in the Bay of Quinte."

Ben reached out with his good arm and took Mollie's hand.

Mollie clenched her teeth and nodded silently.

"Captain Tom's as good a sailor as ever set a jib. He's all right, Mollie. You'll see."

Oh please, dear Lord, she thought silently, let it be so. She dropped his hand and and stared silently at the table.

Dr. Wayne arose, "If you'll excuse me I'll go see the boy up forward."

After he left, she again looked over at Ben.

He said, "Well, I guess we're finished."

Mollie nodded, "I don't care if only Father is safe."

Ben poured another half glass of whiskey and sipped it. Mollie watching him thought his shoulder must indeed be hurting for Ben seldom indulged in spirits when aboard the *Gazelle*.

"We've had a good run," said Ben. "No crew or vessel could have done better. I'll hate turning her over to Sloan, but we did our best and there's no shame in it, I guess. Just the same, I wish we'd done it. The boys will be all right, Nate and I can go to work for Uncle John. But the *Gazelle's* sailing days are over."

Mollie said, "Why do you say that? Someone will buy her from Sloan."

"Darn, I forgot. I was supposed to keep quiet."

"About what?"

"Sloan's son-in-law has already got plans to turn her into a hulk for his new steamer to tow."

Mollie considered. So it really was over now for them all. After her brave fight and grand run before perhaps the greatest storm ever of her life, it didn't seem right. Surely the gallant old *Gazelle* deserved a better fate. She wondered, too, about her own fate without her ship. Was she also doomed to become a consort, pulled here and there subject always to the will of others? What would she do now?

She could go home and move in with Aunt Anna and Uncle Jack on their little farm. But they weren't exactly living in grand style these days. She would have to help out somehow, and there were few jobs in the little bayside village for a single woman.

I could work at the Curtis Hotel, I suppose- maybe as a cook or scullion. Maybe I'd make five dollars a week. I'll never be able to pay Hannah and Uncle John and Father back. That was Uncle John's life savings he used. Then with a chill, Mollie wondered was Father even alive? And working for Billy Curtis- I know what he did to Flora Dates last year. And Louise Adams. They just disappeared after that. What on earth would I do if I got in a family way- how could I support a baby and myself?

I'll work in a factory. It's a more honest form of bondage than marriage to some men would be. Maybe I could go to Rochester or Syracuse and work in one of the factories there. Then Mollie remembered Julie Steele. She'd come home after working in one of those places- thin, and pale, her bones almost poking through her skin, and that dead look in her eyes. Consumption. Coughing blood and gasping for air, she died two months after she came home. How long would anyone live cooped up in those filthy dormitories, working 14 hours a day six days a week, never seeing the sun, never breathing the good clean air, never feeling the sweet wind or the lift of a deck under foot? Six cents a shirt, that's what Julie said she made. And the bosses wouldn't let her even speak to another worker all day.

Mollie studied the table and then said still staring down, "Maybe it just wasn't meant to be. Maybe I wasn't supposed to own the ship." She looked up at Ben and continued, "But we came so close, Ben. We almost did it." Her face twisted in pain.

The two sat in silence for several long minutes before Mollie with slumped shoulders got up. "I'd better start dinner. We're all in need of some real food."

Two days later the *Gazelle* towed into Oswego. The moment her lines were ashore and secured under the elevator and the boarding plank was in place, Hanna came hurrying up it. She crossed the main deck in three strides to where Mollie stood and embraced her in a heart felt hug. Then she stepped back and seeing Ben, his left arm still in a sling, said, "Oh, thank the Lord in heaven you're all safe. But what happened to you, Ben?"

"I pulled my arm out while hanging onto Mouse who wanted to go for a swim. The doc says I can take the sling off in a few days."

Hannah turned back to Mollie. "I just got word not an hour ago that the *Anowa* was safe at anchor in Prinyer's Cove. She's on her way to Kingston for barley, and we expect her here in a day or two."

Mollie smiled, the first real look of happiness on her face that anyone had seen since the gale began. She asked, "What of Isiah, Hannah? When we left, he was off to New York to help a business partner. Was he successful?"

Hannah answered, "He was. And he's coming along right behind me, so you'll see him for yourself in just a few minutes. In fact, he wanted me to tell you to get the crew together as he had something he wishes to tell you all."

Ben and Mollie glanced over ashore at the elevator and then at the hatches. Hanna said, "Your wheat can wait a bit. There's Isiah right now."

"Very well," said Ben. "I'll go get the boys."

Mollie guessed Isiah was coming down to say good bye to them all. It was just the sort of gesture she would expect from the man whom she now knew was as considerate as he was honorable. Mollie took her friend's hands and said, "Hannah, I'm so sorry we didn't make it. Somehow I'll pay you back."

Hannah again reached out and embraced Mollie. "Please don't think of that now. You're here and safe. That's what matters."

They separated and walked aft to the main cabin. Mollie spoke, "You never could find a better crew. I had to take the helm after Ben pulled his shoulder out in the gale. They were all magnificent. And the ship-she flew like a bird. They were all so brave. If we'd had just one more week. We would have done it."

Hannah said nothing, and together they walked the rest of the way in silence back to the deck house.

As Mollie pushed open the companionway doors, she said to Hannah, "Leaving *Gazelle* and the boys is going to be one of the hardest things I've ever done."

A few minutes later Ben had mustered everyone aft. All were seated around the table when Isiah came down the companionway. Isiah looked tired. His face was drawn, and he seemed a bit thinner, but his eyes sparkled, and his back was straight as he stood looking them over.

"Well," he greeted the crew. "It seems we have both had our battles with storm winds of adversity. My battles upon the tempest tossed seas of commerce may not have been quite so rough as yours, though. I trust you'll soon mend, Tommy?"

"My head's too hard to crack, Mr. Fitzhugh."

"And you, Ben?"

"I'll be fit again in a day or two."

Isiah reached into his jacket and pulled out a small cardboard binder and a folded piece of paper.

"Do you have a pen and ink bottle at hand?"

Mollie thought, as she got up to fetch the pen, that there was a peculiar set to Isiah's face. And Hanna seemed oddly preoccupied with fiddling with her fur trimmed hat. When she returned with pen and inkwell and sat down, Isiah leaned forward and placed the paper before her and said, "Please sign the paper there."

He had his hand over the top part so she couldn't make out exactly what it was. It appeared to be some sort of legal looking thing. She carefully dipped the nib in and scratched her name on the line he had indicated. Then, before she could ask anything, Isiah dropped the cardboard binder tied with string on the table beside the paper.

"What is this? What's this paper?"

Isiah pulled his hand away with a flourish and said, "You just signed a credit note to me. And this document here is your deed of ownership. The *Gazelle* is yours, Mollie McIntyre. Sloan has been paid, and I just sold you the *Gazelle* for the remaining balance of the note, three hundred dollars, as it says right there. There is, however, one condition, that being you agree after you've paid her off, to charter your vessel to my service for three years as you did this year-May through September."

A barely audible stir of sound traveled around the table as each of the ship's company reacted. Mollie still staring at the paper before her felt the wind knocked out of her. The cabin seemed to move around her in a peculiar fashion leaving her almost giddy. She looked up and caught Ben's eye. He was looking back, and he gave her a small shy smile. The cabin steadied up around her as she took a deep breath. She didn't deserve this. How could such generosity happen? It was what Isiah wanted. Whether she deserved it or not, the gift had been made. What else could she do but say to Isiah, "Thank you."

"Why, you are most welcome Mrs. McIntyre. Most welcome indeed. I look forward to a mutually profitable association between Fitzhugh Forwarding and the schooner *Gazelle.* I also want you to accept my invitation for you and your entire crew to join me for dinner at my home tomorrow. We'll dine at noon sharp."

Isiah reached for the hat he had put down on the table earlier. "Now I must get on with my day's work. But I'll be expecting you all tomorrow." With that he departed with Hannah at his heels.

After a long pause Ben said, "Well, we've got grain to unload. Others are waiting for this berth so we can't be lolly gagging around. We'd best get the hatches off and the chutes down."

Mollie stood up along with the crew thinking I'd best file these papers in a safe place. As the rest of the company shuffled out silently, still stunned at the sudden turn in fortunes, Ben paused beside her and with his good arm gave her a gentle hug.

"Congratulations. You've got yourself the best manned best sailing little two master on the lake. Now if you can just find yourself an able bodied Captain to go with her…"

Mollie returned the embrace. I've got the right captain now, and there isn't a better one anywhere."

Note from the author and some further reading-

While the characters in "The Widow Maker" are imaginary, the women activists encountered by Mollie were not, and much of their dialogue is taken from their writings. Below are a few sources for more information on their lives as well as suggested reading about the days of sail on Lake Ontario.

Harriet Tubman The Moses of her People by Sarah Bradford   available at www.gutenberg.org

Women and the Lakes   Untold Great Lakes Maritime Tales   Frederick Stonehouse

Coston, Martha J. *A Signal Success. The Life And Travels of Martha J. Coston* available at www.gutenberg.org

The Narrative of Sojourner Truth by Olive Gilbert and Sojourner Truth available at www.gutenberg.org

Hit: Essays on Women's Rights, Walker, Mary Edwards *(1871)* available on line from Google books

Not for Ourselves Alone: The Story of Elizabeth Cady Stanton and Susan B. Anthony   Ward, Geoffrey C., with essays by Martha Saxton, Ann D. Gordon and Ellen Carol DuBois

Tales from the Great Lakes based on C.H.J. Snider's "Schooner Days" edited by Robert E. Townsend Dundurn Press 1995

More Lake Ontario Books by Susan P. Gateley

Passages On Inland Waters local history *Lake Ontario and Erie Canal* isbn 09646149-2-8 144 pages with historic photo section on Fair Haven

Ariadne's Death Heroism and Tragedy On Lake Ontario   96 pages isbn 09646149-4-9 photos

Twinkle Toes and the Riddle of the Lake 234 pages illustrated isbn 978-0-9646149-1-8 2009

Saving The Beautiful Lake a Quest for Hope   *275 pages 2015*

Maritime Tales of Lake Ontario Shipwrecks and survival on an inland sea 128 pp isbn 978-1-60949-684-5   published by the History Press on sale at Amazon.com

Legends and Lore of Lake Ontario published by History Press on sale at Amazon.com

susanpgateley.com for more information on Lake Ontario and our blog

https://www.etsy.com/shop/lakeontarioitems *Visit the Lake Ontario items store at Etsy.com*

Made in the USA
Middletown, DE
21 March 2021